Pawprints & Predicaments

Bethany Blake

KENSINGTON BOOKS
http://www.kensingtonbooks.com

KENSINGTON BOOKS are published by

Kensington Publishing Corp.
119 West 40th Street
New York, NY 10018

All Kensington titles, imprints and distributed lines are
available at special quantity discounts for bulk purchases
for sales promotion, premiums, fund-raising, educational
or institutional use. Special book excerpts or customized
printings can also be created to fit specific needs. For details,
write or phone the office of the Kensington Special Sales
Manager: Kensington Publishing Corp., 119 West 40th Street,
New York, NY, 10018. Attn. Special Sales Department.
Phone: 1-800-221-2647.

Kensington and the K logo Reg. U.S. Pat. & TM Off.

ISBN-13: 978-1-4967-0742-0
ISBN-10: 1-4967-0742-7
First Kensington Mass Market Edition: March 2018

eISBN-13: 978-1-4967-0743-7
eISBN-10: 1-4967-0743-5
First Kensington Electronic Edition: March 2018

10 9 8 7 6 5 4 3 2 1

Printed in the United States of America

To my daughters,
Paige, Julia, and Hope

Chapter 1

The Thirtieth Annual Sylvan Creek Tail Waggin' Winterfest promised to be even bigger and better than the festivals of years past, which was saying something, because the pet-friendly, week-long event had long been *the* highlight of January for many folks in the Pocono Mountains.

And this year, the little village of temporary huts that was always erected at wooded Bear Tooth State Park, on the shore of Lake Wallapawakee, had been completely refurbished; each tiny, heated shack painted a pretty, but wintry, shade of robin's egg blue. There were more vendors, too, selling things like gourmet hot chocolate, s'mores, and cold-weather gear for dogs and cats. For the first time ever, a polar bear plunge would kick off the festivities later that evening, and the bonfire that burned at the center of the ephemeral town crackled in a bigger ring of stones, while the paths through the festival were lit by new glass lanterns. There were even moonlit walks through the woods, led by old Max Pottinger, who told the tale of a legendary spectral Saint Bernard that supposedly patrolled the vast network of cross-country ski trails, guiding those who lost their way.

Strolling through the heart of the festival on a night that threatened snow, I couldn't help thinking the scene was picture-perfect. And yet, something didn't seem quite right.

"It's almost *too* nice this year," I complained to my sister, Piper, and my best friend, Moxie Bloom. Slipping on some ice in my favorite flea-market cowboy boots, I nearly dropped my third s'more. Then I righted myself and added, "Don't you think it's kind of odd?"

"The festival's definitely different," Piper agreed, kicking through the snow in her sensible, waterproof boots, which matched her rated-for-the-Arctic down parka. My sister was a veterinarian who often saw patients literally in the field, and she was always suitably dressed for the weather. And as someone who'd restored an 1800s farm, called Winding Hill, Piper wasn't necessarily opposed to updating shabby structures. "I like the fresh paint," she noted, with a glance at a booth selling hand-knit sweaters for dogs. "And the vendors are better this year. I think it's nice to have more than just the VFW selling hot dogs." She frowned, still staring at the hut, which was strung with clotheslines that sagged under the weight of small cardigans and pullovers. "Although, while I'm a fan of Arlo Finch's crafts, I'm not too fond of his practice."

"You're just too rational," I said, waving to Arlo, a lanky, bearded, graying hippie throwback who practiced holistic "pet healing and energy therapy" when not knitting *adorable* canine garb. I'd already stopped by Arlo's booth and purchased an argyle cardigan for a one-eared, drooling Chihuahua that I used to foster, even though I had trouble picturing the man who'd adopted Artie buttoning the little dog into a sweater. Especially one knitted from free-range yak yarn and delivered in a bag that advertised Arlo's practice, Peaceable Pets. I made a mental note *not* to mention the yarn when I dropped off the present. "I'm definitely open to the idea of alternative medicine," I added. "Some therapies have been time-tested over centuries."

"I agree with Daphne," Moxie said, tucking her hands deeper into a fluffy, white fake-fur muff. "I would totally get acupuncture, if I wasn't scared of needles."

Piper gave Moxie a funny look, then grumbled, "New Age medicine is all mumbo jumbo." I suspected that she was a bit grumpy because her boyfriend, Professor Roger Berendt, was in Europe for the next five months, on sabbatical. She zipped her parka right up to her chin as we all walked on, past ice sculptures that were also new to the festival. The frozen artwork glittered in the moonlight. "And I don't know why you wouldn't like an *improved* Winterfest, Daphne."

"Because even the people look like actors," I complained, sidestepping a twenty-something couple who might've walked directly off the pages of an L.L. Bean catalog. The woman had a tiny, perfectly groomed Yorkie tucked under her arm, and the man sipped cocoa from a commemorative mug. I couldn't ever recall Winterfest having a logo before, but the ceramic cups featured a cartoon image of the legendary Lake Wallapawakee Saint Bernard, who was romping in a snow pile. I watched for a moment as the man and woman stopped to check out the dog sweaters, the woman holding up an even *cuter* cardigan than the one I'd bought. Darn it. Then I returned my attention to Piper and Moxie. "Don't you think the whole thing is kind of . . . *Stepford Wives*-ish?"

"Ooh, I love that movie!" Moxie cried, missing the point. "Although, the festival reminds me more of *White Christmas* than robot wives."

Moxie, of course, knew both movies by heart. She loved all things vintage and, along with the muff, wore a 1940s wool coat that nipped in at the waist, a pair of leather boots with fur trim around the ankles, and a turban-style hat that hid one of her few concessions to modernity, her spiky red hair.

All at once, as I studied my friend's attire, I realized that her outfit, like the too-flawless setting, was a little . . . off.

"Umm, you know you have to ditch all your clothes on the lakeshore, right?" I asked Moxie, with a glance down at my old barn coat, tattered wool mittens, and oversized boots. My long, unruly, dirty-blond curls were tucked under a knit ski cap I'd found on the floor of the pink 1970s VW bus that served as headquarters for my business, Daphne Templeton's Lucky Paws Pet Sitting. In short, I looked like I was about to muck out stalls, while Moxie could've gone shopping on Park Avenue—circa 1945. "Aren't you a little overdressed?" I suggested. "You look awfully nice to jump in a lake."

Moxie stopped in her tracks and pulled the muff back close to her chest. Her green eyes were wide with surprise. "Why would I jump in a lake? In January?"

I looked at Piper, who was rolling her eyes, as if to say, *I knew this would happen.*

Then I turned back to Moxie. "Because we're doing the polar bear plunge this year!" I reminded her. My s'more was oozing, but I hardly noticed the gooey marshmallow dripping onto my mitten. "You're the one who suggested it!"

Moxie shook her head. "Oh, no. I said we should *go to the* plunge. I didn't say we should *do* it."

As I tried to recall a conversation Moxie and I'd had a few weeks before, I heard a soft snuffling sound, almost like laughter, and looked down to see that my canine sidekick, a normally taciturn, introspective basset hound named Socrates, was struggling to contain a rare show of amusement.

"This is not funny," I told him, which didn't stop his tail from twitching, just a tiny bit. His usually baleful brown eyes also twinkled with amusement—until I gave him a warning look, and he hung his head, his long ears dragging in the snow. Needless to say, Socrates had refused to wear a hat, and he'd turned up his freckled nose at the insulated jacket I'd offered him, too. Canine apparel appalled him. "I'm already registered," I added, addressing Moxie again. "I have a number. I have to do the plunge!"

"Moxie is smart to sit the event out," Piper said. "From what I've seen, the organizers slapped the whole thing together at the last minute. I don't think there are even plans to restrict the number of people who enter the lake at one time. It could be a mess."

"I'll be careful," I promised, thinking she was worrying too much. "And it's for a good cause. All the proceeds go to feed the rescue cats at Breard's Big Cats of the World."

"I don't know if I support that 'charity,'" Piper said, continuing to be critical. She'd never admit it, but she was definitely missing Roger, whom she'd been seeing for several months. "Is it a zoo?" she noted. "A shelter? A nonprofit, even? Because you have to pay to tour the place."

I honestly wasn't sure how to classify Big Cats of the World, either. But I knew that Victor Breard, a native of France, had a good reputation for taking in exotic animals that were rescued from bad situations—say, the tiger cub someone illegally adopted, then couldn't handle—and giving them safe, secure homes on his licensed 200-acre preserve, just outside Sylvan Creek.

"Well, regardless, I'm doing the plunge," I said, shooting Moxie a dark look. I was ninety percent sure *she* had misunderstood our earlier conversation.

"I'm sorry, Daph," she apologized. "I'd register now, but I'm not wearing a bathing suit." Then she raised her muff. "Besides, what would I do with Sebastian while I was swimming?"

"What?" Piper seemed puzzled. "What are you talking about?"

I was also confused. "You've *named* that fake-fur thing?"

I was starting to think Moxie had gone over the edge, when all at once a tiny white head popped out of the muff. A small, twitching nose sniffed the cold air, and a pair of intelligent pink eyes blinked at me. I jumped, and Socrates, normally unflappable, took a few steps backward, nearly bumping into one of the ice sculptures.

I had to force myself not to pull away, too. "You adopted a *rat*?"

Moxie raised her hands to let Sebastian brush his little cheek against hers. "Yes! It turns out small pets are allowed in my apartment. And he's *adorable*, don't you think?"

I loved animals, and I'd taken care of everything from pythons to tarantulas, but something about rats spooked me, as Piper knew all too well. She grinned at me. "You look awfully taken aback, for somebody who often quotes the Dalai Lama about the importance of loving all living creatures."

My pragmatic, successful sister loved to mock my admittedly impractical PhD in philosophy.

"I'm sure Sebastian and I will end up being friends," I told Piper and Moxie. I forced myself to meet those pink eyes again, and Sebastian blinked up at me, then squirmed and returned to the warmth of his mobile den. I caught a glimpse of his naked tail slithering away and fought back a shudder, even as I said, "I promise, we'll be buddies, soon."

When the rat was out of sight, Socrates exhaled softly, like he was also relieved.

"I guess you're right about the plunge, Moxie," I added glumly. "You can't take a rat into freezing water." Then I looked hopefully at Piper. "Unless . . ."

"Moxie doesn't have a bathing suit," my sister reminded me. "And I'm afraid I can't hold Sebastian. I'm here on official, if unsanctioned, business, looking out for any dogs that might follow their owners into the water, then get panicked or hurt in the crowd."

"Sorry," Moxie apologized again, as we passed by a hut selling mulled cider and warm donuts. I'd finished my s'more and briefly debated buying yet another treat, in an attempt to fatten myself up, like a walrus insulated with blubber, then decided it was too late. "I wouldn't take part this year, anyhow," Moxie noted. "Not when the whole thing will probably be filmed!"

I grew even more concerned. "What do you mean by *that*?"

"Everybody from the media is here," Moxie explained. Her hands were trapped, so she nodded over at the bonfire, where kids were roasting hot dogs and marshmallows on sticks, while listening to old Max Pottinger spin the tale of the mysterious Saint Bernard, prelude to leading another walk in the woods. Max—wizened, bent, and seemingly oblivious to the cold in a flannel shirt and ball cap—spoke in hushed tones, but his listeners were wide-eyed and rapt. The only exception was the new owner of, and only reporter at, the Sylvan Creek *Weekly Gazette*, who was in constant motion, snapping photos of Max and his audience. "I do not want Gabriel Graham putting my frozen, screaming face on the front page of a paper that people are actually starting to read now," Moxie said. "And you know he'll pick the most unflattering picture for page one!"

"Yes, he probably will," I muttered, as Gabriel—thirty-something, good looking, and perhaps *too* charming—crouched down and snapped away. The flames roared up behind him, and I couldn't help thinking that, with his dark, wavy hair, goatee, and gleaming white teeth, he looked a little bit like the devil.

Gabriel must've sensed that he was being observed, because all at once, he straightened, slipped the distinctive red plaid strap on his hefty Nikon camera around his neck, and began to walk in our direction.

"Hey, everyone," he greeted us, with a nod to Socrates. I wasn't sure if I liked Gabriel, but I appreciated that he included the shortest member of our party, who sometimes got overlooked. Although I couldn't understand how. Socrates had a certain gravitas. Then Gabriel smiled at Piper. "Nice to see you." Before she even replied, he looked me and Moxie up and down and added, ambiguously, "You two look *interesting* tonight."

"Why, thank you," Moxie said, taking the comment as a compliment. "My outfit is vintage forties. And Daphne's dressed to jump in the lake."

Gabriel's brown eyes glittered with amusement. "Always up to something, aren't you, Miss Templeton?" he observed. "The last time I spoke to you, you'd just solved a murder."

"Yes." I crossed my arms over my chest. "I read your article—in which you gave Jonathan Black most of the credit for solving the case."

I'd actually helped handsome, enigmatic Detective Jonathan Black solve *two* homicides during his brief time in Sylvan Creek, but nobody ever seemed to want to acknowledge my contributions. Least of all, Jonathan.

"I'll try to feature you prominently in my story on the plunge," Gabriel promised. "I'll be sure to seek you out when I'm taking pictures. And maybe someday I can do a feature on the pet sitter with the PhD in philosophy who is also opening a bakery for dogs and cats?"

Everybody knew that I was a pet sitter. My van announced my profession and featured a pretty eye-catching painting of a misshapen dog that was often mistaken for a misshapen pony. That was Moxie's handiwork. The fact that I'd rented a small storefront on Sylvan Creek's main street and planned to—hopefully—soon open a bakery for pets was also common knowledge. But I wasn't sure how Gabriel knew about my degree. And I didn't know if I liked his mildly flirtatious, if mocking, tone, either.

"No, please don't feature me . . ." I started to protest, my ears getting warm under my cap.

Piper was clearly amused. And Moxie was oblivious to my discomfort. On the contrary, she seemed increasingly excited about the prospect of seeing *my* "frozen, screaming" face on the front page, and she interrupted me, noting, "Wow, a photo and a feature story!" Her eyes were fairly glowing. "And maybe you'll be filmed by Stylish Life Network, too, when you run into the water!"

I looked down at my barn coat again, then caught Gabriel smirking at me. "I think we've all established that I'm not very 'stylish' tonight," I reminded everyone, while Socrates snuffled again.

Gabriel, meanwhile, surveyed the candlelit village, which had been updated with support from the network, for a show called *America's Most Pet Friendly Towns.* Sylvan Creek had been chosen—some preferred the word *targeted*—for the program the previous year, and a crew had been filming—some said "terrorizing"— the community for nearly six weeks, with no sign of packing up and leaving.

"Stylish Life did help to make this place look pretty nice," Gabriel observed. "Not too shabby, for a festival in a forest."

"Actually, I was just complaining that everything looks *too* perfect," I said, stepping back so two adorable Samoyed puppies could dart past me. I watched the pair tumble in the snow, thinking I'd never seen the dogs before. Was it possible that they'd been planted by the crew, to add even more "atmosphere"? "I sort of miss the shabby, rustic touches Winterfest used to have," I added. "Like the *old* luminarias, made from plastic milk jugs, with candles that kept burning out."

Piper knitted her brows, as if she wasn't quite up to speed. "You're saying Stylish Life funded the improvements?" She suddenly seemed less impressed by the changes. Like pretty much everyone in town who dealt with animals, Piper had suffered some run-ins with the film crew. "I didn't know that."

"Oh, yes, Stylish Life paid for a lot of the updates," Moxie said. As the owner of Sylvan Creek's unique salon for humans and pets, Spa and Paw, Moxie heard all of the local gossip. "Apparently, people who watch that network don't want to see plastic jugs stuck in the snow. From what I hear, some of the older festival organizers were kind of insulted, to be told their event was 'tacky.'"

I could believe that feathers had been ruffled. I'd also had a few encounters with the Stylish Life team, and they weren't exactly tactful. But for once I held my tongue, not trusting Gabriel to keep any tales I told off the record. Piper was wisely staying quiet, too, although I knew she could've gone on for hours about the crew.

"Yes, I've heard that some of the Winterfest folks are unhappy," Gabriel said. "And there's also a rumor that someone at Stylish Life made up the legend about the Saint Bernard, just to make this already pet-centric town even more intriguing for animal-loving viewers." He slipped his hands into the pockets of a rust-colored down vest, and his teeth flashed white when he smiled more broadly. He really was the epitome of "devilishly handsome." "I have to admit, that wouldn't be a bad idea. Everything I print about the 'ghost dog' sells papers."

Socrates whined softly and shook his large head, presumably at the folly of humans. He did not believe in Bigfeet, yetis, monsters that lurked in lakes, or especially spectral Saint Bernards.

"There have definitely been more 'sightings' lately," my equally skeptical sibling agreed, air-quoting "sightings." "But that tale has been around forever."

"Oh, yes," Moxie concurred. "The story, which *I* happen to believe, is older than Mr. Pottinger." She frowned. "But I wouldn't put it past Lauren Savidge to make stuff up. She's horrible!"

Moxie had finally invoked a name that the rest of us had probably subconsciously avoided speaking, just like one might not utter the name of a demon out loud, for fear of summoning the evil spirit.

Small, loud, forceful, and sometimes conniving, in my opinion, field producer Lauren Savidge was the brash leader, and most despised member, of the small TV crew.

Gabriel Graham certainly knew all about Lauren, but he cocked his head, all deceptive innocence. "How so?" he asked Moxie. "What did Lauren do to *you?*"

Piper and I exchanged concerned glances, but Moxie took the bait. "Well, the other day, she barged into Spa and Paw and ordered her crew to start filming, without even asking if I minded. Then I swear, she nudged my arm while I was clipping my landlord's poodle, Marzipan, so his tail lost its little puffball, and I nearly cried—"

"Umm . . . Moxie . . ." There was warning in Piper's voice. Obviously, she'd noticed that Gabriel's eyes were lighting up at the prospect of yet another juicy story about Lauren's heavy-handed attempt to create TV-worthy drama in our sleepy town. One of Gabriel's hands had slipped out of his vest pocket, and he was reaching for something in the back pocket of his worn, faded jeans. Probably a notebook.

Forgetting for a moment that I wasn't eager to touch Moxie's arm, lest I encounter a pink twitching nose, I also tried to silence my friend by reaching out to squeeze her wrist.

But before I could interrupt, someone who'd obviously been eavesdropping barged into our conversation, uninvited, and confronted us all, saying, "If you've got complaints about me, please tell me to my face."

Although I hadn't said a word about Lauren Savidge, I turned around to discover that she was pointing an accusing finger at *me*. Then she announced, in a tone that was almost threatening, "In the meantime, I would like to speak to you, Daphne." And although she was flanked by her assistant, Joy Doolittle, and her cameraman, Kevin Drucker, she added, ominously, "*In private.*"

Chapter 2

"Why do you want to talk to *me*?" I asked Lauren, who continued to give me a dead level stare, her arms folded over her chest. She was shorter than me—which was saying something, since I was a petite five-two, even in my boots—but she looked intimidating in a military-inspired jacket and laced-up Doc Martens. Her pretty features were obscured by large, thick eyeglasses, and her mass of dark hair was piled into a tall, deliberately teased, and, I thought, purposely eccentric rat's nest. Sebastian would've felt quite at home on Lauren's head.

"Did I do something?" I added uncertainly, with a glance down at Socrates, who rolled his eyes, clearly exasperated by the human drama. Then I looked to Joy and Kevin, too, like they might provide some answers to their boss's strange behavior. But Joy—slight, fair, and nervous—clutched a clipboard to her chest and studied her clunky snow boots, while Kevin—squat and wearing a red knit cap pulled low over his brow—placidly chewed gum and swung a big video camera that dangled from his hand. I turned back to

Lauren, who was still staring at me, as Gabriel finally pulled out that notebook I'd known he'd had stashed in his pocket. "Is something wrong?" I asked Lauren one more time.

Before she could answer, Piper wisely excused herself from the conversation. "I'm sorry, but I've got to run," she said, backing away toward a lantern-lit trail that led to the lakeshore. I noticed that a few people were starting to make their way toward the expanse of water, which glittered cold and black in the distance. "I want to let the plunge organizers know I'm available, if needed."

"I've gotta scoot, too," Moxie added, backing up in a different direction, toward the parking area at the edge of the festival grounds. She raised her hands slightly, showing us all the muff. "Sebastian is getting restless. He keeps nibbling my pinkies."

Everyone, including those of us who knew that Sebastian was a rat, took a moment to give my best friend a funny look. It seemed like eventually everybody who spoke with Moxie got that opportunity.

Then, as Piper and Moxie disappeared into the crowd of festivalgoers, Gabriel, ignoring Lauren's bad mood, grinned and noted, "I don't have anywhere to go. I've shot enough pictures of puppies romping in the snow, old Max Pottinger, and kids eating s'mores. I could stick around."

"I want to speak to Daphne *in private*," Lauren reminded him, in an even, warning tone. Apparently, she was also unhappy with Gabriel, probably over one of the many stories he'd printed about the Stylish Life crew, because she added, bluntly, "I don't want to see our entire conversation reprinted—and misquoted—in the *Gazette*."

"Ouch!" Gabriel winced at the insult. But he wasn't really offended. His eyes glittered with amusement when he shifted to address me. "Much as I would like to see what's about to unfold, and save you from Lauren's wrath, if necessary, I suppose I should take a quick hike and try to get a shot of the 'ghost dog' before the plunge." Then he cocked his head at Lauren and smiled, like he knew some secret. "Do you have any thoughts on that, Ms. Savidge? Might I actually spy this mystery pup tonight?"

"Oh, goodness . . ." Joy Doolittle finally spoke up, her pale blue eyes wide and her voice thin and nervous. She clutched her clipboard more tightly to her chest, pressing it against a nylon jacket that was too thin for the cold night, and her hands, not protected by gloves, were white at the knuckles. "That seems unlikely, doesn't it?" Joy looked uncertainly to her colleague, Kevin, and tried to force a smile. "It's just a silly legend, right . . . ?"

I'd met Kevin Drucker a few times, but he never made much of an impression. His eyes, which were dark and impassive, were usually hidden by the big camera that he'd hoisted onto his shoulder, and his entire wardrobe seemed to consist of oversized sweatshirts that advertised his loyalty to the Pittsburgh Steelers. Kevin didn't stand out in terms of personality, either. "I don't know," he told Joy with a shrug. "I just do my job."

"Can we be done with this 'ghost dog' idiocy?" Lauren complained. I thought the comment was mainly directed at Joy. Then she told Gabriel, "I have things to do and places to be, if you don't mind . . ."

"Aw, relax, Lauren," Gabriel cajoled. But all at once, his smile faded away, and he lost his joking tone, addressing her more softly. "You take everything too seriously."

Lauren didn't respond, except to jut her chin defiantly, and I suddenly wondered how well they knew each other. Gabriel's last comment was kind of personal, and there was a familiar quality to their one-sided banter, too, like they'd engaged in similar sparring matches before and knew their roles. Last, but certainly not least, there was something odd—charged—about the way they were staring at each other.

I kept looking between them until Gabriel broke the tense moment by smiling again and telling us, "*I'm* going to catch up with Max Pottinger's walk—even if that makes me an 'idiot.'" Then he pointed his camera at me, as if he was about to take a picture. "But I'll be back in time to get a few shots of you at the plunge, Daphne."

I was about to again protest that I'd prefer not to be on the front page of the *Gazette*, but Lauren spoke up first, to express a similar concern.

"Don't you dare take a picture of me or Joy jumping into the lake," she warned Gabriel. "Don't even think about it."

Lauren's eyes were narrowed, but Joy's were *huge*. "No . . . Please . . . Don't . . ." she begged Gabriel. But her gaze kept flicking to the still impassive Kevin, like she was also appealing to him for some reason. "I'd really rather not have any pictures taken. . . ."

Gabriel didn't make any promises. And Kevin ignored Joy, too. He fiddled with a doohickey on the camera, making an adjustment, like he wasn't even aware of the conversation going on around him.

For my part, I was keenly aware of, and very curious about, the irritable, aggressive TV producer's plan to take part in a chilly, and let's face it, silly ritual.

"Are you really doing the plunge?" I asked Lauren, with an uncertain glance at Socrates, who'd been quietly observing the whole discussion. He huffed loudly, this time at the folly of leaping into lakes. I looked up at Lauren again, asking a question that might've been a little rude. "But . . . *why?*"

Gabriel also seemed surprised by Lauren's decision to take part in a frivolous charitable activity. For the first time since I'd met him, he spoke uncertainly. "You're not really . . . ?"

"Yes, I am." Lauren jutted out her chin again. "Joy and I are both signed up. I like to push myself, physically."

I wondered if Lauren's assistant also liked to "push herself," or if she was under orders to participate. Joy was already pale and shivering, clinging to her clipboard in a futile attempt to ward off the icy breeze from the lake. It was hard to imagine that she was eager to get *colder*. And her expression struck me as more concerned than excited.

Then I looked at Kevin, who continued to fidget with the camera and chew his gum in a slow, steady rhythm.

Why wasn't he participating . . . ?

"Well, good luck, ladies," Gabriel said, interrupting my thoughts. He frowned at Lauren, almost like he was worried about her. Then he nodded at me, Joy, and Kevin. "I'll see you all later."

Apparently, Kevin had been tuned in to the conversation on some level. Although still distracted by his gear, he grunted what I assumed was a farewell, while the rest of us watched Gabriel walk away.

In spite of claiming that he had enough pictures of kids and dogs, he stopped by the bonfire to take a photo of the Samoyed twins, who now both sported sweaters, presumably knit by Arlo Finch. Then he resumed heading toward the forest, his progress carefully observed by Lauren.

"Um, you wanted to talk to me?" I reminded her, reluctantly drawing her attention back to me, although Socrates was nudging my leg with his strong shoulder. I was pretty sure he was suggesting that I also make a discreet exit.

But it was too late.

Lauren jolted out of her reverie and her expression, which had softened as she'd watched Gabriel, grew hard again.

"Joy, Kevin . . . You head down to the lake," she said without taking her eyes off me. "I need to talk to Daphne about how she's *holding up production of an entire television show.*"

Chapter 3

"What in the world did I do?" I asked, trying to pull my cap down lower, because, like Joy, I was getting pretty cold. Unfortunately, my mittens made that task awkward, and I ended up just batting at my head before giving up. "Is this about Whiskered Away?" I guessed. "Or Butterbean? Because I had to slam those doors in your face!"

I'd had two recent encounters with Lauren, and both had ended badly. First, she'd insisted on filming at Sylvan Creek's cat shelter, Whiskered Away Home, where I served on the board of directors. I'd tried to shoo her away, because the old barn that housed the cats was under repair and not quite ready for its close-up. Plus, the shelter's former director, an unstable cat hoarder named Bea Baumgartner, had been there, acting especially ornery and off-kilter that day. I hadn't wanted Bea to embarrass herself in front of a camera. A few days later, Lauren had tried to bully me into giving her access to one of my clients, a slightly bilious and sometimes stinky potbelly pig named Butterbean. I really didn't think poor Butterbean—or his people—would appreciate having his unfortunate condition highlighted on national TV, and I'd semi-forcibly evicted Lauren and her crew from the porker's front porch, although I really didn't like to use phys-ical means to resolve conflicts.

"Butterbean's condition is a serious burden for the family—and to those of us who watch him," I added, waving my hand in front of my nose, just to think about the gassy swine. Still, I defended him. "He's not a curiosity!"

"I don't care about the old lady with the cat issues or that smelly pig right now," Lauren informed me. "Apparently, as things now stand, I'm not allowed to show the world the truth about this pet-*crazy* town!"

I pulled back, confused and slightly concerned. Socrates, by my side, also seemed baffled and maybe borderline worried. His tail was stiff, and his wrinkly brow was scrunched up even more than usual.

"I thought the show was called *America's Most Pet Friendly Towns*," I reminded Lauren, emphasizing the word *friendly*. I watched her face closely, thinking she'd just hinted that the folks at Stylish Life Network weren't being completely honest about how they in-tended to portray my hometown. "And what do you mean by showing the world the 'truth' about Sylvan Creek?"

"Nothing," Lauren grumbled, in a way that didn't reassure me or Socrates. His tail remained rigid and straight. He didn't like getting dragged into people's drama, but he *really* disapproved of deceit. "I'm over the pig and the cat barn . . . for now," she added. "I'm here to talk about your bakery."

It was my turn to scrunch up my brow. "My *bakery*?"

"Yes," Lauren said, jamming her hands into two of

the many pockets on her olive drab coat. "When are you going to open up?" She never struck me as a pleasant person, but she seemed especially irate that night. "Do you even have a name for the place yet?"

"As a matter of fact, I do," I said, although I still didn't understand why my business was her concern. "It's going to be called Flour Power, because I'm going to use healthy, organic, and locally sourced ingredients, when possible. The kind of stuff that 'powers' up pets. Plus the name ties in with my old VW van, so Lucky Paws and the bakery will be connected. . . ."

Lauren obviously didn't care about any of that, and I gave up explaining a name that I thought was kind of clever.

"So when's the grand opening?" she asked again, peering at me from behind those glasses. "Huh?"

"I don't know," I said, getting exasperated. I was already being nagged by my mother, Realtor Maeve Templeton, who'd arranged my lease. I didn't need a TV field producer bugging me, too. "And, no offense, but what does it matter to you, anyhow?"

"If I'm going to make this town look all sugary sweet and pet-perfect, I need footage of your business, which is literally saccharine," she said, her voice dripping sarcasm.

I ignored her snide tone. "Actually, I would never use saccharine, which is terrible for pets," I started to explain. Then I also gave up trying to educate her about pet-safe sweeteners. She clearly wasn't in the mood for a lecture. Nor did I bother explaining that I was trying to finish remodeling Flour Power, but *someone* in town had hired just about every local contractor to overhaul a mansion that I could see right across the lake. As the Chinese philosopher Sun Tzu once said, "He will win who knows when to fight and when not to fight." Nobody was going to win any battles with Lauren Savidge that night. Especially not a peacenik like me. "Don't you already have plenty of proof that Sylvan Creek is pet *friendly*?" I added, again employing that kinder word. "We've got Spa and Paw, Fetch! boutique, the Saint Bernard legend, the Howl-o-Ween Pet Parade, and the Winterfest Cardboard Iditarod, which you can film in just a few days."

The festival always ended with a dogsled race, except the comic "sledges" were made of old boxes and judged on theme and originality, as opposed to speed. Some of the smaller and lazier dogs didn't even run. They were pulled by their owners.

"And you've interviewed our resident holistic pet healer-slash-dog-sweater-knitter, right?" I added, glancing at Arlo Finch's stand again. He was folding sweaters, but watching us. I waved again, but he didn't wave back. I returned my attention to Lauren. "Arlo's pretty unique!"

"Yes, I've spoken with him," Lauren muttered under her breath. She was also looking in Arlo's direction. "Believe me, if I get my way—and I usually do—he and Peaceable Pets will be featured *prominently* on TV soon."

She sounded ominous, and I hoped that she wouldn't portray Arlo, who always smelled of incense and used phrases like "sacred animal energies," as *too* eccentric.

"I really don't think you need my bakery to prove that we love pets here," I said, drawing Lauren's attention back to me. "There's plenty of evidence without my little shop."

She clearly disagreed. "Just try to get your bakery

up and running," she urged through gritted teeth. White powder was starting to coat her rat's nest of hair, and she looked past me again, in the direction Gabriel had just departed, before adding, in a lower, softer voice, "I can't stick around this town forever, waiting for people to get their stuff together."

There was something almost sad, or hurt, about her slightly altered tone.

Or maybe I'd imagined that she'd softened, because the next moment, her eyes were hard again, and her mouth was set in a grim line. "I'd like to film at your shop by the end of next week," she said, starting to walk away. "Please see what you can do."

I glanced across the lake at the mansion, which was dark right then, but where every reputable local painter, plumber, and contractor reported on a nearly daily basis, and I almost did defend myself. Unless I figured out how to install cabinetry and repair a walk-in refrigerator so it didn't freeze everything I put inside of it, my hands were kind of tied.

But before I could say anything, Lauren looked me up and down, adding, "And you might want to skip the plunge tonight. These things are not for the faint of heart. People have *died* jumping into cold lakes."

"Hey!" I finally had to speak up. "I am not 'faint of heart.' I once ran with the bulls . . . by accident, but still . . ."

Lauren wasn't interested in what I considered to be a fairly compelling tale about the dangers of ignoring barricades in Pamplona, Spain. She trudged off toward the lake, leaving me and Socrates standing in a winter wonderland, with snow falling around us. The gently drifting flakes added to the ambiance, but as I watched Lauren disappear into the darkness, I had to admit that I began to suffer a faint sense of foreboding.

"No one's really going to get hurt, right?" I asked, looking down at Socrates. His sober expression was not reassuring, but I forced myself to shake off my concerns. "Let's go see if Arlo will exchange the sweater I bought," I suggested. "I'm not sure I got the right one."

I fully expected Socrates to somehow convey that a return would be even better than an exchange. But his muzzle was pointed toward Arlo's stand, like he wanted me to see something. And when I looked in the direction he'd indicated, I realized that the hut was dark and Arlo was gone.

I had no time to be disappointed. As I stood there already shivering in my cowboy boots, a familiar, thin, and reedy voice cut through the frosty air.

"Attention, swimmers!" Mayor Henrietta Holtz-apple announced, with what I considered to be over-blown enthusiasm. "The first annual Sylvan Creek polar bear plunge will begin in ten minutes!"

I knew that the event I'd signed up for was supposed to be fun, by my heart sank like a stone tossed into the inky waters of Lake Wallapawakee when she added, "Plungers . . . assemble!"

Chapter 4

By the time I made it to the lake, the shore around the expanse of water that was cordoned off for the plunge was crowded with people who were shedding their clothes, although it couldn't have been more than thirty degrees outside.

"You and Piper were right," I told Socrates, while I stuffed the bag from Peaceable Pets into one of my jacket's big pockets, pulled off my mittens, and began to unbutton my coat. My teeth chattered when cold air hit my collarbone. "This was a really bad idea."

Socrates rarely expressed himself vocally, but he gave a low "woof" of agreement, then shambled off to hang out with Piper, who was folding blankets with a guy in a jacket that announced him as "Safety Crew."

"Six minutes!" Mayor Holtzapple announced into a bullhorn, with cheerleader-esque pep. Looking up, I quickly found Sylvan Creek's middle-aged, bumbling leader on the water's edge. She was dressed in a robe, which presumably covered a bathing suit. I wasn't surprised that she was taking part in the plunge. Henrietta Holtzapple—probably in her early fifties, with broad shoulders and frizzy orange hair that matched her Pomeranian Pippin's coat—wasn't considered the most competent public official, but she was Sylvan Creek's most enthusiastic supporter. She'd been mayor for four terms, mainly because no one had the heart to vote against someone who loved the town as much as she did. "Five minutes to go," Mayor Holtzapple added, prompting me to resume struggling with my buttons. My fingers were freezing. "Five more minutes—"

"Yes, yes! We swim in only *cinq* minutes!"

All at once, the countdown took on an air of even greater excitement, not to mention a French accent, and I looked up again to see that Victor Breard had snatched the bullhorn from Mayor Holtzapple. The head of Big Cats of the World was stalking around the small beach, his slicked-back dark hair gleaming, like he'd already gone into the water. And his use of "we" wasn't a slip of the foreign tongue. He was obviously prepared to take part in the event that would benefit his shelter-slash-zoo. Like Mayor Holtzapple, he wore an easy-to-shed robe, but his was silky and red, reminiscent of a boxer's prefight attire. And he spoke like a ringmaster. Raising one hand in the air with a flourish, he cried, "The endangered, unwanted *lions et tigres* at my preserve thank you for your support this *magnifique* evening. *Merci beaucoup!*"

Okay, maybe Piper was right. He did seem a little bit like a snake oil salesman.

Then, while I resumed messing with my buttons, my fingers shaking harder, Victor continued the countdown, calling, "*Quatre minutes!* Four minutes!"

That announcement was greeted by an inexplicable cheer from the crowd, which had caught Victor's excitement, while I silently cursed Moxie. I could've *sworn* she'd *insisted* we participate in what seemed like an increasingly ill-advised escapade. Maybe as bad as accidentally running with bulls.

"Really, Moxie?" I grumbled, finally shrugging out of my coat. "I will get you back for this!"

Then I quickly ditched the rest of my clothes and stood hugging myself and hopping on my bare feet, like everyone else who'd been foolish enough to sign up for an ice bath.

As I jumped up and down, I scanned the crowd and located Arlo Finch, who'd apparently suspended sales so he could join the plunge. He was stripped down to a sleeveless T-shirt and cargo shorts, but he wasn't shuddering or hopping. He stood very still, facing the water, his graying hair pulled back into a ponytail and a meditative look on his lined, lean, bearded face. I envied his ability to put mind over matter in such a challenging situation. Then Arlo raised his hand to smooth his long hair, and I glimpsed an unusual tattoo on his wrist.

I tried to get a better look at the inked design, but my view was suddenly blocked by Joy Doolittle and Kevin Drucker, who were edging to the front of the crowd.

I assumed that Joy was eager to get the whole thing over with, but I thought Kevin should hang back. The big camera that again swung from his hand didn't look waterproof to me.

Joy, meanwhile, looked like she might also short-circuit when she hit the water. She'd taken off her jacket and pants, stripping down to a thin T-shirt and nylon running shorts. Even from where I was standing, I could see her arm shake when she gestured to Kevin, apparently giving him the order to start filming, because he swung his camera onto his shoulder and pressed his eye against the viewfinder.

But what, exactly, did they plan to capture for a show about pets?

I searched the crowd again, noting that there were only a handful of canines there, including a Bernese mountain dog who would probably get his feet wet, a cold-loving Newfoundland, and a very familiar chocolate Labrador retriever named Axis, who sat at the feet of the man who'd reluctantly adopted him.

Detective Jonathan Black.

He was last person I'd expected to see at a frivolous festival event. And, not surprisingly, the ex-Navy SEAL, who had probably logged countless hours in frigid water during his military training and service, wasn't dressed to splash around in Lake Wallapawakee. He wore a pair of jeans and a black down jacket that matched his hair, which was slightly longer than when I'd last met up with him, back in October.

For a moment, I couldn't imagine why he was there, until I also spotted Jonathan's ex-wife, Elyse Hunter-Black, who had likely dragged Jonathan along for moral support.

Elyse, a high-powered executive producer with Stylish Life Network and the driving force behind *America's Most Pet Friendly Towns*, looked predictably stunning in a bona fide, and probably warm, wetsuit that hugged her slender form and accented her delicate curves. For once, however, she wasn't calm and composed. On the contrary, Elyse was in the midst of what appeared to be a heated argument with her underling, Lauren Savidge, who'd shed her military-inspired coat and boots, but still looked like a Marine at boot camp, in a pair of camo shorts and a white tee.

As I observed the two women, Elyse tossed up her hands, clearly exasperated. She held an unusual deep blue bottle, like she was *hydrating* for the event, and some liquid sloshed out when she gestured.

Lauren was gesticulating, too, jabbing her blunt finger at Elyse's face.

I didn't think that was a very smart way to treat one's boss.

Then, since I couldn't hear them, and their spat didn't concern me, I turned toward Jonathan again, only to realize that he was accompanied by *two* dogs: Axis and a one-eared Chihuahua, whom I'd also foisted upon him, over some pretty strong protests.

In spite of how cold I was, I grinned to see Artie happily tucked inside Jonathan's jacket.

The duo had clearly come a long way since the day Jonathan had refused to even look down at the little dog who'd drooled all over his feet, waiting hopefully to be picked up by a man he clearly worshipped.

I was so pleased for Artie that for a moment I kind of forgot where I was, and I almost began to walk toward them, to deliver the sweater I'd purchased, just as Jonathan spied me, too, but Mayor Holtzapple, who'd reclaimed the bullhorn at some point, made a loud and forceful announcement.

"Plungers! Go!"

I didn't even have time to wave to Jonathan, Axis, and Artie.

The moment the excited crowd was released, I was swept backward, toward the icy, murky depths of Lake Wallapawakee, and everything went wrong.

Chapter 5

The first shock of the water took my breath away, and I wanted to run right back to shore and claim one of those blankets Piper had been folding. But I couldn't. My sister had been right. The plunge should've been organized better. The whole scene was chaos, a mess of thrashing, splashing arms and legs, impossible to fight through. And the night air was filled with a raucous cacophony of what I thought was laughter, but there were screams and shrieks, too, as about eighty people collided, running in and out of the black lake. Observers onshore—probably including Gabriel Graham—were taking pictures, too, so the darkness was interrupted by intermittent, strobing flashes of bright light, which only added to the anarchy.

I was a fairly calm person, but I found myself fighting to breathe evenly and stay composed as I got pushed deeper into the water, where the lake bed got softer and more slimy.

I couldn't help flailing my arms, which only made things worse, and in a split second, during which someone else who must've lost her footing grabbed on to me, I slipped in the muck.

Suddenly, I was underwater and struggling to right myself. In seconds, my whole body felt like it was going numb, and when my head, fortunately, popped above the surface, I began to paddle furiously, only to get my hand snagged in something that felt like a huge spider web.

The crowd was receding, everyone else retreating from the water, and I tried to follow. But when I attempted to free my numb hand from whatever was tangled around my fingers, I gasped not with the cold, but with a different kind of shock, as Lauren Savidge's pale—no, bluish—face rose to the surface.

"Help!" I screamed, loudly. And almost immediately, someone came to my rescue.

Actually, two someones.

Detective Jonathan Black, who was missing his jacket but otherwise fully clothed, dripping wet, and calmly in charge as he wordlessly wrapped his arms around me and lifted me out of the water, and a *Saint Bernard*, complete with a barrel under his chin, who showed up seemingly out of nowhere and pulled Lauren's stiff, lifeless body to shore before disappearing into the chaos and the night.

Chapter 6

"Are you okay, Daphne?" my sister asked for the hundredth time, pouring me yet another cup of soothing, warming chamomile tea. Crossing the few steps that separated my cottage's tiny kitchen from the equally miniature living room, she handed me a pretty, blue-glazed earthenware mug. "Keep drinking this, to bring up your core temperature."

Piper wasn't normally maternal, but she was trained to care for shivering, traumatized creatures, and she'd helped me and Socrates get home to Plum Cottage. Then she'd ordered me to change into dry pajamas, set me on the love seat that barely fit into the small living room, wrapped me in two layers of warm blankets, and lit a blazing fire in the arched stone fireplace. My recently adopted, still only semi-friendly black Persian cat, Tinkleston, had deigned to climb under the blankets, too, and he was sitting on my lap like a living, breathing heating pad. Yet I was still shivering. Not so much because I had nearly succumbed to hypothermia for the second time in just a few months, but because I couldn't stop picturing

Lauren Savidge's blue face and recalling how her stiff body had bumped against mine in the frigid water.

Sipping the tea, I tried to shake off the memory and forced myself to smile at Socrates, who wasn't dozing in his favorite spot by the fireplace. He sat rigidly in the center of the room, guilt and regret in his brown eyes. I knew he felt terrible that *he* hadn't come to my rescue.

"You've saved me several times," I reminded him. "And I know you weren't watching the plunge. I'm sure you had your back turned to the whole event!"

Socrates still seemed apologetic, and perhaps unhappy to have been upstaged by a human *and* a Saint Bernard—a breed known for *slobbering*. He plopped down onto his belly and huffed, loudly, to tell me that he was sorry and disappointed in himself.

I knew he'd eventually forgive himself, and I took another sip of tea.

Piper, meanwhile, headed to a coat rack near the door and began to suit up for a short hike through the woods, on paths that led back to her farmhouse.

"If you're okay, I'm heading home," she said, already zipping up her jacket, so it would be hard for me to argue that she should stay. "It's late and really starting to snow out there. It's easy to get disoriented in the dark, even on familiar trails."

As if on cue, a gust of wind smacked against the walls of the cottage, and the plum tree that gave my home its name scratched its limbs against one of the windows. That was always a sign that the weather was getting bad. I knew that Piper should get going, but while she pulled on her hat and gloves, I said, "Speaking of getting lost on trails . . . where the heck did that Saint Bernard come from?" I set my mug on a steamer trunk that served as my coffee table and shook off some of my blankets. I'd buttoned myself into my warmest, softest, striped flannel pj's, and I was finally getting *too* toasty. Tinkleston yowled to let me know he didn't appreciate being disturbed, then hopped to the floor. "The dog ran in out of nowhere and disappeared just as fast."

"Don't start believing in tall tales," Piper urged, wrapping a scarf around her neck. "I'm sure the Saint Bernard was someone's pet, probably there the whole time in the crowd, and then we just lost track of it in all the craziness."

"Craziness" was an understatement. Once the already excited crowd had realized there was a body in the water, the scene at Lake Wallapawakee had erupted into anarchy. Even the poor guy who'd been assigned as Safety Crew had run around like a chicken with his head cut off.

On the off chance that Lauren Savidge's death hadn't been accidental, Jonathan Black would have his work cut out for him. Every plunger on the roster was probably a potential suspect, and the sand had been churned up by hundreds of feet.

"Talk about a messy crime scene," I muttered to myself.

"Daphne . . ." There was warning in Piper's voice. "We've been over this. In water that cold, a slip like the one you suffered could be fatal in seconds. What happened tonight was most likely an accident."

That was probably true, but I couldn't help thinking about all the people who hated Lauren, and I ventured, one more time, "Don't you think there's a *chance* that Lauren was murdered?"

My sister swung open the door, like she wasn't

about to entertain that question again. Then she drew
back, clearly startled. She stood that way for a long
moment, the door wide open and snow blowing into
the cottage.

"I have no idea if Lauren was murdered, Daphne,"
she finally told me. "But I think *you're* about to get a
definitive answer to that question."

Chapter 7

"Are you sure I can't get you something to eat or drink?" I asked Jonathan Black, who stood in my living room, wearing a dry pair of jeans and a gray sweater that gave his dark blue eyes a stormy cast.

My cottage never felt too small to me, until Jonathan visited, which didn't happen often. But when he did cross my threshold, Plum Cottage immediately felt like a dollhouse. Jonathan was over six feet tall, and although he maintained his lean, military physique, he had a way of claiming space. I couldn't quite put my finger on how he did that.

And, of course, my home also felt smaller because he'd brought along Axis, the big chocolate Lab, and my favorite one-eared Chihuahua, Artie, who was currently applying his severe overbite to Socrates's long, droopy ear, in an attempt to cajole the gloomier-than-usual basset hound into a better mood.

I could've told Artie that his strategy wouldn't work. And yet, Socrates was enduring the attentions of the exuberant, mischievous little dog. Talk about opposites who'd somehow attracted, as friends, during the time Artie had lived with us. Then I turned back to someone who was *my* complete opposite—and who might or might not be my friend. "Please, let me get you some coffee. And I made this amazing chocolate-chip bread pudding with a cinnamon rum sauce." My cheeks got warm as I recalled how Jonathan had carried me out of the lake, slogging through the water with me quaking like a human jackhammer in his arms. "It's the least I can do, after how you pretty much saved me tonight." Gesturing for him to follow me, I padded toward the kitchen in my big, fluffy slippers, wishing I was dressed in real clothes, like Jonathan. I also hoped that Tinkleston, who'd once attempted to maul Jonathan, would stay in his favorite hiding spot amid some herbs I grew on my kitchen windowsill. I could see Tinks's unusual orange eyes blinking at me from behind the basil. "Did I thank you for wading in to get me?"

Jonathan had seemed pretty grim since coming in from the storm, but when I looked over my shoulder, I noticed a glimmer of amusement in his eyes, and the corners of his mouth twitched with a suppressed smile. "I don't know, Daphne," he mused, following me to the kitchen. The antique icebox and vintage gas oven seemed to shrink in his presence. "*Did* you ever thank me? Or compensate me for the time you spilled iced tea all over my truck, so I had to have it professionally cleaned? Or pay me back for the restaurant checks you've walked out on, when sudden 'emergencies' arose just before the bills arrived?"

I *might've* stuck Jonathan with the tab at a few eating establishments in the past. Always for legitimate reasons. But I knew that he was teasing me. I'd been trying to repay my debts lately, albeit slowly.

"Have you ever thanked *me* for convincing you to adopt two of the best friends you'll ever have?" I countered, joking with him, too. I poured dark roast, ground Kona beans into a small silver coffeemaker I'd brought back from Italy a few years ago. I knew Jonathan was a fan of strong black coffee, and the little pot would deliver. Then I set three pup-friendly Chicken and Rice Snowballs, formed from poached chicken, rice, and a bit of chicken broth, onto small plates and delivered those to the dogs, who were all communing near the hearth. Returning to the kitchen, I slipped Tinks a little tuna to reward him for not attacking. "I saw you with Artie tucked in your jacket," I added. "So I'm assuming you two are buddies now."

As soon as I said all that, I regretted mentioning the part about "best friends" and "buddies." Jonathan had lost his canine SEAL partner, a Belgian Malinois named Herod, during a battle in Afghanistan. I was pretty sure that wrenching loss had made him reluctant to adopt new pets. But for once he didn't completely shut himself off when talking about dogs. He leaned against what little countertop I had and crossed his arms over his chest, still clearly amused, but pretending to be irritated.

"Artie spent the whole evening shivering worse than you, when I pulled you from the lake," he said, nodding at the Chihuahua, who was helping himself to Socrates's snack. Apparently, Socrates's self-recrimination was affecting his appetite. Axis, who'd already eaten his Snowball, was nodding off by the crackling fire. "I honestly had trouble choosing between continuing to keep that quivering, hyper, pain-in-the-neck warm, and setting him down so I could rescue you."

"Oh, gosh!" I snapped my fingers, suddenly remembering something I'd forgotten during the night's excitement. I hurried over to my jacket, which was hanging by the door, and reached into one of the deep pockets. Locating a bag, I pulled out the contents, concealed my hands behind my back, and returned to the kitchen. "I bought something for Artie to keep him warm. And because it's so cute."

"Cute" was probably not a selling point for Jonathan, whatever the product was. "Thanks?" he said uncertainly. Then he frowned when I handed him a little yellow cardigan with green piping. He held it up for inspection. "Oh, no. You don't really expect me to . . ."

"Yes, I do expect you to put this on Artie," I said, snatching the sweater away from him. I didn't even have to summon the lively Chihuahua, who loved to dress up. He was already prancing toward me, like he knew the cardigan was his. Kneeling down, I draped the soft, yak-hair garment over his shaky little frame, and he was so excited that he could hardly hold still while I slipped his front legs through the appropriate holes. "There you go," I told him, when he was all buttoned up. Smiling, I scratched the spot behind his missing ear. "You look adorable! Like a tiny canine accountant!"

With a quick, grateful yip, Artie pranced off to show his new attire to Socrates, who groaned softly and fell over sideways. He and Artie would *never* agree on clothes.

Jonathan obviously concurred with Socrates. He

was rubbing his forehead, like his head ached, and he sighed, deeply. "That is the most ridiculous—"

"Maybe he can wear the sweater at the Cardboard Iditarod," I said, interrupting again. I doubted that Jonathan had plans to enter Axis or Artie in the sled parade, but I acted like Artie's participation, at least, was a given. Artie loved to be the center of attention, and I couldn't bear to think of him missing one of the year's most fun events. Pretending that I didn't see how skeptical Jonathan was, I smiled up at him. "Won't Artie look cute, riding on a sled in that outfit?"

Jonathan's eyebrows shot up. "*Riding?* What do you mean 'riding'? Dogs *pull* sleds." He glanced at Artie, who was rearing up on his hind legs in front of Socrates, desperate to get the bigger dog's approval of his finery. Socrates, meanwhile, was pretending to sleep. Then Jonathan looked at me again. "There is *no way* I'm going to—"

"Oh, fine, I'll take Artie," I said, waving off Jonathan's objections. In truth, I wanted to take part, and Socrates would never join me. Rising from the kitchen floor, I shoved Jonathan aside so I could reach behind him and get the pan of bread pudding, which was cooling on a rack. The brioche I'd used had soaked all day in a mixture of locally produced eggs, rich half-and-half, and fragrant vanilla, and when I'd returned from Winterfest, I'd popped the waiting dessert into the oven before even changing out of my wet clothes. It was almost like I'd known I would get trampled in a half-frozen lake and need a warm treat at the end of the day. "Moxie and I will make the sled," I added. "It'll take my mind off everything that happened tonight."

Jonathan didn't reply, and I looked over to see that he'd grown serious. On the few occasions we'd stood very close, like we were doing then, I always noted a small scar that ran along his jaw and wondered how he'd gotten it. I was sure there was a story there. But Jonathan didn't like to tell tales about his past. I still couldn't believe I'd gotten him to admit that he'd been forced to leave his career as a SEAL when he'd become gravely ill with a form of cancer he'd never named. But he'd hinted that the disease might come back someday. I didn't know Jonathan that well, but I never thought about him without saying a little prayer to the universe, to spare him that fate. And when my gaze shifted from that mark on his jaw to meet his eyes, I was surprised to see that he was genuinely concerned for me, too.

"Are you okay, Daphne?" he asked quietly. "I know you're—oddly—no stranger to finding bodies, but you went through a real ordeal tonight. Are you all right?"

I tucked some of my curls behind my ear, feeling strangely uncomfortable. "Yes, I'm okay." Breaking our gaze, I reached for the coffeepot and poured some of the aromatic brew into a mug that matched mine. I handed the coffee to Jonathan, who accepted it wordlessly; then I retrieved two similarly glazed, rustic plates and served up the bread pudding. But before I poured the sweet, dark rum sauce over Jonathan's share, he rested one hand on my arm, stopping me.

"What's wrong?" I asked, looking up at him again.

"That looks great." He withdrew his hand. "But I think I'll skip the rum sauce, which smells like it's about eighty proof."

"You're probably right," I agreed, sniffing the

pitcher that held the thick, buttery sauce. "I got the rum in Jamaica, from a guy in an alley, who swore it was as good as Appleton's Exclusive . . ." I started to tell Jonathan a quick story about how I'd tried to save money by buying rum *really* duty free, then thought the better of sharing my tale. He was already giving me a skeptical look. Plus, I didn't need him hauling me and my bottle to a customs agent somewhere. "Anyhow," I said. "It's actually okay in small doses. Are you sure I can't give you a splash?"

"No, thanks." He couldn't quite fight back a grin. "My job would be a lot harder if your *moonshine* blinded me." Then he grew more serious. "And I'm technically on duty and shouldn't be drinking anything stronger than your coffee. Which is also pretty strong."

"What?" I'd been dousing my pudding with the sauce, but when he said that, my hand jerked, and an extra glug splashed onto my plate. "Why are you on duty?"

"I'm waiting for a call from Vonda Shakes," he said, referencing the county coroner. "I'm not sure Lauren Savidge's death was an accident."

My stomach twisted to think that I might've been on the scene of a murder, but I had to admit that part of me was intrigued by the possibility that my hunch was right. Setting down the pitcher, I handed Jonathan his plate, piled high with warm, sweet bread and melted chocolate chips. "Why do you think Lauren might've been murdered?"

Jonathan must've been hungry, because he dug into the bread pudding before answering me. In truth, I didn't really expect him to tell me anything. He didn't like me meddling in his cases. And when he'd finished a big bite, he raised a cautionary hand.

"I'm not *sure* this is a homicide yet, so, please, don't start playing detective."

Ignoring that suggestion, I took my plate and refilled mug of tea over to the kitchen table, where I sank down onto one of the two chairs. I didn't bother urging Jonathan to sit, too. He looked very comfortable standing. "Can you at least tell me why you're thinking homicide? Because I was just talking about that possibility with Piper."

Jonathan hesitated, clearly reluctant to confide in me.

"You might as well spill," I said, through a mouthful of dessert. "I think history proves that I'll get the information somehow."

He sipped his coffee, no doubt recalling my past investigative efforts. Then he must've concluded that I was correct about my snooping abilities.

"When I tried to resuscitate Lauren, I got blood on my hand," he told me. "From cradling the back of her head, as I turned her over. The dog that pulled her from the water left her on her side."

I hadn't seen any blood, although I'd stood where Jonathan had set me down, close to the body. But the beach had been dark, clouds obscuring the moon, and I'd alternated between watching Jonathan kneel on the sand, attempting CPR on Lauren, and glancing around at the crowd of confused, excited people who'd also gathered, forming a circle. I'd noted that some morbid folks continued to snap pictures. The night had been punctuated by flashes, although most had been generated by Gabriel Graham, who must've stepped into the water at some point. His pants were wet up to the knees. And the Stylish Life cameraman had kept his camera on his shoulder and his eye to

the lens, too, as if he'd been *filming*—until Elyse
Hunter-Black had approached him and tapped his
shoulder, shaking her head and forcing him to stop.
Then Elyse had turned to watch Jonathan, although
I thought her gaze had flicked, now and then, to *me*.

Or maybe she'd been checking on Lauren's assistant, Joy, who'd stood right next to me, dripping,
shuddering, and muttering softly into her trembling
hands.

Only the safety crew guy and holistic pet healer
Arlo Finch had run forward to help. Arlo must've
been freezing, because he'd still been wearing his wet
T-shirt. I recalled seeing that strange tattoo on his
wrist as he'd attempted compressions on Lauren's
chest, even after Jonathan had urged him to give up.

Victor Breard had finally shoved through the crowd,
too, dropping to his knees at Jonathan's side. It had
occurred to me that a man who worked with dangerous big cats on a regular basis would probably be
better in that stressful situation than a pet therapist,
however well intentioned.

A few moments later, Piper had hurried over to
me, covering me with a blanket and leading me away.

As I stood in my warm kitchen, picturing Jonathan
attempting to restart Lauren's heart, I realized that
his evening had been as traumatic as mine, if not
worse. I considered asking him if he was okay, then
thought the better of it. I knew he'd insist that he was
fine. He would *always* insist that he was fine.

I also wanted to know if Jonathan had seen the
Saint Bernard run off, but I assumed he'd been solely
focused on trying to save Lauren after setting me
down on the lakeshore. And I had bigger questions
to ask, right then, about Lauren's death.

"So," I ventured, "do you think someone might've hit her on the head? Because of the blood?"

He sipped his coffee and didn't even flinch, although the brew had to be bitter. Then he set down the mug. "Yes, that's what I suspect." He peered more closely at me. "You fell in the water. It would've been difficult to hit your head, right? Hard enough to make it bleed?"

"I'm not sure," I said. "There were some small rocks near the shore. But most of the lake bed was soft. Especially where I found Lauren. And although the water was only a few feet deep, it kind of buoyed me up when I stumbled. I really don't know how your head would hit bottom hard enough to make you bleed."

We both grew silent for a minute, while I tried to figure out exactly how one might get a head wound in the middle of a lake. The only sound in the cottage was the snuffling of the dogs, the crackling of the fire, and the roar of the wind outside.

Then Jonathan broke the silence, setting his empty plate on the counter and noting, "Lauren Savidge had a lot of enemies, didn't she?"

I took a second to study him. "This isn't just a social call, is it?" I finally asked. "You aren't just checking on my well-being, are you?"

"I'm doing that," Jonathan said. "But I'd also like to know what you saw tonight. And I'd appreciate any information you have about Lauren."

He was basically asking for my help with a potential investigation. I wouldn't gloat, though, for fear of chasing him off. And I had plenty to tell him. But before I answered his questions, I had one for him, although I asked it reluctantly.

"Um . . . did you happen to see *Elyse* tonight? Right before the plunge?"

He cocked his head, like he wasn't sure what I was getting at. "Yes, I saw her," he said. "But only for a minute, when she stopped to say hello. Then she disappeared into the crowd."

I hadn't expected that response. I'd assumed he'd attended the plunge with Elyse.

"Why were you even there?" I asked, forgetting, for a moment, that we were discussing a potential murder. I pushed aside my empty plate. "I never expected to see you at something so . . . frivolous."

Jonathan normally didn't explain his motives for doing anything, and he surprised me again by answering. "I heard the event wasn't well organized, and I thought my prior training with cold water rescues might come in handy. I felt a responsibility to go." Of course, he quickly downplayed his history. "But that's not important. I'd rather talk about what *you* observed, right before you found the body." A shadow of concern crossed his face. "You were saying something about Elyse?"

I was trying to decide if I should tell him that I'd seen his ex-wife arguing with Lauren Savidge right before we'd all run into the water, when all at once, his cell phone rang, and he raised one finger, silencing me while politely excusing himself. "Sorry. I need to check this." Then he slipped a sleek black iPhone from the back pocket of his jeans, tapped the screen, and, bypassing pleasantries, said, "Yes?"

He listened for a minute, frowning, then signed off with equal simplicity. "Thanks. We'll talk tomorrow."

A moment later, he returned the phone to his pocket and addressed me again. "Thanks for the dessert and the coffee, which were both great. I think we can consider another part of your debt repaid now." He glanced at the Chihuahua, who had given up preening, but whose eyes still gleamed with pride over his new duds. "And it was nice of you to buy Artie a sweater. I think."

"You are very welcome," I said, ignoring his last, uncertain comment and following him to the door, where he slipped on his down jacket and silently summoned Artie and Axis by holding out his lowered hand. I noted that the formerly incorrigible little dog was continuing to shape up since moving in with Jonathan. Artie trotted right over and raised up on his back legs. At that cue, Jonathan reached down to pick him up. Apparently, the trainer was also a trainee, whether he knew it or not.

"So, do you still want me to tell you what I saw?" I asked, although clearly he planned to leave without interviewing me further.

"Not tonight," he told me. "I will want to get your story, though—when I have my partner with me."

I blinked at him. "What?"

"I'd hoped to ask you a few questions, informally, before this became a full-blown investigation. But Vonda Shakes works quickly. And the next time we talk, I'll be officially investigating Lauren Savidge's murder." He nodded to the doorknob, which he'd updated by installing a lock the last time I'd been involved in a homicide. "And, please, *lock your door.*"

He didn't wait for me to make a promise I probably wouldn't keep. He left without another word, with Artie tucked into his coat, safe from the gale, and Axis trotting happily alongside him, probably enjoying the snow.

Although it was freezing outside, and icy flakes were blowing into Plum Cottage, I watched them disappear into the dark woods while I tried to figure out what, exactly, had just happened.

Had by-the-book Jonathan Black just bent a rule by trying to get some information out of me before the death was officially declared a homicide?

I also wondered if I should've insisted on telling him about Elyse's lakeside argument with Lauren. But Elyse would no doubt admit to fighting with her field producer. I didn't know Elyse that well, but I was fairly certain that the Ivy League–educated TV executive was smart enough to realize that lots of people had witnessed the quarrel.

Last but not least, as cold wind rushed into the room, I started to worry that *I* might've just moved from informant to potential suspect. Because I'd been the one with Lauren's hair tangled in my numb fingers, and he'd mentioned getting my "story" as opposed to my "observations."

There was a subtle, but potentially important distinction between those two terms. And Jonathan tended to choose his words carefully. . . .

My concerns were interrupted by a feeling of pressure against my calf, and I looked down to see that Tinks had joined me at the door and was rubbing against my legs, possibly in a friendly way, or as a precursor to sinking his teeth into me. It was still hard to tell sometimes with Tinkleston.

Socrates was standing right behind me, too. He was watchful, like he wouldn't let anything more happen to me that night.

Not wanting any of us to freeze, I finally shut the door and leaned against it, thinking about poor

Lauren Savidge, lying lifeless on a state park beach, and Jonathan, who hadn't seemed worried about wandering lonely trails in a near blizzard. Then I sent up *three* little prayers to the universe.

One for Lauren, who might've been hard to deal with, but who hadn't deserved the fate that had befallen her that night.

And two for Jonathan: my usual request that the powers-that-be watch over him and an extra appeal, too. Just for good measure.

Chapter 8

When I woke up the next morning, the sun was shining brightly through the window above my bed, which was centered under the peaked eaves in my small loft bedroom. The few noises outside were muffled, so I knew that the cottage was buried under a thick blanket of snow. I was content to linger under my heavy, snowy white comforter, too. And Tinkleston and Socrates weren't moving quickly, either. Tinks was curled at the foot of the bed, sunk down in the feathers so just the tips of his black ears were visible, while Socrates was stretched out on his purple velvet cushion, his eyes closed but his mind likely active. He liked to engage in quiet contemplation before rising to greet the day.

Unfortunately, I couldn't fully enjoy the lazy morning. My thoughts kept returning to Lauren Savidge and the events of the previous night.

Then the peace was also shattered by the ringing of the old landline phone on my nightstand. It was pretty early, and I eyed the black rotary dial phone warily before picking up the heavy receiver. "Hello?"

I was right to be concerned. The person on the other end of the line didn't bother to introduce herself or engage in small talk before asking me, "Daphne, what in the world is going on with you?"

I was about to argue that nothing had been "going on" with me. I'd been quite comfortable in my bed.

Then my mother caused me to jerk upright by adding, "Have you seen today's newspaper?"

Chapter 9

"I can't believe you've gotten yourself involved in another murder," my mother, Maeve Templeton, complained, stalking around the small kitchen in the storefront I'd rented in November. Although it was Sunday and half of Sylvan Creek's sidewalks were still buried under two feet of snow, Mom wore a pencil skirt and a pair of Michael Kors pumps that clicked on the old wooden floor, causing Socrates, who was lying near the warm oven, to wince with every step. I supposed Mom's shoes were a small concession to the snow; on days when the sidewalks were clear, she usually wore even pricier designer heels, like Prada or Saint Laurent. "And this time, your antics are so public!" she added. "On the front page of the newspaper!"

I was rolling out dough for dog treats I called Cinnamon Roll-Overs, but I stole a peek at a copy of the Sylvan Creek *Weekly Gazette*, which Mom had slapped down onto the worn butcher block counter. Catching sight of a large photo on the front page, I cringed again, like I'd done the first ten times I'd seen the image of me being carried out of Lake Wallapawakee. My wet hair was straggly, my eyes were wide with horror, and although the photo was black and white, it was obvious that my bare legs were covered in mud. Jonathan, of course, looked like he'd been styled for an action movie. His expression, shown in rugged profile, was grim but calm; his wet shirt clung to his body in a way that emphasized his strong arms; and a shock of his black hair fell artfully over his forehead.

Gabriel Graham, who was starting to produce the paper on more than a weekly basis, had captured a picture of the Saint Bernard, too. There was a whole sidebar about the dog. I intended to read that story, as soon as my mother stopped nagging me about the *traumatic event I'd endured.*

"What in the world were you doing swimming in the lake in January?" she continued, raising her hands and rolling her eyes up to the ceiling. Maeve Templeton seldom allowed her face to exhibit agitation—emotions bred wrinkles—but she was quite unhappy with me right then. "Who *does* that?"

"Um, about eighty people," I reminded her, as I shaped the Roll-Overs so they'd look like traditional cinnamon rolls. Although Flour Power wasn't open yet, I stopped by several times each week to perfect my recipes, most of which were original. Not that my mother was giving me credit for preparing for a successful launch. "The plunge was a pretty big event."

"And yet, you were the only one to find a body in the lake," Mom noted, helping herself to a mug of free coffee from a machine that she had somehow figured out how to use.

I, meanwhile, was baffled by the massive, complicated contraption I'd inherited from the shop's previous tenant, an Italian woman who'd fled her abusive boyfriend, leaving everything behind, including her imported coffee and espresso maker, which had so many knobs and levers that I sometimes worried I might accidentally time travel if I used the wrong combination. That fear was heightened by the fact that everything was labeled in Italian. And the two clocklike dials on the stainless-steel surface didn't help, either.

My caffeine-addicted mother wasn't the least bit concerned about landing in a different century while making a latte. She brewed herself at least three cups of coffee a day, on a regular schedule, and took a sip before resuming scolding me. "Can you see how your repeated involvement in homicides and your embarrassing hijinks might reflect poorly on me?"

By "me," Mom meant her mini real-estate empire, Maeve Templeton Realty. The two entities were inseparable. And I could not see how my "antics" nor my "hijinks" affected my mother or her business. Would someone refuse to buy a house just because I'd stumbled across a few bodies?

I didn't bother directly arguing that point. It was usually a waste of time to debate with my mother, or with Piper, who shared Mom's determination to win any challenge, at all costs.

That gene had definitely skipped me. Or, more likely, I took after my laid-back, itinerant father, who'd drifted out of our lives when I'd been a kid. Not that I'd ever abandon *my* family. I glanced at Socrates. On the contrary, I had a habit of drawing souls around myself and had difficulty letting them go. I still missed Artie, even though I knew the little Chihuahua was happy with Jonathan and Axis. . . .

"Daphne, are you listening to me?"

My mother's voice interrupted my musings. "Yes," I assured her, sidestepping Socrates. I grabbed some big mitts from a hook on the wall and retrieved my first trial tray of Roll-Overs from the hot oven. The treats, made from whole wheat flour, milk, cinnamon, and honey, looked and smelled delicious. Socrates, who seldom allowed himself to appear enthusiastic about food, lifted his big head, his nose twitching. I slid the tray onto a cooling rack and turned to Mom. "I am listening to most of what you say."

"Please tell me that you are not a suspect in this crime," Mom begged, setting down her mug. "I don't think I could bear to have *another* daughter accused of murder!"

I'd solved my first case because Piper had been implicated in the death of her ex-boyfriend. And I'd spent the previous night parsing Jonathan's words— "observations" versus "story"—and worrying that I really might be a suspect in this latest homicide.

"If you can't bear that possibility, you'd probably better stop reading the *Gazette* for a while," I advised Mom. I began to set the second batch of sweet-smelling treats onto a new tray. "And don't you have any sympathy for Lauren Savidge? This isn't about me. And it's really not about you, at all."

I shouldn't have accused Maeve Templeton of being heartless. She reared back and rested one manicured hand on the ruffles that ran down the front of her professional-looking blouse, blinking at me with disbelief. "I will have you know that I am probably one of the few people in Sylvan Creek who *liked* Lauren. She was a strong, driven woman who got her way. And she was an excellent tenant who paid her rent in advance."

I had forgotten that my mother, who not only sold properties to other people but occasionally invested in them herself, had rented rooms to Lauren on a short-term lease. In fact, the cute efficiency apartment was located right above Mom's offices, about two blocks away from my bakery and across the street from my sister's practice. Most storefronts in Sylvan Creek had apartments overhead.

I was just about to apologize for insinuating that my mother was acting callously about the murder when she had to bring up my potential shortcomings as a tenant. "And speaking of renting," she said, crossing her arms and squashing those ruffles again, "when are you going to open for business? And how are you paying rent here?"

I slid the second tray into the oven. "My pet-sitting business is actually doing well right now," I informed Mom. "In fact, I'll be sitting for Mayor Holtzapple's Pomeranian later this week. And she pays well, to ensure that Pippin gets pampered."

"Oh, Henrietta and that dog," Mom said, with disdain. She waved one hand dismissively. "I swear, that woman is obsessed with that animal—and this town!"

Talk about the pot calling the kettle black. My mother was the most obsessive person I knew. Her real-estate business was everything to her. And, not surprisingly, she quickly steered the conversation back to leases and rent.

"Honestly, Daphne, you need to bake less and renovate more," she advised me, buttoning up her wool coat. I assumed that she was going to show a house and add to her own fortune. "What is taking so long?"

"It's impossible to get anyone to work," I said, looking around at the bakery, which was stuck in mid-overhaul. I'd liked the former café's Tuscan theme, but I wanted to create a more vibrant, yet mellow atmosphere in keeping with my new business's hippie-esque name. In a leap of faith, I'd allowed Moxie to paint the walls with pretty pink and yellow, mod-looking flowers, reminiscent of the late 1960s. And to my delight, my best friend had redeemed herself and could officially be forgiven for painting a horse-dog creature on my van. The walls were beautiful. However, the floors weren't refinished yet, and the cool 1975 olive-green cabinet I'd bought online, to hold the cash register, lacked a countertop. The creepy walk-in refrigerator, which gave me claustrophobia, was also still balky, refusing to maintain a temperature above freezing.

I turned back to my mother. "There aren't that many contractors and handymen in Sylvan Creek to begin with, and they're all busy working for—"

"Excuses, excuses, Daphne," Mom said, cutting off my complaints. She wrapped a Burberry plaid scarf around her neck. "There's no room for excuses in business! Just get the work done!"

Then my mother swept out of the kitchen and straight through the front door, tossing the scarf over her shoulder in dramatic fashion as she left, while I began to tidy up the small kitchen. I was trying to make an effort to be neater, now that I was about to be a commercial baker.

And while I put things away, I thought about what Mom had just said about completing work.

Would someone finish Lauren's job on *America's Most Pet Friendly Towns*?

Or would the remaining crew just pack up and leave?

"What do you think, Socrates?" I asked, although I hadn't voiced my other questions out loud.

My longtime sidekick nevertheless seemed to grasp that I was growing curious about a homicide, and he lowered his freckled muzzle and buried it under his large paws, groaning softly, like he wished I would just mind my own business.

Ignoring him, I wiped my hands on my apron and picked up the newspaper, which my mother had left spread out on the counter.

Eyes moving quickly, I skimmed the article about the tragedy at the lake—cringing when I saw my picture again. I swore, Gabriel Graham had deliberately tried to make me look terrible. The Saint Bernard, while slightly out of focus, looked better than me.

"Seriously?" I muttered, holding up the *Gazette* so Socrates could see my photo. "Isn't this kind of insulting?"

Socrates agreed. He shook his head and snuffled with regret, indicating that he felt sorry about my public humiliation, although I also knew that he'd never supported my decision to jump in a lake.

At least he wasn't laughing at me, like probably everyone else in Sylvan Creek was doing that morning.

"Come on, Socrates," I said, dropping the paper back onto the butcher block. Then I took the second tray of perfectly baked Roll-Overs out of the oven, switched a dial to turn off the heat, and pulled on my big barn coat. "We are going to confront Mr. Graham," I told the basset hound, who was reluctantly rising and joining me at the door. "I'm pretty sure I saw lights on in his building, too."

Socrates hung and shook his head, like he thought I was on another ill-fated mission, but he followed me out into the cold sunshine and across the street, toward the offices of the *Weekly Gazette*.

And when I opened the door, which was unlocked, I discovered that not only was Gabriel Graham at his desk that Sunday morning, but my arrival had apparently been anticipated—and a huge, slobbery surprise was lying in wait for me, prepared to knock me off my feet.

Chapter 10

"Are you okay?" Gabriel asked, barely suppressing his laughter, even as he came around from behind his desk and attempted to *pull a 150-pound Saint Bernard off me*, while I lay flat on my back, fighting off the most slobbery dog kisses I'd ever endured. Normally, I was a fan of canine smooches, but the dog who had tackled me the moment I'd walked through the door didn't know his own strength. Plus he had a wicked case of puppy breath. "Come on, now," Gabriel said, hauling on the dog's collar. "That's enough!"

The massive mutt relented just enough to allow me to slide backward, scooching on my butt and wiping my coat sleeve across my face to clean off the drool. Then, while the dog strained against Gabriel's hold, I quickly stood up and stepped backward. "This isn't really . . . ?"

Gabriel's arms were practically being pulled out of their sockets, but he grinned more broadly with self-satisfaction.

"Yup," he informed me smugly, lurching when the dog made one last attempt to smother me with affection. "Daphne Templeton, meet *the* Lake Walla-pawakee Saint Bernard!"

Chapter 11

"How did you find him?" I asked, stroking the Saint Bernard's broad head, which lay in my lap. I was sitting on an uncomfortable metal seat across from Gabriel, who was behind his desk again, leaning back in a squeaky old leather-upholstered chair, his hands laced behind his head and his feet kicked up on a blotter that featured a calendar from 1979. And the planner wasn't the only thing trapped in time. The *Weekly Gazette*'s headquarters obviously hadn't been updated much since the days of the hand-cranked printing press. Sunlight filtered through smudged, wood-framed windows; stacks of yellowing newspapers teetered on every spare surface; and an ancient typewriter sat on a bookshelf, as if waiting to be called back into service. I even spied a printer's tray full of linotype letters, which were disturbed in their miniature compartments, like maybe they were actually being *used*. Then I glanced between the dozing canine and Gabriel, who was grinning like a big-game hunter who'd bagged a record-setting grizzly. "This really is the dog from Bear Tooth forest, right?"

I'd asked that question several times, and I posed it yet again, mainly because I didn't trust Gabriel. Plus, something didn't seem quite right about "Bernie," as Gabriel was unoriginally calling him. Still, as I ran my hand across a broad white blaze that ran from Bernie's nose to between his ears, I had to admit that the Saint Bernard who was dreaming and drooling on my jeans certainly looked like the dog who'd pulled Lauren Savidge from Lake Walla-pawakee.

"Yes, I assume this is the dog from last night—unless there's a pack of Saint Bernards roaming the woods," Gabriel said. He swung his feet to the floor, so he could lean forward and study Bernie. "Not that I'm an expert on canine identification. Most dogs look alike to me."

Socrates, who'd been staring out one of the dusty windows, watching the street, gave the slightest "woof" of disapproval.

To my surprise, Gabriel seemed to understand that he'd been rebuked. "Sorry, pal," he told Socrates, with a grin. "Didn't mean to insult you."

Socrates, who didn't like nicknames like "buddy" and "pal," ignored the apology, which was basically another insult in his opinion.

"Does Bernie have tags?" I asked, slipping my hand down to the dog's broad collar, which was almost hidden under his thick, reddish-brown fur.

My fingers found the empty metal loop that should have held metal disks with Bernie's real name and an address, as well as proof of immunizations, just as Gabriel said, "No, he doesn't have any ID on him."

"How did you find him?" I asked. For a second, I forgot that the dog whose slobber was soaking through my jeans *wasn't* the stuff of legend, and I added, "No one's ever been able to capture him!"

Gabriel laughed. "You don't really believe this dog is some kind of spirit, do you?"

"No," I said, my cheeks getting warm. "I just grew up with the story, and then to have the old tale sort of come true last night . . ."

My voice trailed off as I once again pictured Lauren Savidge's bluish face and blank eyes, and Gabriel also caught the shift in mood.

"I don't know where he came from, or why he showed up last night, playing the hero, like Jonathan Black," Gabriel said, his dark eyes clouding over. Was that a touch of jealousy in his tone? Did he wish he'd "played the hero" instead of snapping pictures? "But the dog's not mystical," he continued, studying Bernie again. "He's flesh and blood, and I had a feeling that, if I went hiking with some treats in my pockets, there was a good chance I'd find him, if he was still in the woods—as I suspected." He met my eyes again. "I saw him run off last night, and I doubted anyone was waiting for him in a lonely state forest after dark."

In spite of the fact that Bernie was messing up my jeans, I felt sorry for him, alone all night in the woods, and I resumed stroking his head. "And you found him . . . ?"

"About a mile down Blackberry Bramble trail," Gabriel said. "I offered him some food, clipped a leash onto him, and brought him back here." Gabriel smiled again, but it was subdued. The merest lift of the corners of his lips. "He was a semi-willing hostage. I don't think he likes me as much as he likes you."

Bernie snorted in his sleep, perhaps subconsciously agreeing with that statement.

"I know he's not mystical," I said. "But I do wonder why he showed up when he did and ran into the lake. He obviously understood that Lauren was in trouble."

"I have no answers for you," Gabriel admitted. "Maybe it's just the breed's instinct, to save people. That's been their role for a long time."

We both stared at the dozing giant for a moment; then I asked quietly and hesitantly, "Were you friends with Lauren?"

Gabriel leaned his head back and rubbed one hand over his goatee, taking his time before he answered. And when he replied, his response was cryptic. "Something like that."

I had no idea what that meant. He could've been implying that they'd been quite the opposite of friends. Or that they'd been much more. And Gabriel didn't seem inclined to elaborate.

"How about you?" he asked me. "Did you hate her, like nearly everyone else in town?"

All at once, I recalled why I'd come to his office in the first place. "You can't really expect me to answer that, can you?" I asked, pulling my hand away from Bernie's head and folding my arms defiantly and protectively over my chest. "You put *everything* in the *Gazette*. And you don't always portray things accurately."

Raising his eyebrows, Gabriel laughed. "So you weren't 'panicked,' 'foundering,' and 'wide-eyed with terror' when Black hauled you out of the water? You dispute something in that description?" He just happened to have a copy of the day's paper on his desk—of course—and he held it up, so I could see my photo again. "How would you describe the young woman in this image?"

Okay, he had a point. But in my head, I'd been working hard to stay calm. "I didn't feel as 'wide-eyed' as I look there," I muttered. "I was trying to remain centered."

Gabriel dropped the newspaper back onto the desk. "You should write a letter to the editor, complaining that the reporter who wrote that story failed to read your mind. Maybe it would get printed!"

For a split second, I considered that option. Then I remembered that he was a one-man show and realized he was mocking me.

Before I could decide how to reply, he cocked his head at me. "So, Daphne Templeton, will you attempt to solve *this* murder?"

"I don't think so," I said uncertainly, with a glance at Socrates, who had swung his head around to see how I'd answer that question. He appeared to approve of my response, and I turned back to face Gabriel again. "I mean, I don't have any plans to get involved. . . ."

"Good." Gabriel leaned back again. I got the sense that I was being dismissed. "I guess I'll just be competing with Jonathan Black on this one."

I blinked at him, confused. "What?"

"I was an investigative reporter for *The Philadelphia Inquirer* before I came here," he informed me. "One of the best in the business. Google it."

I definitely intended to do that. Mainly because I was very curious about why a big-city, big-shot journalist would leave such a prestigious job and buy a dinky paper in a sleepy town.

Then Gabriel relaced his fingers behind his head.

His feet thunked onto the desktop. "I'll solve this case before you or Black come up with your first theories."

Seriously, did he have something against Jonathan?

And had I just been issued a challenge?

I wasn't a competitive person. I even had a T-shirt that said: I AM IN COMPETITION WITH NO ONE. I RUN MY OWN RACE. But I didn't like the way Gabriel Graham was smirking at me.

"I *may* look into this homicide," I informed him, changing my tune slightly. I didn't look at Socrates, so I wouldn't see the reproach in his eyes. I knew that he wasn't eager to get mixed up in another murder. And, although I didn't like to be boastful, I added, "I have a pretty good track record for solving crimes, too, you know."

Gabriel's eyes were glittering with amusement, and I suddenly started to worry that I would soon be featured in the *Gazette* again, in an article titled, "Local Woman Plans to Solve Murder!" Gently lifting Bernie's head from my lap, I stood up, placed the dog's big noggin on the chair, and summoned Socrates. "We should get going. We have test treats to bake."

But as I headed for the door, Gabriel said, "Daphne, wait."

I reluctantly turned back. "What?"

Gabriel nodded to Bernie, who was awake again, watching me with something like betrayal in his brown eyes. "You forgot the dog."

I hated to sound like a broken record, but I had to ask again. "What?"

"*You* rescue dogs. Not me."

"But . . . But . . ." I glanced down at Socrates, who

was rolling his eyes, as if to say, *Here we go again, taking in strays! Did we learn nothing from Tinkleston?* Then I looked back at Gabriel. He was still reclining—and grinning. "*You* found the dog," I reminded him. "He's your responsibility."

Gabriel was not deterred. "Well, you're also a pet sitter, right?"

We both knew the answer to that question. My distinctive van was parked across the street. The misshapen pony-dog and the bulbous graffiti-like letters that spelled out LUCKY PAWS were visible through the *Gazette* office's windows.

"I'm not equipped to take care of a dog," Gabriel continued. "I work crazy hours. So how about I pay you to take in Bernie? Just until I can solve the mysteries surrounding him, too, and find his rightful owner."

I first looked down at the huge dog, whose eyes now appeared hopeful. But I had no idea how I would fit him into Plum Cottage. And Piper might kill me. I usually sat for pets at the owners' homes, and we'd never discussed how many dogs I was allowed to take into my . . . er, technically *her* . . . tiny house. Meanwhile, while I tried not to get attached to possessions, I had to admit that I was also a little worried about my new love seat. I didn't think the fabric was treated for Saint Bernard–sized slobber stains, like the one on my pants.

Then I looked out the window again, at the storefront I needed to pay rent on every month, even though I wasn't ready to open Flour Power yet, let alone able to turn a profit. My mother's concerns about my ability to afford my rent echoed in my head, and I could just imagine the lectures I'd get if I fell behind and broke my lease.

My shoulders slumped. "Fine. I'll take Bernie. For now."

Somehow, while I'd been staring at the street and silently debating, Gabriel had stood up and clipped a leash onto Bernie's collar. "Thanks," he said, handing me the lead. "You're doing me a great favor."

"I'm going to bill you," I reminded him, as Bernie lumbered up onto his feet. I felt like I had a bear attached to my hand, and Socrates edged aside when Bernie joined us near the door. The low-slung basset hound was probably worried that he'd get squashed under a plate-sized paw. Although I often forgot to bill clients, I warned Gabriel, "I'll be sending you an invoice soon."

"And I'll be happy to pay," he said. Then he smiled. "You *are* doing me—and Bernie—a favor, though, and I'd like to thank you with something other than cash."

I immediately grew wary. "What, exactly, were you thinking?"

The devilish reporter with the intriguing past had a ready answer for that question. Maybe *too* ready.

"How about joining me for dinner?" he suggested. "Monday night?"

Chapter 12

"Thanks so much for helping me get Bernie settled in," I said to Moxie, who was in my kitchen, taking some brie out of the oven. She was also trying to keep a very irate Persian cat corralled on a deep window-sill, where he was sulking among the potted herbs after using his claws on the new addition to Plum Cottage. Holding Bernie's muzzle in my hand, I dabbed at some scratches on his nose with a damp washcloth. "This is not going well so far."

"I don't know how Tinkleston can be mean to such a sweet . . . maybe overly sweet . . . dog," Moxie said, abandoning her post to join me in the living room. She carried a bottle of pinot noir and a hand-carved wooden platter that held slices of toasted baguette and the warm round of baked brie, which she'd drizzled in locally produced goldenrod honey. Setting everything onto the old steamer trunk, she added, "You are going to have your hands full. Bernie is kind of like a bigger version of Artie. Only with no missing pieces."

"They definitely both slobber." I released Bernie's

chin, wiped my hands, and put the cloth in a bowl of warm water. "But Bernie's nowhere near as rebellious as Artie."

"They're both love bugs," Moxie pointed out. Plopping down onto my love seat, she picked some dog fur off her short-sleeved, cashmere cardigan, which looked like something out of her favorite Doris Day movies. Then she kicked off a pair of unusual red pumps with large crystals on the toes and curled her feet up under herself, settling in for a chat. "Bernie nearly knocked me off my vintage Charles Jourdans!"

"Again, I'm *really* sorry about that," I apologized for at least the tenth time as I carried the bowl to the kitchen sink, where I dumped out the water. Glancing at the windowsill, I checked to make sure that Tinkleston was still lurking amid the rosemary and thyme. Unfortunately, he had vanished. That didn't bode well. However, the black cat was impossible to find when determined to hide, so I grabbed two plates containing Hero's Hero dog-friendly sandwiches from the icebox and returned to the living room, where I set the snacks down in front of Socrates and Bernie. Socrates paused for a moment to let me know, as always, that he wasn't the kind of desperate dog who gobbled up food. Then he neatly and slowly consumed his turkey-and-cheddar rollup, which was topped with poached egg "mayonnaise." Bernie, meanwhile, gulped down his treat in one bite. It was gone before I even had a chance to sit down on an elaborately patterned, soft Moroccan floor pillow, which I'd dragged to within arm's reach of the cheese. "Speaking of Artie, would you want to help me create a sled for him for the Cardboard Iditarod?" I added. "You're way more creative than me."

Moxie clapped her hands together. "I would love that!" Then she leaned forward and poured some wine into two waiting tumblers, trying unsuccessfully to act more nonchalant. "I don't suppose Jonathan Black will be involved in this project . . . ?"

Moxie had a slight crush on Jonathan.

Okay, a *huge* crush.

"I'm afraid not," I told her. "He's not a big fan of dogs in costumes, comic sleds—or adorable sweaters."

I looked over at Socrates, who shared those opinions, and saw that he and Bernie were curling up by the fire, fairly close to each other. I was glad to see that Socrates, at least, was sharing his favorite spot with our temporary guest.

"I can't believe you got rescued by Detective Black, *and* you have a date with Gabriel Graham," Moxie noted, with a wistful sigh. I shifted on my pillow to face her again and saw that she had a dreamy look in her green eyes. "You are so, so lucky!"

"Jonathan *pitied* me," I reminded Moxie, because we'd been over all this before. Reaching for a knife, I cut into the brie's snowy rind. A river of pale gold gooey cheese spread onto the wooden tray. "As for Gabriel . . . I don't think it's really a *date*. I always get the sense that he's laughing at me."

"Oh, I'm pretty sure he is," Moxie agreed, with a nod to yet another copy of the latest *Weekly Gazette*, which lay folded on the trunk. She'd brought the newspaper along, just in case I somehow hadn't yet seen my mud-covered, overwrought self being hauled out of Lake Wallapawakee by an action hero. "Gabriel probably shot a dozen pictures, and he obviously printed the most awful one. I don't think you could have looked worse!"

I should've been insulted, but Moxie was right about the photo. And probably about Gabriel's methods, too.

"So, we both agree that he *tried* to make me look bad," I said, spreading a big glob of cheese onto a slice of the toasted baguette. "Why would I want to go out with a guy who tries to embarrass me, when I am very capable of doing that myself?"

"Don't ask me." Moxie lifted her glass and swirled the wine, like we were drinking Dom Perignon, when the label on the bottle I'd found under the sink said OLD ROOSTER, above a picture of a precning chicken. "*I* didn't agree to meet Gabriel for dinner!"

I set down the knife, and my shoulders slumped. "I don't know why I did that," I admitted. "He caught me off guard."

"Handsome men have a way of doing that," Moxie pointed out. "Even the strongest women sometimes fall for a good-looking guy."

"I'm *not* falling for Gabriel Graham," I protested, although I wasn't sure Moxie understood me. My mouth was pretty full. I swallowed before adding, "But I think you're right about even tough women falling for handsome guys. I kind of got the sense that Lauren Savidge had fallen for Gabriel's *questionable* charms."

Moxie's eyes widened with interest. "What makes you say that?"

My best friend was desperate for information that she could take back to her clientele at Spa and Paw, but I was momentarily distracted by two black ears, which poked up from behind the love seat, followed by a pair of unusual orange eyes. At my warning look, Tinkleston sank back down, disappearing. I could never figure out how he managed to seemingly levitate up from the floor. The trick impressed—and sort of scared—me.

"Daph?" Moxie reached down to shake my arm. "What did you see? Or hear?"

I hesitated, then warned her, "You can't tell any of this to your clients. Including the canines."

Moxie looked disappointed, but she crossed her heart. "Okay, I promise. Now spill."

I always trusted Moxie to keep my secrets, and I told her, "I only saw Lauren and Gabriel together for a few minutes at Winterfest, but they had a certain prickly, but teasing, rapport." I dug into the brie again. "Kind of like Spencer Tracy and Katharine Hepburn in *Pat and Mike* or *Desk Set*."

Of course, Moxie was familiar with the classic movies, in which Tracy's and Hepburn's characters sparred endlessly, their banter barely masking simmering passion. Moxie nodded. "That could mean something. Did you notice anything else?"

I thought back to the night of the plunge, and how Lauren's gaze had followed Gabriel as he'd walked away.

"Lauren muttered something about needing to get out of town," I said, trying to recall her exact words. "She told me she couldn't wait around for people to 'get their acts together,' or something like that. She was urging me to get Flour Power open, so she could get footage for her show, but the whole time, she was staring at Gabriel. And I thought she looked sad. Or hurt."

Moxie flopped back, nearly spilling her red wine on my cream-colored love seat.

And I'd been worried about Bernie, who was snoring peacefully on the floor.

"Oh, they definitely had something going on," Moxie declared, with a satisfied smile. "I'm a little surprised, because Gabriel's hair, while on the long side, is actually pretty stylish, while Lauren's hair was always a rat's nest." She seemed to realize that she'd spoken ill of the dead, and she glanced toward the heavens. "No offense."

I wanted to ask Moxie if couples tended to have coordinating hairstyles—if that was something she'd noticed, professionally—but I was suddenly struck by two more important questions.

Was Gabriel a possible *suspect* in Lauren's murder? Because, even though I'd never been to the police academy—as Detective Black liked to point out—I knew that crimes of passion were pretty common. And, as a former big-city investigative reporter, Gabriel probably knew quite a bit about murder. Including, perhaps, how to get away with one.

And, more urgently, where the heck was Moxie's rat, whom I'd completely forgotten about, until she'd described Lauren Savidge's hair?

"Um, Moxie?" I ventured nervously, with a glance at her hands, which weren't hidden by a muff that could conceal a rodent. Nor was there room for a rat to hide in her sweater's sole pocket. "Is Sebastian with you tonight? Do you have him hidden somewhere on you?"

Moxie laughed off the suggestion. "Of course not! Even if there was a place to put him, this sweater is vintage cashmere. What if he snagged it with his claws?"

"Oh, good," I said, with too-obvious relief. I was still getting used to the idea of Sebastian, and I didn't want him to spring out at me, stealing my cheese. I was also worried that, if he was roaming around, Tinkleston might *eat him*. "So he's at your apartment, then?" I asked. "Not here somewhere?"

"Oh, he's here," Moxie said, still smiling. "I told him to stay in my purse."

I looked over at a small table near the door, just in time to spy a little white face with pink eyes and a twitching nose peep out over the clasp on a quirky red handbag designed to look like an old rotary dial phone.

Unfortunately, someone else had noticed Sebastian, too. A small black shadow whose nose also twitched as he stalked closer to the purse on silent, fluffy black paws.

I'd thought Bernie or Moxie would be the first to mess up my poor love seat. But I was the one who spilled the wine when I attempted to stop *another* homicide by jumping to my feet and crying out, "Tinkleston! No!"

Chapter 13

"Tinkleston, I know you were acting on instinct, but I swear, you were also just being difficult," I said, lecturing the cat, who was still acting bratty, after nearly *killing* one of our houseguests. I was kneeling next to my love seat, trying to scrub out the red wine stain with another damp cloth, and when I looked over my shoulder, I saw Tinks poking his paw at Bernie's closed eye. "Stop that!" I scolded him. "You've already chased away Moxie and Sebastian. Don't bother Bernie again, too."

I knew that Tinks had ruled the roost at his former home, where he'd been the sole, spoiled companion of an elderly woman. But I also knew that cats could adjust to live in harmony with a variety of animals. And Tinks was making progress with Socrates. But, as I watched, he stared at me with defiance in his orange eyes and batted at Bernie again.

"Okay, that's enough," I said, starting to rise. I intended to scoop him up, but, as I'd expected, Tinks darted off, retreating to his favorite hiding spot on the windowsill. I was pretty sure he believed he was a fierce jungle cat when he crouched behind the basil.

"Maybe I should hand you over to Victor Breard, and we'll see how you do with *real* lions," I muttered, returning my attention to the stain, which *wasn't* coming out. Tossing the cloth onto the steamer trunk, I sank down next to the love seat, resting my back against the ruined piece of furniture. "I suppose I can toss a throw over the stain," I told Socrates, who was awake and watching everything with a skeptical eye from his spot by the fire. "As Epictetus said, 'Wealth consists not in having great possessions, but in having few wants.' And we have no wants, really. So there's no use being upset."

Socrates, who didn't even own a chew toy, clearly agreed with the ancient Greek philosopher. He curled up on his rug and closed his eyes, content with a small spot by the fire on a cold night.

Soon, the cottage was quiet, except for Bernie's snoring, and I continued to sit on the floor, enjoying the peace while I studied the slumbering Saint Bernard.

It seemed odd to me that no one had put up "lost dog" flyers around town or inquired at Piper's practice, which was always a hub for anyone seeking information on a missing pet.

So where had Bernie come from?

Was anyone worried about him?

I intended to take Bernie to Piper's office the very next day, to see if he might have a microchip, but in the meantime, I climbed onto the love seat and reached for the newspaper Moxie had left behind, after insisting that I might want to frame the offending photo.

"Not going to happen," I said softly, unfolding the *Weekly Gazette* and searching for the article Gabriel had written about Bernie, the night of Lauren's murder. But the story, which was completely overblown, didn't really tell me anything I didn't already know.

"*. . . local legend appeared to come true . . . dog attempted to rescue doomed swimmer Lauren Savidge . . . in two to three feet of water . . . the lumbering beast disappeared into the depths of Bear Tooth forest . . .*"

Folding the paper again, so it was still open to the article about Bernie, I tossed it back onto the coffee table, only to realize that perhaps I had learned something new. Or, at the very least, something nagged at me. But I couldn't put my finger on what seemed out of place.

"Something bothered me about Bernie back at Gabriel's office, too," I whispered, talking to myself, because Socrates was snoring, too, and Tinks was out of earshot. "Something's not adding up."

I glanced at the *Weekly Gazette* again, studying the photo that accompanied the story. The picture showed Bernie standing on the lakeshore after releasing Lauren. He looked deceptively spooky, since the flash made his eyes—and something on his collar— glow. The caption read: "*Ghost dog who haunts the ski trails captured on film . . .*"

Once again, Gabriel had managed to take, and choose, a photo that would sell papers, this time by reinforcing the legend of the spectral dog.

And although he'd laughed at me for implying

that Bernie was "mystical," he was obviously willing to suggest that in print.

Was he a smart businessman or a deceptive journalist?

Or both?

"He worked for *The Philadelphia Inquirer*, not the *National Enquirer*," I muttered. "Did one of the nation's most reputable newspapers really let him get away with, at best, stretching the truth?"

All at once, I realized that I might've been wrong to assume that Gabriel Graham had voluntarily left his prestigious big-city job as an investigative reporter.

Reaching into my back pocket, I pulled out a phone I'd recently purchased, to replace an old broken one that had caused me quite a bit of trouble related to previous homicides. A moment later, I was connected to a search engine. Piper had kindly hooked me up with Wi-Fi, because she was worried about me being isolated out in the woods, and service was actually pretty good. Within a few more seconds, I was reading all sorts of things by and about Gabriel Graham, who was all over cyberspace.

There were lots of links to articles he'd written for the *Inquirer*, and a few pictures of him getting awards for investigative journalism. And then I found what I'd been seeking: the reason Gabriel had probably abandoned his job in the city and moved to Sylvan Creek.

But that story, bigger and more dramatic than anything Gabriel had thus far semi-conjured up for the *Weekly Gazette*, was *nothing* like I'd expected.

Chapter 14

"Bernie seems perfectly healthy to me," Piper said, draping her stethoscope over her neck and taking a step back as the Saint Bernard, who was too big for the exam table, tried to jump up and give her one of his trademark dog hugs and slobbery kisses. Like Moxie, Piper was used to dealing with all kinds of animals, both the hostile and the overly demonstrative, and she deftly sidestepped. "Along with being people-friendly—to say the least—he seems well-fed and even reasonably well groomed, for a dog who supposedly lived in the woods."

"Well, I did brush him this morning," I said, stumbling slightly when Bernie pressed himself against my legs. I stroked his head, which probably reinforced his clinginess. But he was such a sweet, big lug that I couldn't help myself. Socrates, who got uncharacteristically edgy when we visited Piper's practice and had stayed home that morning, wasn't exactly snuggly. And while Tinks would sometimes sit on my lap, he usually sank his teeth into my hand before hopping down. It was kind of nice to have a cuddly dog around, even if he sometimes nearly bowled me over. "Bernie wasn't covered in burrs when I first saw him, though," I added. "And he's pretty clean."

"That's because, in spite of not being micro-chipped, he has a home," my always skeptical sister said flatly. "I bet Gabriel Graham knows more than he's letting on. He's charming, but not completely trustworthy, if you ask me."

I agreed with that assessment, and I didn't tell Piper that I planned to have dinner with Gabriel that very night. Nor did I mention that a small part of me wondered if Gabriel was harboring more than information about a lost dog. I was a little worried that he had a *very* shady secret in his past. I found it hard to believe that he'd committed murder, but there was that strange stuff online, and now Lauren Savidge was dead . . .

"I can't help thinking that Bernie is somehow mixed up in Lauren's murder," I told Piper, shaking off my concerns about Gabriel. "For two such strange things to occur simultaneously . . . It just seems odd."

Piper was washing her hands. "What do you mean, 'strange things'? And what happened 'simultaneously'?"

"A murder, and the sudden appearance, in the flesh, of a dog who used to be just a campfire story," I said, patting the pup in question. I was definitely feeding Bernie's voracious craving for affection, and Piper shot me a warning look, which I pretended not to understand. "Before the other night," I continued, "the Lake Wallapawakee Saint Bernard was just an old legend that, let's face it, nobody but Moxie *really* believed. Now here he is, caught by a reporter who did nothing more than put some treats in his pocket and wander around the woods."

"Yes, you have a point," Piper agreed. She dried her hands with a paper towel, then tossed that into a waiting trash can. "But the two things aren't necessarily related. To be honest, I think somebody—either Gabriel or Lauren—'borrowed' Bernie from heaven knows where, then let him loose in the woods, with plans to get some fake footage or photos of the 'ghost dog.' Then, acting on instinct when he heard people struggling in the water, Bernie likely took it upon himself to run into the lake. He probably wasn't even supposed to be there."

"Most of that makes sense," I agreed. "But if Gabriel knows where Bernie belongs, wouldn't he just quietly return him? Why pay me to keep him?"

"That is a flaw in my theory," Piper conceded. She leaned back against the exam table and tucked her hands into the pockets of her lab coat, taking a moment to think. My sister usually discouraged me from getting involved in murder investigations, but her logical side couldn't resist a good puzzle. "I guess that makes Lauren the more likely suspect," she said. "Which makes sense. TV is a visual medium. She couldn't really feature the 'ghost dog' in her show without running some kind of footage behind the narration. And, now that she's . . . *gone*, the dog *seems* homeless."

"Wouldn't the rest of the Stylish Life crew know where Bernie belongs?" I ventured. "If Lauren 'borrowed' Bernie for the show, to use your term, everybody involved in the production must've known about him."

"You would think so," Piper concurred. "But

they are likely reeling from Lauren's death, both personally and professionally. They're probably in mourning. . . ."

It was my turn to be skeptical, and Piper could obviously tell that I doubted Lauren's underlings were wracked with grief.

"Well, even if they aren't mourning," she amended, "they're likely worried about their jobs, and not even thinking about Bernie."

"I'm going to have to talk to the crew," I said softly. I absently fiddled with Bernie's ears. He was nearly asleep against my legs, and I could feel saliva seeping through the fabric of my tiered peasant skirt. "Maybe Joy or the cameraman knows where you belong," I told the half-dozing dog. "And they might've noticed some things the night of the murder, too."

I'd nearly forgotten that Piper was in the exam room with us, until she said firmly, "Daphne Templeton, don't you dare get mixed up in another homicide. We were just speculating about Bernie's origins. Not launching an investigation of Lauren's murder."

I looked up to see that she was ready to move on to her next appointment. She stood near the door, her laptop cradled in her arm.

"Seriously, Daphne," she warned me. "Don't. Meddle."

Then she left the room before I could even protest that my "meddling" *solved crimes.*

"Come on, Bernie," I said, rousing the dog. "We can probably just leave out the back door. I don't think Piper will bill me."

As I talked to the sleepy Saint Bernard, I clipped his lead onto his collar. And when the latch clicked around the metal loop, something clicked in my brain, too.

Bernie's collar . . . The photo in the Weekly Gazette *. . . A glint of metal . . .*

Dropping the leash, I pulled my cell phone from one of the deep pockets of my barn jacket, searched an online directory for a phone number that took forever to find, and waited impatiently until *someone* answered my call.

"Please put me through to Detective Jonathan Black," I begged the woman who was trying to put me on hold. "I have some information about Lauren Savidge's murder!"

Chapter 15

Jonathan Black was, of course, early for our appointment, while I was predictably late, thanks to my van's touchy ignition system. My usual technique of jiggling the key seven times before slapping the steering wheel twice hadn't worked as well as usual, so I'd been stuck outside Piper's practice for about twenty minutes longer than I'd expected.

As Bernie and I slipped and slid down the last few feet of the icy path that led from Bear Tooth forest to Lake Wallapawakee, I saw Jonathan standing alone on the shore, staring out over the water at the setting sun. His feet were planted wide, his hands were clasped behind his back, and his black hair was riffled by the strong breeze that blew across the lake, creating small whitecaps.

I was really glad that he was facing away from us, because the path was very slippery, and when we were about twenty feet away from him, my cowboy boots went out from under me, and I fell right onto my butt.

Pushing aside Bernie, who was trying to console

me with sloppy kisses, I quickly scrambled to my feet and rubbed my rear end—only to hear Jonathan inquire over his shoulder, "Are you all right, Daphne? Do you need help?"

"No, I'm okay," I promised him, not sure how he knew I'd fallen. I hadn't cried out—at least, not too loudly—and he continued to study the beautiful orange setting sun, from just outside a less aesthetically pleasing temporary barricade of yellow tape, which cordoned off the crime scene.

All at once, the fact that Jonathan wasn't *inside* that tape, poking around for clues while he waited for me, struck me as odd.

"How come you're not combing the beach?" I asked him, when Bernie and I stepped up next to him. "You must've known I'd be late. I'd expect you to make productive use of your time!"

Jonathan didn't answer my question or respond to my teasing. He turned and looked down at Bernie, his expression unreadable. Then he finally met my gaze. "I'm not taking *this* dog home," he noted drily. "My cleaning lady already complains about Artie's issues with saliva retention."

As someone who liked to read, I appreciated Jonathan's interesting phrasing.

I was also shocked to learn that he paid someone to clean his house. I didn't think he'd like anyone nosing around his stuff.

Then again, I'd seen online pictures of Jonathan at a fancy party in the Hamptons. I was pretty sure that, although he'd chosen a career in the military, like his father, and then taken a job in law enforcement, there was money growing somewhere in the Black family tree. Maybe he was used to having servants.

I wanted to learn more about his domestic help, but I was mainly curious about the question he hadn't answered yet, and gesturing to the yellow tape, I posed it again.

"Why are you outside of the crime scene, when the clues are probably *inside*?"

I was half joking, but Jonathan wasn't amused. In fact, his blue eyes were nearly as dark as the night sky that was unfolding above us, as the sun sank below the trees.

"I can't search the site again," he informed me. "I've taken myself off the case."

For once in my life, I had no idea what to say. My jaw actually dropped, and I took a step backward, stumbling into Bernie.

Fortunately, before I could fall again, Jonathan reached out and grabbed my elbow, which he held on to, firmly.

"Come on," he said, guiding me and Bernie toward the path that led to the festival grounds. "We need to talk."

Chapter 16

"Thanks for the snack," I told Jonathan, who was handing me a steaming paper cup full of vegetarian chili, sold at a Winterfest booth operated by one of Sylvan Creek's best restaurants, the Wolf Hollow Mill. Jonathan took Bernie's leash from my other hand so I could use a spoon, and I quickly took a bite of the rich, fragrant stew of tomatoes, beans, and spices. Suddenly, the evening felt much warmer. "Really, I appreciate this," I added, digging into the cup again. "I don't know what happened to my wallet, which I swear was with me when I left Plum Cottage."

"I have a few theories," Jonathan said. He held Bernie's lead loosely, and as I'd expected, the dog fell quietly into step with him. Jonathan acted like he had no more interest in canines, but he was a natural pack leader. He bent slightly to look me in the eye, and I was glad to see that he wasn't quite so somber, even if he was laughing at my—or would that be his?—expense. "It's probably buried under the burrito wrappers on the floor of your van."

"If you had a mobile business, your vehicle would be a mess, too," I said, defending myself.

"I don't really think so," Jonathan countered, his blue eyes twinkling with amusement.

He was right, and I decided to drop the debate.

Besides, we'd reached the bonfire, which was blazing, and he was gesturing for me to take a seat on one of the empty benches that ringed the circle of stones. Tail Waggin' Winterfest was primarily a nighttime affair, much more quaint when the lanterns glowed against the snow, and the festival grounds were still quiet just after sunset. Arlo Finch hadn't even shown up yet to sell his dog sweaters, which kind of surprised me. All of the other vendors were open, if lacking patrons. I also noted that Max Pottinger wasn't there yet to spin his yarn about the dog who was stretching out at Jonathan's feet, oblivious to the cold and snow.

All at once, I wondered if Bernie's appearance in the flesh would ruin Max's story.

"We should probably talk, then move on," I suggested. "I don't think Max Pottinger wants the legendary Saint Bernard to be *quite* so visible. I'm pretty sure he gets paid for leading his walks to 'find' the dog."

Jonathan sat down next to me and finally reached down to scratch Bernie behind the ears. "Yes, you're probably right," he agreed. "Bernie's existence—in furry, quite normal, form—definitely makes the old tale less compelling." He rested back on the bench, turning to me and growing more serious. "Monsters and ghosts, once unveiled as ordinary phenomenon, tend to lose their mysterious appeal."

Wow, he had a nice way of speaking.

"But there is something strange about Bernie," I said, forcing myself to focus. "You need to know—"

Jonathan raised one hand. "I told you. I don't really need to know anything. This isn't my case anymore."

I'd finished my chili, and I set the cup down next to myself. I was almost too warm at that point. The chef hadn't skimped on the jalapeños, and the bonfire was roaring, filling the air with the comforting, familiar scent of burning hickory. "What happened?" I inquired. "Why aren't you investigating?"

"I think you know," Jonathan said, watching my eyes. The fire cast shadows on his face. "I think you tried to tell me, the other night, that I might have a conflict of interest."

I suddenly grasped something that should've been obvious from the start.

Elyse.

Of course, he couldn't impartially investigate his ex-wife.

"So, Elyse told you that she had a fight with Lauren, right before the murder?" I asked, quietly. Not that anyone was around. "You know about that?"

Jonathan's expression was grim again. "Yes, of course, she told me everything. Even if she wasn't an honest person, which she is, Elyse is smart enough to realize that quite a few people saw her and Lauren arguing."

"About?" I ventured tentatively.

Not surprisingly, Jonathan didn't answer that question. He would only indulge my amateur detecting to a small degree.

"It's not important," he said, with a shrug. "But, apparently, the dispute was heated. And Elyse admits that she'd argued with Lauren several times, more privately. An impartial investigator would have to consider her a suspect."

"Are you impartial enough . . . ?"

"That's difficult for me to answer," he admitted, stretching out his long legs, past Bernie, and staring thoughtfully into the flames. "I like to think that I would collect the facts and examine them objectively." He shifted to meet my gaze again, and I saw that his guard was lowered, which only happened on rare occasions. "But she was my wife, Daphne," he said, evenly. "I *know* Elyse. And I find it impossible to seriously consider her capable of murder."

I was the tiniest bit wounded by that comment, because Jonathan had previously, if not too seriously, considered me a potential murder suspect.

Then again, at the time, he'd barely known me.

"I had no choice but to excuse myself from the investigation," he continued. "If only because I would appear biased, and perhaps cast doubt on any resolution that didn't implicate Elyse. If I arrested someone else for the murder, and the case went to trial, any decent lawyer would raise questions about whether I'd looked hard enough at Elyse."

I understood what he was saying. But I wasn't sure why he was telling me any of this. He certainly didn't have to justify his actions to me.

"Why are you sharing all this with me?" I asked, point-blank. "Why did you want to talk to me?"

Jonathan took a long time to answer that question. I could tell that he was, as usual, choosing his words carefully. And while he gathered his thoughts, I looked past the fire to Arlo Finch's stand again, only to see festival organizer Mayor Henrietta Holtzapple hang a cardboard sign on the still-shuttered hut. I could barely make out the hand-lettered words, but I was pretty sure the small poster said, CLOSED INDEFINITELY.

That was odd. And disappointing. I really wanted to buy Artie another sweater as soon as I found my wallet.

Her task complete, Mayor Holtzapple, who looked like a giant grape in a puffy purple down parka, turned to leave, then caught sight of me.

For a split second, she appeared surprised, like I shouldn't have been there. Then she smiled and waved one mitten-clad hand.

I waved back, then returned my attention to Jonathan, studying his face by the firelight. He was almost impossibly handsome, in spite of the darkness that I sometimes glimpsed in his eyes. Heck, the fact that he'd endured, and understood, profound loss only made him more attractive, in a way, and I could understand why Moxie insisted that Elyse had come to Sylvan Creek to win him back.

I'd been studying him so closely that I'd almost forgotten our conversation, until he said quietly and seriously, "I know that we've joked in the past about your attempts to solve murders. Or, at least, you've acted like I was kidding when I've discouraged you from getting involved in homicides." He leaned closer to me, so I could see that he was deadly serious. "But I'm asking you, sincerely, to stay out of this case."

"But . . ."

He squeezed my wrist, silencing me. His grip was

as firm as his expression was grim. "You're already getting involved. If you weren't, you wouldn't have called me here." He released my arm. "But what if your luck doesn't hold out this time?"

"What do you mean?"

"I know you can take care of yourself, and that you have a good partner in Socrates. But you have to admit, it was fortunate that I came along when you nearly got killed in Plum Cottage, and when Larry Fox tried to hurl you down a flight of stairs at Flynt Mansion."

I *was* pretty glib about the dangers I'd faced the last two times I'd investigated murders. And he was right. In spite of having Axis and Socrates to help me when Winding Hill Farm's former caretaker, Mr. Peachy, had tried to knock me out with a hammer, I wasn't sure what would've happened if Jonathan hadn't arrived. Jonathan had been late on the scene when I'd nearly been shoved down a flight of stairs, while solving my next case, but he'd aided me then, too. And yet, I didn't like him thinking that I was some sort of damsel in distress. I was glad when he added, "I'm not asking you this because you're a woman. Or because you aren't strong enough or smart enough to look out for yourself. You are certainly very intelligent, very resourceful, and—much as I hate to admit it—you have a knack for stringing clues together and solving puzzles."

I appreciated the compliments, even though I knew there would be a "but."

"However," he said. "You lack the training, the tools, and—most importantly—the backup to go around solving crimes. I have a human partner, and a whole police force, standing behind me when I confront a killer. You have a basset hound." He must've known I was about to defend Socrates, and perhaps note that he'd relied on a canine partner in a war zone, because he quickly added, "Not that Socrates isn't also clever and good in emergencies. But he lacks formal training and backup, too."

That was the longest speech I'd ever heard Jonathan Black make, and I took a second to let everything he'd just said soak in. Both the compliments and the cautionary words. And while I was considering how to respond, he said softly and sincerely, "Please, Daphne. Don't give me more to worry about, right now. I'm *very* concerned that Detective Doebler won't show up at the right place and time, if you get yourself into trouble."

I was touched to realize that, in his own reserved way, he honestly did care about me. And I wanted to assure him that I wouldn't get myself into any dangerous spots. But I was also practically bursting at the seams to tell him something that might be related to the murder.

"I really appreciate you looking out for me," I said. "And I understand your concerns. But can I at least tell you *one thing* that I noticed, which might be relevant to the investigation?"

Jonathan opened his mouth, and I knew that he was about to remind me that he wasn't on the case. And he almost certainly planned to tell me again that I shouldn't even think about the murder. So I quickly cut him off by blurting, "When Bernie pulled Lauren from the lake, he had a barrel around his neck, like a Saint Bernard in an old movie. Don't you think it's odd that the cask is gone now?"

Chapter 17

Jonathan didn't say much as we walked to the parking lot at the edge of Winterfest. I couldn't tell if he was frustrated with me because I didn't seem to be taking his advice about not meddling, or if he was thinking about the missing collar with the barrel attached.

"You're awfully quiet," I finally said when we'd reached the gravel lot, which was nearly empty and ringed by the thick forest. Jonathan's truck was parked closest to the festival, and we stopped next to it. Bernie came to a halt by my side. I couldn't help noticing that his ears were pricked and alert, and his face was turned toward the trees, like he wanted to run into the woods. Then I looked up at Jonathan. "You're not upset with me, are you?" I asked him. "I just couldn't keep that strange fact to myself."

Jonathan gazed off into the dark forest, too. Then he rubbed the back of his neck and sighed. "To be honest, I've mainly been considering what you told me about the missing barrel. I'd seen that on Bernie at the lake. It had struck me as odd. But I'd just assumed that you—or Graham—had removed the collar."

As we'd walked from the lake to Winterfest earlier, I'd told him about how Gabriel had found Bernie and hired me to watch him. He'd already known half of that story, from reading Gabriel's articles about the dog in the *Weekly Gazette.*

"I suppose whoever removed the cask might've taken Bernie's tags, too," Jonathan added. We'd both been studying the dog, who continued, in turn, to stare into the trees. Then Jonathan's gaze shifted to me. "How long do you think Graham really had Bernie . . . ?"

He seemed to catch himself, like he realized that he was getting dragged back into the case, while I suddenly recalled that I had plans that evening. Using my free hand, I pulled my cell phone from one of my jacket's deep pockets and checked the time.

"Oh, no," I muttered. "I'm going to be late for dinner with Gabriel. I almost forgot, until you mentioned his name."

Dropping the phone back into my pocket, I saw that Jonathan had a strange look on his face. An expression that I couldn't quite identify.

"You should probably get going," he said, bending to pat Bernie, who continued to stand stiffly. "Before this guy returns to the forest. He seems very focused on the woods."

"Yes," I agreed. I tugged lightly on Bernie's leash, trying to snap him out of his trance. "I probably should get moving."

"Have a nice evening, Daphne," Jonathan said, opening to door to his truck. He got behind the wheel, adding, "And, please, listen to me about delving deeper into this case. It's not mine—or yours."

I watched while he drove away, glad that he hadn't given me a chance to respond before closing his door. I couldn't stop thinking about a place I wanted to check out, maybe even later that evening. A spot that might hold some big clues to solving the murder. I would just have to be careful, because he was right. I couldn't always rely on him to show up in the nick of time.

"Come on, Bernie," I said, jiggling his leash again, because his tail was suddenly sticking straight out, and the ridge of fur along his spine was raised, too. That struck me as very strange. Bernie was probably the least aggressive and most affectionate dog I'd ever met.

He was starting to give me the willies, and I pulled harder on the leash, forcing him to walk toward the van. "Let's go," I urged, glancing nervously at the trees.

It was getting pretty dark, and from what I understood, Bear Tooth State Park supposedly harbored quite a few of its namesake creatures.

Plus, someone had just been murdered not too far from the parking lot.

Then, just as we reached the VW, the back of *my* neck began prickling like crazy, because sweet, lovable, protective Bernie hunkered down and *growled.*

Chapter 18

"Thanks so much for loaning me an outfit and for watching Bernie while I'm at dinner," I told Moxie, who was sitting on the floor of her quirky, eclectic garret apartment, which was located on the third floor of a turreted Victorian structure that also housed my favorite book store, the Philosopher's Tome. Moxie was resting against Bernie, who curled around her while she sketched possible sled designs for the Cardboard Iditarod. Stepping over Bernie's fluffy tail, I headed for the alcove that served as Moxie's closet. "I didn't have time to take him back to Plum Cottage, change clothes, and return to Sylvan Creek by seven thirty."

I didn't mention that I also needed a few minutes to conduct what might or might not be a break-in.

"It's no problem," Moxie assured me, her pencil continuing to scratch against her sketch pad. Although she had a look of intense concentration on her face, she managed to follow the conversation. "I can imagine that you lose track of time when you're sharing chili with Jonathan Black."

I pushed aside a mod, floral fabric panel that hid the closet, revealing Moxie's huge wardrobe, which was crammed into a small space under a peaked eave. "Jonathan was warning me not to investigate Lauren's murder," I reminded her. "It wasn't a date."

"Whatever." Moxie waved off my comment. "And he should encourage you to nose around. You noticed that Bernie's barrel is missing. I think that might be important."

"I'm pretty sure Jonathan believes it, too," I said, beginning to flip through Moxie's clothes. I wasn't sure what I hoped to find. We didn't exactly share the same style sense. The alcove was packed with outfits that screamed "Jackie O," while I was more . . . I didn't know what I was. Definitely not someone who would wear the admittedly gorgeous, but scratchy-looking, vintage, red-wool Chanel suit that I was holding up for inspection. "At the very least, the missing barrel indicates that someone met up with Bernie in the woods after Lauren's death and removed it, for some reason."

"Unless Gabriel's got the barrel," Moxie noted. "Maybe, when he caught Bernie, he thought the cask looked uncomfortable, hanging under the poor dog's chin, and he took it off." She stopped sketching long enough to look up at me and prop her fists under her own chin, mimicking a sleeping dog. "It would be hard to rest with a big keg digging into your throat!"

I pushed aside more hangers. "I don't think Gabriel was too worried about Bernie's comfort. But I will ask him if he has the barrel. Although I kind of doubt it. We talked about Bernie's collar, and how he didn't have any tags. I think something as odd as a barrel would've come up."

We got quiet for a moment, both of us no doubt puzzling over the missing cask.

Well, I was puzzling. Moxie put the finishing touches on a sketch, then turned the pad so I could see her design.

Yikes.

"I don't know," I said, trying to be diplomatic. "I think a sled that looks like a giant taco is a bit cliché for a Chihuahua. And the serapes and Mexican hats on the dogs . . . It might be . . ."

I had been about to say "overkill." Or maybe "culturally insensitive."

But before I could finish my thought, Moxie put her own spin on things. "Too warm and sunny for winter festival," she said, flipping her pad to a fresh page. "I see what you mean."

I hadn't said anything about the sled being too "sunny," but I didn't bother pointing that out. Moxie was biting her lip, her brows knit in concentration as she settled back against Bernie to begin a new sketch. I thought most dogs would've objected to being used as a cushion, but he remained curled around her, like one of those pillows with arm rests for reading.

It was hard to believe that Bernie had ever growled at *anything*, and I wondered, once more, what he'd seen back at the forest.

An animal?

Or a *human*, watching us . . . ?

"What if Elyse Hunter-Black really killed Lauren?" Moxie suddenly asked, without looking up from her drawing. "You said she was arguing with Lauren, right before the murder, and that Jonathan basically admits she's a suspect. What if she really did it?"

Of course, I had told my best friend everything I knew about the homicide.

"I don't know, Moxie," I said, resuming my perusal of her closet, where I next found, and rejected, a 1960s jumpsuit in a sunflower pattern. "Jonathan doesn't believe Elyse would commit murder, and I think he's a pretty good judge of character. Plus, Elyse is his ex-wife. He must know what she's capable of."

"*Ex*-wife," Moxie echoed me, emphasizing the first syllable. Her fingers were flying, like she'd hit upon some inspiration. "People change," she pointed out. "And *everybody* harbors secrets."

That was true.

Would I learn more about the strange stuff in Gabriel's past, when we met up later that night?

Was *he* a suspect?

"Where's Gabriel taking you tonight, anyhow?" Moxie inquired, abruptly changing the subject to the guy I'd just been thinking about. I wasn't overly surprised. She could always read my mind. "Why do you have to dress up?"

"Gabriel suggested we meet at Zephyr, that new place in the renovated train station," I said, shoving aside a hanger that held what I believed was a 1940s flight attendant's uniform. "I've heard it's kind of fancy."

Moxie didn't say anything, and I turned to see that she was gawking at me.

"What?" I asked, with rising concern. "Did somebody get food poisoning there or something?"

"Umm . . . not exactly, Daph!"

I knit my brows, confused. "Then what?"

Moxie also seemed baffled—by my ignorance. "You *do* know that Zephyr is *the* most romantic restaurant in the Poconos, right?" she asked. "The dining room is lit only with candles, and you can order *snails*!"

Ignoring Moxie's assertion that slimy, gray mollusks were romantic, I frowned, and not just at the dress with the full skirt and puff sleeves that I was inexplicably holding, like I had the slightest intention of wearing it. "This sounds like it's going to be awkward," I said. "Now I kind of wish we were just going to the Lakeside."

"Oh, Daphne . . ." Moxie suddenly seemed sad. She set down her pad and rose up from the floor, while Bernie stretched out, taking up half of the room. Joining me at the closet, Moxie took the dress from me, replacing it on a rod that sagged under the weight of her extensive wardrobe. Then she turned to me, her expression uncharacteristically grave, although it was hard to take her seriously, given that she wore a pair of Asian-inspired silk pajamas that I swore I'd seen on one of the fictional Haynes sisters in the movie *White Christmas*. "The Lakeside was your place with Dylan," she told me gently. "You need to find new places, with new guys."

All at once, I suffered a pang of sadness, too. Surfer and vet tech Dylan Taggert and I had always been very clear that our relationship would be casual, and probably end when one of us got wanderlust— which struck Dylan just as I was setting down serious roots in Sylvan Creek. But even though I'd been prepared for Dylan to move on, I still missed him, as did lots of patrons at the Lakeside, a dive bar on a pier in

Lake Wallapawakee, where Dylan used to play his original folk songs.

Moxie was definitely reading my mind, right then, and I didn't have to explain what I was feeling.

"Don't look so glum," she urged, pushing me aside and digging deeper into the closet. "You and Dylan weren't meant to be together forever. There's someone else for you. I know it, for a fact."

My best friend was also somewhat psychic. For example, she'd predicted that Artie the Chihuahua would be adopted by someone who'd allow the little dog to remain part of my life. That had turned out to be true. And although I still didn't believe in commitment, I almost asked Moxie if she knew who the "someone else" might be, just for fun. I was sure she could at least offer a description. But before I had a chance to inquire, she pulled an outfit from the very back of the dark alcove and held it up for my inspection.

"Voilà!" she cried, grinning. "This is perfect for you!"

Moxie had done a bad job of painting my van, and she'd once subjected my spiral curls to a disastrous Brazilian blowout, but I had to admit that she'd somehow conjured up a dress that was, indeed, perfect.

"Wow, thanks, Moxie." I accepted a hanger that held a floaty, knee-length cocktail dress in an unusual shade of grayish-green that almost matched my eyes. "This is gorgeous. And totally my style. Whatever that is."

Moxie knelt down and crawled into the closet, searching the floor. "I have shoes to match, too. They'll be a little small for you, but it's only for a few hours."

I stepped back to give her some space, and a moment

later, she emerged, holding an open shoebox that contained a lot of white tissue paper, which cradled a pair of pale green suede kitten heels with a pretty wave pattern stitched on the toes. The heels were a little high by my standards, but I breathed a sigh of relief. Most of Moxie's shoes were four-inch stilettos.

But when I accepted the box, my sigh turned into a small but piercing shriek.

Chapter 19

"Just give him this treat," Moxie urged, trying to hand me some small yellow cubes. For the first time in my life, I didn't immediately accept an offering of cheese. I was warily eyeing Sebastian, who was crawling around on the top of a large cage that Moxie had placed near a window overlooking Sylvan Creek's main street. The view was nice, but I doubted that Sebastian spent much time inside the confines of the well-appointed enclosure, which included three levels for climbing, a wheel for running, and two slides. "You two have cheese in common," Moxie needlessly pointed out, still holding out the snack. "And I think you owe him, after scaring the living daylights out of him. That box is his safe place!"

"*I* scared *him*?" I rested one hand on my chest and took a step backward. Sebastian had reared up onto his haunches and was sniffing around with his twitching pink nose. He stretched out his neck, and his little paws grasped at the air. I had to admit, that was *kind of* cute—if I overlooked his naked tail, which continued to be a deal breaker. "He nearly gave me a heart attack." I suddenly recalled that Moxie also had an irrational fear. "You should understand how I feel. You're afraid of *turtles*, for crying out loud. At least you can outrun those!"

Moxie shuddered. "Turtles are terrifying. They're tiny dinosaurs! Didn't you ever see *Jurassic Park*?"

"I think there's a slight difference between a tortoise and a T. rex," I noted, still watching Sebastian, who was on all fours again, creeping closer to me, his pink eyes blinking. I knew that rats had terrible vision, and that I was probably just a blur to him. I also understood that I needed to coexist with my best friend's new companion, and I finally held out my hand. "Here. Give me the cheese," I requested reluctantly. As she handed over the treat, I noted little dark flecks in the soft cubes. "Really, Moxie? *Pepper jack*?"

She shrugged. "He likes spicy stuff."

"O-o-o-okay." I wasn't entirely convinced that jalapeños were good for animals. Then again, Sebastian was a *rat*. Left to his own devices, he'd eat garbage.

I was suddenly struck by the nightmare image of rats swarming in a Dumpster, their naked tails twining, and I struggled to force the picture out of my mind.

You are being ridiculous, Daphne! You LOVE animals!

I kept telling myself that, but I had to take a deep, calming breath before bending down closer to Sebastian, who'd crept to the very edge of the cage's roof, just a few inches from me. He was on his hind legs again, begging for a treat, and I reluctantly held out one of the cubes for him to take.

But just as his little paws reached out, I dropped the pepper jack, not because I was freaked out by

Sebastian's tiny fingers—okay, I was a little freaked out—but because I'd spied something out the window. A person walking quickly and purposefully down the street.

In my excitement, I forgot about my musophobia and offered Sebastian another cube to replace the one that had bounced to the floor, clearly disappointing him.

Then, while he gulped down the snack, I apologized to him—and to Moxie and Bernie, too—telling them all, "I'm sorry, but I have got to go. Now!"

Chapter 20

Time was of the essence, and I raced across Market Street, doing my best to run in Moxie's heels, which were at least a size too small and pinching my piggy toes.

My mother kept a very rigid schedule, and I knew that her evening coffee run to my bakery would only take about twenty minutes.

Needless to say, caffeine-dependent Realtor Maeve Templeton had not only mastered the complicated Italian coffee machine, but she had somehow secured a key to my storefront.

I kind of wished I'd given myself an energy boost before hurrying through town, no doubt looking like a crazy person in my gauzy dress, which peeked out from under a wool coat that Moxie had also loaned me.

Fortunately, the street was practically empty that cold winter evening, and I didn't see anyone as I ducked past the tasteful black sign with gold lettering that told potential home buyers and sellers that they'd located Maeve Templeton Realty, Inc.

Twisting the knob on a dignified, dark wooden door, I slipped inside the pretty 1800s white clapboard building, which was unlocked, as I'd expected. My mother didn't leave much to chance regarding her empire, but she'd also spent her entire life in Sylvan Creek, and needless to say, she didn't bother sealing her business up tight when she was only going down the street for a few minutes.

Closing the door behind me, I passed through the dark reception area, pausing for just a second to grab a complimentary Belgian chocolate from a basket. Then I made a beeline to Mom's office, where a single light burned on an immaculate desk.

Honestly, aside from the gooseneck lamp, there was nothing on the gleaming wooden surface but an open laptop, a neat stack of papers, a phone, and a holder with business cards.

Although I was trying hard to keep the bakery clean, my Lucky Paws office-on-wheels was a disaster, and I couldn't help wondering, as I often did, how my mother made so much money without making a corresponding mess.

Then I realized I was wasting time, and as I unwrapped my chocolate, I turned my attention to a big rack of keys that dominated the wall behind my mother's desk. I knew that Mom kept spare keys to all of her rentals, and I had a sneaking suspicion that, as she showed properties, she quietly gained *entré* to buildings that were none of her business, too.

Fortunately, the key that I sought was on one of the first pegs I checked; popping my treat into my mouth, I quickly snatched it down. Then I hurried out the back door of the office and rushed up a set of wooden stairs that led to an exterior door on the second floor.

This entrance *was* locked, and my fingers fumbled as I tried to insert and twist the key.

Taking a deep breath, I forced myself to focus. And the next thing I knew, I was inside Lauren Savidge's apartment.

The efficiency was very dark and I couldn't see a thing, so, although I was reluctant to turn on a light, I felt around the wall for a switch.

Finding one near the door, I flipped it, blinked a few times to adjust my eyes to the sudden brightness, then gasped, softly, "Wow!"

Chapter 21

When I first started Lucky Paws Pet Sitting, my mother, hoping that I planned to build my own business empire, had enrolled me in an adult-learner night class called Successful Entrepreneurship at nearby Wynton University. I didn't recall much about that experience—at least, not the parts about accounting and taxes—but I had enjoyed making what the instructor had called a "vision board," which was basically a bunch of pictures and inspirational quotes cut out of magazines or printed off the Internet, then assembled on poster board as a visual reminder of all that we students hoped to achieve.

If I remembered correctly, my board for Lucky Paws had primarily featured pictures of puppies and kittens, interspersed with quotes from ancient Greek philosophers, none of which pertained to commerce. In fact, some of my favorite citations had cautioned against the acquisition of wealth. The instructor, a perky "career counselor" named Jean, had pointed that out, several times, as potentially problematic.

As I stood in the apartment that Lauren Savidge

had occupied for the last several weeks, I found myself wondering what Jean would think of Lauren's version of a vision board, which hung above a small kitchen table furnished by my mother.

"What is the deal with this thing?" I whispered, although no one was around to hear. "What the heck . . . ?"

Clearly, the board, which was littered with sticky notes and photos attached by pushpins, was meant to help Lauren keep track of people and events she'd already filmed for *America's Most Pet Friendly Towns*, as well as plan for future shoots. There was a photo of Moxie's salon, with a date written in Sharpie on the margin. I presumed that was the day poor Marzipan had lost his puffball. I located a picture of my bakery, too, the image of the storefront marred by three big black question marks, which no doubt reflected Lauren's frustration with my failure to set an opening date. And Tessie Flinchbaugh, the kind, matronly owner of Fetch! boutique, had been nice enough to pose for her photo. She stood waving outside her shop, which had apparently been visited by the crew in late December. Not only had Lauren also dated that shot, but Tessie wore one of her trademark seasonal sweatshirts, featuring a dog in a top hat, prancing under the phrase "Yappy New Year!"

In a way, the board was innocent enough. A visual calendar of sorts, created by a woman who worked in the visual medium of television.

But upon closer inspection, there was something unsettling and stalker-ish about the display, too. I found an image of me playing with Butterbean the bilious pig, which looked like it had been taken by someone who'd aimed a camera over the fence that surrounded his home—probably right after I'd told Lauren *not* to film on the property.

"Creepy," I muttered, allowing my gaze to roam around the rest of the corkboard.

Not surprisingly, I quickly recognized more animals I watched, and more people I knew, including Mayor Holtzapple, who was tossing a ball for her Pomeranian, Pippin, in Pettigrew Park. That was a mouthful, and Lauren had expanded upon the "p" theme by attaching the phrase *"Paranoid Wingnut!"* to the photo. I thought that was unfair.

At least, I'd never known Henrietta Holtzapple to be paranoid. Maybe slightly wingnutty, but no worse than most people.

Then I saw a shot of Piper, whose image had been captured as she'd locked up her practice. I doubted that she'd been aware that she'd been photographed, either, and a judgmental sticky note complained that my sister was, *"Uncooperative!! Stubborn!!"*

"Well, that's kind of true," I quietly agreed.

Continuing to search the board, I next found a photo of Victor Breard, head of Big Cats of the World. Only that image was a little different from the rest. Most of the pictures seemed like Polaroids, to me. They were uniformly square, with distinctive, old-fashioned white borders. But the photo of Victor, who wore a dark, sober suit that was at odds with a flashy gold tie, was glossy with ragged edges, and obviously torn from a magazine.

Victor was scowling, his head turned slightly away, like he was avoiding the photographer, and when I peered more closely, I could see part of the accompanying article's headline, although most of the text was torn away.

"Zookeeper Sen . . ."

What did *that* mean?

And why had Lauren circled Victor three times with her Sharpie, making heavy, black concentric circles around his face, like a target with a human bull's-eye?

"I definitely need to look into that," I said, with a glance at the clock on a small microwave.

7:12.

My mother would return in less than ten minutes, and I had a date to keep, so I quickly checked the board again, only to notice two more very interesting things.

The first was a picture of Arlo Finch, who stared straight into the camera, looking less than his usual mellow self. In fact, he appeared quite stern. And although his face was lean and lined, he seemed younger somehow than the man who'd just sold me a sweater. The scenery behind him was plain and largely obscured by one of Lauren's notes, written on a pink Post-it.

"USPT 2016?"

I had no idea what that meant, and I moved on to the last photo that had caught my attention. The world's only unflattering shot of Elyse Hunter-Black, who appeared to be shopping on Market Street, her two greyhounds, Paris and Milan, walking serenely at her side.

Needless to say, Lauren had pasted a comment next to her boss's image—although it was the kind of message that probably would've gotten Lauren fired, if Elyse had ever seen it. And the note wasn't exactly G-rated, either. Lauren had lumped Elyse in with the two female dogs, then added a few of her trademark exclamation points after the expletive.

"Ouch," I whispered, wincing. "That's harsh!"

But perhaps not as harsh as the note that Lauren had stuck at the very top of the corkboard, which apparently summed up her opinion of Sylvan Creek, in general: *"LUNATICS!"*

"That's *really* not nice," I muttered, right before I checked the clock again.

Fortunately, I had a few minutes to spare, and I turned to move toward the door—only to hear footsteps outside on the stairs.

There wasn't time to turn out the light, or even think about hiding. So I simply stood there, frozen in place, in a murdered woman's former home, as someone rattled the doorknob.

I really wished that, for once, I'd taken Jonathan's advice and locked the deadbolt that I could see just a few feet away from me. All it would've taken was a twist of the wrist.

But it was too late to even lunge for the lock, and all I could do was keep waiting, helplessly, while the door swung open and a too-familiar, but still threatening, person joined me in the small apartment.

Chapter 22

"Are you sure you're allowed to be here?" Gabriel teased, sitting back in a burgundy leather booth so a waiter in a crisp white shirt could pour two glasses of wine. Gabriel had chosen a chardonnay from a leather-bound wine list embossed with an old-fashioned train and the golden word ZEPHYR. In fact, he'd ordered both our meals, too, before I'd even arrived. I wasn't sure what I was going to do when my roasted capon with lemon and thyme was set down before me. "You're not grounded, are you?" Gabriel added. "Should I drive you home?"

I was starting to regret telling him the semi-truth about why I'd arrived at the restaurant a half hour late. Although I'd omitted the part about sneaking into Lauren Savidge's apartment, I'd admitted to having a run-in with Maeve Templeton, who'd somehow broken my Italian coffee machine and returned to her office ahead of schedule, only to see the light burning in the efficiency's front window.

In retrospect, it seemed to me that Mom should

apologize for repeatedly breaking into my bakery, not to mention messing up expensive equipment that was probably impossible to get repaired, without shipping it back to Europe.

Of course, she claimed that *I* must've done something to the machine, which had apparently spewed a big puff of steam into the air, then made a clinking sound before giving up the ghost.

Mom was probably lucky she hadn't teleported to the Middle Ages.

"What, exactly, did you say happened?" Gabriel asked, leaning forward, the better to see me. The restored train station wasn't lit only with candles, as Moxie had predicted, but the restaurant was dark and romantic. Large, arched windows framed a full moon and drifting clouds, and the backs of the booths were high and private. Each table held a flickering, antique railroad lantern, which provided just enough light for me to see that Gabriel's dark eyes were gleaming with amusement and curiosity. "What was the argument about?"

I brushed off the questions. "Who can even keep track? My mother and I tend to clash about everything."

That was true. And, thankfully, Gabriel dropped the subject, although I suspected that he might bring it up again at some point. I was pretty sure that, once his interest in something was piqued, he liked to get answers.

For the time being, he raised his glass and smiled. "To Daphne Templeton. Pet sitter. Baker. Private investigator."

I'd been about to reciprocate that toast, but I pulled my wine back, nearly sloshing some of the chardonnay over the rim of the glass. "I'm *not* an investigator," I protested. "Private or otherwise."

Gabriel cocked his head. "Really?"

He had a cat-ate-the-canary look on his face, and I asked, warily, "Is there something I should know about?"

Gabriel sat back again, set down his glass without taking a sip, and stroked his goatee, laughing at me. "I saw you running through town when I was driving here."

Oops. I'd noted that the sidewalks had been empty of pedestrians, but I hadn't thought much about passing cars. And there had been a few.

"You looked so odd, wobbling along in your heels and your dress, that I had to slow down and watch," he continued, while my cheeks grew red with embarrassment and indignation. Who was he to spy on me? He didn't seem to notice that I wasn't enjoying his story, though. Or, if he did notice, he didn't care. "I saw you furtively duck into your mother's real-estate office. Then the next thing I knew, a light went on in Lauren Savidge's apartment." He smiled with self-satisfaction. "I can only assume that you were investigating. Privately."

For a second, I didn't know how to respond. Then I leaned forward, crossed my arms on the table, and—ignoring everything he'd just said—narrowed my eyes at him. "How do *you* know where Lauren lived?" I demanded. "Did you spy on her, too? Or did you spend some time in her apartment? Maybe as more than friends?"

I had a feeling that few people got the upper hand with Gabriel Graham. But I had definitely struck a nerve. His smile faded away and the glimmer in his eyes dimmed. Then he said softly and seriously, "Maybe I've underestimated you, Daphne."

Chapter 23

"I found Lauren interesting," Gabriel told me quietly. All of his smug bravado seemed snuffed out, and I had to say that I liked him better without the cocky, mocking attitude. He took a sip of wine, then set down his glass. "When she first came to town, we did spend some time together. As 'more than friends,' as you put it."

"So . . . what happened?" I was dying to know more about his relationship with Lauren. And dying of hunger. Our food was running late, and I'd already eaten my share of warm brown bread with rich, Irish butter from a skimpy bread basket. "I take it you two broke up . . . ?"

He shook his head. "We were never a real 'couple.' At least, I didn't think so."

"But Lauren did?"

Gabriel had been fiddling with—and staring at— his wineglass, but he met my gaze again. "Yes. And, as you know, she was a forceful personality. She assumed that she would get her way at some point. Even though

I'd tried to make it clear that I never wanted a serious relationship to begin with."

Gabriel didn't seem interested in his slice of bread, so I reached for the remaining piece and buttered that, too. Then I asked, sort of offhandedly, "Did you two fight a lot?"

Gabriel laughed too loudly for the hushed room. Glancing around to see if anyone had noticed, he lowered his voice and apologized. "I'm sorry. But that was the *least* subtle question I've ever been asked. Why don't you just come out and ask me, 'Did you kill Lauren Savidge?'"

Since the question was already out there, I figured it couldn't hurt to ask. "Did you?"

I couldn't help but notice that Gabriel didn't exactly answer that simple inquiry.

"I didn't take part in the plunge," he reminded me, leaning back again, this time so the waiter could deliver an appetizer that I hadn't been warned about—except by Moxie. *Escargot.* Gabriel waited until the server retreated before adding, "As you, of all people, should know, Lauren was killed in the water. Probably by someone who used a rock, grabbing it from the lake bed and acting on impulse in the midst of the chaos, according to the prevailing theory."

I hadn't heard anything about a weapon, and I leaned forward, talking through a big bite of bread, which was probably going to be the only thing I ate that night at the rate things were going. "Are the police sure the killer used a rock?"

"No." Gabriel picked up a set of tongs that looked like a medieval torture device and deposited a snail, complete with shell, onto a small plate the waiter had placed in front of me. "But that's Detective Doebler's best guess at this point."

"Interesting," I said. "And it makes sense." I suddenly recalled that I needed to ask Gabriel a question. "Did you remove anything from Bernie's collar after you found him?"

His interest was immediately piqued. "No, I didn't. Why do you ask?"

I almost told him about the missing barrel, but he obviously prided himself on being a crack investigator, and I decided that he could figure things out for himself, if he was curious. Gabriel had printed a picture of Bernie wearing the barrel at the scene of the crime, and he'd clipped a leash onto the dog's other collar, several times. I didn't need to spell things out for him. Plus, I wasn't sure he was being honest with me. I still thought he might have the little keg.

"It's nothing," I said. "No big deal."

Gabriel didn't believe me, but he didn't press me to explain further. He grabbed a snail for himself and resumed speculating about the murder. "So, ruling *me* out as a suspect . . ." He looked across the table at me. "Not that you necessarily have."

I didn't hurry to assure him that I'd crossed him off my list of potential killers yet, because I hadn't.

He didn't seem bothered and dug a tiny fork into the shell on his plate, pulling out a limp, gray mass. "Assuming I'm not the killer, who do you think murdered Lauren? What's your best guess at this point? Colonel Mustard with a fistful of limestone?"

I drew back, surprised and disappointed by the callous joke.

"You know, this isn't really a contest or a game," I

reminded him. "Someone you used to care about, at least to some degree, is dead."

Apparently, snails were chewy, because he raised one finger, asking me to wait while he ate, which took a long time. Then he swallowed, dabbed his mouth with a napkin, and said, with obvious remorse, "I'm sorry, Daphne. I've covered so many homicides that I'm afraid I'm pretty matter-of-fact about murder. But you're right. That comment was out of line." He grew pensive and gazed across the room. "This is probably sad to say, but it's the *very* rare homicide that can get under my skin."

I was pretty sure he was referring to a case I'd read about when I'd researched him online. But I didn't feel like I could ask him about that, even though he'd invited me to Google him.

Taking a sip of wine, I studied Gabriel over the rim of my glass. He looked especially handsome that night in a dressy, but casual, shirt and suit jacket. As Moxie had noted, his longish, dark hair was actually cut in a stylish way, and he could pull off the goatee. His eyes were his most intriguing feature, though. They radiated intelligence and could, at times, reveal more depth than I'd initially believed him to possess.

He definitely had charisma, and I could imagine how an equally strong personality like Lauren might have been drawn to him—and not want to let go.

Just how hard had Lauren Savidge clung? And what might I find if I saw *all* of the pictures Gabriel had taken the evening of her death? Because he'd snapped a lot of shots with that heavy, professional-grade Nikon. I could recall him bobbing around in the crowd, the camera's unusual plaid strap around his neck. And his pants had gotten wet, up to the knees, like he'd stepped into the water at some point.

But why . . . ?

"Is something wrong?" Gabriel asked, interrupting what had become a long reverie. For a moment, I worried that he'd somehow sensed that I'd been questioning his potential involvement in Lauren's death. Then I realized that he was gesturing to my uneaten appetizer. "You don't like escargot?"

I had been so lost in my thoughts that I'd forgotten about the snails. I glanced down at the butter-soaked creature on my plate, not sure if I'd find it appetizing even if I ate meat.

"I should probably tell you that I'm a vegetarian," I confessed, continuing to study the snail. "Although, I'm not really sure if this is technically 'meat.' It kind of reminds me of this eel I ate once in Tokyo. By accident, but still . . ."

"It's okay." Gabriel grinned and reached across the table to take away my appetizer plate. "You don't have to eat it, on purpose or by accident . . ." His voice trailed off, and he looked past me, like something to my right had caught his attention.

Leaning out of the booth, I followed his gaze, which had grown intent. And when I located what—or who—Gabriel was watching, I nearly slipped off my seat.

Victor Breard.

The big-cat rescuer, whom I'd last seen at the scene of a murder, then on Lauren Savidge's bulletin board, where his face had been the bull's-eye in a Sharpie'd target, stood just inside the door, next to an empty hostess station.

As Gabriel and I both watched, Victor, apparently

tired of waiting to be greeted, walked farther into the dining room. Then he paused to scan the dimly lit, private tables, his chin lifted high and his neck craning.

"He's looking for somebody," Gabriel observed. His journalistic antennae were clearly standing straight up. I was pretty sure he was also thinking about Victor's presence at Lake Wallapawakee on the night of Lauren's death. "I wonder who he's meeting."

I started to tell Gabriel that I had no idea, and that Victor Breard's dinner plans were really none of our business, so we should probably quit gawking.

But before I could say anything, or scooch back into the booth where I belonged, Victor stopped searching and started striding through the restaurant, winding his way around the tables.

"Um, Gabriel?" I ventured, uncertainly—and a bit nervously, for some reason. "It looks to me like Victor's here to see . . . *us.*"

Chapter 24

"Good evening! *Bonsoir!*" Victor greeted us bilingually, and with a big grin that revealed a mouthful of white teeth that his lions probably envied. The flashy smile matched his pinstriped suit, red silk tie, and pointy-toed leather shoes. Just as I was wondering if he knew who I was, the smile turned upside down, and he addressed Gabriel. "I do not believe that I have met your lovely lady friend."

"Oh, I don't think I'm a *lady*—"

"Victor, this is Daphne Templeton," Gabriel interrupted me, before I could explain that we weren't a couple. I wished he'd let me get the word *friend* out. "If you ever need someone to watch the tigers and leopards while you're out of town, she's a professional pet sitter."

Victor's eyes lit up with recognition. "Oh, yes!" he said. "I have seen your van." He grew serious and nodded approvingly. "You care for disabled and disfigured horses, yes? That is a beautiful and noble calling."

Gabriel knew why Victor was under the impression

that I was some kind of equine therapist, and he stifled a laugh, coughing into his fist.

"Actually, I . . ." I started to explain that the animal on my VW was supposed to be a dog, then decided not to bother. At least he thought my "calling" was "noble."

"Please, join us," Gabriel said, gesturing to my side of the booth. "Have a seat."

I slid over, making more room for Victor, although now that I had a chance to meet him up close, I realized that he was actually surprisingly short and slight. And his face, which was tanned in an orange, artificial way, was also deeply lined. When I'd seen Victor at the lake, addressing the crowd in ringmaster style, I would've guessed that he was in his forties. But as I studied him by the flickering glow of our tabletop lantern, I revised that estimate upward, perhaps into the late fifties. I could also smell his cologne, which was sweet and too pungent, in my opinion.

Luckily, I wasn't going to have to endure the overpowering scent while I picked at the garnishes on my chicken dinner, whenever that arrived.

"*Non, non, merci.*" Victor raised his hands. "I am meeting someone soon. I merely stopped by to say hello." He spoke to Gabriel again. "And I wish to invite you, as a journalist, to visit Big Cats of the World, for a tour that would be . . . How do you say it in English?" He looked to the ceiling and rubbed his chin until he found the phrase he wanted. He snapped his fingers. "Behind the scenes!" Then Victor frowned, the lines around his mouth deepening. "There is some misunderstanding of my mission, and I would like to explain, to the public, what I do for *les lions et tigres.*"

I was among those who didn't understand Victor's mission. "I would actually like to read that article," I told Gabriel. "It sounds pretty interesting."

Smiling triumphantly, Victor waved his hand with a lion tamer's flourish. "You see? Already a reader is intrigued!"

I got the sense that Gabriel didn't like being manipulated by a public relations pitch. But he also wanted to sell newspapers, and there was no denying that a lot of Sylvan Creek residents would like to know more about Big Cats of the World, where a man who was something of an enigma lived with some of nature's most dangerous creatures. At the very least, I was sure local folks would buy the paper in hopes of learning whether Victor's fencing system was adequate. Still, Gabriel didn't immediately agree to write the article.

"I'll take the tour," he said, raising one finger before Victor could extend his hand to shake on the deal. "On one condition."

Victor arched his eyebrows. "And that is . . . ?"

"Daphne gets to come along." Gabriel smiled at me. "You'd like an up-close and personal look at some exotic cats, right?"

I wasn't sure if I was being invited on a second date, or if Gabriel really just thought I'd enjoy the tour. Regardless, I definitely wanted to go.

"Yes, I would like that," I agreed, looking hopefully at Victor. "If you don't mind me tagging along?"

"You are most welcome," he promised, smiling at me, too. "Surely, working with damaged horses, you will appreciate *my* humble efforts to help unfortunate creatures." While I again debated setting him straight, he turned back to Gabriel. "I will contact you to set up a day and time convenient for all." Then Victor took a step backward, so the waiter could set a sizzling filet mignon in front of Gabriel and a capon before me. "For now, I will leave you to your meals," Victor added, with a glance over his shoulder. "While I go to join *my* dining companion, who has finally arrived."

My brief conversation with Victor Breard had pretty much confirmed my—and Piper's—opinion that he was a somewhat slippery showman. But when he mentioned his "dining companion," I was pretty sure that I glimpsed the real person behind the public façade.

And the look in Victor's narrowed eyes, as he turned to greet *Lauren Savidge's assistant, Joy Doolittle,* reminded me of a panther stalking its prey.

Chapter 25

The full moon I'd seen through the windows at Zephyr shined like a spotlight on the path that Bernie and I followed from Piper's farmhouse, where I'd parked my van, to Plum Cottage, on a night that had grown still and icy cold. My sister was building an access road from the main farm to the old caretaker's cottage, but the project wouldn't be done until late spring. In the meantime, I had to hike to my house, regardless of the weather or the time of day.

"Come on, Bernie," I said, tugging lightly on his leash to get him moving and pulling my coat closer around my chin. I'd changed back into my usual clothes at Moxie's, when I'd picked up the dog. Moxie had also supplied me with a peanut butter sandwich, in exchange for the capon, which the waiter had packed up in a doggy bag. "Let's go," I urged Bernie, who didn't seem to be in any hurry. "It's pretty late."

Needless to say, Moxie had held me hostage for a good half hour, refusing to hand over the sandwich until I'd told her everything about my evening. She'd been most eager to get my impressions of Gabriel, but had been pretty interested in Victor Breard and Joy Doolittle's meeting, too.

Or had that meeting been a *date*?

I wasn't sure, but I had to admit that I was also curious.

Victor and Joy made a strange pair, even discounting the disparity in their ages. Victor always commanded attention, while Joy had been ghostly pale and painfully easy to overlook in a dowdy taupe skirt and a plain cream-colored top that washed out her ash-blond hair, which was cut into a basic bob.

Yet, the two had seemed to have a lot to talk about—although I got the sense that they disagreed on whatever topic was up for discussion. They'd both leaned over the table, Victor gesturing animatedly, while Joy had repeatedly answered with pursed lips and short, sharp shakes of her head.

"Were they talking about the murder?" I mused aloud, breaking the silence. My voice, though hushed, sounded loud in the quiet woods. I spoke even more softly, looking down at Bernie. "Because they were both at the lake when you pulled out Lauren. And Victor was on the corkboard, in that bull's-eye."

Of course, Bernie didn't comment, and we resumed walking quietly through the trees.

I didn't usually get nervous on the trails, especially if I had a canine companion, but as I recalled that a killer was on the loose—and remembered how Bernie had growled, back at Bear Tooth forest—I gradually started to grow uneasy.

Reaching down, I stroked Bernie's head, grateful that he wasn't on the alert, like he'd been earlier. That was probably a good sign that we were alone.

Still, I was relieved when we rounded the final bend in the trail, and I saw the windows of Plum Cottage glowing with a welcoming light that I'd left on for Socrates and Tinkleston.

Then I stopped short and grabbed Bernie's collar, my heart racing with fear as a *large shadow*—far too big to be cast by a basset hound or a Persian cat—moved inside the house.

I probably should've whipped out my cell phone and called the police, but my first thought was for Socrates and Tinkleston, who were apparently trapped inside my cottage with an intruder, and on instinct, I ran to the porch and hauled open the door.

Bernie once again proved that he could sense when something was wrong, and he pushed past me, galloping inside a step ahead of me.

"You'd better watch out!" I warned whoever was inside. "Bernie is trained to . . ."

I was about to say "attack," although I doubted that the sweet Saint Bernard who was scrambling across the cottage's old plank floors knew the command or would follow it, if he did.

But when I burst through the door, too, the word died on my lips, and instead of confronting the person who was crouched in my kitchen, I cried with dismay, "What in the world happened here?"

Chapter 26

"Tinkleston, I am very disappointed in you," I told the little black Persian, who was crouched on top of the icebox, probably because he'd destroyed the windowsill herb garden where he usually hid. Tinks had also knocked over some cactus-shaped salt-and-pepper shakers I'd picked up in Dallas and spilled a glass of water I'd left near the sink. "And don't try to pretend you didn't do all this!"

Socrates, sitting by the fire, shook himself vigorously, like he was physically distancing himself from the vandalism. And I knew that he wasn't to blame. Although Socrates didn't care about possessions, he didn't believe in wanton destruction, either.

Plus, he was way too short to get up on the countertop.

"What got into you?" I asked Tinkleston, planting my hands on my hips. "Huh?"

The surly cat merely blinked at me, as if he didn't understand the questions, so Piper, who was kneeling on the floor, cleaning up soggy potting soil, answered for him.

"He's probably either upset that you left him alone all evening, or that you brought a new animal into the house." She scooped damp dirt into a 1920s Chase & Sanborn coffee can that used to hold a fragrant thyme plant, which lay limp on the floor. "You're lucky I stopped by to drop off your mail this evening. Who knows what else he would've gotten into?"

I opened a drawer, retrieving a clean dishcloth. "He must be upset about Bernie, because I've left him alone before with no problems." I glanced at Tinks, who flexed his claws. "In fact, I think he likes his alone time."

"Maybe he didn't approve of your *human* company tonight," Piper ventured, rising and setting the thyme, which she'd repotted, back on the windowsill. "Maybe Tinkleston doesn't like you seeing Gabriel Graham."

I'd been wiping up the water and stray grains of salt, but I stopped and looked at my sister. "What does that mean? And how do you know who I was with tonight?"

"Mom told me, when she called to complain about you *breaking into Lauren Savidge's apartment*," Piper informed me. Stepping over Bernie, who lay in an awkward spot between the kitchen and living room, she headed for the coat rack near the door. "Plus, when I left your mail on the counter—and it looks like you're behind on your student loans—I saw your reminder scrawled on a napkin, '*MEET GABRIEL GRAHAM 7:30 ZEPHYR!!*'"

"Oh, I forgot about that." I rinsed out the dishcloth and draped it over the faucet to dry. Then I followed Piper to the door. "I guess that was a pretty big clue."

"Speaking of clues . . . What were you doing in Lauren's apartment?" Piper was zipping her coat, but she raised a hand. "And, please, don't tell me that you're investigating her murder."

"Okay, I won't tell you that," I agreed. "And do I detect disapproval, on your part, of my meeting with Gabriel, too?"

Piper stepped into her snow boots, which she'd left by the door. "I've told you. I'm just not sure I trust him." She peered at me through her wire-rimmed glasses. "Are you dating him? Or was this 'meeting'— at a romantic restaurant—somehow related to the investigation that I *know* you're conducting?"

I had been pondering those very questions on the way home, and I answered honestly. "I'm not sure if it was a date or part of his investigation of the murder, for the paper. We mainly talked about Lauren's death, but he did ask me out again." Of course, our next outing, to Victor Breard's sanctuary, might also be considered investigative. I, at least, hoped to learn more about why Victor was highlighted on Lauren's corkboard. "I think it's all kind of tangled up right now," I told Piper.

"I get the sense that things with Gabriel Graham tend to get 'tangled up,'" Piper warned me. "If I were you, I would be careful."

My sister left without another word, stomping out into the dark night in her big boots, and I turned to

Socrates, who always gave me wise counsel. "What do you think about Gabriel?"

Socrates furrowed his brow, which might've indicated disapproval, or uncertainty on his part, too.

"Well, I do know one thing for sure," I told him. "I am still starving. Let's get a snack."

Socrates obviously agreed that I'd suggested a wise course of short-term action, and he followed me to the kitchen, where I stepped over Bernie. Opening the icebox, I located some leftover Mutt Loaf and popped the lid off the container. At the smell of the doggy meatloaf, made with ground beef, carrots, and eggs, Bernie roused and shook himself, clearing the path for Socrates to enter the kitchen, too.

"Enjoy, guys," I said, patting Bernie as I set the dogs' snacks on the floor. Then I shot Tinkleston an aggravated look, only to melt slightly at the sight of his puffball paws.

"Oh, fine," I grumbled, opening a glass apothecary jar and offering him two homemade Reel-y Good Tuna Tidbits. "Not that you deserve anything!"

Tinks flattened his ears, like he didn't appreciate being criticized, but he gobbled down the treats.

I, meanwhile, was still hungry, so I whipped up one of my favorite late-night snacks: toast with avocado and fried eggs. As the crusty bread warmed in the toaster and the eggs sizzled in the skillet, filling the kitchen with a homey aroma, I located a notebook and pen.

A few minutes later, I sat down at the spindle-legged table, a plate and my writing materials in hand. And while I savored the fresh eggs from Piper's own chickens, the creamy avocado, and crispy toast, I paused now and then to write in the notebook, trying to reconstruct everything I'd seen on Lauren's corkboard. Although I was a terrible artist, I even attempted to re-create the photos. And when I was done, I studied the page.

Arlo Finch. And the cryptic note, "USPT 2016."
Victor Breard's image torn from a magazine and circled, like a target. "Zookeeper Sen . . ."
Elyse, with Paris and Milan, next to an expletive.
Me, with Butterbean.
Tessie Flinchbaugh, waving.
Spa and Paw.
Piper. "Uncooperative! Stubborn!"

All under the scornful heading *LUNATICS!*
I sat up straighter, suddenly wondering why Lauren hadn't posted any pictures of Gabriel.

Then I recalled that he wasn't integral to *America's Most Pet Friendly Towns.*

Still, it struck me as strange that Lauren hadn't tacked his photo up somewhere, maybe inside another bull's-eye. The board definitely reflected her grievances, some of which I thought were as much personal as professional.

"What—or who—else isn't there?" I whispered, eating the last bite of my toast. I studied my sketches again. "I feel like something big is missing, either from my memory—or Lauren's corkboard."

Socrates couldn't offer me any guidance, because he was sound asleep by the fireplace, a few feet from Bernie. And Tinkleston had no intention of being helpful. He was licking his paws again, with a snooty attitude.

Rising, I collected all of our empty plates and set them in the sink. Then I settled onto the love seat, pulled a soft throw over my legs, and sat quietly, still puzzling over the corkboard. Outside, the wind rose, causing the branches of the plum tree to scratch against the window. I used to find that sound unnerving, but the more I grew used to it, the more I found it soothing. And before long, I gradually felt my eyes drifting shut and my mind wandering, like a Saint Bernard lost in a dark forest.

"Bernie . . ."

I was pretty sure I uttered his name out loud, just as I drifted off to sleep.

And I said it again when I sat bolt upright in the morning, awakened by pale sunlight that filtered through the windows.

"Bernie. That's who's missing from the corkboard!"

The big dog snuffled in his sleep at the sound of his name, while Socrates, who was wide awake and listening from his spot by the hearth, cocked his head, indicating that he didn't understand my outburst.

"Lauren used the corkboard to organize the taping of the show," I told him. "If she'd known that Bernie was going to be at Winterfest and planned to get footage of him—like Piper suspects—wouldn't Lauren have placed his picture on the board? With a date? Like she did with Fetch!, Spa and Paw, and practically everything else the crew filmed? But Bernie—and Max Pottinger—were missing."

Socrates didn't share my excitement over those

revelations. And he definitely wouldn't take part in the adventure that I hoped to plan for that very afternoon.

Locating my cell phone, which had fallen between the cushions of my love seat, I dialed Moxie's number.

"Hey," I said, the moment the connection was made. "How would you like to go skiing today?"

Chapter 27

I hadn't hit the cross-country trails in years, and my barn jacket wasn't exactly the latest in high-tech ski wear. But my Rossignol skis, matching boots, and insulated gloves, all borrowed from Piper, made me look like an Olympian compared to Moxie, who'd arrived at Bear Tooth forest wearing a white wool coat and plaid pants and dragging along ancient *wooden* skis.

"Are you sure you shouldn't rent new skis?" I suggested, watching her struggle to secure her boots into twisted, looped spring bindings that looked like she'd plucked them from the seats of my van. My skis weren't brand new, but at least I was able to clip my toes securely in place. Looping Bernie's leash around my wrist, I carefully slid myself a little closer to Moxie, grabbing on to a rustic, wooden trail sign for support when my feet nearly flew out from beneath me. Apparently, skiing wasn't like riding a bike. Resisting the urge to lean on Bernie, who watched me with worried eyes, I clutched a crude arrow that pointed the way to a trail with the ominous name Black Ice. "Maybe this is one time you should sacrifice form for function," I added, bending down carefully to unclip Bernie's lead from his collar. Happily, he didn't dart into the forest, like part of me had feared. "They rent skis at the park ranger's lodge. . . ."

I didn't finish that thought, because Moxie, still crouched down at the edge of the trails, was staring up at me, clearly aghast at my suggestion that function *ever* trump form. And, I had to admit, she looked pretty cute. Like she'd stepped out of an old poster for a long-forgotten resort in the Adirondacks, where the walls would be paneled in knotty pine, a big set of antlers would hang over the roaring fireplace, and happy skiers would gather for hot cocoa in the evenings.

Jeez, I kind of wanted to use my coffee machine to step back in time and spend a weekend at that imaginary place, myself. Especially when the wind off the lake blew icy snow into my face. I peered down the trail, into the forest, which was gloomy that day, the gray light dimmed further by thick stands of pine trees that creaked and moaned every time the cold air shook them. Then I looked over at Winterfest, where the little huts glowed cheerfully and the bonfire blazed.

"Maybe we should just forget about skiing and go to the festival," I suggested to Moxie and Bernie. Needless to say, Socrates had never even considered cross-country skiing with us. His legs were far too short for logging miles on trails, and he disapproved of excessive exertion in general. "I haven't had a chance to try the Snow-Capped Funnel Cakes yet," I noted. "I'd hate to miss out on fried dough smothered in vanilla pudding and powdered sugar."

I had just convinced myself that skiing, no matter how well-intentioned, was a bad idea when I heard Moxie's cheerful voice calling to me. "Daphne! Are you coming?"

I turned to see that she was smiling and waving a mittened hand from about fifteen yards down Blue Moon trail, according to the sign that was still anchoring me in place. Bernie was at her side, with something like a goofy grin on his face.

It struck me then that we should've stopped at the ranger's lodge to at least get a map. But it was too late. Moxie was gliding off with surprising grace, given that her boots were held in place by sprung springs and her warped wooden poles looked like an extra pair of bowed legs on either side of her. Bernie ran next to her.

"I'm coming," I called to them both, reluctantly letting go of the sign.

Unfortunately, the path wasn't as level as it appeared. There was a deceptively steady downward grade that began right at the trailhead, and before I knew what was happening, I was moving at quite a brisk clip, right toward Moxie, Bernie, and *disaster*.

Chapter 28

"You're doing much better," Moxie assured me, as we all crested the top of a rise on a trail called Big Drop. I probably should've considered that name before choosing to follow the path, which consisted of a series of switchbacks up a long, steep hill, leading, not surprisingly, to the "big drop" ahead of us. Although I couldn't recall Moxie ever skiing before that day, she was barely out of breath and smiled at me like an instructor whose student has shown modest improvement. "You've only fallen five times since you hit the tree!"

I rubbed my head, which had conked into the trunk of a white birch when I'd swerved to avoid plowing down Moxie and Bernie, right near the trailhead. "Fifty thousand soft pine trees"—I was winded, and took a moment to breathe before concluding— "and I hit the birch." Glancing at Bernie, who was still full of energy, I sucked air again. "This sport . . . is tougher . . . than I remember."

"You've done this before?" Moxie asked incredulously. "Really?"

"Yes, I used to come here . . . all the time with Piper when we were kids . . ." I bent over for a moment, catching my breath, then righted myself, shooting Moxie a quizzical look. "You've skied here before, too, right?"

"No, this is my first time on skis, ever," Moxie informed me. She planted her poles in the snow, triumphantly surveying the forest, while I warily studied the slope in front of us. Then Moxie grinned at me, her cheeks flushed with cold and happiness. "I didn't know it would be so much fun."

"Yeah, it's a blast," I agreed glumly, rubbing my head again. I had snow down my pants, too. I was starting to recall that I'd never been very good on skis, even as a kid, and I glanced over my shoulder. "Maybe we should turn back. This doesn't seem very productive. I'd really hoped Bernie would lead us to his barrel, or we'd see it lying in the snow somewhere," I added. "But I guess that was unrealistic—especially since I can't focus on anything but staying upright." I looked around and saw nothing but trees. "I also haven't seen Max Pottinger's house, which I thought Bernie might sniff out. The place must really be hidden."

"Oh, gosh . . ." Moxie slid sideways so we could talk more easily. She seemed oblivious to the fact that we teetered on the edge of a steep hill. Well, I was teetering. "I completely forgot that we're looking for Max's cabin, and any clues that might help you get poor Bernie home," she said. "I'm so sorry!"

"Don't feel badly," I assured her. "You've been really nice to endure my screams of terror all afternoon."

"They have been piercing," Moxie admitted matter-of-factly. "But I thought you were just exhilarated by the speed we picked up, especially on Yo-Yo. There were some pretty big dips there!"

"Yes, I was exhilarated," I assured her, bending down, very carefully, to pat Bernie's head. The big dog seemed to sense that I was worried about the precipitous incline and had placed himself between me and the drop ahead of us. "Or something like that."

Moxie planted her poles again, this time so she could push back her coat sleeve and check her Minnie Mouse watch. Then she made a sad face. "I wish I could keep hunting, but I have to get back to town. If Sebastian doesn't get his midday snack, he'll chew the furniture. He's already left teeth marks in my Eames chair."

"He's not here?" I asked, straightening. I'd been wondering the whole time if Moxie's rat was tucked into one of her pockets. "Sebastian's at your apartment?"

Moxie blinked at me with surprise. "Of course, I left him at home. I thought anyone new to skiing was bound to fall. I didn't want to risk squishing him. You should've told me he would've been perfectly safe. He *loves* speed, almost as much as he loves jalapeños!"

I didn't even know what to say to all that. I just carefully sidestepped in my skis, trying to turn myself around so we could all head back to Winterfest, where I intended to console myself with a funnel cake.

But as I spun slowly and awkwardly around, something in the distance, at the bottom of the long hill, caught my eye.

Bernie noticed it, too, and he stiffened at my side, his tail straight out, like a banner.

I stopped scooching around and looked more closely.

Then I sighed and told Moxie, "You go ahead and feed Sebastian. I have to ski down this killer hill with Bernie."

"Why?" Moxie asked, sounding genuinely jealous. "Are you finally starting to like skiing again?"

"No," I told her, pushing off before I could chicken out. Bernie was already racing ahead of me, his tail wagging. Then I called back over my shoulder. "I think I finally found *one* of the things I've been looking for!"

If Moxie replied, I couldn't hear her over the sounds of my screams.

Chapter 29

If I hadn't seen a thin trail of smoke rising from a thicket at the bottom of the hill, the gray wisps blending into the gray day—and noticed Bernie's attentive behavior—I wouldn't have ever spied Max Pottinger's cabin, which was camouflaged by brush and brambles. In fact, as we approached the house, after I'd slid down most of the slope on my rear end and done one complete somersault that I couldn't even explain, I wasn't sure if the place was deliberately concealed, or just being swallowed by nature.

Knowing what I did about the Pottinger clan, either scenario seemed possible. The Pottingers had squatted on the property for generations, since long before Bear Tooth forest was declared a state park, and they'd battled to stay put when authorities had taken control of the land. Everyone in Sylvan Creek knew that the Pottingers lived like mountain men and despised the government—although Max had been willing to put aside some of his enmity and accept a taxpayer-funded job as a custodian at my high school, a few years back.

"I hope he remembers me," I told Bernie, shuffling off the trail and toward the cabin. "This place doesn't look very welcoming."

In fact, the closer we got, the creepier Max's shack looked. It was almost impossible to tell where the forest left off and the house began. The structure seemed to being growing out of—or receding into—the ground. Years', or perhaps decades', worth of fallen, rotten leaves weighed down the sagging roof, and the trees had closed in around the walls, which were smothered by a twisting, impenetrable snarl of choking vines and spiky thistle. The foliage was all bare, mid-winter, so I could see a man-made door and window, but in midsummer, I could imagine that a hiker could pass right by and never realize he or she had been close to a human's dwelling.

That thought was pretty scary, and I stopped in my tracks, really regretting that I hadn't told Moxie where, exactly, Bernie and I were going before I'd plummeted down the hill.

"We're going to head back," I said aloud, alerting Bernie to my change in plans, and to assure anyone who might be listening that we planned to peacefully retreat. But Bernie ignored me, looking back once over his shoulder before resuming trotting toward the shack, while I slid my skis backward. The move wasn't very effective, but better, in my opinion, than turning my back on the forbidding little house. "Bernie, come," I called the dog, adding, "people are waiting for us at the top of Big Drop, so we'd better get going!"

I didn't like to lie. As the great philosopher and statesman Francis Bacon once said, lies "doth so cover a man in shame."

But better to be covered in shame than rotten leaves and a few shovelfuls of dirt in a shallow grave, right?

"Gotta get back to our friends!" I said more loudly, because Bernie was ignoring my summons. I also had the spooky feeling that someone was watching us from behind the dark windowpane that peeked out from the vines. "Can't keep people waiting!"

"Umm . . . Your friend took off a while ago."

The voice came from right beside the door of the house, and I realized that I'd been wrong about being watched from a window.

No, Max Pottinger had been observing us the whole time from a makeshift seat on the rotting boards that served as his porch.

In fact, he was just a few feet away from me, and even closer to Bernie, who was hurtling toward him at full speed.

Chapter 30

"I'm so sorry Bernie knocked you off your overturned bucket chair," I told Mr. Pottinger, who was puttering around his home, which was surprisingly clean and cozy inside. Bernie had crossed the threshold and was lying near a wood stove, but I stood in the open doorway, waiting while the wiry old man brewed some tea from fresh mint. I thought I had a decent indoor herb garden, but Mr. Pottinger's shack was filled with potted plants, which only enhanced the illusion that the structure was being consumed by nature. But the ramshackle house was very warm, thanks to the stove. My cheeks were actually getting hot, even though I continued to wait on the porch. Fortunately, Mr. Pottinger, who did recall me from high school, as a "girl who spilled a lot," seemed to understand that I might be reluctant to enter his isolated, crumbling home and hadn't urged me to come inside. In fact, I got the sense that he preferred I stay just beyond the door, although he hadn't objected when Bernie had trotted right over to the fire. "Bernie sure seems to like you, and your place," I added. "Maybe a little too much!"

I was joking, but I did think Bernie seemed strangely at home in the shack. Like maybe he'd been there before.

But Max was acting like he'd never seen the dog. He smiled at me, and although he had hair the color of a crafty fox's fur and that creature's pointed nose, I saw that his eyes were kind. "Your pup is just friendly," he said. "And he didn't hurt me. I'm old, but pretty tough."

"He's not really my dog," I told him, trying to study Mr. Pottinger more closely. But he'd turned his back to me while he poured the tea. "I'm just watching him."

Mr. Pottinger didn't reply, so I added, "You *do* know that he's the Saint Bernard who pulled Lauren Savidge from the lake, right? The one whose picture was in the *Weekly Gazette*?"

I still couldn't see his face, but Mr. Pottinger's bent back stiffened, and his wrist twitched, so he spilled some of the hot water. Then his spine curved again, and he finished filling two mugs that sat on a cluttered counter. "No, I didn't know that," he said. "Don't read that newspaper everybody's talking about lately." Then he turned around, smiling again, but in a way that seemed forced. "Not much use for news out here!"

"No, I guess not," I agreed, again looking around his home, which was filled with stuff that indicated he was pretty self-sufficient. Large sprays of dried herbs hung from the ceiling, and every wall was lined with wooden shelving that bowed under the weight of not only his extensive botanical collection, but Mason jars filled with home-canned goods. I spied summery yellow peaches, ripe red tomatoes, and gorgeous purple beets. Although the crowded shelves made the space seem cramped, I realized that there wasn't really much furniture to speak of, with the exception of a crude table that was nearly buried under scattered papers and pens. Clearly, Mr. Pottinger was in the midst of some sort of writing project. All in all, with the right lighting and styling, Elyse Hunter-Black probably could've featured the place in a show that would appeal to folks who dreamed of going off the grid and writing the great American novel in rustic solitude. So long as she didn't use any exterior shots. I turned back to Max, who was shuffling in my direction, mug in hand. "You do know about Lauren Savidge, though, right?"

Mr. Pottinger grew somber as he handed me the tea. "Yes, yes, of course," he said, taking my elbow and quickly guiding me away from the door. He glanced over his shoulder, almost nervously. "That was a terrible tragedy. Poor girl drowning like that." He shook his head. "City folks underestimate nature sometimes."

Apparently, Mr. Pottinger didn't know that Lauren had been murdered. And I didn't set him straight, for some reason.

Maybe, although I got a good vibe from him, I just didn't like the idea of bringing up the topic of homicide in such a remote place. And, even for a hermit, he was acting kind of cagey about letting me see his home. That seemed odd to me.

Still, as he guided us both outside, I asked him, "Did you know Lauren?"

I wasn't sure how I expected Mr. Pottinger to answer. He hadn't been featured on Lauren's corkboard, but I couldn't imagine how she could've produced a show about Sylvan Creek and pets without featuring the Lake Wallapawakee Saint Bernard.

"Did Lauren ever interview you for *America's Most Pet Friendly Towns*?" I added, because Mr. Pottinger hadn't answered me.

"No, no," he said, waving off the question. "I told her I'm not much for television. Don't even own one!" All at once, I saw something like a glimmer of anger in his eyes. "Don't trust the people who make the shows to get things right!" He looked out at the woods, and I got the sense that he almost forgot that I was there for a second. His voice grew softer, and he shook his head, mumbling, "Tried to tell that to the other kids, but they wouldn't take no . . ."

He must've said more than he'd planned, because he abruptly stopped talking, his jaw hanging open, and I could tell that he regretted his words, although they made no sense to me. I had no idea who the "kids" were or what they'd tried to force him to do.

Were they, perhaps, children who'd come to Winterfest and heard the story of the Saint Bernard, then urged him to share the tale on TV?

That didn't really make sense, but I didn't think Mr. Pottinger was going to elaborate, so I changed the subject, if only slightly. "Well, are you *sure* you don't know anything about Bernie, or where he came from?" I asked again. "Because he ran out of the woods the night Lauren was murdered. Didn't *anybody* on one of your walks mention seeing him?"

For a split second, I didn't understand why Mr. Pottinger stiffened again, visibly, like I'd struck him. Then I realized that I'd accidentally used the very word I'd planned to avoid uttering.

"*Murder?*" he asked, his eyes growing wide. Then he staggered back a step, reaching blindly behind himself for one of two overturned buckets that served as seats on the sagging porch. As he sank down onto his makeshift chair—the Pottingers had probably been repurposing before *repurposing* was a word—I noted that his legs seemed unsteady. "Are . . . are you saying that young lady was *murdered?*"

"Yes," I confirmed, since there was no backtracking from what I'd just blurted. He didn't invite me to sit, too, but I carefully crouched down on the matching, wobbly perch, so we were eye to eye. "Someone killed Lauren. It wasn't an accident."

Mr. Pottinger grew very quiet while he digested that news. He gazed out into the forest again for a long time before turning back to me. "I'm so sorry about Ms. Savidge," he said softly and with more composure. "But I didn't really know her. And I can't tell you anything about the dog you have."

As if on cue, the Saint Bernard in question ambled out of the shack, a massive bone clamped in his big jaws.

I really hoped that Mr. Pottinger hadn't planned to make some sort of stock or soup.

Fortunately, he didn't seem to mind that Bernie had helped himself to the pantry. Maybe because, while more outwardly calm, he was clearly still shaken by my inadvertent news—and guarding some secret of his own.

"Are you *sure* you know *nothing* about Bernie?" I asked one more time, in a quiet voice. I glanced at the big dog, who was happily gnawing on the already half-chewed bone, then met Mr. Pottinger's eyes again. "Because I thought maybe Bernie was part of Winterfest. Maybe let loose so kids would spy the 'ghost dog' when you led walks through the woods. It could've been a fun touch, you know? And completely innocent . . ."

I was trying to assure Mr. Pottinger that, if he had tried to "embellish" his moonlit hikes, perhaps without the approval of the Tail Waggin' Winterfest organizers, it probably wouldn't be a big deal. In fact, I thought Mayor Holtzapple and the rest of the committee would likely applaud the harmless charade.

But Mr. Pottinger was shaking his head. "No, it wasn't like that," he muttered, abruptly rising, although we'd just sat down. "Now, if you'll excuse me, I need to get inside. I . . . I've got some work to do."

I seriously doubted he had a pressing deadline to meet, but I stood up, too, and handed him my mug. "Thanks for the tea, which was delicious," I said honestly. The simple brew of mint and honey had been the perfect antidote to the cold, damp day. "What kind of mint do you grow?"

"That's apple mint, also known as woolly mint," he informed me. He was still impatient for me to leave, but clearly couldn't resist talking about his herb collection. "Grow seven kinds of mint," he said. "Woolly mint's best for tea, in my opinion."

I looked past him into the shack, with all the canned goods, plants, and papers and pens.

"Well, you seem to have a green thumb and a knack for 'putting up' the stuff you grow," I said, smiling, like I hadn't noticed that he was still agitated.

Mr. Pottinger shrugged. "Plants are like friends, out here. I take care of them, they take care of me."

"Are you writing a book or something?" I added, nodding toward the table. "Maybe on recipes using homegrown ingredients? Because I would be interested in reading that."

"As a matter of fact, I am writing something," he informed me, jutting his chin, like he thought I might find the prospect of a former-custodian-turned-author absurd, which was not the case at all. As the great British thinker Edward Gibbon once noted, "Solitude is the school of genius." If that was true, as I suspected, Max Pottinger probably had an IQ equivalent to Einstein's. "But it's not a book about plants, much as I love 'em."

"No? Then what . . . ?"

"It's a history of the legend," Mr. Pottinger said, puffing out his chest, too. "I'm recording all of the sightings, throughout the years. Telling the story the *right* way. Because so much knowledge will be lost when I'm gone . . ." He'd been almost defiant, but his shoulders slowly caved in and his voice trailed off. "So much, just gone . . ."

Although I'd grown a bit nervous when Mr. Pottinger had become upset, my heart suddenly ached for him. In the blink of an eye, he seemed less like a self-sufficient pioneer and more like a lonely old man who lived in woods that were swallowing him and his house. A soul whose only hope for a legacy was an old talc that, let's face it, would probably be buried with him.

"I'm sorry we bothered you," I said quietly, while I summoned Bernie by tapping my hand against my thigh. This time, he obeyed, although he hesitated before dropping the bone. Then he rose and followed me off the porch. Finding my skis, which I'd left in the snow, I snapped my boots into the toe clips. "I shouldn't have come here."

"It's okay, Daphne." Mr. Pottinger pulled himself straighter again. "I wish I could've helped you more." He frowned at Bernie with what I thought was genuine sadness. "And I hope that dog finds his home. 'Cause everybody needs a home."

That was a wistful, borderline melodramatic comment, and yet, there was a bitter tinge to Mr. Pottinger's voice, too. I wasn't sure why, since he lived on land that had been passed down through generations. If anybody had roots, it was Max Pottinger. And some of those roots were literal, growing down through whatever corrugated material was serving as a roof over the makeshift porch.

"Take care, Mr. Pottinger," I told him, starting to shuffle-ski back toward the trail. Bernie followed me, looking back once, like he regretted leaving the bone. Or the shack. Or Mr. Pottinger? "And if you think of anything that might help me find Bernie's home, please let me know," I added. "I don't think I can keep him too much longer. He's too big for my cottage and upsetting my already belligerent cat."

Mr. Pottinger didn't say anything for a moment, and I thought he'd gone inside. Then I heard him call to me. "There is one thing," he said. "Although, it won't help you find Bernie's owner. I just think it's curious. . . ."

I turned back to see him watching me and Bernie from the porch, one hand resting on the ivy-covered walls of his house, like he needed to prop himself up.

I cocked my head. "What's that, Mr. Pottinger?"

"In . . . in older versions of the legend," he said, just loud enough for me to hear, "the Saint Bernard always appeared *right before someone died.*"

Then Max Pottinger vanished soundlessly into his strange home, leaving me to ponder his equally strange words—which had almost sounded like a *warning*—while I skied awkwardly back into the forest, with no clear recollection of how to find my way home on the twisted, endlessly looping maze of trails.

Chapter 31

It took Bernie and me about two hours to make our way back to Winterfest, which *I* located by a combination of dumb luck and by following the smell of hot dogs, because, although the festival was more upscale that year, the VFW still had its annual stand.

"You really aren't . . . the Lake Wallapawakee . . . Saint Bernard," I wheezed to Bernie, who pranced ahead of me, still full of energy, while I clumsily waddled up the rise I'd first tumbled down. "You were . . . supposed to . . . lead us . . . home!"

Bernie woofed, the deep, happy sound of a dog who's been in his element.

I was pretty sure he could've guided us directly from Max Pottinger's house to civilization, but had led me in circles so he could keep enjoying the snow.

"We'll see . . . if you get . . . a hot dog," I warned him, cresting the hill, where I grabbed on to the wooden trail sign. "I don't . . . think . . . you deserve . . . a treat!"

Bernie woofed again in protest, his deep bark echoing loudly at the quiet edge of the forest.

We both knew that I'd cave in and buy him something, but I refused to make any promises.

Sinking down, I began to remove my skis, unlacing the boots without even unclipping them from the bindings, which were covered with ice. At one point, Bernie had led me off the trail, and we'd bushwhacked through a small stream.

Only when I was free of the skis did I realize that I'd left my other boots—the cowgirl type—stashed under a crude wooden bench, which, according to a sign, some Boy Scouts had crafted as part of a trail beautification project.

"Great," I grumbled, because the bench was about fifteen feet away and I was in socks. Then I looked hopefully at Bernie and said, "Boots, Bernie! Get the boots!"

The big dog looked directly at my footwear—and sat down.

"Thanks a lot," I grumbled. Then I glanced around, checking to make sure that no one was watching before I started crawling toward the bench, since Piper's ski pants were waterproof and insulated against the snow, unlike my wool socks.

I'd been sure that I was alone, not counting Bernie, who was rolling happily in the snow. But before I'd gone three feet, another skier soared up the hill and skidded to a stop next to me like an Olympian after a record-setting run. "Are you all right, Daphne?" she asked me. "Should I call for help?"

Still on all fours, I twisted to look up at Elyse Hunter-Black, who wore a sleek pair of black ski pants; a red down vest that probably cost more than my van, based upon the discreetly displayed label;

and a matching headband that held every strand of
her glossy blond hair in place.

"There's no need to call for help," I assured her.
Then, because it was obvious that I was struggling, I
admitted, "But I wouldn't exactly say that I'm 'all
right.'"

Elyse stared down at me for a long time. I was
pretty sure she wanted to leave me to finish crawling
toward my boots. But her whole life was based upon
acting with grace and style, and after a moment, she
forced a smile. "Would you and your dog like to come
to my house and warm up for a minute?" she offered,
with a glance at Bernie, who was covered in snow. I
saw a momentary flash of dismay in her eyes, but she
added, "I could put your things in the dryer, so you
don't have to drive all the way to Winding Hill in
wet socks."

I bent my spine to look back at my feet, which were
crusted with snow, although the whole reason I'd
been crawling was to keep that from happening.

Then I slowly stood up with as much dignity as
possible. And, ignoring the fact that Elyse's invitation
had been a polite gesture, meant to be refused, I
grinned and said, "Sure, that would be great, thanks!"

Chapter 32

The moment Bernie and I stepped into Elyse Hunter-Black's hilltop mansion overlooking Lake Wallapawakee, I understood why every electrician, plumber, handyman, and contractor in the Sylvan Creek area was booked solid with work, so my little bakery project remained incomplete.

"This is amazing," I had to admit, following Elyse into a foyer that had been dim and cramped just a few months earlier, when the property had been owned by an elderly spinster named Lillian Flynt. Lillian—Tinkleston's former person—had let her family's estate slide into disrepair, but Elyse was rebuilding the whole place, starting, apparently, with the foyer, which no longer had walls. The entryway was open to a massive parlor, which was filled with sawhorses, paint cans, tarps, and toolboxes. I wondered how Lillian, whose murder I'd solved, would feel to see her home changed so dramatically. To be honest, I wasn't sure how I felt about Elyse's decision to tear apart the historic building. But, having seen her magazine cover–worthy renovations to Jonathan's

A-frame home in the woods, I knew that the results would be impressive. Absently patting Bernie, who was still damp, I looked at Elyse again. "You're really gutting the place."

"You have no idea," she said, leading the way through the cluttered parlor, toward a tarp that hung over a doorway. It was dusk by then, and the room was dim, so it took me a few seconds to realize that her two greyhounds, Paris and Milan, had emerged from the shadows on silent paws and flanked Elyse, as they always did. The dogs were gorgeous and perfectly behaved, but they kind of spooked me, with their impassive eyes and absolute, almost preternatural silence. Elyse pulled aside the tarp and gestured for me and Bernie to step through. "When you start ripping apart these old places, you always find more than you bargained for lurking behind the walls."

I cringed, recalling how Lillian's electrocution in her bathtub had revealed problems with the wiring.

Then, as I ducked to step under the tarp, I let out a low whistle, to discover what waited behind the plastic sheet.

"This is phenomenal!" I straightened, gawking at the kitchen, which Elyse had already finished remodeling. "Holy cow!"

"Why, thank you." I turned to see that, for once, Elyse looked genuinely pleased by something I'd said. "I'm pretty proud of this space."

"You should be." I still had reservations about her decision to completely alter a local landmark, but there was no denying that Elyse had made the most of what had been an outdated room. The kitchen's focal point, a bank of tall windows that offered stunning views of the water, remained the centerpiece of the space. But Elyse had replaced the old cupboards with an artfully eclectic, purposely mismatched combination of classic white cabinetry and freestanding pieces that looked antique, but were probably modern and fully functional. The gleaming, six-burner gas range was a home chef's dream. And the marble countertops would've made Michelangelo drool. I loved my humble abode, but I had to admit that Jonathan's ex-wife had designed a show-stopping space that honored the mansion's style while bringing the house into the twenty-first century. As Bernie stretched out on an intricately patterned, antique Turkish rug, which I never would've thought to use in a kitchen, I turned to Elyse, who was putting a gleaming silver tea kettle onto one of the burners. "I know you must hear this all the time," I told her, "but you are *really* talented."

She must've received the compliment quite often, because she didn't bother thanking me again. She just smiled and gestured for me to sit down at a long white table that was positioned to overlook the lake. "Please. Let me take your wet socks. And any other damp things you have."

I took a seat on a chair painted in a pretty shade of pale green and removed my boots, while Elyse placed some muffins on a delicate china plate, which she delivered to the table. I couldn't recall the last time I'd been somewhere so upscale, without a speck of dust or a single object out of place, and I felt funny handing over my soggy socks. Especially since Elyse didn't seem to have worked up a sweat in her perfect outfit. But she was waiting with one hand out, so I gave her my laundry.

"Thanks," I said, sheepishly.

Elyse allowed the socks to dangle from her thumb and forefinger, so I knew that she wasn't pleased to handle them, but she did her best not to wrinkle her perfectly straight nose.

"I'll be right back," she promised, turning on her heel. "Please, make yourself at home."

I doubted that was possible, since I'd never lived in a five-star hotel, but I was willing to give it a try, and I settled into my chair, watching the sun set over the lake.

A few moments later, I heard Elyse's footsteps—and only hers, although Paris and Milan had followed her—crossing the upstairs hallway, toward the master bedroom, where I'd first seen Tinkleston hiding in a slipper.

I wondered, for a second, if Elyse was bothered to live alone in a huge house where someone had been murdered.

I kind of doubted it.

Unlike me, Elyse didn't seem like the type of person who would entertain thoughts of ghosts, the occult, or bad juju, all of which I was very open to believing in.

Then my stomach started to grumble, and I decided that making myself at home probably included helping myself to the muffins while I waited for the kettle to whistle.

Deciding upon what appeared to be blueberry, I broke off a piece and popped it into my mouth, only to clap my hand over my lips.

It was quite obvious that Elyse, or whoever had baked the muffins, had mistaken salt for sugar.

I was looking around for a napkin, hoping to spit out the awful bite, when Elyse ducked under the tarp and caught me even more off guard by noting, "So, Daphne, why don't we cut to the chase? Because I know you're *dying* to ask me what I know about the murder, correct?"

Chapter 33

"So, what *do* you know about the murder?" I asked Elyse, who was pouring tea into a classic, classy white china cup. She'd changed out of her ski clothes into an outfit that was probably technically a sweat suit. However, unlike my sweats, Elyse's black velour hoodie and pants weren't baggy and worn, and a big gold zipper that ran down the front of the jacket was definitely a designer touch. Paris and Milan, who padded softly behind her as she moved about the kitchen, wore matching black velvet collars. I was also getting a taste of Elyse's luxurious lifestyle. She'd loaned me a pair of thick, soft cashmere socks to wear while my old wool pair dried. I shifted in my seat so Elyse could set the steaming tea down in front of me. "Did you see anything the night Lauren was killed?"

"You know that I told Jon everything I saw," Elyse reminded me, opening a refrigerator that I hadn't even noticed, because it was concealed by cabinetry. Pulling out a deep blue bottle, she closed the door and joined me at the table, sliding gracefully into an upholstered banquette that ran below the windows.

"And Detective Doebler has questioned me several times since Jon took himself off the case." She twisted a silver cap off the bottle. "But I suppose you won't rest until I answer your questions, too."

"Probably not," I confirmed, but absently.

I was distracted by Elyse's beverage. The bottle's thick, heavy glass was the color of the sky at dusk, and the label was written in French: *Eau de Vaucluse.* I didn't speak much French, but I recognized the name of a town in the fancy Côte d'Azur region, on the Mediterranean. I'd traveled through that area once and gotten stuck just outside Vaucluse overnight, when my train had mechanical problems. I hadn't even been able to afford regular water there, let alone the stuff Elyse was drinking, and I'd spent a long, thirsty, stinky night on a sticky vinyl seat, next to another broke backpacker whose last hostel had lacked a working shower.

"I'm sorry, Daphne," Elyse said, breaking my reverie. I finally looked up to see her observing me with concern, and for a second, I thought she somehow knew about my sad experience in the South of France. Then I realized I'd been staring at the bottle for too long. "Did you want water instead of tea?" she inquired politely. "I just assumed that you'd want something warm, while I'm sort of addicted to Eau de Vaucluse. Enough that the little specialty market in town, Epicure, orders it for me by the case. Even though I'm the only person who buys it."

"Yes, I saw you drinking that at the plunge," I noted, finally sipping my tea. It was so weak that I couldn't tell if I was drinking chamomile, lavender, or Earl Grey. No wonder Elyse preferred European water. And how could someone known for living stylishly mess up *tea and muffins*? Trying hard not to make a face, I swallowed quickly. "I'm pretty sure you were the only person who brought a *cold* drink."

Elyse smiled, almost guiltily. "I really only planned to dip my toe in the water, then step right out. I was mainly there to be part of my new community, you know? Show myself as a Sylvan Creek 'team player.'" All at once, she stopped smiling. "Then, of course, everything went wrong."

"Yeah, very wrong," I agreed quietly, studying her face. I'd never had a chance to sit down with Elyse before, and she was even prettier than I'd realized. Her fair skin was flawless, her cheekbones high and angular, and her blue-gray eyes as big as a Disney princess's. Well, almost that big. I had a feeling those wide eyes probably caused some of her competitors in the television industry to underestimate her intelligence and determination, which could be advantageous to Elyse. "I know you've already been debriefed," I said, continuing to watch her eyes. "But I'm still curious . . . Did you see anything out of the ordinary the night of Lauren's murder?" Then I pressed my luck by adding, "And—not to be too nosy—but what were you and Lauren arguing about before the plunge?"

To my surprise, Elyse didn't tell me to mind my own business. She grew thoughtful, like she was taking my inquiries seriously.

"As hard as I try to recall, I honestly can't remember seeing anything strange," she finally said, resting back and curling one foot under herself. Outside, snow began to fall past the windows, and across the lake, I could see the lights of Winterfest glowing in the heart of Bear Tooth forest. Elyse looked out the windows, too, and frowned. "As for the argument . . ."

I leaned forward, unable to contain my interest. "Yes?"

Elyse met my gaze again. "We'd actually been clashing for weeks," she admitted. "Nearly from the moment Lauren arrived in Sylvan Creek."

I pushed aside my tea and half-eaten muffin. "About what?"

Elyse smiled faintly and wryly. "Everything. But mainly about the direction that Lauren was trying to take *America's Most Pet Friendly Towns.*" She pulled the bottle of pricey water closer to herself, wrapping her delicate fingers around the glass. "I told her that Stylish Life Network was expecting a show about a pretty place, with pretty pets and pretty people. That's our brand."

"I take it Lauren had other ideas?"

"Oh, yes." Elyse rolled her eyes. "She considered Sylvan Creek *too* obsessed with pets. She wanted to focus less on the quaint setting and more on the town's colorful, quirky characters, highlighting their eccentricities and digging deeper into their stories, to expose them as . . ."

Elyse struggled for a word, but I could easily supply one, because Lauren had already used it, when we'd last spoken. And I'd seen the word *Lunatics!* pinned to her corkboard.

"Crazy," I said. "Lauren wanted to portray people like Arlo Finch and Bea Baumgartner . . . maybe the whole town . . . as pet 'crazy,' as opposed to pet 'friendly.'"

Elyse nodded. "Exactly. But Stylish Life viewers

don't want to watch an investigative piece on Big Cats of the World, or an exposé that debunks holistic pet healing."

I felt a tickle of excitement in my stomach. Or maybe it was just the muffin, sitting wrong. Regardless, I asked, "Was Lauren really investigating Victor Breard's zoo-shelter . . . hybrid? And Arlo Finch's practice? Was there *reason* to investigate either of those things?"

Elyse seemed to realize that I was starting to think in terms of suspects, and she backed off her statements, just slightly. Raising one hand, she said, "I don't know how much Lauren was really digging or what she might've found. Whenever she even mentioned 'investigating' anything, I repeated my mantra: Pretty places. Pretty people. Pretty pets."

All at once, I got kind of confused. "Did you hire Lauren to be field producer? Or was that somebody else's decision?"

Elyse's mouth set in a firm white line. "Unfortunately, I was the one who hired her and brought her here. Which I suppose means that, even though I didn't wield whatever weapon was used to kill her . . ."

I couldn't help jumping on that comment. "The police still don't know?"

Elyse shook her head. "No, they don't." Then she concluded, "Even if I didn't directly harm Lauren, I suppose I do share some responsibility for her death."

That admission surprised me. I'd always assumed that Elyse was a little . . . *cold.* She had a reputation for getting whatever she wanted and letting nothing stand in her way. But she was clearly remorseful, for no good reason.

"You are not responsible for Lauren's death," I

assured her. "As Jean-Paul Sartre said, individuals are 'condemned to be free' and ultimately responsible only for themselves. Lauren chose to come here, and not to say that she deserved her fate . . ." I reared back a little. "I would *never* say that! But she did stir up trouble in Sylvan Creek. That wasn't your fault."

Elyse blinked at me. "Jon wasn't kidding when he said you have a philosophical quote for every occasion."

I couldn't help wondering whether Jonathan had been complimenting me or complaining about the quotes. Then I turned the conversation back to Lauren, because I felt like I was on the verge of getting some potentially useful information.

"So, why did you hire Lauren?" I asked. "Because, just based on her appearance, she didn't look like *she* fit the Stylish Life brand." I didn't mean to disparage Lauren, who'd cultivated an intriguing look, in my opinion, and I gestured to my old sweater and the ski pants I was still wearing. "Not that I know what it's like to be 'stylish,' either!"

"I think you sell yourself short, Daphne," Elyse said quietly, looking me up and down. "I think you know that you're very pretty, with your gorgeous curls and effortless Bohemian style that can't be purchased off a rack. You either have it, or you don't."

I didn't really consider myself pretty, at least not in the traditional sense, like Elyse, and I wasn't sure why she suddenly seemed unhappy.

There was a moment of somewhat awkward silence, interrupted by Bernie's deep snores. Apparently, our adventure had finally worn him out. He was sound asleep—and drooling—on the no doubt expensive rug.

"So, why choose Lauren to head up *America's Most*

Pet Friendly Towns?" I finally repeated, ending the uncomfortable moment. "Had you worked with her before?"

Elyse broke out of her reverie and shook her head again. "No, I hadn't. But I'd heard very good things about her work for one of Stylish Life's sister networks, Real Crime."

I cocked my head, surprised. "Those two networks have the same parent company?"

"Yes." Elyse had grown very serious during our conversation, but she couldn't help smiling at my naïveté. She also seemed to warm to the topic of television, more than murder. "The global corporation that owns both networks doesn't care if their content meshes. It's all about the bottom line, and Real Crime is a moneymaker. The shows are cheap to produce, since most of them revolve around prison interviews, and viewers never seem to tire of peeking inside the hidden world of the cellblock."

I could imagine Lauren Savidge dealing successfully with inmates. She wouldn't have let them intimidate her. In fact, I suddenly felt like I understood Lauren a little better. If she'd really worked in prisons all the time, she would've had to gain a tough exterior.

"What was Lauren's role at Real Crime?" I asked, forcing myself to take another bite of the salty muffin, just to be polite. I nearly chipped my tooth on a blueberry. At least, I'd thought the dark bits were blueberry. "What did she do there?"

"She was field producer for a series called *Life on Death Row*," Elyse said, idly pushing aside the plate of muffins that she couldn't have tasted. If she had, she never would've offered one to a guest. "She'd visit maximum security prisons and get killers—the worst

ones, who were sentenced to die—to tell their life
stories and describe their crimes." Elyse frowned,
then shuddered. "Rough, ugly stuff. I can't believe
anybody wants to delve into that world. But the show
has consistently high viewership."

I thought about Jonathan's latest career choice.
Had Elyse also failed to understand why a former
Navy SEAL might be interested in investigating "ugly"
homicides, when there were no doubt more aesthetically pleasing career options available to him? If so,
that might help to explain their split.

Elyse and I seemed to be gaining a rapport, but we
certainly weren't close enough for me to play mar-
riage counselor, so I returned my attention to Lauren
Savidge's career.

"I didn't know Lauren that well, but it seems to me
that she was way better suited to Real Crime than Stylish Life," I noted. "So, why leave *Life on Death Row*?"

Elyse answered me with a question of her own.
"Wouldn't you choose filming puppies over killers,
given the chance?"

Elyse obviously thought the question was a no-
brainer, and I knew that I would also take that deal.
But I was a sucker for animals. Lauren Savidge hadn't
seemed to particularly like puppies, the few times I'd
met her. And, clearly, she'd had trouble making the
transition to the less exciting network. I could honestly imagine that the woman who'd claimed to enjoy
challenges like jumping into cold lakes might pick
killers over cockapoos and kitty cats.

Or *big* cats.

I suddenly pictured Lauren's corkboard and the
photo of Victor Breard in a bull's-eye, with the curious caption *"Zookeeper Sen . . ."*

Might that last word have been "sen*tenced*"?

Victor had looked pretty upset in the picture.

What if he'd been headed to *prison*, where he might've crossed paths with Lauren Savidge somehow?

If so, and Victor was hiding some past wrongdoing for which he'd served time, he might have had reason to silence Lauren.

"Are you sure Lauren never said anything about why she might want to 'investigate' Victor Breard and Big Cats of the World?" I asked Elyse, who was staring out over the lake, nibbling a fingernail lightly enough to protect her manicure. "She never gave a real reason?"

Elyse returned her attention to me. She seemed confused. "No. Why?"

"It's nothing," I said, not wanting to unnecessarily impugn Victor's character. For all I knew, the magazine article had been titled "Zookeeper Sensational Hit in Vegas!" Although I doubted it. And I had a feeling that Lauren's work with Real Crime was somehow connected to her murder. "Did anybody ever threaten Lauren when she was with Real Crime?" I ventured. "It seems like some people on death row might not want their stories to be told. Or, with her forceful personality, she could've easily rubbed some of her already homicidal subjects the wrong way."

I was just making guesses, and Elyse was unsure. "I have no idea," she said. "I imagine that's a risk one would take in that line of work. As I noted, Lauren— and her crew—weren't exactly dealing with pleasant subjects."

I edged forward on my seat, intrigued by her mention of the television crew. "You don't mean the same people who are here, right? The cameraman and the assistant, Joy?"

But Elyse was nodding. "Yes, that was part of the deal to get Lauren. She insisted that we also hire her favorite cameraman, Kevin Drucker, and her assistant, Joy Doolittle. And that actually impressed me— until I realized that Lauren wasn't acting out of loyalty. She mainly found Kevin and Joy easy to boss around and didn't want to break in new minions."

I was about to ask her more about Joy and Kevin when a buzzer went off upstairs, and Elyse tilted an ear to the ceiling. "It sounds like your socks are dry." She slid out from behind the table. "I'll go get them."

I was pretty sure that I'd be dismissed once I'd exchanged cashmere for itchy wool, so I posed one last question as the greyhounds emerged from beneath the table.

"What will happen to *America's Most Pet Friendly Towns* now that Lauren is gone?" I asked, trying to choose the most delicate word possible. "Will the crew pack up and leave?"

Elyse seemed surprised by the question.

"No, of course not," she told me. "I've already promoted Joy. She's quiet, but actually seems quite capable. She can finish what's left of the job."

Then Elyse, flanked by Paris and Milan, ducked under the tarp and disappeared into her huge, dark mansion, leaving me to ponder that revelation while I poured the remainder of my weak, cold tea into the sink and buried the muffin in a trash can.

I had just closed the lid and was nudging Bernie awake when Elyse returned with my socks, which had shrunk three sizes, so I could barely pull them on. In fact, they slipped halfway off my feet while Bernie and

I followed her to the door. Stopping in the renovated foyer, I said, "I know you don't owe me any favors, but I'm going to ask one anyhow."

Elyse watched me warily. "And that is . . . ?"

"Can I borrow some of your workmen for my pet bakery?" I requested. "I need to have my grand opening soon—so Joy Doolittle can film it before she leaves town forever."

Chapter 34

"Come on," I urged the VW, patting the dashboard as the van lurched into Sylvan Creek after coasting downhill from Elyse's mansion. We rolled in fits and starts onto Market Street, managing to drift past Templeton Animal Hospital and my mother's real-estate office, although the engine was making an alarming coughing sound. "You can do this," I promised my semi-trusty vehicle. "Just a few more miles to Winding Hill!"

We had slowed down to about three miles per hour on the dark, flat, largely empty street, and in my heart, I knew that my encouragement wasn't going to be enough to power us up the daunting hill that lay ahead.

Apparently, I wasn't the only one who'd noticed that my poor VW wasn't feeling very well. As the van drifted to a stop conveniently close to Flour Power, someone stepped off the curb, knocked on the driver's side window, and said, with a resigned sigh, "Let's go, Daphne. I'll give you a ride home."

Chapter 35

"You honestly don't have to walk me all the way home," I told Jonathan, who was maneuvering his black pickup truck into a spot near Piper's barn, after declaring my carburetor deceased and giving me a ride to Winding Hill. In retrospect, I was lucky that he'd been walking Axis and Artie in town. I glanced over my shoulder at Bernie, who was riding in the backseat with the other dogs. "I feel pretty safe on the trails, especially when I have a big dog like Bernie with me." I faced forward again. "Plus, I took a class in *Krav Maga* when I was stuck in Israel for a few months."

Jonathan faced me in the dark. "I'm not even going to question why you were 'stuck' in the Middle East. I'm just going to assume that you lost your passport."

"Yes, in a kibbutz . . . !"

I started to tell Jonathan that he was correct, but he continued talking.

"However, I can't help asking why you—a self-proclaimed peacenik—studied a particularly aggressive form of self-defense used by the Israeli Army."

"I thought I was signing up for a cooking class," I informed him. "The brochure was a little misleading." I shrugged. "And once I got there, I figured I might as well stay, since I'd spent quite a few shekels to register."

Jonathan didn't seem to know how to respond. He stared at me for a long time in the darkness. Then he opened the driver's side door. "Well, I'm going to walk you home, regardless," he said, getting out of the truck and opening the back door to release Axis and Bernie, who both bounded down onto the snowy ground. As I exited the truck, too, Jonathan lifted Artie and set him down before slamming the door. "Bernie might be good in a water rescue, but I don't think he'd do more than slobber on an assailant."

I drew back. "Why would there be an 'assailant' at Winding Hill? That's an ominous word."

"You once again found a homicide victim, this time moments after the murder," Jonathan reminded me. He took my elbow lightly in one hand and began to guide me toward the paths. The dogs were already running ahead. Axis and Artie were familiar with the route to Plum Cottage, and I hoped that Bernie would stick with them and not run off into the woods. I probably should've leashed him. "Maybe someone would like to see you out of the picture, too," Jonathan added. "Someone who's worried about what you might've seen that night."

Much as I hated to admit it, I realized that he might be right, and we grew quiet as we entered under the canopy of trees. We walked along in silence for a few minutes before Jonathan said, "You didn't take my advice, did you?"

I jolted, but he continued to hold my elbow. "What?"

"Elyse called to tell me that you'd been at her house, asking questions. She was worried that she'd talked too much about Lauren and some of the other people who were at the scene of the murder."

"I didn't seek her out," I told him, defending myself. "We were both skiing at Bear Tooth forest, and she invited me to her house so I could dry my socks. I couldn't help asking questions."

"Daphne." Jonathan's voice was even and his grip was firm. "I'm not going to lecture you again. I did the best I could to warn you about the risks of investigating a homicide. But I am going to ask . . . Why were you skiing in a forest where a mysterious Saint Bernard was recently on the loose? A dog who *might be related to a murder*?"

"I thought Mr. Pottinger might know something about Bernie's origins," I admitted. "Or the missing barrel. But he claimed he didn't know anything."

"You shouldn't have gone there, Daphne." Jonathan shook his head. "I don't know exactly where Pottinger lives, but I know the house is remote. And he has a reputation for being eccentric."

"He was acting strangely," I agreed. "I probably *should've* been scared to be at his decaying shack in the woods, but he was the one who seemed nervous. He didn't want me to step inside, any more than I wanted to do that. And when I told him that Lauren's death wasn't accidental, he got very pale. Then he said this odd thing, about Bernie."

"What?" Jonathan's tone was sharp, and he bent so he could see my face. "What did he say?"

I stepped carefully over an icy patch on the trail. "When I asked Mr. Pottinger if maybe the dog had been released into the woods on purpose, as a stunt for Winterfest, he got shaky and mumbled, 'No, it wasn't like that.' I got the sense that *something* had been planned—and gone wrong."

Jonathan finally released my arm and dragged his hand through his hair. He didn't speak for a moment, and I could hear the dogs running ahead of us. "Daphne," he finally said, as Plum Cottage came into view. The dogs were scrambling up on the porch. "I'm not on this case. If you have information, you need to tell Detective Doebler."

"I will," I assured him. "But I'm honestly not sure if Mr. Pottinger was behaving strangely because he's somehow involved in the murder, or if he's just eccentric, as you noted. Because he said something *really* strange when I was leaving. Something almost spooky."

Jonathan met my gaze again. Even in the darkness, I could tell that he was worried. He spoke more softly. "What, Daphne? What did he say?"

The temperature was below freezing, and I shuddered with cold and at the eerie memory. "Mr. Pottinger told me that, in the oldest versions of the legend, the Lake Wallapawakee Saint Bernard only showed up *right before someone died.*"

Jonathan was quiet for a long time. Above us, the trees creaked more loudly as the wind picked up. I tried to gauge his expression, to figure out what he was thinking. It was often difficult to read Jonathan's moods, and that task was almost impossible when I couldn't really see his eyes. I was just about to ask him what was going on in his head when he broke the silence, saying, "I think you do need to talk to Detective Doebler."

"I will," I promised. "I'll contact him tomorrow."

"Good." Then Jonathan looked at the cottage, where Axis, Artie, and Bernie were waiting patiently on the porch. "I can't believe I'm saying this," he added, muttering under his breath. "But I'm *taking all of those dogs* with me tonight."

Chapter 36

"What do you mean, you're taking Bernie?" I demanded, following Jonathan up onto my porch. Artie began twirling around, no doubt eager to visit with Socrates, while Axis and Bernie stood up and faced the door. The handsome Lab probably expected a treat, because I always gave him snacks when he visited, and Bernie seemed eager to get inside the cottage, too. "Bernie's doing just fine here," I said. "And I'm being paid to take care of him. He's my responsibility until his rightful owner is found."

Jonathan was bending over to pick up Artie, who'd started scratching at his knees. "Yes, I know," he reminded me, straightening. Artie wriggled happily in his arms, the dog's mood in sharp contrast to his person's. "You've been hired by Gabriel Graham. Which doesn't reassure me, either."

"What does *that* mean?"

He didn't answer.

"Taking care of Bernie is helping me to pay my rent on Flour Power," I told him. I reached down to stroke Bernie's broad, soft head, and I couldn't help smiling when the dog gazed up at me with his big brown eyes. "And I'm kind of fond of him now, to be honest. I want to keep him here."

Jonathan lowered his voice. I looked up to see that his expression had softened, too. "There are just too many questions surrounding the dog, Daphne. What if he really is linked to Lauren Savidge's murder somehow? And what if the killer decides that he or she would like to reclaim him?"

"Oh, I don't think that's likely at this point," I said, waving off his concerns. "Why would the killer want to claim Bernie now?"

"You, at least, seem to think he's a clue of some sort," Jonathan pointed out. "And killers tend to eliminate clues. Especially if they get wind that an *amateur detective* has been poking around, asking questions, instead of letting sleeping dogs lie. No pun intended."

I started to protest that I'd only speculated about Bernie's origins and possible involvement in Lauren's murder with Piper. Then I realized I'd also spoken with Max Pottinger, Gabriel, and Moxie.

"Okay, you have a point," I conceded, feeling a little chastened.

"Look, Daphne," Jonathan said. "I believe that Bernie will be safer with me. And you'll be safer, too, when he's out of your house. So let's just gather up anything he needs, and we'll be on our way."

I appreciated Jonathan's concern, but I still thought he was being paranoid. "Bernie is perfectly safe here," I assured him. "And so am I."

Jonathan arched his eyebrows. "Really? Because you don't ever lock your doors. And, not to denigrate your *Krav Maga* and kreplach-making class at an Israeli rec center—"

"Actually, it was a senior center," I corrected him. "And how did you know I thought we'd be making kreplach?"

Jonathan ignored my question. "I've spent the greater part of my adult life learning how to protect myself and those around me," he advised me. Then he cocked his head. "How long did you say you studied martial arts?"

My cheeks got warm. "Umm . . . two afternoons," I admitted. "But it was pretty intense. Some of the more frail seniors dropped out after the first day."

"I'm taking the dog," Jonathan informed me firmly. He set down Artie. "This is no longer up for debate."

Without giving me a chance to object again, he opened my door, which, needless to say, wasn't locked, and before we even stepped inside Plum Cottage, I cried out, "Tinkleston! No!"

Chapter 37

"First you break a lamp, then you attack *another* guest," I chided Tinkleston, who was glowering at me from beneath the small table, just inside my front door, that used to hold a lamp. The light was now on the floor, broken by Tinks when he'd launched himself, claws out, at Jonathan. "Unfortunately for you, Jonathan Black actually *knows* martial arts."

I heard snuffling coming from near the fireplace, which was giving off a cheerful glow and warming the room, and I turned to see that Socrates was trying to stifle his amusement. He was laughing at the recollection of Tinks getting caught in midair and plunked down onto his butt. Or maybe he was amused because Artie had just fallen over while trying to chase his own tail, in a surprisingly successful attempt to entertain the normally reserved basset hound.

"Thank you for getting along with everyone," I told Artie, whom Jonathan had left behind so Moxie and I could design his sled for the Cardboard Iditarod. We were running out of time, and so far, the taco theme was still Moxie's best idea. I turned back to

Tinks. "You could learn a lot about being friendly from Artie."

The diminutive, flat-faced Persian clearly disagreed, because he suddenly darted out from his hiding spot and plunged his teeth into my calf.

"Ow!" I cried, sinking to the floor as Tinkleston beat a hasty retreat to the loft.

And as I sat there near the broken lamp, rubbing my leg, I noticed a crumpled plastic sack, which Tinkleston had also knocked off the table.

Grabbing the bag, I smoothed it out and saw a telephone number printed on the plastic.

Reaching into my back pocket, I retrieved my cell phone and, checking the number one more time, dialed the seven digits.

Almost immediately, someone answered, which was surprising, given that it was pretty late for a business to be open, and I inquired hopefully, "Do you have any appointments available tomorrow?"

A few minutes later, when the call was ended, I stood up and moved to slip my phone back into my pocket. Then I changed my mind and tapped the screen again, calling up a search engine and typing in "clock with no hands tattoo."

As the results popped up, each link offering the same interpretation of the strange symbol, I figured out why Lauren might've written *USPT 2016* under Arlo's picture, and I sank to the floor again, whispering, "No way!"

Chapter 38

Arlo Finch's holistic therapy center, Peaceable Pets, was located in a heavily forested area just outside Sylvan Creek, accessible only by a twisting, unpaved lane that was so narrow I feared the trees might scrape against Piper's Acura, which I'd borrowed while my van was in the shop for the day, getting a new carburetor.

My sister would not appreciate a scratch on her pristine sedan, which had already suffered one mishap that day, when Tinkleston, who was sulking behind me, had reached his little paw through the air holes in his carrier and snagged the upholstery.

Luckily, Piper seldom used the backseat, where Artie was also riding— and drooling.

Of course, Socrates was behaving himself up front, next to me. He stared straight ahead, quietly studying the bumpy path, while I dared a quick glance in the rearview mirror to check on Tinks. And, sure enough, a black puffball with claws darted out of the carrier and felt blindly around for something to ruin.

"Keep your paws to yourself," I urged the irritable Persian. "Stop that!"

Then I quickly looked forward, just in time to steer the car through a particularly tight bend in the lane.

And when we rounded that curve, I gasped with surprise as Peaceable Pets came into view.

"This is so cute," I told Socrates, Artie, and Tinks, although the cat couldn't see anything from his carrier. "It's like a gingerbread house in the woods!"

Tinkleston yowled, like he understood that he was missing out on the view, while Artie strained in his harness, trying to see out the window. Socrates, meanwhile, rolled his eyes. He was a fan of spare architecture, and I knew that he thought Peaceable Pets was a little over the top.

"I disagree," I said, parking the car in a waiting spot, next to a blue van that was almost as old and derelict as my VW. The vehicle's back doors were wide open, and I saw boxes stacked inside, like Arlo had either just ordered a bunch of yak yarn—or was in the process of moving. Then my attention was drawn back to the building, which was about the size of a large shed, but trimmed with elaborate, Victorian-style woodwork and painted in a soft rainbow of pastel hues. A rooster weathervane spun cheerfully at the peak of the pitched roof, and colorful wind chimes made from glass and wood and old forks and spoons dangled from the eaves, creating merry, yet soothing, music. As I opened the door and got out of the car, something at my feet caught my eye, and looking down, I discovered that dozens of whimsical, if crudely made, statues of frogs and bunnies and gnomes were tucked around the property, their heads poking out of the snow. Arlo had posted some hand-painted signs, too, urging visitors to FOLLOW YOUR BLISS! and LIVE FREE, LOVE LIFE!

"It looks like Arlo tried every free arts-and-crafts class offered at the Sylvan Creek rec center and only knitting took," I admitted to Socrates, in a whisper, when I let him out of the car. "While I like the building, most of his handiwork *is* kind of bad."

Dropping to the ground on his big paws, Socrates woofed softly in agreement.

Opening the sedan's back door, I also released Artie, who bounded out of the car. When he darted past my feet, I paused to again read that second sign, about "living free," and I suddenly got a cold feeling of apprehension in the pit of my stomach.

Does that sign have special meaning to Arlo?

Does he know what it's like to be denied *freedom?*

Standing in the snow, I suddenly debated skipping the appointment I'd made the night before.

Unfortunately, it was too late to hop in the car and return to Winding Hill.

As Artie darted toward the colorful building, the pink door swung open, and Arlo stepped out to greet us.

"Welcome, Daphne and friends," he said, without smiling. Although he was carrying a bulky cardboard box, he freed one hand and gestured behind himself to the open door, adding, "Please, won't you come in out of the cold?"

Chapter 39

The few times I'd met Arlo Finch, I'd always found him to have a very soothing, peaceful vibe, befitting a man whose mission was to help stressed-out and reactive animals become calm and centered. But on the day of Tinkleston's appointment, Arlo was the one who seemed agitated.

"Are you sure you have time today?" I asked for at least the third time, as Arlo knelt to open the carrier that I'd set on the floor of Peaceable Pets. The room where Arlo held therapy sessions didn't seem too "peaceable," either, although I suspected that the space had been quite tranquil before Arlo had started *packing it up.* A deep pile throw rug, in soothing, natural shades of rust and moss green, covered the floor; a small stone fountain still gurgled in a corner; and the scent of citrus-and-sage incense hung in the air. But I felt a jarring sense of impermanence and haste as I stepped around a box that held a bunch of office supplies. I looked down at Arlo, who fiddled nervously with the latch on the crate's gate. "If you're busy, we could reschedule."

Arlo didn't answer, and I glanced first at Artie, who was running around the room, sniffing all the cartons, then at Socrates, who swung his big head toward the door, indicating that we should all leave. I doubted he cared that Arlo seemed tense. I was pretty sure Socrates objected to the idea of holistic cat therapy in general, and thought Tinkleston would benefit more from some old-fashioned punishment. The quiet-loving basset hound was also likely irritated by the relentless sound of wind chimes outside.

"Can you please help me with this?" Arlo requested, still jiggling the latch with fingers that shook just enough to be noticeable. Although Tinks kept swiping at Arlo's hand, I didn't think that Arlo was worried about getting clawed. From what I understood, he'd handled everything from dysfunctional Dobermans to former bomb squad dogs with PTSD. I couldn't imagine that he was unnerved by a little cat. Yet I swore I saw fear in his gray eyes when he looked up at me, requesting my assistance again. "If you don't mind, Daphne. . . . The latch *really* seems to be sticking!"

I knelt down beside Arlo—healer of troubled pets, knitter of free-range yak-hair dog sweaters, and hanger of cheerful wind chimes . . . perhaps too many wind chimes, in retrospect. Although I knew that I was taking a big risk, I rested one hand on his wrist, where he had a strange tattoo under his tie-dyed shirt, and tried to calm him, while getting some information, too.

"Arlo," I said very quietly, looking straight into his eyes. "Are you leaving town because you're afraid you'll be arrested for murder—*again*?"

Chapter 40

"Lauren Savidge knew you'd spent time in a penitentiary for murder, didn't she?" I asked Arlo, who was offering me a clay tumbler full of green juice that he called Soothing Serum. As I warily accepted the pungent beverage, he gestured for me to take a seat on the carpet remnant. I wasn't sure if I should get too comfortable in the presence of a killer, but he was already sitting down, and it would've seemed rude to keep standing there, so I sank down, too, being careful not to spill my drink. Then I awkwardly crossed my legs, while Arlo, whose lined face and graying ponytail told me that he was at least twice my age, easily twisted himself into a full lotus position. Although the day was very cold, he wore battered Birkenstock sandals and a pair of ratty old cargo shorts that revealed his knobby, but apparently flexible, knees. The moment Arlo was settled, Tinkleston, who'd been lurking behind some boxes, jumped into his lap and began to purr. That was kind of irritating, given that I'd spent months trying to befriend the sulky cat. However, Tinks's behavior was actually my secondary concern right then. "Lauren met you when she was working for Real Crime Network, didn't she?" I asked Arlo. "Maybe while profiling another inmate for her show *Life on Death Row*?"

Arlo nodded, looking miserable, and not just because he'd taken a sip of the stinky smoothie. "Yes, that's exactly what happened, about two years ago," he confirmed, setting down his drink and absently petting Tinkleston, whose eyes were getting glassy. Artie trotted over to Arlo, too, and offered his good ear for a scratch, which Arlo provided with his free hand. "Lauren and her crew—Joy and the cameraman, Kevin—were interviewing one of the guys in my cellblock, at the federal pen in Tucson—"

I didn't mean to interrupt, but I suddenly pictured Lauren's corkboard, and I snapped my fingers. "Tucson! Of course! That's the *t* in USPT! United States Penitentiary – Tucson!"

Arlo gave me a funny look. "What . . . ?"

Something told me not to mention Lauren's display, and I tucked some of my curls behind my ear, fibbing nervously. "Nothing. I was doing this crossword puzzle, and the clue was USPT. . . . It's really nothing."

That made absolutely no sense. But Arlo didn't seem to care. He was wrapped up in his own story, which he'd kept locked away for nearly two years, until Lauren, and now I, had uncovered it.

All at once, I got even edgier, although Arlo seemed oblivious. He continued to pet Tinks and Artie, who were both getting glazed-over eyes. Only Socrates, who'd edged closer to me, was also tense. I could tell by his alert expression and the way his ears were slightly less droopy than usual.

"How did *you* know I did time for murder?" Arlo asked, peering at me more closely. "Did Lauren tell you? Because I don't think she was certain. I kept telling her that she was mistaken, and we'd never met. I don't think she'd even tracked down my real name . . . yet."

That word *yet* hung out there ominously.

Had Arlo, or whatever his real name was, silenced Lauren before she could dig deeper?

I got an icy feeling in the pit of my stomach, and although I wanted to untwist my legs, I couldn't quite get them to work.

"Lauren didn't tell me anything," I said. "I just saw your tattoo at the plunge, and I got curious. So I did a little research. And I learned that the clock with no hands is usually worn by lifers, because time becomes immaterial when you're never getting out of prison."

I shouldn't have used prison slang in front of a former inmate. I was pretty sure I'd sounded stupid. And had I really needed to explain the tattoo to a man who had the mark permanently displayed on his body?

But Arlo didn't even crack a bemused smile. He remained deadly serious. "I knew I should've kept my arm covered, like I usually do," he muttered, more to himself than me. "If there's one thing I should've learned in prison, it's never to let your guard down. But I got so comfortable here, and most folks are so nice. . . ."

He sounded wistful, not angry, and I let him sink into a pensive silence that made the tinkling wind chimes seem even louder.

Then Arlo met my gaze again, and the pain in his eyes took away my fear.

"People make mistakes, you know," he said, his voice tight with emotion. "And they can reform." He stopped stroking Tinks long enough to point at his own chest. "*I* reformed. I learned that I was really good with the therapy dogs that came to prison. I liked them, and they liked me. I worked hard to prove that I deserved a second chance. . . ." He looked down at the tattoo that was peeking out from under his sleeve. "A chance I once believed I'd never have." Then he raised his face again, and I saw guilt and misery written in every deep line. "I've dedicated what's left of my life to making the world a more peaceful place," he told me. "I can't bring back the life I took, but you have to believe that I am a different— better—person than I used to be."

I pictured Arlo standing on the beach at Lake Wallapawakee, his expression tranquil as he looked out over the water, and recalled how he'd rushed to help Jonathan perform CPR on Lauren. Then I glanced at the normally intractable cat and hyper Chihuahua, both of whom remained half hypnotized by a man who also knit adorable sweaters to keep pets warm.

I met Arlo's gaze again. "I believe you," I assured him honestly. My legs finally seemed to work and I stood up, nearly knocking over my drink, which I still hadn't tried. Bending down, I picked up the tumbler. "And I won't tell anyone about your past. I promise. Not that I even really know what happened. I only looked up the meaning of the tattoo. I don't know anything more, and I don't need to."

"Thank you, Daphne," Arlo said. His eyes were actually watering, and his voice was a little choked. He gently pushed aside Artie, then cradled limp and dazed Tinks in one arm and stood up, too, with surprising grace and strength. "I'd like folks around here to remember me as a nice guy who tried hard to help their pets."

"Arlo," I ventured, uncertainly, "you didn't do anything. But it might look like you did if you take off in a big hurry."

"That's a risk I have to take," he told me, slipping Tinks into the carrier in one smooth motion, before the cat even had a chance to yowl in protest. When Arlo had latched the gate—this time with steady fingers—he bent to pick up his own drink and straightened, frowning. "You don't understand what it's like to have a record, like I do."

Actually, I did know what that was like. I had been advised never to return to Kenya after being wrongly accused of shoplifting at a fair trade shop in Nairobi. But I didn't mention that to Arlo. I didn't think he'd consider our pasts comparable.

"The police are already asking questions," he added. "I'm sure they'll figure out the truth soon and try to pin Lauren's murder on me, since I have a record *and* motive." He looked around the room, his thin shoulders caving, like he was suddenly aware of everything he was leaving behind. "But I'll be long gone by then," he told me sadly.

I wasn't sure how to respond, and I stood there in silence until Arlo raised his tumbler and smiled wanly. "To yet another new beginning!"

His cheer was forced, but I raised my cup, too, and clinked it against his. Then I reluctantly sipped the "serum," which was surprisingly delicious. I tasted kale, ginger, celery, and apple, along with some other stuff that I couldn't identify, but which added up to a pretty yummy drink.

In fact, I downed the whole thing in two more gulps, then picked up the carrier that held Tinks, who immediately began clawing at me. Holding him at arm's length, I led Socrates and a still groggy, wobbly Artie to the door.

We all went outside, and although I was pretty convinced that Arlo was reformed, I still felt a rush of relief when the cold, fresh air hit me.

"I'm sorry that I didn't really help Tinkleston," Arlo noted, following me to Piper's car. "I hope you can figure things out with him. Because he seems like a good cat, at heart. Just a little jealous of the other animals in your life, if my instincts are correct."

I loaded Tinks into the car, still being careful to avoid his claws, which were swiping at me. "You really think so?"

"Yes," Arlo said. "He didn't really want me to pet him at first. He mainly wanted your attention, and to make *you* jealous." Arlo cocked his head. "Do you have any new animals in the house?"

I nodded. "Yes, the Lake Wallapawakee Saint Bernard has been staying with us recently."

Arlo smiled with what looked like genuine amusement. "I'd say that's your . . . or his . . . problem."

"Well, thanks," I said, holding out my hand. I glanced quickly at his van, which was nearly filled with boxes, and debated trying again to convince him to stay in Sylvan Creek. I also wondered if I was obligated to tell Detective Doebler that one of the potential suspects in Lauren's murder was fleeing town, because I did plan to talk with Jonathan's partner that very day, as I'd promised. But I had a feeling that, even if I went directly to the police station, Arlo would be gone before Detective Doebler could do anything.

I was pretty sure that Arlo would hit the road the moment I drove away. He wouldn't have risked telling me that he was leaving if he wasn't ready to take off. So I simply said, "Good luck, Arlo. I wish I could've bought a few more sweaters at Winterfest. You have a real gift for knitting."

He shook my hand, still smiling. "Thanks, Daphne."

Then he turned to go back inside Peaceable Pets, while I opened the passenger side door to let Socrates lumber up onto the seat.

When I'd secured his harness and slammed the door, I was surprised to realize that Arlo was still outside, watching me from under the wind chimes.

"Do you want to know the real secret?" he asked.

I hesitated, suddenly uncertain again. "Umm . . . I guess so?"

"Kiwi," Arlo said solemnly.

It took me half the ride to Sylvan Creek to figure out he'd been talking about the smoothie.

And as I pulled up to the police station, where I hoped to find Detective Doebler, I also realized that Arlo Finch had never told me his real name.

Moreover, although he'd protested that he was a "changed man," he'd never *directly* denied murdering Lauren Savidge, either.

Chapter 41

"Well, Daphne, I'm pleased that you've finally taken the bull by the horns and have some men with boots on the ground, putting the finishing touches on your business," Mom said, twirling around the small space with her eyes on the ceiling, like she was touring the Sistine Chapel, as opposed to surveying a still-under-construction pet bakery. A workman who was getting ready to sand the hardwood floor gave her a funny look, which my mother didn't seem to notice. She stopped spinning, clasped the counter—because she'd obviously made herself dizzy—and did her best to focus on me. "You should be up and running in no time!"

"Wow, you just strung together quite a few clichés without hardly taking a breath," I noted. I wiped some sawdust off the counter with a damp rag. "And one of them pertains to military operations. Not construction."

I probably shouldn't have mentioned any of that. And I probably *should've* confessed that Elyse Hunter-Black had grabbed the bull's horns and put the boots on the ground, quickly making good on her promise to share some of her best contractors with me.

I had to admit, Elyse knew how to get things done. She'd even located an extremely old man named Salvatore, who'd fixed the Italian coffee machine and taught me how to use it.

"Don't be critical when I'm complimenting you," Mom scolded me. She absently picked up a bright green fish-shaped melamine platter, which would hold samples of cat treats, and turned it back and forth in her hands. "I am *trying* to encourage this endeavor—which, I will admit, I initially considered a fool's errand, but which I now believe has potential." She looked around again at Moxie's mod, hand-painted pink flowers; the space-age 1970s starburst light fixture that Elyse's electrician had suspended from the ceiling; and the olive-green cabinet that held my recently installed cash register. Then she set down the fish. "It's a quite lovely space, which makes me harken back to my teenage years!"

I gave my mother a skeptical look. I was pretty sure she'd been past her teenage years in the 1970s.

"What brings you by here?" I finally asked, deciding not to challenge her asserted age, which was surely off by a good decade or so. Although I could never be certain. Even Piper and I weren't allowed to know Maeve Templeton's true birthdate. I spoke more loudly over the sudden whine of the sander. "Did somebody tell you that the coffeemaker's working again?"

My mother's eyes lit up. "No! But that's wonderful news. I have sorely missed my evening cappuccino."

"Actually, I'd really appreciate it if you wouldn't mess around with the machine anymore," I requested, giving up on wiping the counter, because the sander was kicking up more dust. I gestured for Mom to follow me to the kitchen, where things would be quieter. When we were in that small, bright room, which smelled of yeast and cinnamon, I explained, "I'm not sure how long Salvatore will be around to repair the thing if you break it again. *He* was definitely way older than a teenager, back in the seventies."

Ignoring everything I'd just said, including my thinly veiled reference to her recent fib, Mom made a beeline to the shiny machine, which Salvatore had also cleaned. "Nonsense, Daphne," she said, waving a dismissive hand at me. "I know exactly what I'm doing. And I didn't break anything."

I knew there was no arguing with her, and I watched helplessly as my mother proceeded to wrench the silver basket that I now knew was a *portafilter* from its housing, cram it full of ground espresso beans, and smash the powder down with three hammer-like blows from a heavy object called a *tamper.*

"So much for Salvatore's suggestion that I treat my 'priceless' vintage Faema Urania 'like a delicate woman,'" I grumbled, leaning against one appliance that still didn't work: my despised, claustrophobic walk-in fridge. I crossed my arms over my apron. "I wouldn't blame that poor machine if it really did teleport you back in time some evening, when you sneak in here."

"I don't know why you're complaining, or what you're talking about, using words like *teleport*," Mom said, ramming the portafilter back into place and hitting random buttons. "We're not on *Star Trek*." The coffeemaker began to hiss, like it was upset. Mom ignored that warning, too. "And as for 'sneaking in here . . .'" She finally managed to get the machine brewing and turned to face me. "You are the one who needs to quit creeping around in the dead of night. Which is why I stopped by today." She placed her hands on her hips, which were straitjacketed in one of her many pencil skirts. A suitably espresso-powder-brown wool version that matched her Hermes equestrian-print scarf. Then Mom stared hard into my eyes and demanded, "What in the world were you thinking, outright *breaking into* poor, deceased Lauren Savidge's apartment—*again*? And breaking the lock on the door?"

"I . . . But I . . ."

I had no idea what she was talking about. I'd only sneaked into the apartment once, and I'd confessed the whole episode to Detective Doebler, who actually seemed to appreciate my insights. I got the sense that he was foundering without Jonathan on the case.

"Well, Daphne?" Mom said, jutting her chin. "What do you plan to do about the property you destroyed? The lock is ruined!"

I was still confused and struggling to respond when someone else entered the kitchen.

Gabriel Graham, whose keen ears had apparently overheard everything, because the sander had stopped at the most inopportune time.

"I hope you're not grounded, Daphne," he joked, grinning first at me, then at Mom, like he was oblivious to the tension in the room. "Because, if you've read any of the texts I've repeatedly tried to send you, in spite of getting no response, you'd know that we've been invited somewhere today."

Chapter 42

Big Cats of the World was located about two miles from downtown Sylvan Creek, but as Gabriel's red Jeep Wrangler bumped off the main road and passed through a dark, wooden gate that was at least ten feet high, the familiar hardwood forest in the heart of the Pocono Mountains suddenly took on a menacing aspect.

"Did you see that?" I asked Gabriel, who was mainly focused on navigating the rutted road through the woods. I shifted in the passenger seat to peer out the window, searching for another glimpse of tawny, striped fur. "Was that a *tiger*?" My breath fogged the glass, and I wiped away the condensation with my sleeve, then narrowed my eyes, searching the trees. "Seriously, I'm pretty sure I just saw an honest-to-gosh tiger wandering in the forest!"

"Umm, this is a preserve for big cats," Gabriel reminded me, sounding much less impressed than I was. "Didn't you see the warning sign near the gate? 'Do NOT touch or attempt to scale electrified fencing.

Predators roam free over five acres. Proceed at your own risk.'"

Of course, I'd had plenty of time to read that sign while we'd waited for Victor Breard to buzz us through the gate, but somehow—having been disappointed by most zoos and preserves, where animals always seemed to be sleeping in dens—I hadn't really expected to see anything more than a few squirrels scampering around the forest.

"I thought the sign was probably exaggerated, to make visitors think they were going on a big safari," I explained, locating another tiger, which stalked even closer to the Jeep, just beyond what I assumed was a deceptively skimpy-looking wire fence. The animal was majestic—almost magical. It strolled languidly through the woods on its massive paws, its muscular shoulders and haunches rolling with each step. When the great cat stopped and turned to stare at us, I saw snow in its whiskers—and an unnerving curiosity in its eyes. "Wow," I whispered, in awe. "I kind of forgot how beautiful big cats are. This makes me wish I wasn't banned from Kenya!"

"You're banned from Kenya?" Gabriel asked. I heard laughter in his voice. "What the . . . ?"

I reluctantly turned away from the tiger, which remained still, observing us as we drove on. "It's a long story that I don't want in the *Weekly Gazette*," I said. "Plus, if I ever tell it again, which I may not do, I think Jonathan Black gets first dibs on the tale."

Gabriel, who wore a blue down vest over a plaid shirt on that unseasonably warm day—meaning temperatures were slightly above freezing—knit his dark eyebrows. "What does *that* mean?"

I waved off the question with a hand covered by a wool mitten, knit in a zigzag pattern. "Jonathan's waiting on a whole anthology of travel anecdotes that we never have time to finish. We always get sidetracked talking about murder."

The Jeep bumped over a deep rut, and Gabriel steadied the wheel with gloved hands. But he dared another glance at me. "Are you discussing Lauren's murder with Black? Because I thought he was off this case." I already knew why Jonathan had withdrawn from the investigation, but Gabriel explained, "Conflict of interest, since his ex is a prime suspect." He snorted a laugh. "Although, I know some guys who'd frame their ex, given half the chance."

"Jonathan's not like that," I told Gabriel. Then I realized that I probably shouldn't risk saying anything about Jonathan, for fear of accidentally divulging something he'd consider private, and I shrugged. "I'm pretty sure that Detective Black is a very principled, trustworthy guy."

Gabriel turned to me, arching one eyebrow, but speaking in a level, even tone. "Are you sure that your Detective Black is 'principled' and 'trustworthy'? Are you positive about that?"

There was something unnerving about the question. Something lurking underneath the seemingly innocent query, like a tiger padding silently through a quiet forest, and I studied Gabriel's dark eyes.

Was he trying to make me doubt Jonathan's integrity for some reason?

Or did he know some secret about Jonathan that I wasn't privy to?

I couldn't tell, and a moment later, Gabriel faced

the road again as we crested a small rise. Ahead of us, a cabin-like wooden structure came into view, under a bright green-and-yellow sign that announced BIG CATS OF THE WORLD in a vaguely African font.

"Have *you* done much investigating?" I asked, suddenly remembering Gabriel's boast about solving the case before Jonathan. We were nearly at our destination, but I ventured, quickly, "Do you have any theories about Lauren's murder?"

"Yes, I do," he informed me.

"Really?" I scooched around on the leather seat to see him even better and caught a glimpse of his 35 millimeter digital camera with its distinctive plaid strap, which he'd tossed to the backseat when I'd gotten into the Jeep. I really wished he would've let me hold, and perhaps examine, that camera during our drive to the preserve. I would've liked to have scrolled through the archive of photos, to see what he'd shot the night of Lauren's death. But for now, I would have to pry information out of *him*. "What have you learned?"

Gabriel wasn't really listening to me. He was distracted, staring straight ahead and frowning. Then he muttered, more to himself than to me, "I thought this was supposed to be a *private* tour."

I'd been focused entirely on Gabriel, looking for clues to his still elusive character and trying to get his insights into the murder. But when he said that, I faced forward, too, and saw that Victor Breard had apparently invited other "media" to witness what happened behind the scenes at his enigmatic operation.

And while Gabriel might've been irked to have his scoop undermined, I was happy to discover that we'd be joined by cameraman Kevin Drucker and the new producer of *America's Most Pet Friendly Towns*, who was obviously stepping right in to fill Lauren Savidge's big Doc Martens, before Lauren's body was even in the ground.

Chapter 43

"I don't see how this tour is very 'exclusive' or informative," Gabriel complained, speaking over the loud hum of a golf cart, which he was driving along narrow paths that wound through the extensive Big Cats compound. Not all of the animals were allowed to roam as widely as the tigers, and we made our way slowly past smaller, but still spacious, enclosures. These were all filled with climbing equipment and toys to entertain the lions, jaguars, and leopards that Victor had rescued from circuses and unlicensed, abusive zoos, if his introductory lecture, delivered back at the cabin-like gift shop and snack bar, was to be believed. Gabriel gestured to the gaudy, tiger-striped cart ahead of us, where Victor, Joy, and Kevin Drucker were deep in conversation. "I can't believe he's driving the TV people around—talking their ears off—while we're stuck back here together."

"Hey!" Acting purely on reflex, I lightly slugged his shoulder, my mitten further softening the blow. "What do you mean, you're 'stuck with' me?" I asked incredulously. "You're the one who insisted that I come along!"

"Sorry." Gabriel rubbed his arm like I'd really clubbed him and nearly crashed into the cart ahead of us. Victor had stopped abruptly, mid-path, under a thick canopy of trees that obscured the sun. We bumped to a halt, too, and the camera that I still wanted to see slid on the pleather seat between us. I grabbed the Nikon, which was surprisingly hefty, before it fell to the floor of the cart. Then I reluctantly offered it to Gabriel, who was holding out his hand. Slinging the camera over his shoulder, he grinned sheepishly. "That came out wrong. The reporter in me is just frustrated to be missing out on a lot of information when Victor's ridiculous bullhorn fritzes out."

"Yes, his attempts to lecture us while moving aren't working very well," I agreed, glancing at the bullhorn, which Victor kept in a special holder on the side of his ostentatious, noisy vehicle, when he wasn't using the balky amplifier. "I guess, if I hadn't tagged along, this would be a lot more productive for you. There was room for one more in Victor's cart."

"No, Daphne." To my surprise, Gabriel reached over and clasped my wrist. "I am *very* happy that you joined me today. Please believe that. And I'm sorry if you were hurt by my offhand comment. I should edit my speech as carefully as I edit my articles. But don't think for a second that I'm not glad you agreed to come here with me, after my attempt to impress you with dinner went so wrong."

I didn't accept his apology right away, mainly because I was a little confused by his almost vehement, if brief, speech, and by the feel of his hand on my arm, not to mention the way he was looking at me right then. He'd grown serious, and there wasn't a hint of sarcasm in his tone or the usual mocking glimmer in his dark eyes. In fact, I almost thought he was regarding me with genuine appreciation. Maybe even something more . . .

"It's . . . it's okay," I stammered, feeling my cheeks get warm. I averted my gaze, gently pulled my wrist free, and picked at a loose loop of yarn on my knit scarf. "I'm sorry I punched you," I finally apologized, too. "That was completely out of line. Especially since I normally eschew violence, on principle."

"Daphne."

I stopped babbling and looked up to see that Gabriel was still very solemn. But there was warmth in his eyes, which were searching mine. He was always a good-looking guy, but I thought he became downright handsome when he lost the arrogance and cynical attitude. Even his goatee came across as less devilish.

"What?" I asked, getting sort of nervous.

Had he leaned closer?

Yes. Yes, he had.

But did I want him to do that?

Especially at an *animal shelter*, while we were *on a tour*?

My gaze flicked to the camera.

Did I want that anywhere, given that I wasn't sure I trusted him completely?

Not to mention other conflicting, confusing feelings I sometimes suffered . . .

I drew back, and my voice sounded squeaky when I repeated, "What? What's up?"

Gabriel didn't answer me. He just leaned a little closer, and I wasn't sure if I was disappointed or relieved when we were interrupted by a Frenchman, who bellowed into a bullhorn that was obviously working again, "Daphne, Gabriel . . . Please, join us to meet my very best friend, *le très magnifique* Genghis Khan!"

Chapter 44

The lion with the imposing name Genghis Khan must've weighed 450 pounds. His mane was like a thick brown thundercloud swirling around his massive head, and he blinked at us with eyes that reminded me of the strange yellow color the sky had turned, right before I'd nearly been caught in a tornado while crossing Oklahoma on the back of a motorcycle. Which was a really bad idea, because Oklahoma is not only windy, but pretty dusty in August.

A worse idea, in my opinion?

Standing inside an enclosure with a gigantic male lion and absently hand-feeding the great beast chunks of raw beef from a large bucket.

I loved animals—was even bonding a tiny bit with Sebastian over our shared love of cheese—but I had to keep stifling the urge to beg Victor Breard to get the heck out of that pen before *he* was nothing but a meaty memory.

I shot Gabriel a worried look. But, like Joy Doolittle and Kevin Drucker, he was focused on the spectacle unfolding on the other side of a fence that I knew surged with electrical current, but which still seemed too skimpy to contain the animal Victor affectionately called Khan. Ducking down to get a better angle, Gabriel raised his Nikon to his face and snapped a few pictures, his camera making faint clicking sounds as the images were recorded.

I continued to watch Gabriel for a moment, wondering if Detective Doebler had thought to take a look at Gabriel's photos from the night of Lauren's death.

Then I returned my attention to Khan, who was accepting another hunk of beef from Victor's fingers. And out of the corner of my eye, I caught sight of Kevin Drucker. He hadn't said three words since we'd all hopped out of our carts, but he also had his camera on his shoulder, filming Victor as the wiry man told us all about Khan's past.

"It is hard to believe that such a beautiful creature could be considered, how do you say . . . ?" Victor set down the bucket, which was empty, and scratched the cat's forehead with what had to be a sticky hand while he searched for the right word in English. "Expendable!" He glanced down at Khan, and the lion raised his face to look up at his "best friend." I had to admit, the two seemed pretty chummy. "Can you believe that, after many years spent dutifully jumping through fiery hoops—a terrible activity for any animal," Victor continued, with what I thought was genuine outrage over a practice that I agreed was cruel. "After years of loyal service with a circus—one of renown, which I shall not name—poor Khan is considered worthless! Or, should I say, worthy . . . of *destruction*! Until *I* pled to bring him here, where he is 'retired' in peace!"

It was obvious that Victor had given this spiel many times, and the way his chest puffed with self-congratulation was kind of obnoxious, but the tale was powerful, and he told it with passion.

Was there such a thing as a sincere huckster?

It seemed possible. Or maybe I was just falling under the spell of a gifted and charismatic storyteller. If so, I wasn't alone. Joy Doolittle was also captivated by Victor's speech.

She stood next to me, wearing a navy wool coat that I assumed was supposed to make her appear "professional," but which was a touch too big on her size zero frame. She reminded me of a little girl playing dress-up in her mother's clothes. And Joy's sympathetic sigh, on behalf of the lion who was lying down at Victor's feet, was soft and childlike, too. Shivering slightly, she turned to me, her fair cheeks rosy with the cold and sorrow in her pale blue eyes. "Poor Khan!"

I opened my mouth to agree that the lion's past plight was sad, but before I could say anything, I flashed back to the beach at Lake Wallapawakee, where I'd also stood next to Joy while Jonathan had tried to resuscitate Lauren Savidge.

Joy had been trembling and speaking softly then, too. Not talking to me, but to herself, muttering into her shaking hands.

Was she really a fragile waif?

Or did her appearance and mannerisms mask—

perhaps somehow aid—an ambitious, grasping agenda?

Because Joy was surviving in a very competitive industry.

Not only surviving, but moving up at Stylish Life Network, now that Lauren Savidge was out of the way.

And what had Joy said, over and over, that night at the beach . . . ?

"What did you say, Joy?" Victor Breard asked, so for a second I thought he'd been reading my mind. Then I snapped out of my reverie and realized that he was walking closer to the fence, his clean hand cupped behind his ear. The lion, behind him, was still reclining, but watchful. Victor, no doubt used to being vulnerable to Khan, seemed oblivious to what I thought was real danger. Especially given that Victor's other hand was freshly stained red with blood that was making my vegetarian self queasy, but which was no doubt a lip-smacking temptation to a carnivore. I exchanged glances with Gabriel, who was no longer taking pictures. He also seemed to think that Victor was crazy to turn his back on a predator that still had blood on its muzzle. But Gabriel shrugged, as if to say, "Not my problem!" Or, perhaps, "This will make great copy!" I noted that he kept his Nikon at the ready, no doubt in case he had the chance to get some action shots. But Khan continued to lie still while Victor stepped even closer to the fence. "You had a question, Joy?"

"No, no." She smiled and tucked some of her ash-blonde hair nervously behind her ear. "I was just sympathizing with poor Khan's plight."

"You have a kind heart," Victor said softly. I got the sense that, if there hadn't been about five thousand volts between them, he would've patted her hand. At least, I hoped there were at least five thousand volts. "Just remember that, thanks to the generosity of caring people like you, Khan has a safe home now."

Victor managed to make a subtle pitch for a donation and successfully flirt, if I was reading the signs correctly. And I thought I was.

I looked between the older man and the much younger woman, remembering the night I'd seen them together at Zephyr, the most romantic restaurant in Sylvan Creek. But they'd appeared to be at odds that evening.

What was really going on with Victor and Joy?

Then I stole a glance at the guy who'd taken *me* to Zephyr, and who was also observing the unlikely couple with unabashed curiosity. I could tell that Gabriel also believed there was a story behind Victor's odd smile and the increasing flush on Joy's cheeks.

And speaking of stories . . .

"You must get a lot of media attention when you rescue a lion like Khan, who starred in a circus," I noted, not certain where I was headed with that comment. I just hoped to steer the conversation toward the magazine article I'd seen on Lauren's corkboard. And, since I wasn't sure what to say next, I decided to take the direct route. "I remember seeing an article about you once. There was a picture of you, wearing a dark suit and very interesting gold tie. And you looked incredibly unhappy, like maybe a rescue hadn't worked out. . . ."

My voice faltered, because, in the course of about one second, I saw at least four emotions flash through Victor Breard's eyes. First, there was recognition. He knew what I was talking about. Followed by surprise. And a hint of concern. Then . . . *anger?*

At me?

Or at someone else, like Lauren, who might've brought something unsavory from Victor's past to light again, just like she'd tried to do with Arlo Finch?

"What was that article about?" I inquired, meeting Victor's gaze, which was locked on mine, although his expression was already neutral again. I doubted that anyone else had even noticed the rapid-fire barrage of emotions I'd just witnessed. Even Gabriel, who was perceptive and always on the alert for potential news, seemed unaware. He was looking past me, still observing Joy, like she was the story. And maybe she was. "Do you know what I'm talking about?" I asked Victor, more quietly. "It seemed like a pretty big article, in a glossy publication."

"Yes," Victor said, forcing a smile. The slightest twitch of his lips. He continued to meet my gaze, but I wasn't sure, at that point, what he was trying to convey. "Perhaps we can discuss the article at another time?" he suggested. "For it is *une histoire longue.*"

He'd just told me that the story was a long one. I could translate that phrase in about ten languages, because I used it quite a bit myself, as Jonathan Black could attest.

"I'd like to hear it sometime," I said softly. "I really would."

Victor nodded. "*D'accord.*" Then he broke the odd tension between us by stepping back, grinning his showman's grin, and asking Gabriel, "Do you have questions for me? I am, today, an 'open book'!"

Gabriel finally stopped staring at Joy and retrieved his notebook from the back pocket of his jeans.

"Yeah, I do have a few questions." He clicked open a pen that he'd tucked in the thin pad's spiral wire binding. "Let's start with funding," he suggested, peering closely and somewhat suspiciously at Victor, who remained separated from us by the fence. I believed we should move the interview to a safer place, but Victor didn't seem in any rush to leave Khan's enclosure. And the lion remained at ease, his long, sinewy body stretched out on the cold ground. "Did you say this place is funded entirely by donations?" Gabriel asked, poising his pen over the paper. "Or do you get government support? Maybe state or local tax dollars?"

Victor had fully recommitted to the role of pitchman, and he smiled more broadly. "Mayor Holtzapple is one of my biggest supporters," he informed us. "But only on a personal basis. I am afraid that this entire rescue operation is financed by individuals who donate directly or pay the modest fee to tour the property, and the occasional corporate sponsor."

"Interesting," Gabriel said, scribbling. He jerked his head toward the carts that waited on the paths behind us. "I wasn't sure I heard you right, when you explained your funding sources, while driving ahead of me and Daphne."

Gabriel was lodging another not-so-subtle complaint about the golf cart situation, but Victor didn't seem to notice. Although he did apologize, if only for a technical glitch.

"I am sorry," he said, with an exaggerated frown. "I tried to use my bullhorn, as I often do during tours like this. But she is no longer *fiable* . . . reliable . . . since the terrible night at the lake. I believe she got some water in the electrical parts, during *le chaos*."

He made a motion like snapping something in two. "There is a crack, and I must buy another, with my limited money." His frown dragged down to his shoes. "Which is better spent to feed poor Khan and friends."

I hadn't realized that the faulty, handheld loud-speaker he'd been trying to use all afternoon was the same one that had been at the lake the night of Lauren's murder.

And had he just begged us all to outright buy him a new one?

How much would that even cost?

Gabriel and I once again exchanged glances, silently asking each other if we should hand over some cash.

I had a huge soft spot for animals, and I was definitely feeling pressured to make a contribution. In fact, I was reaching into one of my coat's pockets for the wallet that I was actually carrying that day, when all at once, silent Kevin Drucker spoke up from behind the camera that was still on his shoulder, noting drily, "I think that lion's gonna eat for free, if you don't get out of that pen in about seven seconds, Mr. Breard."

Chapter 45

"I can't believe you almost saw someone get eaten by a lion on your second date!" Moxie marveled. At least, I was pretty sure that's what she'd said. Her lips were clamped around straight pins that were making me nearly as nervous as Khan, when he'd crept up behind Victor Breard on silent, stealthy paws. Well, not quite that nervous. But I was still glad when Moxie spit the pins into her palm so she could speak more clearly from her spot on the floor of Piper's spacious living room. We'd met there a few days after my visit to Big Cats of the World to work on Artie's and Bernie's cardboard sled, because Plum Cottage was too small to accommodate the old refrigerator box I was carving up. Moxie shook her head ruefully. "That would've been a disaster!"

"For Victor, or Daphne and Gabriel?" Piper asked sarcastically, without looking up from her laptop. She was, as usual, working on her bookkeeping that icy evening, although she'd moved from her traditional seat at the kitchen counter to an overstuffed chair near the fireplace. Socrates also sat by the fire, glumly watching me cut up the box with a utility knife, while Moxie hand-stitched Artie's costume. The Chihuahua seemed to grasp that the frilly bonnet and velvet dress were being crafted for him. He spun happy circles around Moxie, a string of drool hanging from his mouth. The spittle made me miss Bernie, who was probably leaving puddles all over Jonathan's home, vexing the cleaning lady. "And was this really a date, Daphne?" Piper inquired, reaching for one of the mugs of Belgian hot chocolate with homemade marshmallows I'd whipped up to thank her for allowing us to mess up her house. I'd also brought a batch of still-warm peanut butter oatmeal chocolate-chip cookies, half of which were already gone. "Have you figured out Gabriel's intentions yet?"

"Intentions?" I laughed, avoiding her questions. I knew that Piper, whose boyfriend seemed like an uncomplicated, genuinely nice guy, wouldn't like to hear the truth, which was that Gabriel would've kissed me goodbye if I hadn't insisted that I was freezing and ducked inside Plum Cottage. Kneeling, I began to cut what I hoped would look like a window into the box. "That's a really old-fashioned word," I added, shaking off the memory of Gabriel's and my awkward parting. "You sound like *you've* been watching *Stagecoach*!" I glanced quickly at my best friend. "Which is a brilliant theme for a sled featuring a horse-sized dog and a pint-sized pup like Artie. He'll be such a cute 'passenger' in his little western outfit!"

Moxie stopped sewing lace onto the bonnet long enough to give me a quizzical look. "*Stagecoach*?"

"Um . . . yeah," I said, also confused. "You said the

theme is *Stagecoach*, right? As in the classic movie from the 1930s?"

"Oh, that was a great film!" Moxie agreed, resuming her work on the bonnet. "But I said we're making *a* stagecoach—to reenact 'The Julia Bulette Story,' which, as you probably know, is an episode from the first season of the 1960s television show, *Bonanza*."

Piper and I exchanged puzzled looks, while Moxie held up Artie's dress. "Artie will be the gold digger, originally played by Jane Greer, who attempts to seduce Little Joe and steal the Cartwright's family fortune." She frowned at me and Piper. "I really thought it was all pretty clear from the context clues."

Piper rolled her eyes, and Socrates covered his muzzle with his paws and groaned.

"Oh, it's all very clear now," I said. Sometimes it was just easier to play along. "At least I understand why he's wearing a dress instead of, say, a cowboy hat and tiny chaps."

"I did think about dressing him as Little Joe," Moxie said, patting the tiny, excited dog on his shaky head. "But Julia Bulette is the one who arrives by stagecoach, and I was afraid people wouldn't get the reference, if we weren't as true to the story as possible."

"Nobody's going to—"

Piper started to argue with Moxie, but I cut her off, sitting back on my heels and changing the subject entirely. "You know, it really was scary, when we all realized that Khan—the lion—was sort of stalking Victor. Although he insisted that the cat just wanted a scratch behind the ears."

"He's being a fool," Piper declared flatly. "I don't

care how experienced he is with big cats. In fact, people who work too closely with them often get lulled into a false sense of security. The caretakers grow fond of the animals and think that feeling is reciprocal. Which may be true. But a lion isn't like a dog. It doesn't have centuries of domestication hardwired into its brain. At any moment, its natural instincts could override any genuine affection it has for a human."

"Maybe even domestic cats have a dual nature," I said, giving up on cutting out the window, which so far looked like a jagged-edged, three-dimensional Rorschach test. Heading to the kitchen, I retrieved a plate that held four dog-friendly, chocolate-free peanut-butter oatmeal Off the Leash treats I'd also made and set those on the floor. I trusted that Socrates would divide the snack equally. Then I picked up my mug of hot chocolate and one of the ooey, gooey, melty cookies, which had the added bonus of a full bag of chocolate chips, and curled up on Piper's deep, cozy sofa. Outside, sleet pelted the dark windows of the snug 1800s farmhouse. "Even though I've made progress with Tinks, he still takes a swipe at me now and then," I noted. Then I shrugged. "Although Arlo thinks he has a good heart."

Piper had resumed working, but she gave me a quick, sharp glance. "You took Tinkleston to see *Arlo Finch*?"

"Yes," I told her, not sure why she was so surprised. I'd made my positive opinions about holistic medicine pretty clear. "But he was packing to flee town and couldn't really do more than serve me a delicious, if stinky, smoothie." Piper appeared baffled by everything I'd just said, so I added, "The secret ingredient was kiwi."

My sister didn't seem to know what to say, while Moxie, of course, had latched on to the incriminating phrase I'd accidentally used.

"Arlo was 'fleeing town'?" she asked, clearly not interested in the smoothie recipe. I looked down to see her struggling to tie the sweet little bonnet under Artie's recessive chin, while the dog was still chewing his treat. "Why was he 'fleeing'?"

I normally shared all of my secrets with Moxie, but I had no intention of breaking my promise to keep quiet about Arlo's past, and I changed my tune slightly. "He was just moving out quickly," I fibbed reluctantly. Socrates shot me an accusing look, which made me feel even worse. Cringing, I tried to cross my fingers while holding a mug. "I guess 'fleeing' was the wrong word."

Piper could tell I was prevaricating. She continued to observe me with a shrewd, skeptical eye. "Were you trying to help Tinkleston, or investigate Lauren Savidge's murder?"

"Maybe a little bit of both," I admitted, uncrossing my fingers. I spoke pointedly to Moxie. "And I honestly don't think Arlo was involved. So please don't spread any rumors around town."

"I won't say a word," Moxie promised. She held the dress up to Artie's chest, so the outfit's lacy frill was right under the dog's chin. He really was going to be adorable, although I could already imagine Jonathan's negative critique. "My lips are sealed!"

"Thanks, Moxie." I dipped my cookie into the hot chocolate and took a bite, savoring the perfect combination of fluffy marshmallow, sweet peanut butter, and warm chocolate layered upon warm chocolate. Licking my fingers, I added, "I do have to say, there is a lot of weird stuff going on, and I have a feeling that, if I could piece it all together, I'd solve the crime."

"Daphne . . ." Piper's tone was disapproving, but Moxie was intrigued.

"What kind of weird stuff?" she asked, setting aside the dress, which was apparently finished. I wished I could've said the same for my project. The Iditarod was coming up soon, and I wasn't sure how I'd create wagon wheels out of cardboard. And the stagecoach was basically still a box, complete with the words "Amana 36 Inch Cubic Side-by-Side." Not exactly authentic to the Old West. "Daph!" Moxie said, interrupting my thoughts. "What, exactly, is happening?"

"We don't need to know," Piper said. "It's Detective Doebler's problem."

Socrates agreed. He was whining softly and shaking his head, urging me to drop the subject. Which I did not intend to do.

"I'm not sure Detective Doebler is on top of things," I informed everyone. "I spoke with him the other day, and he seemed completely overwhelmed by the investigation." I set down my mug and cookie so I could start ticking things off on my sticky fingers. "Meanwhile, Bernie's barrel is still missing. Victor Breard is acting strangely around Joy Doolittle. Who is, in turn, acting strangely around Victor. Mom says somebody *else* sneaked into Lauren's apartment. Max Pottinger is hiding a secret. And there's something mysterious in Victor's past, too. Not to mention that his bullhorn is broken. And then there's the whole thing about Joy muttering at the plunge." I raised my eyes to the ceiling, trying to again jog my memory. "If only I could remember what she'd said . . ."

"I don't get any of that, especially the part about Victor's poor, injured bull," Moxie interrupted. "I thought he mainly dealt with lions." She began to pack her sewing supplies into an old hatbox printed with images of the Eiffel Tower. "Although, if there's something going on with Victor and Joy Doolittle, that might be interesting."

By "interesting," she meant "worthy of sharing at Spa and Paw."

"Sorry," I told her. "I have no details."

"And you should *stay out of Lauren's murder*," Piper cautioned me, more firmly than before. "Especially when you have lots of treats to make for the Cardboard Iditarod—and a bakery for pets to open in just three days!"

I'd been slouching, on chocolate overload—maybe chocolate, like wind chimes, could be overdone—but I sat up straighter. "What? I've never set a date. . . ."

"I know," Piper agreed, offering me her laptop. "You wouldn't, so I did. It's time to stop stalling, Daphne. You're ready, and you can do this."

I glanced at Socrates, who was avoiding my gaze, like he was in on some secret with Piper. Then I accepted the thin computer from my sister and scanned the screen.

"This . . . this is an advertisement . . . which says I'll have a grand opening for Flour Power . . . in *three days*!" I cried, although Piper had already said all that. I read more closely, my jaw dropping. "And I'm *giving out free samples* at the Iditarod?" I tore my gaze away from the screen to see that Piper was smiling smugly. "I never agreed to that!"

"Wow, congratulations, Daph," Moxie chirped, somehow overlooking the fact that all the blood had drained from my face. Lacking a glass, she raised her scissors. "Mazel tov!"

"Thanks?" I said weakly and uncertainly, staring again at the ad, which was actually quite nice. Piper had used Moxie's hand-painted flowers as the background. Then I frowned at my sister. "You didn't already place this . . . ?"

"You owe me for a full-page ad in the *Gazette*. And I paid extra to have it posted today on Gabriel's new online edition," Piper informed me, gesturing for me to return the laptop. "Although, now that you and the editor in chief are quite obviously an 'item,' I suppose you'll get a discount."

Handing over the computer, I sank down on the couch again, my stomach really hurting. I nevertheless reached for another cookie, stress-eating out of habit.

How was I going to finish a fake stagecoach, bake enough treats to hand out at Winterfest, open a new business—and solve a murder? Because I really felt like I was on to something. . . .

I was so lost in thought that I didn't even notice a light touch on my shoulder, until Moxie said, "Oh, that's so sweet, Daphne! Sebastian wants to share your cookie. I *knew* you two would be friends!"

Chapter 46

I wasn't the best at prioritizing, but shortly after Piper informed me about the looming grand opening—and the fact that I'd be giving away free pet treats on the last day of Tail Waggin' Winterfest—I put away my utility knife and hopped into my van, leaving Socrates and Artie with Piper, because I expected to work long into the night at Flour Power.

"Thanks a lot, Piper," I complained under my breath, as my old VW, with its new carburetor, rolled into Sylvan Creek on streets that were still icy, although the storm was over. I was aggravated with my bossy sister, but part of me knew that she was, as usual, right. The work crew that Elyse had assembled on my behalf had finished all of the big projects at the bakery, and while the walk-in continued to malfunction, I was used to working around that by bringing fresh eggs and other refrigerated goods from home on the days I baked. Still, I could've used a few more days to prepare Flour Power, given that I also had Artie and Bernie's sled to work on, and some upcoming pet-sitting jobs, too.

"You could've given me until Monday," I told my sister, who was far out of earshot, no doubt drinking hot chocolate in her warm, snug farmhouse. All at once, I shuddered with more than the cold and, taking one hand off the steering wheel, I absently brushed at my shoulder, because I swore I felt little paws tapping there. It was going to take me a while to get over the fact that Sebastian had crept right up next to my face, without me even knowing it, while I'd eaten my cookie on Piper's couch. That stealthy move had set our budding friendship back a few steps. Then I used my coat sleeve to wipe at the condensation that always formed on my windshield when the weather dipped below freezing, because the van's heater was as unreliable as my oversized, frozen crypt of a fridge. My hand scraped ineffectually at the ice that had formed inside the VW, and I shook my head. "Nobody wants to be out tonight!"

I was convinced that I was correct about the evening being fit for neither man nor beast when suddenly I saw both man *and* beast walking down Market Street.

The night was dark, the moon obscured by clouds, and the streetlights cast only a dim glow on the sidewalk, but I was certain that I recognized the trio of human and dogs. The man's tall frame and bearing were distinctive, and one of canines was so big and bulky that I didn't exactly need a spotlight trained on him to know who he was.

Rolling up beside them on the otherwise empty street, I hand-cranked my window as far down as it would go, which wasn't that far. Then I lifted my chin and asked, "What in the world are you three *doing*?"

Chapter 47

"Are you supposed to cook for humans in a facility that's licensed—at least, I hope it's licensed—to serve animals?" Jonathan Black inquired skeptically, as I whipped milk into eggs to make a cheese omelet, using some ingredients I'd picked up at the store on my way into town. Coffee brewed in the machine that Mom, thankfully, hadn't managed to break, although she'd done her level best. "Isn't this some kind of code violation?"

"For your information, I actually know the rules," I said, stepping over Jonathan's chocolate Lab and Bernie, who gazed up at me with affection in his brown eyes. I smiled to let him know that I'd missed him, too, although I would've been okay with a less enthusiastic reunion on his part. My butt was still wet from hitting the pavement. I rubbed it absently before pouring the egg mixture into a pan that already held sizzling butter. "There's nothing to prohibit me from giving away food and drink to humans, for free."

At least, I thought I'd read that part of the huge code book correctly, before admittedly closing the cover and deciding I'd mainly hope for the best.

Not surprisingly, Jonathan continued to look doubtful. But I noted that he was nevertheless taking off his coat and hanging it on a peg near the back door. His long wool overcoat looked like something he'd wear on duty, but his jeans and gray V-neck sweater over a white tee signaled otherwise.

I thought the sartorial mixed message was interesting, and perhaps telling.

"Why are you in town, walking around in such terrible weather?" I asked, layering some mellow Swiss and sharp Wisconsin cheddar cheese onto the omelet, which would be big enough to share. It seemed like a good night for a late, hearty breakfast. I was also toasting up two thick slices of whole grain bread that I was keeping on hand for myself. I anticipated that I'd need to eat during my workdays. "Why aren't you at home in your gorgeous A-frame chalet, which was built specifically for hunkering down on winter evenings just like this one?"

I wouldn't have left Jonathan's house that night. I would've built a fire in the massive stone fireplace, snuggled up under one of the many thick, soft throws that Elyse had artfully placed around the overstuffed, welcoming furniture, and stared out the huge windows overlooking the forest.

But Jonathan obviously hadn't been tempted by that scenario.

"Bernie needs exercise, and I was restless," he said, helping himself to the coffee, which I knew would suit his taste. I'd need about five glugs of cream to make the inky brew palatable, but Jonathan took a sip straight from one of Flour Power's new signature mugs, which featured the bakery's name and logo, a pastel peace sign with a paw in the middle. Pouring me a mug, too—and adding milk—he set both drinks on the butcher block counter, drew up a seat, and smiled. "I'm going a little stir-crazy, to tell you the truth, Daphne."

"You can't stand to be off the case, can you?" I asked, sliding the bright yellow omelet onto a pretty Italian pottery plate that the building's previous tenant had left behind. Taking the toast out of the oven, I slathered both slices with creamy butter and placed them next to the eggs. Then I set four Off the Leash treats, which I'd brought to stock my glass counter, onto two smaller plates with the same design as the mug, and set those on the floor for Axis and Bernie. Rooting through some drawers, I next found two forks and sat next to Jonathan, offering him one. When he accepted the utensil, I started to dig into the omelet, then hesitated. "I've only got one 'human' plate. Are you okay with sharing?"

Jonathan laughed. "Daphne, you've helped yourself to food on my plate several times. It's a little late to ask if I mind sharing."

I met his deep blue eyes, which glimmered with amusement. I also noted that his jaw was dark with stubble, indicating that he hadn't shaved that day, and he hadn't cut his hair recently, either. It remained a bit on the long side, by his standards. Even the way he sat seemed more relaxed. While he still had a reserved, military bearing, Jonathan wasn't quite as rigid as he used to be.

And I was changing, too, in the opposite way. Taking on more responsibility, signing a lease that would keep me in town, considering actually using a calendar . . .

"You're staring at me and letting cheese get cold," Jonathan observed. "Is everything all right?"

"Yes, yes," I assured him, although I didn't stop studying his face.

The first time I'd seen Jonathan walking through town, I'd been struck by his good looks. And I'd come to admire his intelligence, his sometimes biting wit, and his strength of character, too.

Or was the still sometimes enigmatic man who sat across from me everything I believed him to be? Because, all at once, I recalled Gabriel's cryptic question about Jonathan.

"Are you sure that your Detective Black is 'principled' and 'trustworthy' . . . ?"

"Something is definitely wrong." Jonathan frowned. "Why are you not eating? You're not having any trouble related to the murder, are you? Is someone following you again?"

He was referring to how I'd been stalked the last time I'd solved a homicide.

"Nothing's wrong," I assured him. But I broke our gaze and finally dug into the omelet, not wanting him to somehow see that I'd suffered a momentary shadow of doubt regarding his integrity. A shadow that vanished as quickly as it had materialized. Because, while he liked to maintain his privacy, Jonathan *was* honest and honorable.

Right?

"I'm pretty good at reading people," Jonathan noted matter-of-factly, while I shoveled eggs and cheese into my mouth with a little too much enthusiasm. "If there's something that you want to talk about . . ."

I set down my fork and looked up again to see him watching me closely. I could tell that he genuinely wanted to listen. And for a split second, I considered blurting out that I thought he was phenomenally handsome, frequently irritating, still too guarded, and just plain confusing to me at times.

But something stopped me from speaking my mind, like I usually did. A fear that I'd mess up a relationship that was important to me, in a strange way. Instead, I told him, with a shrug, "I'm just worried about opening my bakery on time, and getting Artie's sled ready for the Cardboard Iditarod." I brightened at the thought of the theme. "He's going to be riding in a stagecoach, dressed as an actress from the old show *Bonanza*."

Jonathan's eyebrows arched with bemused confusion. "An *actress*, as opposed to an actor." He grinned. "I suppose he won't look any more ridiculous than he did on Halloween, when you dressed him in a clown costume."

I thought Artie had looked adorable when Piper and I had dressed him for Sylvan Creek's Howl-O-Ween Pet Parade.

Then I thought about the refrigerator box waiting at Piper's house, and my shoulders slumped. "Well, don't expect too much. I'm really having trouble making the stagecoach."

Jonathan finally cut into the omelet. Not that much was left. I'd managed to cram in quite a few bites. He looked at me over a forkful of eggs. "To be honest, I thought maybe the whole project had gone by the wayside, after seeing the ad for your grand opening on the *Weekly Gazette* site."

"You check that site?" I asked, surprised. I took a sip of coffee. "Why?"

"I'm part of this community now," Jonathan reminded me. "I, of all people, need to know what's going on here." He hesitated, and I wasn't sure if he was teasing or serious when he noted, "Such as why you were on an 'exclusive tour' of a facility run by a murder suspect, in the company of other murder suspects."

I dropped my fork. "Gabriel already wrote—and ran—an article?"

"Yes." A glint of amusement returned to his eyes. "There was a picture of you recoiling from a kitten."

I knew what Jonathan was talking about. Victor had unexpectedly shoved a six-month-old lynx in my face, and, on instinct, I'd withdrawn. Especially since I'd nearly seen Victor get eaten a few minutes before.

I hadn't known that Gabriel had snapped a picture, and I could imagine how I looked.

"Victor caught me off guard with a wild animal," I protested. "I think he's a little too reckless with the cats under his care." Jonathan continued to smirk, while I suddenly focused on something more important than another terrible photo of me. "And what did you mean by 'suspects'? Which of the people on the tour are officially 'suspects'?" All at once, I got worried and pointed to myself. "Am I under investigation? Because Detective Doebler didn't indicate that when I *did* go talk to him, as I promised you." I picked up a piece of the toast and took a big bite. Placing a hand in front of my mouth, so I wouldn't spray Jonathan with crumbs, I added, "He seems a little overwhelmed."

Jonathan shook his head. "Well, there's nothing I can do."

He sounded like he wished that wasn't true.

"You know, somebody broke into Lauren's apartment—"

"Aside from you?"

My cheeks got very hot. "I had a key! And how did you know about that . . . ?"

"I ran into your mother. She asked me if there was a reform school for adults. Needless to say, the story came out."

I hung my head. "Oh." Then I set down the toast and brushed crumbs off my hands. "Anyhow, someone *else* went there, after me. My mother says the lock was broken."

Jonathan looked like he wanted to jump off his seat and go see that lock himself. His fingers flexed restlessly around his fork. But his tone was neutral. "Your mother reported that incident, right?"

"Yes, I'm pretty sure she did," I said, trying to recall what Mom had said about the break-in. She'd grown more circumspect after Gabriel had entered the room, but she'd told us both a few details. "Although, Mom didn't think anything had been taken. Things were just a little disturbed."

Jonathan frowned. "Interesting."

I fiddled with my coffee mug. "Jonathan?"

He was distracted. "Hmm?"

"Is it okay for us to talk about the case? I don't want to put you in a position where you break any rules. . . ."

"There are no hard and fast rules." He set down his fork, pushed away the plate, and stretched out his long legs. "I don't think I'm prohibited from discussing the murder privately with someone who's not on the force."

I felt better about repeatedly bringing up Lauren's death, and I risked doing that one more time.

"Well, from what Gabriel told me, the prevailing theory is that Lauren was hit with a rock that somebody picked up on the spur of the moment."

Jonathan nodded. "Yes, that's what I understand."

"But, like I told you on the night of her death, the beach isn't rocky there," I reminded him. "I really think it's unlikely that someone who decided to kill Lauren in a fit of rage or passion could've reached down into the dark water and found a suitable weapon." I wrapped my hands around my mug and shrugged. "It just doesn't add up."

"So you think somebody carried a concealed weapon into the water?" he asked, immediately finding a hole in my theory. "Because most people were in bathing suits. It would've been difficult to hide anything." The corners of his mouth turned up with a barely suppressed smile. "Especially not in the bikini you inexplicably wore to a polar bear plunge."

I felt my ears get warm again. Then I tried to picture the scene at the lake before everything had gone crazy. And I quickly realized that the other plungers had actually worn quite a variety of outfits.

Elyse had wisely donned a wet suit, which had hugged her tiny frame. Even if I'd suspected her of killing Lauren, I couldn't imagine where she'd hide anything in her neoprene body glove. Joy Doolittle, meanwhile, had worn running shorts and a T-shirt. She was small, too, and the outfit had been baggy on her. Maybe loose enough to hide a weapon. And Arlo Finch . . .

I sucked in a sharp breath, and although I'd honestly believed Arlo was innocent when I'd spoken with him at Peaceable Pets, I blurted, "Arlo wore cargo shorts! With big pockets!"

But Jonathan shook his head. "I don't think Arlo Finch is currently guilty of anything but crimes against canine fashion."

I wouldn't break my promise to keep Arlo's past a secret, but I *had* to drop a hint. "You know, just because Arlo loved wind chimes, incense, and tie dye doesn't mean you should just assume that he couldn't act on impulse. He was . . . is . . . human. Wherever he is."

"Sedona, Arizona," Jonathan said flatly. He crossed his arms over his chest. "I expect that he'll be happy there among the UFO watchers, psychic channelers, and spiritual questers. Although, I imagine that there's a lot more competition for business in Sedona, if you're a holistic pet therapist."

I knit my brows. "How do you know where Arlo went? And why don't you think he killed Lauren, given that he left Sylvan Creek pretty hastily?"

"I've been keeping an eye on *Samuel Beechey* ever since I saw the note about him on Lauren Savidge's vitriolic corkboard, which I assume you also saw at her apartment," he said. "I had a chance to examine it before I took myself off the case. And I quickly followed up on the mug shot—and the note linking Beechey to a federal penitentiary."

Of course, Jonathan had deciphered the initials under Arlo's photo. But I didn't understand how he'd figured out that the terrible picture of Arlo had been taken by the police.

"How did you know the photo was a mug shot?" I

asked, speaking over Bernie's snores. Both dogs were sound asleep by the warm oven. I knew that I was delaying my own slumber by discussing the homicide instead of baking or cleaning, but I couldn't resist picking Jonathan's brain. "Arlo wasn't holding a placard with numbers. I just thought it was an unflattering portrait, taken on a bad hair day."

"Not all mug shots look like the ones you see on TV," Jonathan explained. "But the bland background, the blank stare, and the plain orange shirt, reminiscent of scrubs . . ." He shrugged. "I've seen enough photos like that to know that Arlo had been arrested, at some point. And the tattoo on his wrist, which I saw at the plunge, not to mention the ridiculously made-up name—"

"You saw the clock with no hands, too?" I interrupted. I didn't know why I was so surprised. Jonathan observed everything. I slouched as I thought about how I'd had to research the clock's meaning. "And, of course, you knew what it symbolized."

Jonathan nodded. "Of course."

I could've saved a lot of time and effort by asking Jonathan about Arlo instead of poking around at Peaceable Pets. I sighed, figuring I might as well get the whole story. "And Arlo's name, which never struck me as unusual . . . ?"

Jonathan grinned. "Really, Daphne? A holistic healer whose first name just happens to pay tribute to one of the nation's greatest folk singers—an icon best known for using music to fight for social justice? And whose last name is taken from *To Kill a Mockingbird*? It's clearly a name created by someone hoping to reinvent himself as a paragon of virtue. Which made me very curious about what Mr. Finch's *past* held. Especially since Elyse had once mentioned Lauren's work on *Life on Death Row*."

I cocked my head. "So, if you know all that about Arlo, why would you ever rule him out as a suspect?"

"I'm not 'ruling' anyone in or out," Jonathan reminded me, setting his empty mug next to the plate. "That's up to Detective Doebler. But I do have a lot of experience with inmates, and ex-inmates, and I don't think Finch would risk going back in prison. Not when he beat the odds to get out." Jonathan grew somber as he recalled the night of the murder. "I also worked with him, trying to resuscitate Lauren. I saw the look in his eyes when I told him to stop CPR." He shrugged, but he wasn't making light of the memory. He was trying to shake it off. "I suppose my belief that he's innocent is based solely on my gut instincts, but I trust them. It's up to my partner to figure out if I'm right or wrong."

"I also believe Arlo's innocent," I said, rising and carrying the empty plate and forks to a big silver sink. "I just wish I'd gotten his recipe for stinky smoothies before he left town."

"*Stinky* smoothies?"

I turned to see that Jonathan was giving me a funny look.

"Yes," I said. "The secret is kiwi."

Jonathan stood up, too. "Don't take this the wrong way, but you might be spending a little too much time with Moxie."

"Yeah, that's probably true," I agreed, bending down to scratch Bernie, who'd left a sticky puddle of slobber on my floor. That might violate some health codes, even in a pet bakery. I looked up as Jonathan took his overcoat down from the hook. "And speaking of friends . . . How are you and Bernie getting along? Do you want me to take him back?"

"No." Jonathan shrugged into his overcoat. "He's fine with me, for now. Although my housekeeper is threatening to quit." He glanced at the Saint Bernard, who was rousing, jostling Axis with his big paw, so the Lab woke up, too. "Hopefully, this thing gets solved soon."

I followed Jonathan and the dogs to the door. I knew that Bernie was in good hands, but seeing the Saint Bernard's confused look, as he tried to figure out if he was going with Jonathan or staying with me, tugged at my heartstrings. "Yes, and I hope Bernie gets back to his home, if he even has one."

Jonathan stopped at the entrance to Flour Power, which now featured the same logo as my mugs and advertised my hours of operation. And when he turned to face me, I saw that he appeared uncharacteristically uncertain.

"Is something wrong?" I asked, with a worried glance at Bernie. "Did you learn something about Bernie's owner?"

"It's not about the dog," he said. "I just want you to be careful around Gabriel Graham. At least until Lauren's murder is solved. Because he *was* there, and had a past with Lauren. Not to mention a history in Philadelphia—"

"Are you on this case or not?" I teased, because, along with checking into Arlo's past, he'd obviously done some digging into Gabriel's history, too. "Shouldn't you be kicking back with a good book? Or investigating some old cold case?"

Jonathan didn't respond right away. In fact, he looked away for a moment and rubbed the back of his neck, a gesture that told me he was uncomfortable. Then he admitted, "My research into Graham's life was more personal than professional. The night of your open house at Plum Cottage, back in October, he mentioned being an award-winning crime reporter for the *Inquirer*."

I could recall the conversation Jonathan was describing. I'd seen the two men talking at a small gathering I'd held to celebrate my new home.

"Back then, I was curious about why somebody with Graham's—let's be honest—substantial ego left that job to run a weekly paper with such a small circulation," Jonathan continued. "And when Lauren was killed, that curiosity turned to suspicion—and finally concern, when you started spending time with him. Enough that I did a little research."

I wasn't sure I'd heard him right. "You . . . you were mainly *worried about me*?"

He smiled in a way that told me he couldn't believe what he'd just said, either. "Yes, Daphne. Worrying about you seems to be becoming a hobby of mine."

In the past, when Jonathan had tried to protect me, I'd always promised him that I could look out for myself. But that night, I simply said, "Thank you, Jonathan." Then, to reassure him, I added, "I've done a little research into Gabriel's past, too. I know about his work for the *Inquirer*—and what happened to his former girlfriend."

I could tell that Jonathan was relieved not to have to say more and risk impugning Gabriel's character, when the facts surrounding Gabriel were murky. He nodded. "Good."

"Thanks again for looking out for me," I repeated, reaching down to stroke Axis's smooth fur and rumple Bernie's big head. Both dogs were waiting patiently at our feet. "It was nice of you."

I was tempted to stand on tiptoes and kiss him on the cheek, but I resisted the urge. He seemed to be holding something back, too. But he finally said, "Good night, Daphne." Then he opened the door. I noted that he didn't clip a leash onto Bernie's collar, and the big dog followed him outside, looking back once at me. I felt a surge of guilt, as if I'd abandoned Bernie. Jonathan glanced over his shoulder, too. "I suppose I'll see you at the Iditarod, if not before."

I smiled, although I got a knot in my stomach just thinking about that messed-up cardboard box. "Yes. You won't be able to miss us!"

I saw Jonathan grin as he turned away, and I watched him and the dogs walk down the dark, wet, shimmering street until they were out of sight.

Then I closed the door, turned around, and exhaled with a whoosh to see all of the work I still had to do, from cleaning pretty much every surface to baking and stocking the shelves.

As I worked, I thought about Detective Doebler's assertion that the killer had probably picked up a rock, on impulse—in a swimming area where rocks were few and far between. And about how few of the plungers could have carried concealed weapons.

So what, exactly, had been used to commit the murder?

The question kept my mind occupied while I labored until nearly dawn, at which point, exhausted, I put away my cleaning supplies and grabbed my coat from a peg in the kitchen.

But, although I was tired, I didn't head right home.

I had one quick, secret stop to make before the sun rose.

Chapter 48

My mother was normally on top of maintenance at her various properties, so I crossed my fingers as I mounted the exterior steps to Lauren Savidge's former apartment, hoping that Mom hadn't yet hired someone to repair the lock that she'd accused me of breaking.

And, luckily, at least for me, when I reached the efficiency's small, covered porch, I discovered that the doorknob was hanging loose and silver duct tape covered the faceplate.

Forgetting that I should probably avoid leaving fingerprints, I grasped the wobbly knob and pulled. The door swung right open, and I stepped into the kitchen, which wasn't much warmer than the outdoors.

My thrifty mother was probably keeping the thermostat on a setting that would just barely keep the pipes from freezing. I flipped the switch near the door, and the kitchen's overhead light came on.

"Wow . . ."

The place seemed more disturbed than my mother had led me to believe.

In fact, the entire corkboard was gone.

Then I realized that Detective Doebler had probably taken the pictures and sticky notes, maybe even before my mother had reported the break-in.

Regardless, I was disappointed. I'd hoped to examine that board one more time, just to make sure I hadn't missed or forgotten anything.

"Oh, well," I sighed, spinning on my heel to survey the rest of the spare space, which still held some things that I assumed were Lauren's, like an olive drab cap that sat on the kitchen counter, next to a microwave that was probably furnished by my mother.

Scanning the counter, I continued trying to separate Lauren's possessions from those supplied by Maeve Templeton.

The four-piece canister set with the clamp top lids? That screamed Mom.

But the half-empty bottles of wine and the case of bottled water had obviously been purchased by Lauren.

I checked the label on the water, noting that it was generic and packaged in plastic bottles. Then I thought about Elyse Hunter-Black's Eau de Vaucluse, which she drank from heavy blue glass bottles that looked like works of art.

"Weird how *water* can be a status symbol," I whispered, although no one was around to hear me.

Feeling a tickle in the pit of my stomach, I glanced at the broken doorknob. At least, I hoped I was alone in the apartment. Anyone could come and go. Then I reassured myself that the place was so small that a person would have to hold his or her breath to go undetected.

Moving away from the water, I next noticed a wilting, half-frozen spider plant that sat next to the sink.

I wasn't sure who had purchased *that*.

I couldn't imagine my mother supplying a tenant with a houseplant. Nor could I imagine Lauren Savidge buying something to nurture during her brief time in Sylvan Creek. I could only assume that the plant had been left behind by some previous tenant.

"You poor thing," I told the sprawling, spiky mess of foliage. Then, forgetting that I had no right to take anything from the apartment, I reached for it, planning to take it home with me and nurse it back to health. But as I lifted the terra-cotta pot, I discovered that the soil was actually damp. The plant was mainly suffering from the cold, not from lack of water. Still, I didn't intend to leave it behind. "You are coming with me—"

All at once, that promise froze in the chilly air as I spied something that had been hiding behind the planter.

A dog collar.

With a *barrel attached.*

Chapter 49

The sun wasn't yet peeking over the horizon as I stood bleary-eyed in Lauren's former, temporary home, studying the barrel and trying to figure out what to do next. I didn't want to leave the collar in the unlocked apartment, for fear that it would disappear as mysteriously as it had shown up. Because I was pretty sure the cask on the leather strap hadn't been in the kitchen the first time I'd been there. I was almost certain that the plant hadn't been near the sink, either.

Why—and how—had the collar materialized on Lauren's countertop?

I really wanted to take the barrel home with me, get some sleep, then call Detective Doebler at a more reasonable hour.

Actually, I wanted to call Jonathan right then and wake him up. But I knew that he'd first be groggily irritated, then angry to learn that I'd entered the apartment again, before telling me that the collar was Detective Doebler's problem. Assuming that the barrel was even related to the murder.

I again looked between the spider plant and the collar.

Was there a chance that the plant and the cask had been in the kitchen all along?

Had I just not noticed either thing, somehow . . . ?

All at once, I jumped, and my heart started racing, because I heard something outside. Heavy footsteps, clomping up the stairs to the apartment.

I instinctively moved toward the door, but this time, there was no way to lock myself in. The knob was just hanging there.

The footsteps got louder, and closer, and my heart began to pound so hard that I swore I could feel it thudding against my rib cage.

"That's not Mom," I muttered nervously, my eyes fixed on the door. It sounded to me like the person was wearing clunky shoes, like boots. My mother never wore heavy boots, even in snowstorms.

Backing away again, I reached into my pocket to get my phone so I could call for help.

But before I could even tap the screen with my shaky fingers, the door swung open and in walked Gabriel Graham.

"What are you doing here?" I demanded, too loudly. I rested my free hand against my chest, trying to calm my thumping heart. "You scared me half to death!"

Gabriel ignored my questions and my complaint.

In fact, he didn't say a word. He just frowned and stalked farther into the apartment. Closer to me. But his gaze was fixed on the countertop. And I didn't know why his voice was so low—almost threatening—when he ordered me, "Tell me how—and where—you found the collar, Daphne. I need to know *now*."

Chapter 50

"I have disturbed quite a few crime scenes, and I'm telling you, you shouldn't have taken the collar from the apartment," I told Gabriel, who was hunched over his desk, poking at the barrel.

He hadn't been kidding when he'd told me that he worked odd hours. He'd been headed to his office before dawn to fire up the old presses for the next edition of the *Gazette* when he'd seen the light I'd turned on in the efficiency. Curious about who would be in a murder victim's rental in the wee hours, he'd hurried to investigate. And when he'd seen the collar, he'd practically pounced on it, over my objections, then taken it back to his office, with me trailing behind, protesting the whole way.

I knew that *I* was going to get blamed for messing up any fingerprints if the collar turned out to be significant.

"Seriously, I don't think you should touch that," I said nervously, as Gabriel continued to peer at the keg. "You're going to get *me* in trouble!"

"I'm not touching anything with my hands." He

paused in poking at the collar with a pencil to look up at me. I was standing on the other side of the desk, too worried to take a seat. Even by my loose standards, he'd gone too far by taking the collar from the apartment. "You saw me use my handkerchief to pick it up," he reminded me. "And I've covered plenty of homicides. I know what I'm doing." He sat back and shrugged. "Plus, for all we know, the barrel has nothing to do with the murder."

I shook my head, disagreeing. "I feel like it does."

Gabriel grinned, then bent over the desk again. "To be honest, I do, too. And I'd like to write a story about the mysterious whisky cask that went missing after a murder, only to show up in the victim's apartment. And I'd like to run it today."

I stifled a groan. My mother would no doubt read that article. Not to mention Jonathan. "Please, keep my name out of the story," I begged. "My mother thinks my involvement in murders is bad for her business."

Gabriel didn't make any promises. He didn't even look up at me.

"Tell me again how you found this," he urged, using the pencil to spin the collar, so he could see it from a different angle. "Was it really just lying on the counter?"

"Yes, I found it behind the spider plant . . ." I started to answer him, but all at once, I thought about how Gabriel had found Bernie in the woods. And although he'd claimed the dog hadn't been wearing anything unusual, I narrowed my eyes at him, suspiciously. He could've been pretending to be surprised by the discovery of the collar. In fact, he'd acted pretty strangely when he'd first entered the apartment.

"When's the last time *you* were at Lauren's, before this morning?"

Gabriel raised his face again and smiled at my less-than-subtle question. "If you're trying to ask me if I planted the collar at Lauren's—and I'm pretty sure you are—the answer is, no, I've never seen this thing before, outside of a few photographs." A shadow crossed his face. "I haven't been to Lauren's place in quite a while, before today."

Given how tense things had seemed between Gabriel and Lauren on the night of her death, I was pretty sure I believed that last statement at least. I also realized that, for better or for worse, a potential clue to the crime was right in front of me, waiting to be examined. I finally took a seat in the metal chair and joined Gabriel as he resumed poking at the cask, like it was some sort of bomb that might go off.

However, under close inspection, the barrel wasn't very impressive. In fact, it wasn't even made of wood, just thick plastic, made to look like wood grain and looped with some kind of cheap, tinny metal. There was a curious slit on one end, and a black rubber stopper, plugging a hole in the plastic, on the other end. The end with the stopper was covered with a lot of thick, dried-up glue.

"Isn't the hole supposed to be on the *side* of the barrel?" I asked, knitting my brows. "Wouldn't all the whisky pour out the bottom the moment you pulled out the cork?"

"I really don't know much about crafting barrels," Gabriel said. "But I don't think whoever made this one intended it to hold liquid—unless whisky suddenly becomes currency. Which wouldn't be a bad idea, in my opinion." He smiled at his own joke. "Distill your own dollars!"

He was laughing, but I had no idea what he was talking about. And he clearly saw that I was confused.

"This is a *bank*, Daphne," he informed me, using the pencil to spin the barrel. "Coins go in the narrow slot. And you can shake them out the bottom, after you remove the stopper. I had one of these when I was a kid."

He resumed peering closely at the keg, and I was glad he was distracted. My face had to be beet red. Of course, the cask was a child's novelty bank. If I'd dared to touch the barrel, back at Lauren's, I probably would've figured that out. And I would've noticed another small hole that Gabriel was pointing out, slowly spinning the cask again so I could see a dark spot in the plastic. A spot that glittered, like glass.

Dark, polished glass . . .

All at once, as I stared into what looked like a tiny, gleaming eye, I sucked in a sharp breath. Then Gabriel and I announced, at the same time, "This thing is also a *camera*!"

Chapter 51

"That's why the glue job on the bottom is so bad," Gabriel noted, both of us bent down again, even closer to the cask. We were circling like vultures—or members of an actual bomb squad, both eager to understand the mechanism and half afraid the whole thing would blow up in our faces. At least, I was kind of afraid. "Somebody must've cut off the bottom, put a camera inside, and sealed the thing back up." He nodded in an approving way. "Homemade spy—or nanny—cam. I like it. Much more original than the standard teddy bear on a shelf."

I wasn't so sure I agreed, and I gave him another suspicious glance. "What's so great about *surreptitious surveillance?*"

Gabriel laughed. "What's *not?*"

I drew back, even more wary. "Are you sure you've never seen this . . . ?"

"Relax, Daphne." He nodded to his trusty Nikon, which was also on the desk. "I'm pretty up front when I take photos. I'm not a fan of lawsuits."

And yet, I thought he tempted that fate all the time, with his barely-this-side-of-the-truth articles and his *not quite* misleading photos.

I stared at the hefty digital 35 millimeter.

And what sort of images waited in that black box . . . ?

"The big question is, who created this thing?" Gabriel noted, so I returned my attention to the biggest mystery on his desk. "And why?"

I suddenly remembered the picture that Lauren had snapped of me, without my knowledge or permission. And the photo of Piper locking her door. I was pretty sure my sister had no idea that image existed.

"Maybe Lauren," I suggested. "She wasn't above undertaking the occasional covert camera operation."

"Yes, she wasn't too squeamish about violating privacy rights," Gabriel said, leaning back on his chair. The old springs squeaked. I sat back, too, but my chair didn't give. "However, I don't see Lauren doing a craft project." He waved at the barrel, almost dismissively. "And she wasn't the cloak-and-dagger type." Then he smiled wryly. "Well, she was the dagger type. But she wielded them pretty directly."

I could've sworn Gabriel admired the ruthless aspects of Lauren's nature.

So why did he have the slightest bit of interest in *me*?

Not that he was acting like he'd ever tried to kiss me, right then. His gaze was trained on the cask again. Then he looked at me, briefly. "Of course, Lauren wasn't the only person with some professional expertise regarding video equipment."

I leaned forward. "You mean Joy Doolittle? And—or—Kevin Drucker?"

He nodded. "Especially Kevin. The silent observer with the omnipresent camera perched on his shoulder . . . Think about it."

Gabriel had a point.

"But why?" I asked. "Why stash a camera in a barrel? And put the barrel on a dog. And let the dog loose in a forest. Then find the dog, steal the barrel from his collar, break into Lauren Savidge's apartment, and ditch it there . . ." I shook my head. "It seems like a lot of effort for . . . what?"

"That's what we're hopefully going to find out, by busting this thing open—"

Gabriel was actually reaching for the retrofitted bank, and I leaped out of my chair and grabbed his arm, stopping him. "What in the world are you thinking?" I demanded. I realized that I was starting to sound like Jonathan, but I kept protesting. "This is evidence. I keep telling you. We have to turn it over to Detective Doebler. We can't destroy it!"

"I'm not going to destroy anything," Gabriel promised. I was still clutching his wrist, and he looked up at me, his eyes all innocence, but his grin pure devilment. "I'm just going to see if there are any images captured on the camera, reassemble everything, then turn the whole thing over to the police."

That still sounded like a bad idea to me, and I broke the rules all the time. I released his arm and pulled out my cell phone. "I'm sorry, but I'm calling Detective Doebler. Now."

"Go ahead," Gabriel said, grinning. "I work pretty quickly. By the time he gets here, I'll be ready to write a story about *our* discovery for the *Gazette*."

Chapter 52

"Do you think Gabriel *really* would've tampered with possible evidence?" Moxie asked, as I whipped up some batter to make a test batch of Woofles waffles for dogs. We were video chatting, and I had my phone propped against an old cookbook on the kitchen counter at Plum Cottage. Moxie was at her apartment, painting her nails an unusual shade of green. Stirring a big bowl full of rice flour, eggs, and cinnamon, I glanced at the screen to see that she was frowning. "Or do you think he was just pushing your buttons by threatening to take apart the barrel? Because that wouldn't be very nice."

"I think he honestly wanted to see the camera," I said, dropping some batter onto the surface of my hot waffle iron. I'd picked up Artie and Socrates from Piper's house early that morning, and Artie was dancing around, licking his chops. Socrates was waiting patiently for his snack. "But we still had a few tense moments before he agreed that we should call Detective Doebler."

In fact, Gabriel and I had ended up having a pretty

big argument, which I'd won. Not that I felt a great
sense of triumph. Gabriel, who had insisted upon
being there when the police took apart the barrel,
had recently called me to apologize for being over-
zealous in his effort to get a scoop. He'd also informed
me that no images had been found on the small, but
high-quality, video camera that had been discovered
in the cask. As things stood, Detective Doebler didn't
really think the barrel was a clue to solving Lauren's
murder.

"How would somebody even work a camera that
was stuck in a barrel?" Moxie mused. I looked over to
see her holding up her nails, examining her Martian-
colored fingertips. She blew on her hand, appearing
satisfied. "Would, like, an elf crawl inside to take the
pictures?"

Was it strange that I honestly wasn't sure if she was
joking?

"According to Gabriel, it's easy to connect most
cameras to a remote control," I told her, flipping the
ancient cast-iron waffle iron. "Anybody with even a
little technical know-how could do it, then videotape
from a pretty fair distance from the camera."

"But why . . . ?" Moxie sounded baffled.

"I don't know." I opened the waffle iron and saw
that the Woofles were perfectly golden brown. Artie
started jumping up and down, his tongue hanging
out, and even Socrates moved closer, his nose twitching at the scent of cinnamon. "I guess it doesn't
matter," I added with a shrug. "Detective Doebler
doesn't think the camera will help solve the case."

"I still think the whole thing is weird," Moxie said.

I had to agree. I still believed that the plastic keg

was connected to Lauren's murder. Why else would it have gone missing after the crime, then show up in her apartment?

I also couldn't stop thinking about two people who could easily connect a remote control to a camera: Kevin Drucker and Gabriel. . . .

"Why were you even at Lauren's apartment again?" Moxie asked, interrupting my thoughts. "Are you trying to make your mother—and Jonathan—angry?"

"No!" Using a knife, I gently pried the warm Woofles, which had the perfect amount of crisp on the edges, out of the waffle iron and set them onto two plates. Then I spread peanut butter into the crannies, so it would melt and get gooey, and topped both treats with "whipped cream" yogurt, sweetened with honey. Artie started popping around like a cork, nearly knocking his plate out of my hand before I could set it on the floor. And Socrates was licking his chops. I had a feeling Woofles would be a hit at Flour Power. As the dogs dug in, I straightened and wiped my hands on my apron. "I had hoped to see Lauren's corkboard, with all the photos, one more time," I told Moxie. "I didn't intend to touch anything. But I happened to see a dying plant, and I couldn't just walk away without at least watering it."

"That sounds like you, Daphne," Moxie noted. "All my plants would be dead if you didn't stop by now and then."

That was true. Moxie had a good heart, but she never watered the few ferns and the ficus she kept in her apartment. I guessed some people weren't as fond of plants as others. . . .

"Daph, are you listening?"

I'd been drifting off again, my mind still struggling to connect a bunch of dots that seemed random, but which I knew would reveal a picture of Lauren Savidge's killer, if I could just draw the lines between them.

"Look at your phone," Moxie said, summoning my attention again. "I want to show you something."

I stepped over to my phone and bent down. "What's that?"

Moxie picked up her own cell and swung it around, so for a second, I got queasy when the colorful, mismatched décor in her eclectic apartment swirled like paint dumped on an old spin art toy. Then she stood still and pointed the camera at a very authentic-looking, if somewhat small, *stagecoach* standing in the middle of her cramped living room.

"Oh, Moxie!" I cried. "It's perfect!"

"You really like it?" I heard pride in her voice as she moved her phone around so I could see the cardboard vehicle from all angles.

I got a little seasick again, but forced myself to check out the sled's glossy red paint and yellow wagon wheels, which were mounted onto Moxie's vintage skis, so Bernie could pull the contraption across the snow. Moxie had also crafted a rear-facing "rumble seat" in the back, where I presumed Artie—in character as Julia Bulette—would sit, surprising the crowd as he glided by in his velvet dress.

There was even an upholstered seat for a driver. . . .

I turned to look hopefully at Socrates, who'd finished his Woofle. He shook his head and growled under his breath. The sound wasn't vicious, by any means. He was just putting down his substantial paw.

"Oh, fine," I told him. "You don't have to take part." I turned back to Moxie, whose face was on-screen again. "How can I ever thank you enough? Because the stagecoach was supposed to be my responsibility."

"We're best friends, Daph," she reminded me. "I know your priority has to be the bakery right now." I was basking in the warm glow of friendship when she also noted, "Plus, you were really wrecking the refrigerator box. It was like you'd never held a craft knife before!"

I supposed that honesty, even the brutal kind, was a good quality in a friend, too.

"Well, thanks," I said. "That is a load off my mind. I can't wait for the Iditarod!"

"Me, neither." Moxie waggled her fingers, signing off. "In the meantime, I've got to go fit Sebastian for his cowboy vest and boots."

"Vest?" I asked uncertainly. "And *boots*? For a rat? But why . . . ?"

Moxie was nodding with enthusiasm. "Yes! I've decided he'll make a perfect Little Joe Cartwright!"

I seriously doubted that anyone would understand that a rodent in a cowboy outfit and a hyper dog in a velvet dress were supposed to be an ill-fated couple from a 1960s TV show. I was also trying to figure out how Moxie would put boots on a rat when a white face with a wriggling pink nose and bright pink eyes popped up on the screen, obliterating my view of Moxie.

"Sebastian!" I rested one hand against my chest. "Don't video bomb! It's rude!"

I didn't think Sebastian heard me, because, all at once, an even *ruder* black cat darted out from his mini-jungle and pounced on my new phone, ending the call—and sending a bunch of plants crashing to the ground.

I opened my mouth to scold Tinkleston, then froze in place, staring at the poor, battered herbs on my floor. And as I stood there, my thoughts flashed back to Lauren Savidge's apartment. I remained still for a long time, my brain again struggling to make those connections that stayed just out of reach.

What was odd about the spider plant?

Chapter 53

"You *had* been doing so much better since Bernie's been out of the house," I told Tinkleston, as I set the potted herbs back on the windowsill. The little cat, who had reclaimed his spot, was blinking up at me, like he didn't even realize that he'd made a mess. But I saw a hint of self-satisfied defiance in his orange eyes. Picking up a cracked terra-cotta planter that overflowed with fragrant lavender, I dusted some dirt off the rim. "I am going to ban you from this hiding spot, if you can't behave . . ."

I wasn't done scolding Tinks, but as I held that clay pot, I again pictured the spider plant that had been wilting next to the sink at Lauren's apartment. If Moxie had been there, she would've walked right by it. . . .

I felt like I was finally on the verge of a revelation, when all at once my cell phone rang.

"Darn," I muttered, thinking Moxie had probably forgotten to tell me something. But when I picked up the phone, I saw an unfamiliar number on the screen. However, I immediately recognized the caller by his accent and unusual greeting.

"*Bonsoir*, Daphne!"

Chapter 54

"Will you please stop looking at me like that," I asked Socrates, who rode shotgun next to me in the VW on the dreariest winter day I could remember. It wasn't snowing. Snow would've been pretty. The morning was just *dark*, the sky filled with low, churning, nearly black clouds that seemed to press down from above, like a cracked and slowly collapsing ceiling. I flipped the switch to turn on my unreliable headlights. But the dim glow they produced did little to help offset the gloom, which deepened as I turned onto the forested road leading to Big Cats of the World. "I really don't think this is a mistake," I told the basset hound, who was warily scanning the trees. "I'm sure Victor just wants to talk. And it's not like we'll be all alone there. He said the shelter is open to the public today, and might even be busy."

Socrates rolled his eyes and huffed, softly, to let me know that he thought I was being potentially dangerously naïve.

And, the truth was, he was probably right.

But how could I resist Victor's suggestion that we

meet, especially since I'd seemed so eager to hear all about the mysterious article the first time I'd visited his rescue? We'd shared that strange moment of mutual understanding. . . .

"Woof!"

I'd been lost in my recent memories, but Socrates's deep, unexpected, and rare bark brought me back to reality.

"What's wrong?" I asked, shooting him a worried look. I knew he wouldn't speak up unless something was really troubling him. That definitely concerned me, given that we were headed toward a preserve filled with some of the world's biggest predators. In fact, although I'd seen Victor's extensive security system firsthand, I'd still left Artie at Plum Cottage. He was just too friendly, impulsive—and perfectly snack-sized—to be anywhere near a beast like Genghis Khan. Steering using only my peripheral vision, I kept watching Socrates. "What's the matter?"

"Woof!"

He barked louder and pointed his nose forward, indicating that I should look ahead again.

And when I did, I saw what he'd perceived as amiss, although, as far as I knew, he'd never been to Big Cats of the World.

I hit the brakes, and my bald tires skidded on the icy, narrow road.

And when I got the VW under control, my heart still racing, I turned to Socrates, whose eyes were asking the same question that I vocalized, my voice low with growing unease.

"Why is a gate meant to keep unwanted visitors out—and big cats in—*swinging wide open?*"

Then I looked to the alarmed call box with the keypad that Gabriel had used to contact Victor, so the zookeeper could buzz us into the compound, and a cold trickle of sweat ran down my spine.

"And why the heck is the call box just a *tangle of wires?*"

Chapter 55

For a split second, I wasn't sure what to do, aside from panic to think that tigers might be roaming loose in the Pocono Mountains. An electric fence ran around the property and kept the tigers off the road, but looking at the open gate and broken call box, I had a terrible feeling that the whole security system had been compromised.

"I suppose Victor could be having the intercom system repaired," I ventured, keeping a wary eye on the gate, in case something big came wandering out. "Maybe he—or the technician—didn't realize that the gate would hang open if the call box was removed . . . ?"

I thought that was possible, but Socrates was skeptical. He furrowed his already wrinkled brow, expressing doubt.

Not wanting to overreact, I first dug into my back pocket to retrieve my cell phone.

"Darn it," I grumbled, tapping the screen three times, like that would change the "out of service range" message I was receiving.

Still watching the gate, I slipped my phone back into my pocket, while Socrates made a low, soft, sound deep in his throat. When I looked over at him, he nudged his nose forward.

I understood exactly what he was trying to say.

"We have to go in there, don't we?" I asked, not sure how I'd become the reluctant one.

But I knew that Socrates was right.

We had no choice but to drive onto Victor's property, close the gate behind us, and find either Victor or the nearest working phone. I couldn't risk the safer option of shutting the gate from the outside and taking the time to drive back to town. Not if there was even a tiny chance that a single tiger was roaming free in woods used by hikers. I shuddered to think of the possible consequences.

Glancing again at the broken call box, I swallowed thickly.

And, on the off chance that something had happened to Victor, time might *really* be of the essence. . . .

Taking a deep breath, I exhaled and put the van in gear, telling Socrates, "As Confucius said, 'Faced with what is right, to leave it undone shows a lack of courage.'"

Socrates nodded in agreement and faced forward, too, as we rolled through the open gate into a forest that seemed even deeper, darker, and more eerily quiet than before.

That might've just been my imagination, but I couldn't help suffering a terrible sense of foreboding— then outright fear—as I put the van in neutral, hopped out, and scrambled like crazy to shut the gate behind us. Fortunately, there was a low-tech latch, presumably to be used if the power went out, and I set the metal bar in place with trembling fingers, unable to shake the feeling that keen and hungry eyes were watching me from the trees.

I sat for all sorts of animals, including a few dogs who were less than friendly, but I couldn't imagine coming face-to-face with one of the tigers I'd seen stalking through the forest on my last visit.

"Please, don't eat me," I whispered, running the few feet to the VW, hopping inside, and closing the door behind myself.

Socrates was remaining calm, but I thought I heard him exhale softly with relief once the bus was in motion again.

Then we both grew silent and watchful as we made our way through the preserve. The only sound was the slow rumble of tires on gravel. I knew that nothing in the woods could get to us, as long as we stayed in the van. And I could see the thin wires of the electric fence. But I was still on edge, and I started at every shadow and jumped each time a branch creaked in the breeze.

I was also increasingly concerned that my unreliable vehicle would choose to conk out halfway to Victor's headquarters.

Then what?

Would we have to spend the night in the forest, if Victor didn't find us?

Or would we be stuck even *longer*?

I started scanning the trees, when I should've been paying attention to the narrow road.

And should I be worried that I *wasn't* seeing any tigers, this time . . . ?

"Woof!"

Socrates's third bark of the day jolted me and I

faced forward, only to see that we'd reached yet another gate. The one that separated the free-range tiger preserve from the parking lot, the gift shop, and the smaller pens.

That gate was swinging open, too.

I had been holding out hope that nothing was really amiss, but as my van rolled into an eerily empty parking lot, I suddenly got a metallic taste in my mouth. The taste of real fear, even more intense than what I'd suffered when I'd closed the main gate.

"Something's wrong," I whispered to Socrates. I wasn't sure why I felt the need to be quiet. "Really, really wrong." I parked the van as close to the building as I could, right next to Victor's tiger-striped golf cart. I looked at the elaborately decorated vehicle for a second, thinking something seemed amiss with *that*, too. Which was probably just my imagination starting to run wild. Then I turned to Socrates, who had a steely look in his eyes. "You stay here, okay? I'm going to run into the gift shop and try to find Victor."

"WOOF!"

Socrates's deep bark was *thunderous*, and he pawed the seat, his broad chest straining against his harness.

"There's really no need for both of us to go," I assured him, trying to act unconcerned. "I'm just going to be gone for a minute. . . ."

"WOOF!"

His second protest was even louder, but I still hesitated.

I didn't want to put him in any danger.

Then I studied Socrates's wise, loyal eyes and realized that he would never forgive me, or himself, if I didn't let him come with me. It would shatter his dignity, to be restrained when he wanted to help. And I was pretty sure that, for an existential, stoic dog like Socrates, that would be a fate worse than death. Not that we really faced *that*.

"Fine," I agreed, unhooking him. "But come out my side. It's closer to the door. And run for once, okay?"

Part of me thought I was overreacting, my worries heightened by the gloomy day and the curious circumstances. For all I knew, Victor had penned the tigers while doing some repairs to the gate and call box. But part of me was pretty sure that some of the world's most cunning predators were on the loose, either inside or outside of Big Cats of the World. Maybe both.

It was that gut instinct that sent me tearing toward the falsely rustic, wooden door to the gift shop, with Socrates hot on my heels. Daring to look down to make sure that he was safe, I actually saw him *leap over something* in his haste to follow me. A bottle, discarded in the parking lot. It wasn't very big, but it was like a hurdle for his short legs.

"Come on," I urged, hauling open the door, which was thankfully unlocked. I waved my hand as Socrates passed by me, his big paws thudding with each step he took. "Get inside!"

And when we were safely inside the building, I slammed the door and quickly found a deadbolt, which I slid into place.

"Okay . . . Okay," I gasped, resting my back against the door. I tried to catch my breath, not sure how Socrates was already breathing steadily, given that he seldom exercised anything but his intellect. "I think we're safe."

Socrates seemed to agree. He began to tentatively

sniff around the building, heading toward the area that housed the gift shop, where schoolkids and other visitors would normally stop to buy postcards featuring Khan, or tiger key chains, or bumper stickers that boasted, "I Survived Big Cats of the World!"

I seriously hoped Socrates and I would qualify for one of those stickers by the end of our visit.

Then I turned toward the other part of the structure, which held the snack bar. The room was dark, and I felt along the wall until I found a light switch. Flipping that on, I immediately felt safer as several wall sconces, designed to look like torches, flickered to life.

"Victor?" I called softly, reluctantly moving farther into the room. I no longer believed that I was about to be consumed by a tiger, but I couldn't shake the feeling that the place was too quiet. The boards creaked under my feet as I searched for a telephone. I couldn't recall seeing one on my previous visit, but I was almost certain there would be a landline somewhere. "Victor?" I called again uncertainly. "Are you here?"

He didn't answer. But he'd clearly been in the room recently.

One of the tables, set in a dark corner, was strewn with papers.

I moved in that direction, only to discover that the documents included a magazine. A glossy periodical that was open to the same article I'd seen at Lauren Savidge's apartment. Only this story was intact, so I could read the entire headline, by the faux flame of the sputtering sconces.

ZOOKEEPER SENTENCED FOR ASSAULT OF POACHER.

I took a second to check the subtitle.

INCENDIARY ACTIVIST RETURNS TO PRISON, VOWS TO CONTINUE FIGHT FOR BIG CATS.

"Wow," I muttered, under my breath. "He's done jail time, in service of animals."

I didn't approve of violence, but I couldn't help admiring Victor Breard's commitment to saving endangered species.

Setting down the magazine, I saw other documents that Victor must've intended to show me, to tell his story. Citations—the bad kind, from law enforcement agencies—for disturbing the peace and unlawful protest. And more citations—the good kind, from animal welfare groups—for his work on behalf of threatened species.

"I bet he's like Arlo," I guessed, fanning out the documents. "I bet he came here to continue his work, but to escape parts of his past, too. That's what he wants to tell me. . . ."

All at once, I heard Socrates's tags jingle and his toenails click as he joined me in the snack area, and I realized I'd lingered too long at the table.

"I'm going to find a phone," I assured him. "I'll be right back. . . ."

But something in Socrates's expression stopped me. A look in his eyes that I'd never seen before.

Then he turned and began to walk with purpose back toward the gift shop.

Something told me that, much as I needed to place a call, I should follow him. A sick, yet almost resigned feeling in the pit of my stomach.

And that sensation grew more profound when he padded up onto a platform that I'd forgotten about. A small viewing area with a big window that allowed visitors a bird's-eye view—into *Khan's pen.*

I knew what I was about to see, based upon the things that were wrong at the compound, and Victor's curious absence at our appointed meeting time, not to mention a heavy, oppressive feeling that I'd been trying to shake off, but which had already warned me that death had recently visited Big Cats of the World.

Yet I still reeled backward, just a step, when I joined Socrates at the glass and looked down.

Chapter 56

I didn't want to watch as Coroner Vonda Shakes, Detective Doebler, and a bunch of uniformed officers and EMS workers paced around Genghis Khan's pen, examining Victor Breard's body, which lay curled up and stiff in the center of the enclosure.

Yet I couldn't pull myself away from the observation deck—or stop reliving the memory of first seeing the lion batting Victor around, like the corpse was a new toy.

Socrates was also staring out the window, probably pondering the inevitability of death, or the folly of believing that one could be best friends with a lion. I doubted that he was very shaken—he didn't rattle easily—but he must've realized that I was unnerved, because he rested lightly against my leg, just letting me know that he was there. I appreciated the rare public show of affection, but I didn't even acknowledge it. I knew he wouldn't want me to make a big deal out of his gesture.

My sister was also concerned about me.

"Are you okay, Daphne?" Piper asked, resting one

hand on my shoulder. She'd been called to the scene to tranquilize Khan, who had then been hauled into one of several trailers Victor kept on-site to transport animals. I always knew that Piper was capable and could wield everything from a scalpel to a hammer, but it had still been odd to watch her put one of Victor's arsenal of tranquilizer guns to her shoulder, coolly take aim, and pull the trigger. She gave me a squeeze, then removed her hand. Like Socrates, she wasn't one for big shows of affection. "Maybe you should stop watching . . ."

"Probably," I agreed, without taking my eyes off the scene unfolding below. Vonda Shakes was conferring with Detective Doebler, standing in front of Victor and blocking my view of the body. Which was okay. I'd seen enough of poor Victor's cadaver, which looked relatively peaceful, given the terrible circumstances. I would've expected to see blood, or bite marks, but Khan seemed mainly to have played with the corpse. I turned to Piper, concerned, suddenly, for the lion. "What do you think will happen to Khan?"

"I'm not sure," my sister admitted. "There are, unfortunately, too many cases like this. Sometimes the animals are euthanized, but more often than not, they're allowed to live."

That answer surprised me. "Really?"

Piper nodded. "The deaths are usually attributed to human error. It's irrational to kill a wild animal that we brought into captivity, just because it acts upon its true nature."

"People aren't always rational," I noted, earning a snort of agreement from Socrates, who'd also peeled himself away from me, now that I was settling down.

"But I hope whoever decides Khan's fate takes into account that *Victor* probably wouldn't want him to be put down."

"You're overlooking something, too, Daphne," Piper said, nodding toward the enclosure, so I looked outside again. Detective Doebler and Vonda Shakes had moved aside so the EMTs could place Victor's body on a gurney. "There's a *detective* here," my sister pointed out. "And the gates were left wide open, the electric fence shut off, and the intercom system tampered with. Not to mention the fact that Victor doesn't look like he suffered trauma from a lion attack."

"Oh, my gosh," I muttered, finally able to think clearly. "You're saying that he might've been murdered *by a human* and dumped into the enclosure. Which is probably correct." I wrapped my arms around myself, no less horrified by Piper's theory. In fact, the possibility that Victor had been killed by someone with the ability to reason and make moral choices only heightened the tragedy, in my opinion. "How did I overlook all of those things you just pointed out?"

"You saw a dead man in a lion's pen," Piper reminded me. "I would've assumed the same thing. Especially since you saw Khan stalking around behind Victor the other day."

I resumed watching the EMTs, who had loaded a gurney carrying Victor into the ambulance and were shutting the rear doors. "Still, that was pretty stupid of me."

Piper didn't disagree. In fact, she didn't say anything. We both just watched in silence as the ambulance drove slowly down paths designed for golf carts.

Victor's golf cart . . .

I was picturing that flashy little vehicle, trying to recall what had struck me as odd about it when I'd parked next to it, when Piper finally asked a question that was probably long overdue.

"What, exactly, brought you here today, Daphne?"

I opened my mouth to explain that I'd been invited by Victor Breard, presumably so he could tell me about his past, then request that I stop digging into his personal history. Just like he'd probably asked Lauren to stop nosing around, too. But before I could say anything, the door to the gift shop swung open and in walked a person who'd been conspicuously absent from the scene.

Jonathan Black, who carried not a detective's notebook, but a *high-powered rifle*.

Scarier than the gun, though, was the look on his face.

Chapter 57

"Daphne," Jonathan grumbled ominously. He paced around the snack bar, while I sat at a table, a few feet away from the materials that Victor Breard would never get to explain. Then he stopped abruptly and faced me. "Where do I even begin?"

"You could start by putting down the gun," I suggested, eyeing the weapon nervously. "Why do you even have that?"

"I was doing a head count of loose tigers in a heavily forested compound," he informed me, nevertheless setting the gun down on the sales counter, next to a festive red-and-white popcorn machine. The rifle actually seemed more in keeping with the safari theme than the cheerful popcorn maker. "Although I'd been assured that the animals are used to humans and largely docile, I—like the other volunteers— wanted to make sure I came out alive."

I drew back. "*You* were counting tigers . . . ?"

"Yes," he confirmed, finally sitting down across from me. He seemed slightly less upset now that we'd started talking. Of course, taking the rifle out of the conversation helped to make him less threatening, too. "We requested volunteers among the local hunters, but not too many people stepped forward to help, once we explained that the prey might be hunting them back."

"I guess I can understand the low turnout," I agreed. "I was pretty scared, the few moments I thought I was vulnerable."

Jonathan rested back in his seat. "Fortunately, the fence is electrified again and all four of the tigers are accounted for—with no *additional* loss of human or animal life."

Something about his tone made me feel like I was responsible for everything. The broken gate. Victor's death. The potential destruction of majestic animals. "I'm sorry. . . ."

He leaned forward, resting his forearms on the table and tenting his fingers, the better to peer into my eyes. "What were you doing here, Daphne?" He wasn't one to get carried away by emotion, but there was an edge of frustration in his low, soft voice. "Why are you—again—the first to find a body?"

"I came here at Victor's request," I defended myself, searching around for Socrates, as if he could back me up, but the sagacious basset hound had made himself scarce. He was not a fan of confrontation or firearms. I reluctantly faced Jonathan again. "I wouldn't be here otherwise."

Jonathan spoke evenly. "Why did Victor invite you?"

I tucked some of my curls behind my ear, growing nervous, because I'd suddenly realized that I was being *interrogated*. This was a new murder, and while I'd assumed the two recent killings were related, that probably hadn't been established yet. "You're not off this case, are you?"

"Not at this point," he advised me. "Now, please, tell me why you came here today."

It seemed like he was growing more distant with every second, putting up that wall between his personal and professional personas. I couldn't read anything in his eyes, and that made me even more uneasy. I took a deep breath, trying to focus, then told him, "When I took the tour with Gabriel, Joy Doolittle, and Kevin Drucker the other day, I mentioned an article about Victor that I'd seen on Lauren's corkboard—"

"The piece that was torn out of a magazine," Jonathan interrupted. I'd forgotten that he would've seen the story, too. "With half the headline missing."

I nodded, then pointed to the table that held all the papers. "A copy of the article is right over there, with some other documents."

Without a word, Jonathan rose and went to the table that held the magazine and Victor's citations. He quickly found the article, which was on top of the papers, and skimmed it. Then he returned and sat across from me again. He didn't say anything about what he'd just read. He just nodded and said, "Continue. Please."

I licked my lips, nearly squirming under his coolly professional gaze. "Well, Victor acted strangely and said he'd like the chance to explain that story. I didn't really expect him to call, but he did. And I was curious, so I took him up on his offer to talk."

Jonathan sat back and crossed his arms, observing me closely. "Did you get a chance to have this 'talk'?"

I felt my eyes grow wide. "You don't really think I killed Victor . . . ?"

He didn't respond. He just kept watching me. He was no longer irritated, but completely dispassionate. And that was somehow worse.

My cheeks got warm under his level stare. And although I knew that he could—and probably should—logically have doubts about my involvement in Victor's death, I was stung by his failure to assure me that he would never believe me capable of murder.

Then I felt a pang of guilt, because I had experienced moments of doubt about Jonathan, ever since Gabriel had asked me if I was sure Jonathan was trustworthy.

But I'd never suspect him of *murder*.

"I don't think I want to talk anymore until I call my lawyer," I finally said quietly, trying not to let him know that I was hurt. I was also keenly aware that I had no lawyer to call. And Jonathan probably knew that the threat was empty.

Still, he told me, "Fine, Daphne. That's your prerogative."

I stood up to leave, but I didn't get three steps before Jonathan rose, too, and clasped my shoulder with his hand. I hadn't even heard him push back the chair to stand up.

I started to pull free; then I saw the apology in his eyes, and I stopped tugging.

"I'm sorry," he said softly, although we seemed to be alone in the building. Piper had left at some point, and Socrates had probably gone outside to watch the remaining officers search Khan's pen. "I don't really believe that you killed Victor Breard.

Although I probably shouldn't admit that to you." He took his hand off my shoulder, then closed his eyes for a moment and rubbed them. "I'm just very frustrated. . . ."

He didn't finish that thought, but I knew what he meant.

He was unhappy to be off a case that he probably could've solved by now. Plus, I was nosing around in another homicide investigation and had found another body.

"I'm sorry, too," I apologized. I wasn't angry anymore and regretted my rash comment about hiring a lawyer. "If you have more questions for me, I really don't mind answering. I think we both know that I don't have legal counsel."

"Thanks, but I think we're done for now." Jonathan stepped away from me to reclaim the rifle. He hesitated, then added, "You're lucky, Daphne. Things could've really gone wrong today for you and Socrates."

That was an understatement, and images that I'd shoved to the back of my mind came flooding back in vivid detail.

My mad dash to shut the gate . . .

My ragged breath as I'd run to the gift shop . . .

Socrates, jumping an object that had rolled away, revealing a distinctive label . . .

"Oh, my gosh!"

I hadn't even realized I'd spoken until Jonathan asked, "What? What's wrong?"

I'd started getting excited when I'd realized that Socrates had almost stumbled over what might be a clue to solving both Lauren's and Victor's murders.

Then, as I calmed down and considered how the possible evidence might impact Jonathan, I felt terrible. But I had to show him what I'd found.

"Just come with me," I urged, lightly tugging his sleeve.

He drew back. "Why?"

"Because . . ." I hesitated. Then I took a deep breath and told him, "A potential weapon in Lauren's murder—an object I hadn't even considered before—has shown up, out of the blue, and is rolling around just outside the door."

Chapter 58

"Well, Daphne, I honestly think this place might be a success," my mother said, sipping coffee while I used ribbon to tie my newly printed business cards to little carob-dipped peanut-butter Barkin' Good Bones that I planned to hand out at the Cardboard Iditarod. Mom and Piper had stopped by Flour Power, which was ready for its grand opening in two days, and I couldn't help feeling proud of the space. The retro sunburst light fixture glowed over the cash register, the hardwood floors were gleaming, and the glass case was nearly filled with treats. Artie kept jumping up to sniff the display, leaving drool marks that I needed to wipe off, and I caught Socrates surreptitiously checking out the tempting selections now and then, too. "It's very nice, dear," Mom added, looking around and nodding with approval. "Evocative of the early seventies, without being kitschy or cliché."

Piper and I exchanged surprised glances, and I didn't even dare to thank Mom, for fear that she'd realize she'd offered me a compliment and quickly find something to criticize.

"I can't believe you're running two businesses," Piper said, joining me at the counter and picking up one of the promotional cards. Although she probably also meant to compliment me, her comment was a bit disparaging. "And one of your enterprises *isn't* run out of a van," she added, flipping the card back and forth. One side featured Flour Power's logo, and the other advertised Lucky Paws. "I guess you're really settling down."

The thought of being tied to one place—even a place as great as Sylvan Creek—sometimes caused my chest to tighten, the way it did when I was in any enclosed space, but I was also happy to be putting down roots. Still, I reminded Piper, "I'm only leasing this space. I didn't buy the building. And Lucky Paws is still my primary business." I glanced at my one admittedly kitschy piece of décor: a classic 1970s clock shaped like a cat, with rolling eyes and a swinging tail. "I have to walk Martha Whitaker's bloodhound this afternoon, and I'll be taking care of Mayor Holtzapple's Pomeranian, Pippin, again next week, too."

"Oh, that silly little dog." Mom sniffed derisively.

I suspected that Mom's disdain was still directed more toward the mayor than her pet.

"Speaking of dogs, how is Bernie doing with Detective Black?" Piper asked, wisely changing the subject before our mother could start complaining about Sylvan Creek's leadership. "And has there been any progress in finding his home, now that his collar's turned up?"

"No, no one has claimed Bernie yet," I said, tying

yet another card to one of the bones, which were made with peanut butter and whole wheat flour. "And I guess he's getting along with Jonathan. Although Bernie's slobber is a bit of an issue, from what I understand."

"That is so strange about the camera in Bernie's barrel," Piper noted. "I read the article in the *Gazette*."

My hands, trying to knot yet another ribbon, froze in place. "Gabriel ran a story already?"

"Yes," my mother confirmed. Apparently, reading the *Gazette* was becoming a habit for my mother and sister. I held my breath, waiting for Mom to snap at me about entering Lauren's apartment again. But she simply said, "It was a rather interesting article."

I breathed a sigh of relief. Obviously Gabriel hadn't written anything about me, and I made a mental note to thank him for honoring my request.

"I was more interested in his coverage of Victor Breard's murder," Piper added, reaching for one of the treats and a piece of ribbon. She'd already helped me assemble a few of my giveaways, and her knots were, not surprisingly, surgically precise. "I'm still ambivalent about Gabriel, but it's kind of nice having a real journalist in town, writing about actual news."

I'd been so busy that I hadn't picked up the latest issue of the *Gazette*. But I was curious about his coverage of the recent homicides. "Did he report anything new about either of the murders?"

"Only that Vonda Shakes has decided that Victor *wasn't* killed by Khan," Piper said. "The official cause of death is blunt force trauma, just like in Lauren's case."

I accidentally snapped one of the fragile dog

cookies in two and dropped the pieces down for Artie, who gobbled them up. "That's pretty interesting."

Piper must've seen the wheels turning in my head as I linked the two murders, because she was quick to add, "Detective Doebler hasn't said that the two crimes are related." She shrugged. "Beyond that, Gabriel's recent coverage mainly recounted the events that took place at Big Cats of the World, the day of Victor's death."

"That was a nice quote from you, Piper," Mom said with a smile, patting my sister's hand. "You were very well-spoken when you explained how you tranquilized that beast." She turned to me, adding glumly, "And, of course, there was a brief mention of how you *found another body*."

I didn't even acknowledge her comment, or remind her that Socrates and I could've been killed that day. I was too shocked to learn that my circumspect sister had agreed to speak to Gabriel on the record.

"Gabriel interviewed *you*?" I asked Piper. "And you let him?"

"Yes." Piper answered both questions with one word. She placed a neatly tied card and bone on the growing pile of treats. "I knew he'd mention that I was at the scene, and I wanted to explain my role in my own words. I didn't need him printing something about how I 'shot' Khan. I can't have my reputation as someone who *protects* animals compromised."

I understood Piper's concern. And, I had to admit, the fact that she'd felt compelled to make sure Gabriel didn't sensationalize her actions again undermined my fragile trust in Sylvan Creek's new reporter.

I was also surprised that Gabriel hadn't tried to convince me to talk, since Socrates and I had found Victor's body. But I was okay with being overlooked.

"Did the article say anything about a bottle?" I asked, picking up a pair of scissors and cutting a few more pieces of ribbon. "A blue water bottle?"

The puzzled expressions on Piper's and Mom's faces answered that question.

"A bottle?" Mom echoed me. "Why in the world would he mention a bottle? Victor Breard wasn't poisoned!"

"It's nothing," I said, averting my gaze. Piper was peering at me, and I could tell that she knew I was withholding information. I started to gather up the treats. "Forget I said anything."

"Well, it's too late for that now," my mother noted. "What in the world are you talking about?"

I hesitated. "If I tell you, you can't tell another soul."

Piper didn't bother making any promises. She never spread rumors.

And Mom drew back, clearly insulted. "I don't go about gossiping, Daphne. A Realtor must be incredibly circumspect."

My mother had more faults than she had silk scarves in her walk-in closet, but she was discreet.

I checked with Socrates, who shook his head, like he nevertheless thought I should stay quiet.

I ignored his advice, because I really wanted to hear what Piper, in particular, would say when I told her and Mom, "When Socrates and I ran from the van to Victor's gift shop, Socrates jumped over a very distinctive blue bottle, which somebody had dropped in the parking lot."

Piper knit her brows. "And this is significant because . . . ?"

"The water is a special imported brand called Eau de Vaucluse." I felt kind of guilty, but I explained, "It's only available at Epicure, and I've only seen one person around here drink it."

"Who?" Mom asked. I could tell that she was still skeptical.

"Elyse Hunter-Black," I said quietly, although there was no one around. "I saw her drink it at her house— and at the lake, the night of Lauren's murder." I pictured the blue glass. "And the bottle looks pretty hefty. . . ."

Piper's eyes widened. "You think *Elyse* could've hit Lauren over the head with a bottle?"

My mother waved her hand dismissively. "That's ridiculous, Daphne. Elyse Hunter-Black is a successful, composed, and charming woman. She would not go around knocking people out with imported water."

"I don't really think so, either," I agreed. "I just think it looks bad for Elyse. But you're right. I don't believe she's a killer."

Piper, always rational, wasn't so quick to overlook hard facts. She spoke thoughtfully. "And, yet, the presence of an unusual bottle at two murder scenes *is* strange."

I knew that Jonathan agreed. I'd seen his face grow pale, for the first time I could remember, when I'd shown him the discarded bottle of Eau de Vaucluse, which he'd immediately recognized as the brand Elyse drank. Then he'd reluctantly gone to tell Detective Doebler. . . .

I was getting lost in that memory, when all at once Artie ran to the door and started to yip like crazy. Looking through the glass, I saw that someone was standing outside Flour Power, his hand cupped around his eyes as he tried to see into the bakery.

"It's pretty obvious I'm not open yet," I noted, even as I rose to open the door. I looked down at Socrates, who also seemed confused. "Can't he see the sign, with the hours?"

Then, before anyone could answer me, I gently nudged aside Artie, spun the lock on the door, and swung it open, only to discover not a customer, but a delivery man from the local florist's shop, Betty's Bouquets.

"Are you Daphne Templeton?" he inquired, stepping backward, because Artie was bopping up and down at his feet, trying to get his attention.

"Yes . . . ?" I sounded uncertain about my own identity. I wasn't used to getting flowers.

"Here." He handed me a colorful bunch of daisies and chrysanthemums, arranged with lacy sprigs of baby's breath.

"Thank you," I said, as he hurried back to his van, probably to escape Artie.

"What a lovely gesture," Mom said approvingly, after I'd closed the door and turned around. "Flowers are always an appropriate way to wish a new business owner success."

"I guess so," I agreed. To be honest, I wasn't a huge fan of cut flowers. I set the vase on the counter, finding room among the scattered dog treats. Then I stepped back and cocked my head. "They are pretty, I suppose."

Piper reached out to grab a card that was tucked into the bouquet. "Who are they from?"

Socrates was also intrigued. He'd inched closer and raised his muzzle to give me a curious look.

"Here, let me." I plucked the envelope from Piper's fingers. Not that I thought the message would be private. In fact, when I took out the card, I read aloud. *"Best wishes for success with your new business . . ."* Then I skipped a line and went straight to the slanting signature. *"Gabriel."*

"Well, that's very nice," Mom said. I could tell that Gabriel Graham had just risen a few notches in her estimation.

Artie also seemed to approve of the gesture. His tail whipped back and forth.

However, Piper still seemed skeptical. And Socrates wandered off, clearly not won over by Gabriel's gift. Which was exactly why I hadn't read the second line. *"Join me for a pre-opening celebration dinner tonight?"*

Sticking the card in the back pocket of my jeans, I lifted the vase again and began to carry the bouquet to the kitchen. "I guess I should make sure these have enough water. . . ."

All at once, as I thought about the futility of watering flowers that would die in a few days, at most, I jerked to a halt, my mind racing.

The spider plant on the counter in Lauren's apartment.
A houseful of well-tended "friends."
A gnawed bone in a home without a dog . . .

"Could you please watch Socrates and Artie for a

while?" I asked Piper, seemingly out of the blue. "I need to go somewhere. Right away."

My mother and Piper both gave me quizzical looks. "What is the rush?" Mom demanded. "Where are you going?"

"Skiing," I told her and Piper. "I need to go skiing again. Now!"

Chapter 59

I wasn't much better on skis the second time around, but I did have the good sense to stop by the Bear Tooth State Park ranger station and pick up a trail map—after finally getting myself one of those Snow-Capped Funnel Cakes with vanilla pudding and powdered sugar, to fuel my adventure. The fact that I didn't have a Saint Bernard deliberately misleading me all over creation probably also helped me arrive at the top of Big Drop trail's aptly named hill within a reasonable amount of time.

"Here goes," I muttered, resisting the irrational urge to close my eyes as I pushed the tips of my skis over the lip of the steep rise.

Moments later, I was flailing, falling, and ultimately skidding on my butt—while screaming—as I hurtled downward, the pine trees on either side of me whizzing by in a green blur.

"Help!" I cried to no one in particular, right before I did shut my eyes tight. Wincing, I braced for impact with a tree or rock, only to feel myself gradually slow down when I veered off the trail into deeper snow near the bottom of the rise. Then, still sitting on my skis and dragging my poles, I skidded to a very ungraceful stop and fell backward, grateful to be alive.

A few moments later, I dared to open my eyes and realized, with a start, that someone was standing over me. A person who looked down with an expression of concern on my behalf, mingled with fear and maybe a touch of guilt.

"Hey, Mr. Pottinger," I said, without even trying to rise. I wasn't sure if I'd broken anything yet. He didn't greet me, so I added, "You probably know that I'm here to ask you why you broke into Lauren's apartment, right?"

Chapter 60

"How did you know it was me?" Mr. Pottinger asked as we walked through the woods toward his house. I'd left my skis right where I'd crash-landed, and I limped along in Piper's boots, while Mr. Pottinger seemed oblivious to the fact that snow had to be getting into his old brown shoes, which were full of holes. He shifted to look at me quizzically. "Even if you knew how to find fingerprints, I tried to wipe 'em all off the collar." He frowned. "Did them kids finally say something . . . ?"

That was the second time he'd mentioned "kids," and I still didn't know whom he was talking about. "Kids?" I asked. "What kids?"

"Nobody," he muttered, looking down at his feet. "Just tell me how you figured out I had somethin' to do with the camera."

"I was mainly guessing, based upon what I observed when I went to Lauren's apartment," I admitted. I probably should've been scared to confront him, but I was pretty sure that he was harmless. Mixed up in a bad situation, somehow, but not violent himself.

"Clearly, whoever had planted the collar—no pun intended—had taken time to water the spider plant. I started thinking about how you called your plants 'friends' and took such good care of them."

"Lots of people take care of plants," Mr. Pottinger reminded me.

We'd reached his shack, and as I stepped up onto the sagging porch, I noticed that he'd left his door open again, no doubt because the woodstove was cranking out an excess of heat. Peeking quickly inside the house, I saw the tangle of well-tended foliage. "Not many people love plants quite as much as you," I observed. He gestured for me to take a seat on one of the overturned buckets, and I obliged, happy to rest for a few minutes. "I kept thinking about Bernie, too. How he ran right to your house and seemed so excited to see you. So comfortable to be here. And you had that half-chewed bone, too, just waiting for a dog . . ." I shrugged. "I put that all together and figured Bernie really does belong to you." I watched Mr. Pottinger as he sat down on the other makeshift seat. He moved slowly and shakily, his age showing. "You must miss him."

"I do miss Bubba," he said, surprising me by using a different name for the Saint Bernard. I'd come to believe he'd always been "Bernie." And Mr. Pottinger shocked me more when he added, "But he's not really my dog."

I cocked my head. "No?"

"Well, I have been taking care of him for a few weeks," he said. "Since he showed up, out of the blue, back in December."

I nearly fell off my wobbly seat. "Are you saying that

a *Saint Bernard* materialized in the woods near Lake Wallapawakee—just like the legend says?"

Mr. Pottinger nodded. "Yes, at first I was half scared, thinking a ghost had come to life. Because I *have* seen the ghost dog." His leathery, lined face grew pale. "I thought it was a bad omen. That someone . . . maybe me . . . was gonna *die*."

He still looked spooked by the memory, and I had to prompt him to keep talking. "But . . . ?"

He shrugged. "Time passed, and nothing happened. I started to think maybe somebody dumped Bubba in the woods, to get rid of him—and as a joke. He can make a mess, and what better place to get rid of a Saint Bernard than in a forest known to be haunted by one?"

"Yeah, I see what you mean," I agreed. "He does drool, and he takes up a lot of space. And somebody with a twisted sense of humor might have gotten a kick out of stirring up the old legend."

Mr. Pottinger smiled crookedly. "You know, Bubba's really a smart dog. He knows all kinds of tricks. Fetch, sit, stay. I even taught him how to retrieve a duck or a rabbit, so he could help me when I went hunting."

I was impressed, because Saint Bernards weren't traditionally hunting dogs. However, I wasn't there to talk about Bernie's hidden talents. "Um, was Bernie . . . er, Bubba . . . wearing the collar with the barrel on it when you found him? And why haven't you come forward to claim him?"

Mr. Pottinger grew guarded. "I don't know if I should tell you. I don't want to get in trouble."

I'd skied a long, treacherous way in hopes of solving the mysteries surrounding Bernie, and I was practically dying for answers. "Just tell me the rest of the story," I urged. "I promise, I won't go to the police, unless you tell me, outright, that you killed Lauren Savidge." He jolted, clearly alarmed, and I raised a hand, trying to calm him by quickly adding, "But I don't believe you did that. You looked far too shocked when I told you she'd been murdered."

"I wasn't shocked," he said softly, looking off into the woods. "I was just sick. I'd hoped it was an accident. . . ."

My heart started racing. "The dog, the collar, and the murder . . . They really are tangled up together, aren't they?"

"I think so." Mr. Pottinger's face was ashen, and his voice trembled when he whispered, "It was all supposed to go differently. . . ."

"What was?"

Mr. Pottinger finally looked me in the eye again, and I saw that he was miserable. "It all started when those kids, Joy Doolittle and the cameraman . . ."

"Kevin Drucker," I reminded him, leaning forward. It was cold outside, but my palms were getting sweaty. I tried to calm down. "What about them?"

"One day, when I was helping set up for Winterfest, they showed up at the lake, saying that Lauren Savidge wanted them to film me. Wanted me to tell the legend for that show they're making." He shrugged again. "I don't know much about TV—don't even own one, like I said. And I'd already told Ms. Savidge, right to her face, that I wasn't interested."

It was difficult for me to imagine Joy Doolittle being forceful, but I ventured, "Joy wouldn't take no for an answer, though, huh?"

Mr. Pottinger shook his head. "No. She told me she'd be in big trouble if I didn't 'help her out.' And she's such a wee, timid thing, while Ms. Savidge really did seem like somebody who'd lose her temper . . ."

Was Joy really timid? Or did her shy persona mask a manipulative side? I was starting to wonder. I couldn't speculate right then, though, and I let Mr. Pottinger continue.

"Well, I told the story, just the way I always do," he said. "But Ms. Doolittle still wasn't happy. Not so much with me, I guess. But with her boss. She kept complaining that there was no 'footage,' and that it wouldn't make sense to just show an old man talking." He laughed. "She called me that, right in front of my face. Not that I don't know I'm old!"

"So what happened?"

The brief flicker of amusement that I'd seen in his eyes disappeared. "Both her and Kevin started grumbling about Lauren. Talking about how she thought she was still at something they called 'Real Crime,' and mumbling about how she was going to mess up their chance to work at a better network." He shook his head. "It was mainly gibberish to me. But I understood that they wanted to get film of the ghost dog, to show during my story. I've *seen* TV, even if I don't own one."

My heart was pounding in my chest. He'd just told me that Joy, especially, had even more motive to kill Lauren. As part of Lauren's team, Joy might've lost her job, too, if Lauren had gotten fired for failing to create a show that fit the Stylish Life brand. But with Lauren out of the way, Joy's job was not only safe, she'd earned a promotion.

And Kevin had obviously been unhappy with Lauren, too.

I edged my seat closer to him. "You offered to let them film Bubba, didn't you?"

"Yes," he told me, rubbing his hands on his stained pant legs. A nervous gesture. "I almost didn't say anything 'cause I was thinking that maybe I'd keep Bubba a secret until Winterfest. Then use him during my walks. I was sure I could train him to show up if I whistled, then disappear again."

"Surely somebody knew about Bubba," I said, interrupting his story. "Somebody must've seen him before."

"Nope." Mr. Pottinger shook his head. "I only go into town a few times a year. Hadn't left the woods from Christmas until it was time to set up for Winterfest. I always help with that."

He jerked his head, gesturing inside the house. "Got most of what I need to live right in there."

I could believe that. I could see all of his canned goods, and he'd mentioned hunting, too.

"You can imagine that Joy and Kevin were pretty happy when I told them about Bubba," he continued. "They wanted to come all the way here to meet him." He grew thoughtful, his focus turning inward. "And when they saw how smart he was, and how I'd trained him, they came up with this plan. . . ."

I was pretty sure he'd forgotten I was there. "What plan?" I prompted, nearly falling off my seat again.

Mr. Pottinger snapped back to reality. "They thought it would be 'great TV'. . ." The phrase sounded funny coming from his mouth. "To actually show the 'ghost dog' rescuing somebody, with some of the video taken from a dog's-eye view." He frowned at the memory. "It sounded loony to me. But, like I said, what do I know about TV?"

I fought to keep my voice low and even. "What did they ask you to do?"

"They wanted me to keep staying quiet about Bubba for a few more days. Until the night of the crazy swim at the lake. Then, that evening, they would give me a special collar to put around his neck."

"Did you know it would have a camera?"

"Yes," he admitted. "I was supposed to put the camera on him and bring him to the edge of the woods. Get as close to the water as possible without being seen."

Mr. Pottinger was starting to sound hoarse and haunted, like the story was strangling him. But I let him keep telling it.

"Joy was signed up for the plunge," he continued. "She was supposed to go in with Lauren, while Kevin filmed dogs that took part. At least, that's what Lauren thought."

"But Kevin wasn't really focused on the few dogs who swam that night, right?"

Mr. Pottinger twisted his gnarled hands. "No. The plan was, once everybody ran into the water, Joy would thrash around and call for help."

"What was supposed to happen next?" I asked.

Mr. Pottinger frowned. "I'd release Bubba, commanding him to retrieve."

I was confused. "How would Bubba know where to go, in a crowded lake?"

"We'd worked on it, one day, right here," he explained. "Trained Bubba to run to Joy and pull her to 'safety'—out of a snow bank—at the cues 'help' and 'retrieve.' He caught on right away." Mr. Pottinger beamed with pride for a moment. "I'd told Joy and Kevin that Bubba knew how to get ducks in water, and was sure smart enough to 'save' a person in a lake. To be honest, I didn't even think I'd have to give a command. Bubba's a protective dog. I fell in the woods once. Twisted my ankle, bad. And he helped me home. Wouldn't leave my side. I knew that, if Joy really acted like she needed help, he'd rescue her. The whole thing seemed harmless enough."

I was dying to hear what happened next, but a question kept nagging at me. "And Lauren honestly didn't know about this plan?"

Mr. Pottinger blanched again. "No. Joy said, if it didn't work, Lauren would never let her live it down. Maybe even fire her. From what I gathered, Joy had gotten in trouble before for trying out different ideas."

"I see," I muttered, thinking that now Joy would be able to think outside the box whenever she wanted. Try new things all the time. Then I forced myself to focus on the conversation and asked another question that was bugging me. "Who was supposed to turn on the camera?"

"Me." Mr. Pottinger pointed to himself. "Kevin gave me a little black doohickey. I was supposed to press a button, right before I released Bubba." He swallowed thickly. "But everything went wrong."

I scooched back farther, giving him more room. I was pretty sure that he was about to name Lauren Savidge's killer, and my heart was in my throat, but I tried to sound casual. "How so?"

"The swimming party . . . It was more crowded

than I think anybody expected. I couldn't even find Joy and Lauren when everybody rushed into the water. I couldn't see what was happening. But Bubba—and me—heard *someone* cry for help, above all the other noise. And it didn't sound like Joy."

I wondered if that person had been *me*.

"Like I'd expected, I didn't even give him a command," Mr. Pottinger continued. "Bubba just tore free of me and went running. I didn't click the doohickey, either. I could tell that something had gone wrong when other people started screaming, too, and I dropped the little device in the woods. My fingers just fell open when I saw Bubba drag that poor girl out of the water, and I started to back away, not sure what I'd just been part of . . ." His voice was a thin whisper. "When Bubba ran back to me, I took the collar and, as soon as the sun came up, shooed him away, thinking he really did bring death to the forest." He buried his face in his hands. "What have I done?"

"What happened to Lauren—that *wasn't* your fault," I assured him, although he had exercised bad judgment, teaming up with Joy and Kevin for a risky stunt. And he shouldn't have pushed poor Bernie away. But I didn't think he'd done anything criminal. Unless he'd seen more than he was telling me, the night of the plunge. Because I could imagine Joy running into the water, and suddenly seeing an opportunity to eliminate a boss who'd verbally abused her, dismissed her ideas and stood in the way of her possible promotion. Edging closer to Mr. Pottinger again, I rested one hand on his shoulder until he raised his eyes to meet mine. "You're *sure* you didn't see anything?"

He shook his head, which was covered by a threadbare knit cap. "Not a thing. It was crazy at the lake. You know how it was."

Yes, I remembered the scene all too vividly.

"Why did you really do it?" I asked, with a glance at his home. He lived so simply, and he seemed content with his solitude. It was hard to imagine the old man who sat across from me being lured by money or the "glamour" of television. "Why would you even take part in their stunt?"

Mr. Pottinger hung his head. "I didn't think any harm would come from it. And they said they could help me get my book published, too. That they had lots of connections." His voice was almost a whisper. "I want my story told, Daphne. I *am* an old man, and I don't have long here."

My heart was breaking for him, but he needed to do the right thing. I dared to reach out and squeeze his hand. "You have to tell the police everything you just told me. You know that you do."

He drew back, his expression guarded. "I don't like the government. . . ."

I shook my head. "No, you have to come forward."

"It's not just the government," he said, pulling free of my grip. All at once, I saw fear in his eyes again. "What if those kids *killed* that young lady? What if they lied to me, and planned all along to murder her, and get it on film. I know some people make movies like that! What if I turn them in and they come after *me*?"

I wasn't sure how a man who lived alone in the woods knew about snuff films, but he was genuinely scared. And, I had to admit, as I thought about Joy and Kevin's plan, I couldn't help wondering if Joy, at least, had ended up doing more than just fake an accident, that night.

"If you honestly suspect that Joy or Kevin might've committed murder, you really need to talk to the police," I told Mr. Pottinger. "You know it's the right thing to do. Your conscience is eating at you. If it wasn't, you would've just tossed the collar in the woods. Made it disappear forever. But you left it somewhere it would be found."

His voice shook. "I couldn't give it back to those kids. I don't want to see them again. But you're right." He buried his face in his hands again. "I feel so guilty every day. I was afraid if I tossed that collar in the woods, I'd never feel at peace here again."

I stood up to go. "Then tell the police. Go to Detective Doebler. He's pretty nice." I hesitated, then offered, "I could even go with you."

Mr. Pottinger raised his face, and I saw that he was near tears. "You'd do that?"

"Sure." I already had a pretty packed schedule, but I smiled encouragingly. "I'd be happy to."

We took a moment to figure out a time that we could both go to the police station; then I stepped off the porch into the snow. I was a little bit worried about my legs, which had gotten stiff while I'd been sitting awkwardly on the low bucket. And a light snow was falling as the sun began to set. I'd need to hurry home. But as I went to retrieve my skis, I asked Mr. Pottinger one last question. "So you really don't know where Bubba came from? He really just showed up, out of the blue?"

I could barely see Mr. Pottinger in the increasing gloom. He was just a shadow under the sagging porch roof. And his voice was muffled by the snow, which was falling faster, when he answered me.

"I really don't know where he belongs," he said. "And I don't know, now, if I ever want to see him again. I love that dog, but I think he just brings . . . death!"

Chapter 61

It was dark by the time I crested the small rise at the trailhead and Tail Waggin' Winterfest came into view. There was only one evening left to enjoy the festival, and the grounds were crowded. The cute blue shacks were all busy with patrons, and dogs romped in the snow amid the glowing lanterns.

I was starving, and as I released my boots from the skis' bindings I debated whether to buy another funnel cake.

Although I'd promised Mr. Pottinger that I wouldn't contact the police before we went to the station together the very next day, I also kept trying to decide whether I should talk to Jonathan. He *was* taking care of Bernie, and he probably deserved to know that I'd located the dog's last caretaker, even if Max also considered Bernie a lost dog and wasn't sure he wanted to see him again.

"I think I'll just sleep on that information," I muttered. "It's not like Jonathan will hike into the woods tonight to return the dog."

As least, I didn't think he'd do that.

Then, as I bent to pick up the skis, I started thinking again about everything that Joy had probably gained now that Lauren was out of the way.

A promotion. Freedom from an irascible boss who stifled her creativity. And almost certainly a raise.

But was there still a chance that the whole thing had been an accident?

The result of a plan that had been flawed to begin with, and had gone awry in a cold, crowded lake . . . ?

I was still deep in thought when I realized that my cell phone was pinging in my coat pocket, alerting me to messages that had probably been delayed while I'd skied in the remote forest, where I doubted there was service.

Dropping the skis again, I pulled my phone out of my pocket and tapped the screen, being careful to shield it from the falling snow.

The first text was from Piper, who had, of course, typed in her precise, grammatical, and perfectly punctuated way.

I took Socrates and Artie back to Plum Cottage. Tinkleston seems to have behaved in your absence. Nothing appeared to be broken.

"Well, that's good," I muttered, as my stomach growled loudly.

Ignoring my hunger pangs, I opened the next message, from Moxie, who had texted me a photo of Sebastian, wearing a tiny cowboy hat and a vest.

"Well, I'll be," I said, smiling. "He actually looks kind of cute!"

Then I closed out that text and tapped the screen one more time. Whoever had sent the message wasn't in my contacts, and I wasn't sure I recognized the number. But I could easily identify the sender based upon context.

You didn't respond re: dinner. Offer still stands.

And, just to make sure I knew that he wasn't upset or offended, Gabriel Graham had added an emoji. A bright yellow smiley face with a very devilish wink.

Chapter 62

"Are you hungry, Daphne?" Gabriel asked, grinning. He was laughing at me because I had just crammed half of a basil spring roll with hoisin peanut sauce into my mouth, after polishing off a plateful of lemongrass tofu skewers. I had agreed to join him at Bamboo, a little Thai restaurant on the outskirts of Sylvan Creek. From the outside, Bamboo looked like a shack. But whenever I stepped inside, I felt like I'd been magically transported back to Thailand. The walls were hung with elaborately patterned tapestries featuring elephants and lotuses, brightly colored paper mobiles dangled from the ceiling, and candles glowed on each of the teakwood tables. The food was also amazing and, starving after my day of skiing, I couldn't seem to stop eating. "Easy, there, Daphne," Gabriel cautioned when I gobbled up the second half of the spring roll. His eyes twinkled with amusement. "Don't choke!"

I didn't mind that he was teasing me. I knew that I was eating with too much gusto. But, as I wiped my fingers on a deep red cloth napkin, I couldn't help thinking that Gabriel *always* seemed to be making fun of—and provoking—me.

I leaned forward, folding my arms on the table and looking him in the eye. "Can I ask you something?"

He set the sweet chili chicken wing he'd been eating onto his plate and wiped his fingers, too. He seemed guarded. "I suppose."

"Why have you asked me to dinner twice? And invited me to take the tour at Big Cats of the World? Is it because you think I'm in some competition with you to solve Lauren Savidge's murder, and you want to pick my brain?" I felt my cheeks getting warm, because if he had no romantic interest in me, I was probably about to embarrass myself. Still, I asked, "Or do you have a more personal reason for asking me out?"

"I did want to ask you about everything that happened during your second visit to Breard's zoo," he admitted. "And I'd like to know why you went back there alone. I'm sure you were following up on something you noticed when we took the tour." He smiled again, but it was an out-of-character, almost sheepish grin. "But I also just like you, Daphne Templeton. You stand up to me, which most people don't do. And I think you're uniquely pretty and uniquely . . . you." He rested his arms on the table and leaned forward, too, growing more serious. "I thought I'd made my interest in you pretty clear."

In a way he had. He'd taken me to Sylvan Creek's most romantic restaurant, and I was pretty sure he'd tried to kiss me on two separate occasions. But he'd also acted like a schoolboy who pulls a girl's pigtails by printing that awful photo of me in the *Gazette* and sparking one real argument.

And, although I couldn't deny that I found Gabriel attractive—he looked very handsome that night in a cream-colored sweater that accentuated his dark skin and eyes—I didn't like that I couldn't trust him. I would've liked to tell him all about my sad, frightening misadventure at Big Cats of the World, and everything I'd just learned about Bernie, too. I was pretty sure he'd be able to offer some interesting insights into Victor's murder and Max Pottinger's confession about being at the lake the night of Lauren's death. But, while he hadn't mentioned me in his article about Bernie's collar, I still wasn't convinced that Gabriel would keep everything that I could tell him about Mr. Pottinger, especially, in confidence. Nor was I sure that he was being open and honest with me about other things.

I'd already asked some pretty blunt questions, but all at once, I narrowed my eyes and leaned even farther across the table, the better to see his reaction when I inquired, point-blank, "What happened in Philadelphia, Gabriel? Why did you leave the *Inquirer*—and what, exactly, happened to the last woman you dated *there*?"

Chapter 63

"How much do you already know?" Gabriel asked. He averted his gaze for a moment while our server placed his entrée, red curry mussels, on the table. I thought he was relieved to have a moment to re-group. I seemed to have caught him off guard with my very direct questions. The waiter set my vegetarian curry in front of me, and I was also momentarily dis-tracted by the sight of colorful carrots, eggplant, and peppers and the aroma of ginger, garlic, and Kaffir lime. I couldn't wait to eat, and I picked up a fork as Gabriel pointed out, "You must have already done some digging, or you wouldn't have asked that second question about my former girlfriend."

"I did do some research," I admitted, after swal-lowing a bite of the curry. The dish was just spicy enough, and the crisp vegetables were a bright con-trast to the rich, creamy coconut milk in the silky orange sauce. "But only because you invited me to do that."

He arched one eyebrow, like he didn't believe me.

Then he must've recalled our conversation, because his shoulders relaxed and he laughed. "Yes, I did say you should Google me, didn't I?" He shook his head and poked a fork into one of the mussel shells. "I should learn to keep my mouth shut."

"Gabriel . . ." I set down my utensil, my appetite suddenly dulled. "Did you leave the *Inquirer*—and Philadelphia—because—"

"I left after Sarah Bankman's murder," he said, correctly assuming that I would recognize his former girlfriend's name. He was staring down at his plate, possibly to hide his emotions from me. At least, I hoped that was why he wouldn't look me in the eye. I hoped it wasn't because he was hiding the truth. But when he finally did raise his face, I saw that he was genuinely sad, and maybe a bit angry. "When the case was deemed cold—unresolved, for now—I couldn't take the suspicious stares of my colleagues anymore. And I wasn't quite so enamored of the city anymore. Or my beat, covering crime."

"You don't have to say more," I assured him. His mood had changed abruptly. He was agitated, picking at his food without eating anything. "I probably read enough—"

"To suspect me of murder," he interrupted again. His lips twisted into a bitter smile. "Funny how *you* can find bodies and nobody assumes you killed anyone. But I find myself alone with one victim, and suddenly I'm a killer."

"I never had motive . . ." I started to defend myself; then I changed my mind. Gabriel didn't really want to compare his circumstances to mine. I suspected that he wanted to tell his side of the story. Clear his name, at least with me. "Maybe you should talk to me," I suggested gently. "I would like to hear the story directly from you."

He'd finally taken a bite of his meal, and he watched me as he chewed. I got the sense that he was trying to decide whether I'd really listen, or if I'd already made up my mind about his guilt or innocence. And he must've seen that I hadn't judged him. Yet.

"Fine." He nodded and rested his fork next to his plate. "Sarah was a colleague of mine. And, obviously, more. We both covered crime in Philly. The worst stuff. Homicides, arson, domestic violence. Sometimes we even teamed up." He smiled faintly at a memory. "Sarah was a relentless digger." The smile faded. "At the time of her death, she was working quietly on her own, on a very hush-hush story. Something about the Harriman family." He paused and raised his eyebrows. "You know the name, right?"

I nodded. "Yes, everybody in Pennsylvania knows all about the Harrimans. They've been prominent since the state's coal mining heyday, more than a hundred years ago."

"Prominent—and corrupt as hell," Gabriel said. "They always have been, from the days they sent miners into unsafe holes in the ground, setting records for lives lost." He lowered his voice, although no one was listening to us. "And today, they have sketchy connections everywhere, from Congress to every branch of the mob you can imagine."

"So what, exactly, had Sarah uncovered?"

Gabriel shook his head. "I have no idea what her angle was. She would only say that she was on to something new—and big. But before anything could come of her investigation, someone silenced her. Killed her while I was out taking a walk late at night, cooling down—"

"Because you'd argued. I read that."

He nodded. "We were both hardheaded people. We fought quite a bit. And one night, we argued loudly enough for the people in the neighboring apartment to hear. I stormed out, needing to calm down, and when I came back, the place was a mess, and Sarah was lying on the floor. Bleeding from the head . . ."

"I get the picture," I promised him. I had to admit, I was also imagining Lauren Savidge, lying in the sand with a head wound. I hadn't seen the blood, but Jonathan had. And although I would've liked Gabriel to explain himself more, I felt like I'd already pushed him pretty hard. His mouth was drawn down and his eyes appeared tired, like he was sick of the story and the emotions that telling it conjured in him. "It's okay."

But he wasn't quite finished with his tale. "I was never able to find her notes about the Harriman story. And I knew she must've had notebooks full, as well as computer files. And, of course, the neighbors told the police about the argument." I saw a flash of anger in his eyes. "Or someone *paid them* to tell their tale, because they conveniently didn't hear me slam the door and storm down the hall—before someone ransacked the apartment."

My eyes widened. "So you think her murder was part of a conspiracy?"

"I'm sure of that," he said matter-of-factly. He picked up his fork again and began eating. He suddenly seemed to be starving. "I have no doubt. And that's the other reason I left the *Inquirer*. Even after I was cleared, by the skin of my teeth, my editor wouldn't let me *really* dig into Sarah's murder. I decided it was time to run the whole show, even if I could only afford to do that in a small town. For now." He smiled again, but in a way that told me he wasn't really amused. "Funny that I got a murder to investigate, almost right away."

I watched him closely. "Yeah, funny."

Gabriel knew what I was thinking. "I know that Black and Doebler—and probably you—suspect me of killing Lauren *and* Sarah," he said. "But I'm telling you, I'm innocent of both crimes."

"Jonathan's off the case," I noted, neither confirming nor denying my suspicions.

Gabriel snorted. "Sure he is."

I pushed some of the vegetables around on my plate. My stomach suddenly felt funny. "Did you and Jonathan know each other before you moved here?"

"No." Gabriel's tone was clipped. "I just know his type."

"Which is . . . ?"

"The silent war hero, who probably has more secrets than I ever will."

Jonathan did have lots of secrets. But I thought Gabriel was wrong to assume that people only hid things out of guilt or shame. Wasn't it possible that some things were buried just because they were too painful to share? Or because the person was too humble to brag about *good* things he or she had done?

"I think people have all sorts of reasons for staying

quiet about their pasts," I observed. "Did you know that Victor Breard was once arrested for assaulting a poacher and did jail time?"

Gabriel was prying open a mussel, but he looked up at me, frowning. "No, I never even heard a rumor about that, and this town seems to thrive on gossip."

"Like all small towns," I said, defending Sylvan Creek. "Anyhow, Victor might've kept that quiet because he was ashamed—or, conversely, because he didn't want to boast. For all I know, he thought his violence was justified. He did keep a clipping about his arrest."

In the blink of an eye, *I* was the one under a microscope. "How did you end up at the scene of that homicide?" Gabriel asked, popping the mussel into his mouth. He covered his mouth with his hand, chewing while he talked. "You never did explain why you went back to Big Cats of the World."

I took a sip of water from a pretty silver cup with a raised design, stalling while I decided how much to tell Gabriel. "He invited me," I finally admitted, setting down the cup. "While we were all on the tour, and you were distracted, observing Joy Doolittle's odd behavior—"

"You noticed that, too?" Gabriel interrupted. "The way Joy looked at Breard like a teenager with a crush?"

"Yes, I did see that. And they had dinner at Zephyr, too," I reminded him.

He scowled, like he didn't approve of May-December romances. "You don't think . . . ?"

"I don't know." I shrugged and speared some of

the red and yellow peppers. "I wouldn't find it odd or inappropriate, though. Age is just a number."

Gabriel didn't seem convinced. "Let's get back to why Breard invited you to his compound," he suggested.

"Oh, yeah." I'd almost forgotten about our original topic. "I'd seen a picture of Victor at Lauren's apartment," I explained. "A torn clipping, from a magazine. He'd looked very unhappy in the photo. I mentioned the story during the tour, and Victor promised to tell me all about it. And, to my surprise, he did call. But when I got there, the magazine was on a table—and Victor was dead."

"Wow. You couldn't have missed the murder by too long," Gabriel said, reminding me of a fact I kept trying to forget. We'd both finished our meals, and the server laid the bill on the table before clearing away our empty plates. I reached for the check, but Gabriel grabbed it first. "And the article was about the assault on the poacher?"

I nodded. "Yes."

He watched me while he pulled his wallet from his pocket. "Did you notice anything else?"

I paused, then told him, "There was something weird about Victor's golf cart. But I can't figure out what was wrong. It's like one of those puzzles where you try to find the differences between two photos. But the images are both only in my memory, and I can't spot what's changed."

"If you figure it out, give me a call," Gabriel urged, placing his credit card on the table for the server to retrieve. "I'm intrigued."

I didn't make any promises. I kind of feared I'd

already told him too much, without clarifying that anything I said was off the record. And as I drove home, I rehashed his story about his former girl-friend's murder over and over again, still not sure if I believed everything he'd told me.

In fact, I was so deep in thought by the time I reached Winding Hill Farm that I actually yelped with surprise when I hopped out of the van and heard Piper call to me from her dark porch, "Daphne, wait! I have a package for you!"

Chapter 64

I waited until I got to Plum Cottage and had brewed a cup of hot, fragrant Ceylon tea before I opened the package, although the moment I'd seen the return address, I'd started itching to see the contents.

"Please let this be what I hope it is," I said, crossing my fingers and smiling at Socrates, Artie, and Tinkleston, who had obviously coexisted without incident while I was away. The dogs were by the hearth, enjoying the fire I'd just lit, and Tinkleston was curled up on the love seat. He yawned, showing his little fangs and letting me know that he didn't care about the envelope that I was ripping open with eager fingers. Reaching inside, my hand met free-range yak hair, and I pulled out a tiny red sweater with white stripes and a bright yellow button, right on the chest. I held up the gift for the dogs and cat to see. "Is this adorable or what?"

Socrates, who'd stood up when I'd entered the cottage, groaned and collapsed, his eyes rolling back

in his head, while Artie spun like a gleeful canine
tornado, his toenails clicking merrily on the wooden
floor.

Tinkleston merely yawned again.

"Well, Artie, I'm glad you share my excitement," I
said, kneeling down. He ran over to me, his eyes practically popping out of his head, and shivered with
happiness as I put his little paws through the arm-
holes. When he was all dressed, I chucked him under
his recessive chin. "You look *wonderful.*"

I watched him trot off to model his new duds for
his less-than-eager audience; then I stood up and took
the package to the kitchen. Sitting down at the table,
I shook the bubble-wrap envelope until a piece of
paper fluttered out. Squinting at Arlo Finch's shaky,
slanted handwriting, I read the note.

Daphne,

    *Enclosed please find a sweater I knitted for Artie,
during rest stops on my long drive. I used vivid
colors to match his bright and multi-hued aura,
which radiates like a pulsating rainbow. Although
the gift is for the irrepressible Chihuahua, I'm
sending it to thank YOU for believing in me. Your
trust stayed with me during my whole journey to
Arizona, and will buoy me as I begin my new life
here. While I miss Sylvan Creek, I have to say that
this climate and its vibe suit me well, too. I look
forward to spotting my first alien!*

I drew back, not sure if he was kidding. Then I finished reading what little was left of the note.

Namaste, Daphne Templeton!

P.S. I would've gladly knit something for Tinkleston and your most dignified companion, Socrates, too. But Tinkleston will never be tamed enough to wear a sweater. And Socrates . . . Only a toga would suit the reincarnated spirit of an ancient Greek philosopher!

I folded up the letter and looked over at Socrates, who had his nose in the air, pretending not to notice that Artie was strutting around the room, putting on a one-dog fashion show. I also didn't know if Arlo had been joking about Socrates being reincarnated, but I agreed that my favorite canine curmudgeon had an old soul.

Rising, I yawned and stretched, my muscles aching from skiing. Then I glanced at the clock. It was nearly eleven p.m., and I had a big day tomorrow, debuting my treats at the Cardboard Iditarod and making sure that Artie and Bernie were dressed and ready to go at the appointed time—after I took Max Pottinger to the police station.

"Come on, everybody," I said. "Time for bed."

A few minutes later, we were all in the loft, where Socrates lumbered over to his purple velvet pillow and lay down. Artie insisted upon sleeping in his sweater and curled up on a smaller cushion I'd placed near Socrates's bed. When the dogs were settled, I finished getting ready and climbed under my warm down comforter. The night was supposed to be exceptionally cold, with snow arriving after midnight, and I wriggled far under the covers before reaching out one hand to turn off my bedside lamp.

Almost immediately, I felt something land at the foot of the bed, and I started. Then I smiled in the darkness. "Good night, Tinkleston."

He didn't reply, and my home grew quiet, except for the crackling of the fire downstairs and the occasional creak of the cottage's old roof as the wind rose ahead of the storm. Before long, I found myself drifting off to sleep, even though my mind was whirling with questions.

Do I believe Gabriel is innocent?

What was wrong with Victor's golf cart?

Why was the blue bottle at Big Cats of the World?

I had no answers, though, and I was so tired that I soon fell asleep to the sound of the plum tree knocking at the window, telling me that the weather was changing.

And when I awoke, I thought the tree was still rapping—until I realized that the morning was overcast but still, and the knocking noise was coming from *outside my door.*

Chapter 65

Max Pottinger had arrived at my house at the crack of dawn. But by the time I'd taken him to the police station and he'd given a long statement to Detective Doebler, I was running late to get to Tail Waggin' Winterfest, where Moxie was already preparing for the Cardboard Iditarod. And I still had one task to complete before I could head for the spot near the woods where the entrants were assembling.

"I hope Moxie has everything under control," I told Socrates and Artie, as I hoisted a big basketful of Barkin' Good Bones onto a counter that used to hold cute hand-knit pet sweaters, until Arlo Finch had fled town. I'd contacted Mayor Holtzapple, who'd been nice enough to let me use Arlo's vacant booth for the last day of the festival, so I could advertise Flour Power. Along with attaching business cards to the bones, I'd made some flyers announcing my grand opening, and I arranged those near the basket, next to a sign that urged people to help themselves to the pet treats. Then I stepped back, frowning at my display, which looked skimpy. I'd left some of the ribbon-wrapped bones at the bakery, so I'd have something to hand out at my opening event, too. Gnawing my lower lip, I looked down at the dogs. "I also hope I brought enough bones."

Socrates and Artie weren't paying attention to me. Artie was still trying to convince Socrates, with a series of yips and twirls, that dogs should, indeed, wear sweaters, like the colorful one he was still sporting that morning, after sleeping in it all night.

Someone was listening, though.

A person I'd sort of hoped not to run into, after hearing Max Pottinger practically accuse her of murder, in his conversation with Detective Doebler.

I felt my spine stiffen and my stomach drop to my toes when Joy Doolittle stepped up behind me, telling me, "I think those bones will go fast. And I can't wait to film at your bakery tomorrow!"

Chapter 66

"I didn't realize you planned to film tomorrow," I told Joy, who wore her professional-looking wool coat again. Only, this time, she stood a little straighter, so she didn't appear to be drowning in the garment. And her eyes seemed brighter, too, probably because she was wearing eyeliner and eye shadow. Joy had also dusted a touch of pink blush across her normally pale cheeks. It was almost like she was maturing into her new role as field producer in just a few days. And more than her appearance had changed. Joy was acting kind of pushy, too. "No offense, but I don't know if I want you and Kevin at my grand opening," I added, pulling my wool cap down over my ears. The day was pretty cold. "I'm going to be nervous enough without a camera following me around, and the place is small. I want to make sure the customers I *hope* will show up have room to look around."

"Oh, we won't be a nuisance." Joy smiled brightly and gestured for me to look over my shoulder. I turned and saw Kevin Drucker crouching on the ground, getting footage of Artie, who was running circles around one of the ice sculptures, showing off his sweater. Kevin was blocking the footpath, and people looked annoyed as they stepped around him. Joy didn't seem to notice that Kevin was clearly in the way. "See?" she said, as I faced her again. "He's practically invisible when he's behind the camera. You won't even notice us when we *are* at Flour Power tomorrow."

Joy wasn't being abrasive, like Lauren had been, but she was acting very differently from the girl I'd seen trembling on the lakeshore, and I took a moment to look past her makeup and into her eyes. Then I glanced down at Socrates, who was watching Joy with his head tilted, like he also didn't understand how someone could change so dramatically over the course of a week.

I met Joy's gaze again.

Which was the real person?

Had this more assertive Joy been hiding herself, just biding her time until she got her opportunity to be in charge?

Or was the newfound confidence an act, born out of necessity, as Joy tried to fill Lauren's shoes and prove herself?

"It must be a lot of pressure, trying to finish a big project that your boss started and make a bunch of TV executives happy," I said sympathetically, stepping aside so someone could take one of the treats I'd made. I was mainly focused on Joy, but out of the corner of my eye I saw the man read my card and nod approvingly before walking away. "You must be under a lot of strain to wrap up the filming quickly and move on to your next venue, huh?"

The words were barely out of my mouth when I saw

the *real* Joy: a shy, overwhelmed young woman who was trying hard to be a leader, after having her confidence undermined by a tough, abrasive employer.

"It is hard," Joy admitted, speaking more softly. She tucked her hands into her pockets, rounding her shoulders, and the coat suddenly seemed oversized again. She turned pleading, almost desperate, eyes on me. "Can we *please* film tomorrow? Because the network is breathing down my neck. They say we're going over budget here. And I don't even know what our budget is!"

I still didn't want a camera at my grand opening, but I felt sorry for Joy. I wasn't too good with budgets, myself, and employed a newly minted accountant, Fidelia Tuttwciler, to keep my books.

"Sure," I said, as two more people took treats from the basket. I looked over at Kevin, who was still blocking the path, filming while Artie jumped up at the camera, trying to get his close-up. I turned back to Joy and told her, reluctantly, "You guys can come whenever you want."

"Oh, thank you," Joy said, smiling in a more genuine way. "You're doing me a huge favor."

I knew that I should get Artie over to the Iditarod course, which was really just a big circle tramped down in the snow, but I took a moment to study Joy again.

Could she really have killed Lauren?

Because it didn't seem possible, right then— although she'd certainly had motive.

And what sort of relationship had she shared with Victor Breard . . . ?

"Is everything okay?" Joy asked. I must've been staring at her for too long. Her eyes grew round with concern. "You're not changing your mind, are you?"

"No, no," I assured her, with another quick glance at Socrates. He seemed to think I was making a mistake, but I couldn't go back on my promise. I addressed Joy again. "I was just thinking about how, the last time I saw you, we were at Big Cats of the World, and Victor was alive."

The moment I mentioned Victor, all of the color drained from Joy's face, and every last bit of her false front fell away. "Yes, I can't believe he's gone," she said softly.

I knew that Joy's relationship with Victor was none of my business, but I said, "I saw you two at Zephyr. And you seemed to have a special connection, during the tour. Were you two . . . ?"

Two bright red spots formed on Joy's fair cheeks, and I thought she wasn't going to answer me. But she must've been eager for someone to confide in— someone who wasn't a silent cameraman—because she told me, nervously and quietly, "We met that first time, right after Lauren's death, because he wanted a favor." She licked her lips and looked around herself, to see if anyone was listening. When she was convinced that no one was paying attention to us, she added, "Lauren had learned some stuff about his past. About him being arrested for assault, and some other shady things he'd done in the name of rescuing animals. Lauren wanted to make his history public."

I frowned, confused. "How would she have used any of that information in a show about pet-friendly towns?"

"I don't think she could've," Joy agreed. "Lauren was just fascinated with crime. Digging up dirt on people was like a hobby for her. She never should have taken a job with Stylish Life."

"Yes, I get that impression." I tilted my head. "So, did Victor convince you to ignore his past?"

Those little spots of red formed on Joy's cheeks again. "Yes, of course. And by the end of that dinner, we were actually having a really nice time." Although I hadn't said anything disparaging about Victor, Joy seemed to feel the need to defend him. "He was a hero, to animals. He did some things illegally to save them. But his heart was in the right place."

"You really liked him, didn't you?" I asked.

She nodded slowly, like her attraction for the older man confused *her*. "I didn't know him for that long, but, yes, I had developed some feelings for him."

I didn't know what to say. Then I realized that I should probably offer her my condolences. But before I could say anything, Detective Doebler emerged from the crowd, seemingly coming out of nowhere and announcing, quietly but firmly, "You need to come in for questioning, Ms. Doolittle. *Now.*"

I would never forget the shocked, terrified expression on Joy's face as Detective Doebler led her away, followed by Kevin Drucker, who'd been summoned, too. Kevin acted like his usual placid self, but Joy looked back over her shoulder at me, her eyes huge, pleading with me to help her. "What's going on?" I heard her ask, right before she, Detective Doebler, and Kevin were swallowed up by the crowd. "What's happening . . . ?"

All at once, I flashed back to the night of Lauren's murder, when Joy had stood trembling on the lakeshore, and I could finally recall the then-cryptic, muffled phrases she'd kept repeating.

"Bubba and ME . . . It was supposed to be me . . . Bubba and me . . . What's happening . . . ?"

I looked down at Socrates and Artie, who both seemed to understand that something serious had just occurred. Artie was no longer jumping around. He stood stiffly next to a very grave Socrates, both dogs looking up at me for an explanation.

"She's definitely in trouble," I told them. Then, speaking just from my gut instinct, I added, with a confidence that surprised even me, "But I don't think she killed anybody. I think Joy just needs to tell Detective Doebler the truth about the night Lauren died and she'll be fine."

Artie still looked baffled, but Socrates dipped his head twice, like he agreed.

Then the somber mood was broken by the sound of Mayor Holtzapple's cheerful voice over a loudspeaker.

"The Cardboard Iditarod will begin in fifteen minutes!" she announced. "Please join us at the snow track for this favorite Tail Waggin' Winterfest tradition!"

"We'd better hurry," I said, quickly checking my basket of treats. A few more of the bones had disappeared while I'd been absorbed in conversation with Joy, but there was nothing I could do. Moxie was probably going crazy, wondering where Artie was. "Come on," I told both dogs. "Let's get a move on!"

Artie and I trotted through the crowd, while Socrates took his time. I knew he'd catch up with us, and I bent down and scooped up Artie, thinking we could move even faster if I carried him. Plus, he liked to hitch a ride. He bounced happily along in my arms, his mouth hanging open and his tongue flapping over his chin.

It only took us about a minute to reach the track, which was surrounded by a crowd.

Pushing my way through, I quickly found Moxie, who was conversing with Jonathan and Piper next to the cardboard stagecoach, to which Bernie was hitched, like a horse.

I was pretty impressed with our entry—until I spotted another sled that practically made my jaw drop.

Chapter 67

"I've seen a lot of interesting spectacles in my travels, but this is truly . . . something," Jonathan observed, as a parade of costumed pets and people made their slow way around a snowy track. As usual, only a few dogs were actually pulling sleds. Most of the canines were being dragged along by their owners. Jonathan crossed his arms over his chest and tried to frown, but his eyes were twinkling with amusement. "I don't know if this is more humiliating for the dogs—or the humans."

"I'd say the humans," Piper noted. "Tom and Tessie Flinchbaugh look ridiculous!"

I had to agree that the proprietors of Fetch! pet boutique and the Philosopher's Tome looked a little silly in their matching mime costumes. And their ancient, beret-wearing poodle, Marzipan, seemed ashamed to sit on a piece of cardboard next to a really bad replica of the Eiffel Tower. But, for the most part, I found the event charming.

"It's all in good fun," I reminded Jonathan and Piper. "And Moxie looks adorable!"

I waved to my best friend, who wore a plaid shirt, a circle skirt with about ten petticoats, and a white cowboy hat. She waved back as she led Bernie around the track. Sebastian sat on top of the stagecoach, looking cute in his cowboy suit. I'd helped to dress him, and after a few minutes, I'd forgotten about his tail. He was kind of a charmer. And Artie, of course, was winning over the crowd in his outfit. I knew that the Chihuahua would make the front page of the *Weekly Gazette*. Gabriel was following the carriage around, half bent over and holding his big camera up to his face as he snapped picture after picture of the preening pup.

"I guess I will finally dare to ask why Artie is wearing a blue velvet dress," Jonathan said, looking down at me. He was still trying to act like he disapproved, but he was very close to laughing. "Who is he supposed to be?"

"Julia Bulette, a character in an obscure episode of the old TV show *Bonanza*," I informed him.

Jonathan sighed and shook his head. "Of course."

Then we all resumed watching the Iditarod, just as Elyse Hunter-Black entered the course with her two greyhounds, Paris and Milan. I'd thought Moxie was bound to win best overall entry—until I'd seen Elyse's jaw-dropping entry, when I'd first arrived at the track.

Was the fairy-tale coach—a crystal-encrusted, pumpkin-shaped vision straight out of Cinderella—even *cardboard*?

And how had she attached white flowing manes

and tails to the already equine-looking dogs who pulled the sled?

"Elyse created quite an entry," Piper observed, voicing my thoughts. She tucked her gloved hands into the pockets of her warm down jacket. A light snow was beginning to fall from the leaden sky. "Wow."

"Elyse plays to win," Jonathan said. His gaze was trained on the carriage. "No doubt about that."

His expression was suddenly grim, and although I knew it wasn't the right time or place, I tugged his sleeve, compelling him to look down at me again.

"Did you ever hear anything more about the bottle?" I asked quietly. I didn't want Piper to overhear. Not that she was nosy. "Were there fingerprints—?"

"I don't know anything, Daphne," Jonathan interrupted me, also speaking softly. I could tell that he was worried about his ex-wife. "I haven't spoken with Detective Doebler about that since I showed him the bottle. And if Elyse was questioned, she didn't tell me about it."

"Oh." I glanced down to see that Socrates had finally joined us. He'd definitely taken his time, probably hoping that he'd miss the whole event. He got a pained expression on his face when Artie and Sebastian drifted by again, led by Moxie, who did a little do-si-do in front of us. I returned my attention to Jonathan. "Did you know that your partner just led away Joy Doolittle, to question her?"

"No," he said again. "I'm telling you, I have no information about either of the murders. I'm completely out of the loop."

"Then I should probably tell you that Max Pottinger

has been keeping Bernie—whom he calls Bubba," I said, with a quick glance at the Saint Bernard. "He took care of him for weeks, before Lauren's murder."

"What are you talking about?" Jonathan demanded, still whispering. But there was an edge to his voice. "The dog is *Pottinger's?*"

"Yes. And he was part of this scheme, with Joy Doolittle and Kevin Drucker. But I don't think they really did anything wrong . . . I have a different idea. . . ."

I was getting excited, and Jonathan rested a hand on my arm. He looked around, reminding me that we were in public. "This isn't the right place. But we do need to talk. At the very least, I need to know what's happening with the dog."

I was about to suggest that we go someplace more private, perhaps after stopping to buy one last Snow-Capped Funnel Cake before the festival ended, when someone interrupted us, squeezing my other wrist and telling me, in her enthusiastic way, "Daphne! Your basket of treats is completely empty!" Mayor Henrietta Holtzapple made a sad face. "Festivalgoers are walking away disappointed. Don't you have any more of those adorable little bones?"

"Um, yes," I said, pulling free of both Mayor Holtzapple and Jonathan, who seemed unhappy about the interruption. I knew that he was dying to know why he'd been stuck with another man's drooling dog for the last few days. "But the treats are back at my bakery."

"Don't you think you should get some more?" Mayor Holtzapple suggested. "It's such a wonderful opportunity to advertise, and I'm so eager for your bakery to be a success." She smiled. "You know how I hate empty storefronts!"

We were speaking in normal voices again, and Piper leaned around Jonathan, so she could see me. "I think you should listen to Henrietta. You can always give away something else tomorrow. This is an opportunity to market Flour Power to people from all over the Poconos."

I really wanted to stick around Winterfest and celebrate whatever trophy Moxie *would* win for her sled, not to mention talk to Jonathan, but I knew that Mayor Holtzapple and Piper were right.

"Oh, fine," I agreed. I turned to Jonathan. "We'll talk soon, okay?"

He nodded, and after giving Moxie an apologetic wave, I headed for my van with Socrates in tow. He seemed more than eager to leave the Cardboard Iditarod behind, although I doubted he'd ever get the image of Artie in the dress out of his mind.

As I drove back to Sylvan Creek, *I* kept thinking about Joy Doolittle's expression when she'd been led away, and the blue bottle that had been rolling around in the parking lot at Big Cats of the World— as well as Victor Breard's golf cart.

I hardly noticed how quiet the town was until I was opening the door to Flour Power. But as Socrates and I stepped inside the bakery, I got a little spooked. Maybe because the last time we'd been in a dark, silent building, Socrates had found Victor Breard's body. And Sylvan Creek's shopping district was completely, eerily empty on that snowy, late-Sunday afternoon. Even the windows at the *Weekly Gazette* office, across the street, were dark. Which made sense, since I'd last seen Gabriel at Winterfest.

Fighting off the uneasy feeling, I closed the door behind me and Socrates, and the silence seemed even more oppressive. Not unlike the silence at Big Cats of the World, right before Socrates had trotted into the snack bar, compelling me to follow him to the window overlooking Khan's enclosure.

That hollow lack of sound had been in sharp contrast to my first visit to the sanctuary. As I went behind the counter to get more treats, I recalled how Gabriel had complained about the noise of the golf carts. We hadn't been able to hear Victor half the time.

The bakery was warm, and although I didn't intend to stay long, I absently shrugged out of my coat and tossed it onto the counter, still lost in thought.

Victor had apologized, several times, for the fact that we were missing out on information, due to technical difficulties. . . .

All at once, with my hand poised to flip on a light in the kitchen, I sucked in a sharp breath and looked down at Socrates, who'd followed me.

"The murder weapon!" I said, whispering for some reason.

Before I could explain, I heard the front door open, and forgetting about the treats, I turned around, eager to tell Jonathan about my latest revelation.

I'd half expected him to ditch Winterfest in favor of satisfying his curiosity about Bernie, and I stepped past Socrates and rushed to the counter, blurting, "Jonathan! I think I figured out what the killer used to hit Lauren over the head—"

I stopped in midstride, because Jonathan Black hadn't followed me to town.

"Mayor Holtzapple?" I heard the confusion in my voice. "What are you doing here?" Then I glanced at her hand. "And why do you have a *gun*?"

Chapter 68

"I . . . I didn't really run out of treats, did I?" I asked nervously. I dared to take my eyes off Mayor Holtzapple's little pistol for just a moment and looked over my shoulder at Socrates, who was behind me in the kitchen. I doubted that Henrietta had seen him there, and I silently willed him to stay out of sight. I was pretty sure he understood. He stood stock-still, his tail rigid, indicating that he grasped that we were in danger. But his brown eyes were calm as he assessed the situation. As always, he was a soothing presence. Then I quickly turned back around to discover that Mayor Holtzapple had taken a step closer. She was just across the counter from me, and her hand, holding the gun, was remarkably steady. I raised my hands, on instinct, and took a step backward. "You wanted me to come here, didn't you? Where I'd be alone in a storefront in a town that you knew would be nearly empty of people. Because you killed Lauren Savidge—and you were afraid I'd figured it out."

Mayor Holtzapple offered me a regretful smile. "I'm sorry, Daphne. But this is really your fault. You seem to have this knack for solving murders, and when I overheard you talking with Detective Black about the recent homicides plaguing our fair community, I thought I'd better silence you."

I scrunched up my brows. "When and where did you hear . . . ?"

"At Winterfest, the other day," she informed me. "You and Jonathan Black spoke in the parking lot. He warned you not to investigate. But I could tell you had other plans."

I stared at her in disbelief. "*You* were the reason Bernie got so agitated the other night?"

"Yes, I saw you chatting with Detective Black when I hung a sign on Arlo's booth, and I followed you both. Even before then I suspected that I'd have to end your speculation at some point." The corners of her mouth drooped. "Murder has a funny way of snowballing, you know? No Winterfest pun intended!"

I wasn't laughing.

"You killed Lauren with the bullhorn, didn't you?" I asked, slowly lowering my hands. "That was the weapon."

Mayor Holtzapple looked almost impressed. "How did you figure it out?"

"I saw you using it at the plunge," I explained. "And when I was at Big Cats of the World a few days later, Victor complained that his bullhorn had gotten cracked. I should've realized then that someone had used it to hit Lauren over the head. Because there were so few weapons available at the lake. And then, when I returned to Victor's compound, the bullhorn was gone, missing from its special holder on his golf cart. I'd known something was different about the cart, but I couldn't figure out what it was, until just a few minutes ago."

"You're pretty clever for a pet sitter," Mayor Holtzapple noted, insulting me before she killed me.

"Well, I have a PhD, too," I reminded her glumly. "And I haven't exactly figured out why *you* killed Lauren."

Mayor Holtzapple's eyes grew hard, with glints of anger. "That girl was a menace. I can't tell you how many people complained to me about Lauren Savidge. The way she filmed them and their pets without even asking, and stomped all over people's property, and insulted Winterfest, even! And Lauren was bound and determined to make Sylvan Creek, and everyone who lives here, look like lunatics—on national TV! She was going to ruin our community's reputation. Drive away the tourists who are the lifeblood of this town—which *I've* built up, for years!" She laughed, a rueful sound. "And the worst part was, some people blamed *me*—like I was responsible for bringing Lauren and her whole crew to Sylvan Creek!" The fingers of Mayor Holtzapple's free hand flexed, as if she still felt like punching Lauren. "I didn't intend to kill her that night. But when I saw her standing in the lake, with a smug look on her face, I just snapped and smacked her in the head with the bullhorn from behind. It was so easy, in all the chaos of that disastrous event. Everyone was flailing around. I didn't really expect her to *die*, but then she crumpled down under the water. . . ."

"And you left her there?" I was incredulous.

Mayor Holtzapple didn't seem remorseful. She shrugged. "Yes, I guess I did."

Mom had told me that Henrietta Holtzapple was

obsessed with Sylvan Creek. I guessed she was right. Mayor Holtzapple had probably "snapped" long before she'd committed murder.

All at once, I felt a chill run down my spine, and not just because I was staring down the barrel of a gun. I also felt a chilly breeze coming from behind me, and I looked over my shoulder again.

Socrates was gone. And, judging from the icy air seeping into the bakery, he'd exited out the small back door, which led to an alley full of Dumpsters used by all the businesses along Market Street. I never locked that door, but I still had no idea how a basset hound had spun the knob. Leave it to Socrates to find a way.

However, he did have physical limitations, and his short legs would never get him as far as Winterfest, where Jonathan Black or Piper might actually understand when he tried to indicate that I needed help. I doubted anyone else he ran across would know what he was trying to communicate. Still, I was happy that he would be safe.

"What—or who—is back there?" Mayor Holtzapple demanded. I must've kept my back to her a second too long. I turned around to see that her eyes were narrowed with suspicion, and she'd moved again. Come around to the side of the counter, so nothing separated me from that gun. "Is someone in the kitchen? Why is it getting cold in here?"

"There's no one here," I promised her. Then I told a big fib, if only to save my skin. "I always leave a window cracked, because the kitchen gets too hot when I bake." I fought the urge to turn and run myself. I was afraid Mayor Holtzapple might have good aim. She seemed pretty comfortable holding a gun. "Why didn't you just shoot Victor?" I suddenly asked, puzzled by her decision to bludgeon him, too, not to mention her motive. "And why kill *him*?"

"That bullhorn . . ." Mayor Holtzapple grew thoughtful, and she spoke more softly. "It haunted me. I knew it was in Victor's hands, and I couldn't sleep at night, wondering if he'd ever figure out that he was holding—probably using—the murder weapon all the time. I had, of course, visited Big Cats of the World many times, and I could picture the bullhorn in its holder on that garish golf cart." She shuddered, maybe at the memory of how the bullhorn's existence, right out there in the open, had troubled her, or because Victor's golf cart really was gaudy. Then she added, "I had to get the bullhorn back—and shut up Victor, too."

"But why not shoot him?" I asked again, although I was somewhat reluctant to remind her that she was holding a gun. But I had to know. "Why stage an accident?"

"Bullets can be traced." She shrugged. "And why not lead the authorities to believe that Victor's death was an accident? Everyone expected that lion to kill him someday."

"So you . . . ?"

"Showed up at his preserve, under the pretense of making a donation," she said. "I often did, because that place was a big tourist draw. Good for the town."

She really was obsessed with Sylvan Creek.

"And when he had his back turned, I hit him with a marble bookend I'd brought from home. Hit him harder than I'd hit Lauren. And when I was sure he was dead, I dragged his body to the lion's pen." She rubbed her neck with her free hand. "That was the hardest part, although he wasn't a big man."

I couldn't believe how tough she was. I'd always thought she was just a kind, somewhat bumbling woman. "Weren't *you* terrified to face Khan?"

"Not really," she said. "I knew where Victor kept the raw meat. I made sure Khan was distracted during the brief time I was in the enclosure. And it was easy enough to find the control panel for the electric fencing system." She frowned, because part of her plan had gone wrong. "Only I couldn't seem to get the fences working again. So I gave up and ran to my car."

"Why did you tear apart the call box at the gate?" All at once, I remembered the Eau de Vaucluse bottle. "And why did you try to frame Elyse Hunter-Black? Because you dropped the blue bottle, didn't you? Knowing that police would find it and link it to Elyse."

Mayor Holtzapple's eyes glittered with something like misplaced pride. "Yes, I bought some of that fancy water and purposely left one of those *pretentious* bottles in the parking lot."

"Why?" I repeated.

"Because Elyse brought this whole scourge upon our town!" Her anger spiked so quickly that I thought Elyse was lucky to be alive. "Her and her Stylish Life Network!" Mayor Holtzapple spat the words. "And I knew that Elyse was a suspect in Lauren's murder. Everyone saw them fighting at the lake." She shrugged. "Why not cast more doubt on her?"

That was *really* ruthless. "And the call box?"

She pursed her lips and made a frustrated huffing sound. "I couldn't get the gate to shut, either. I must've done something wrong when I turned off the fencing. I got so mad that I used the bookend to smash the call box, too!"

Wow. She was a ball of rage.

Who knew?

"You could've killed innocent people," I reminded her, backing up in preparation to dart away. I was running out of time. She'd advanced again, and her fingers were twitching on the trigger. I raised my hands again, even as I accused her. "Your own citizens could've been *eaten by tigers!*"

"I told you," she said evenly. "Murder tends to *snowball!*"

We had run out of things to say, and there was nothing left to do but spin around and run like crazy—while hunched over, on the assumption that she'd aim for my head. Which she did. I heard a loud bang and felt the bullet whiz past me as I scurried into the kitchen, headed for the door that Socrates had left ajar. But before I could reach it, she pulled the trigger again, and without even thinking, I darted to a closer sanctuary: the dreaded, unreliable walk-in refrigerator.

I didn't want to go there, but I had no choice, and I hauled open the door and jumped inside. As I slammed the door shut, another bullet zinged against the thick metal.

Grabbing the handle, I held on tight. And, of course, Mayor Holtzapple started pulling from the other side. The handle was rattling.

"Unlock this thing now!" she demanded. "NOW!"

The funny thing was, the door didn't have a lock.

I didn't say anything, and there was a long silence, during which I tried to breathe. I desperately wanted to test the handle myself, because if something had gone wrong, and I was actually locked inside . . .

I couldn't bear to think about it. My breathing was already getting shallow, the darkness closing in on me. And the cold was penetrating my thin shirt.

I remained still, trying to listen through the thick walls of the walk-in. But I couldn't hear anything. Not even footsteps receding. And after what felt like about a half hour, but was probably only ten minutes or so, I couldn't take it anymore. I decided I would rather risk being shot than freeze to death—or go out of my mind from claustrophobia—and I dared to rattle the handle, myself.

It wouldn't even move.

"No . . ." My voice was the merest choked whisper, and I sank down to the floor.

Henrietta Holtzapple wasn't going to shoot me.

She'd left me to an even worse fate. Because even Socrates wouldn't look for me in a refrigerator that everyone close to me knew scared the bejeepers out of me.

As I wriggled on the floor, I could feel ice crystals under my hands, because the unpredictable fridge created a lot of frost when the temperature dipped low.

Murder . . .

It really did snowball.

Chapter 69

I kept staring into the darkness, my teeth chattering as at least an hour passed. If only I hadn't taken off my coat. The temperature in the broken refrigerator couldn't have been above twenty degrees, and I was only wearing a light peasant blouse. I could feel my lips getting numb, and pictured how they were probably starting to turn blue. Like Lauren's face had been, back at the lake, when Mayor Holtzapple had walked away from her, too.

I'm going to be blue . . . Blue like Lauren . . . Stiff like Victor, in the lion's pen . . .

I couldn't even come up with a philosophical quote to calm myself. My phobia of tight places was overriding my ability to reason.

And then I heard it.

Something scraping against the door.

Something that sounded an awful lot like a dog's toenails, scratching—digging, if futilely—to get me out.

"Socrates!" I cried. I rose and tested the door handle for the hundredth time. "Are you out there?"

I heard a loud, rare, and blessedly welcome "WOOF!" which was followed by the sound of the handle rattling from the outside and a human voice.

"Hang on, Daphne. I've got tools in my truck. I'll get you out of there. Just hold tight, okay?"

"Okay," I promised.

I didn't cry very often, but I was close to tears then. And, I'll admit, I melted down entirely when Jonathan Black smashed the handle with the blunt side of an axe and hauled the door open, so I could stumble out of that frozen crypt and collapse in his arms.

I was sniffling so hard that I could barely see Socrates through my tears, but I was pretty sure he was dancing around like Artie would've done.

Chapter 70

"How did you find me?" I asked Jonathan, who was offering me one of two steaming mugs of coffee that he'd brewed using the Italian machine. He'd had to follow my instructions, because my hands were too numb to work the dials. We were still in Flour Power's kitchen, sitting on stools at the butcher block counter while Detective Doebler and pretty much every uniformed officer around searched the area for Henrietta Holtzapple. I knew that Jonathan would have to leave soon, too, but for now, he was staying with me, in case Mayor Holtzapple returned to make sure I hadn't escaped my frosty tomb. I was pretty sure Jonathan was sort of hoping she'd come back, so he could confront her. I glanced at Socrates, who was resting by the oven and enjoying a Cinnamon Roll-Over. "Socrates couldn't have run all the way to Bear Tooth State Park. So how did you two meet up?"

"Actually, I saw him on the road to the park, halfway to Winterfest," Jonathan said. He looked at Socrates with admiration. The taciturn basset hound acted like he didn't notice we were even talking about him. Socrates didn't like praise, and I was pretty sure he was embarrassed by his earlier show of relief. Jonathan returned his attention to me. "Fortunately, I had left the festival earlier than expected—"

"So you could track me down and ask for the full story on Bernie," I interrupted, wrapping my hands around the warm mug.

Jonathan took a sip of coffee, then shook his head. "I planned to go home. But when I passed by the booth with your basket of free treats, I noticed that there were still a few bones left. That struck me as odd, since Henrietta had said disappointed people were walking away empty-handed."

I'd taken a sip of coffee, too, and I could feel the warmth suffuse my still chilly body. "So *then* you came here . . ."

Jonathan shook his head again. "Nope, I was still headed home. Until I started thinking about everyone who'd been at the lake the night of Lauren's death. I kept trying to recall any objects that might've served as weapons. Because I never could accept my partner's assumption that the killer had used a rock."

"And . . . ?"

"Of course, I'd seen the blue bottle in Elyse's hand," he said, dragging his own hand through his thick, dark hair. "But even when a similar bottle showed up at Big Cats of the World, I knew she hadn't killed anyone. Especially since I doubted that she even knew Breard."

"Then you remembered the bullhorn."

"To be honest, I next considered Gabriel Graham's

heavy camera," he said. "I knew that could've done the job."

"I'd thought about that, too," I agreed, immediately feeling guilty, like I'd betrayed Gabriel by voicing my doubts about him, even if they'd proven unfounded.

"But I was pretty sure he'd kept the camera's strap around his neck the whole time," Jonathan explained. "Probably so an expensive piece of equipment wouldn't be ruined if he lost his grip. And his pant legs were wet—but barely to the knees."

"I observed all that, too," I said proudly.

Socrates whined softly, cautioning me against getting too puffed up. Especially since he'd just seen me stumbling, wide-eyed and panicked, out of a refrigerator.

"Go on, please," I urged Jonathan.

He grinned, like he'd understood that Socrates had just knocked me down a peg. Then he said, "I wasn't getting anywhere, so I took a different tack, trying to recall events in order, leading up to Lauren's death. That's when I remembered seeing Mayor Holtzapple with the bullhorn. I hadn't even considered her a suspect—until I realized that the bullhorn was linked to Victor Breard, too. He'd also used it at the plunge. There seemed to be a connection there. And then Henrietta apparently sent you on a wild-goose chase. . . ."

"THEN you came to find me?" I asked, getting exasperated. My fingers also tingled in an unpleasant way as they thawed. "You were finally worried about me?"

"Yes, and when I saw Socrates running along the road, I was sure that something was wrong. So I stopped to pick him up, and, I swear, he nodded approval every time I made a correct turn toward the bakery."

I pictured how dog and man must've tried to communicate, and I turned to Socrates. "Is he saying that you were allowed to *ride in the front seat of his truck?*"

Socrates's mouth opened into what was clearly a doggy grin. I wasn't sure I'd ever seen him smile before.

Jonathan was grinning, too, at Socrates. "I make an exception for dogs who are acting heroically," he said. Then he rose and picked up his empty mug to carry it to the sink. I knew he probably had to leave. But all at once, his phone buzzed with an incoming call, and he pulled it out of the back pocket of his jeans and tapped the screen. "Black, here." A moment later, he said, "I'm on my way."

"What's up?" I asked, eager for news about Mayor Holtzapple. I would feel better if and when she was in custody.

"That was Doebler," Jonathan said, tucking his phone back into his pocket. "They found Mayor Holtzapple—having a breakdown in her office."

"What?" I'd kind of assumed she'd flee town, in case her plan to freeze me to death didn't pan out. "She went to her *office?*"

"Yes," Jonathan informed me as he reached for his coat, which hung on a peg near the back door. "Apparently, she couldn't bear to leave 'her town'."

Chapter 71

"Well, I would say that your grand opening was a great success, in spite of the weather," Piper said, turning a sign on the door of Flour Power from OPEN to CLOSED. Outside, big, fat snowflakes were floating down from a leaden sky, but the little storefront was warm and cozy and smelled of coffee that Mom was brewing to celebrate a successful first day. Moxie, who'd helped me all day, was already restocking the glass counter, which had been all but emptied out. Piper locked the door. "Between Lucky Paws and Flour Power, you're turning into quite the entrepreneur."

"Don't forget, I lost a Lucky Paws client yesterday, when Mayor Holtzapple *tried to kill me*," I noted, with a glance over my shoulder at the kitchen, where the broken walk-in refrigerator lurked. It was going to take me a while to get over the trauma of being locked inside, and I shuddered before I turned back to Piper. "I don't think I'll be sitting for Pippin very soon."

"Actually, you'll probably be watching him at

your expense," Piper said, joining me at the cash register, where I was cashing out the drawer. I planned to make a concerted effort to manage my bakery's finances in a responsible way. "Pippin will probably become a ward of Fur-Ever Friends, while Henrietta's . . . indisposed," my sister added, referring delicately to Mayor Holtzapple's almost inevitable incarceration. Apparently, she'd already confessed to murdering Lauren Savidge and Victor Breard. "And they'll be looking for a foster home for him."

I stopped counting money long enough to look at Piper. "Are you saying I could take in Pippin?"

"Oh, I love that little dog," Moxie interrupted, withdrawing from the glass case. She stood up, dusting her hands on a big apron that protected her dark pants. She had surprised, and sort of dismayed, me by dressing as a cat for the grand opening. Along with her all-black outfit, she wore felt cat ears and a tail. I was afraid she'd enjoyed dressing up for the Iditarod a little too much. Fortunately, customers had been charmed by the getup. Still, I thought it was a bit ironic when Moxie added, "Pippin's nearly as nuts as Artie!"

"At least he's small," Piper said, earning a soft groan from Socrates, who lay behind the counter, listening to our conversation. He clearly didn't want a new roommate. Piper ignored him. "Pippin is one tenth of Bernie's size."

I shut the cash drawer and sighed. "Bernie . . . Another client I lost."

At that inopportune moment, Mom came out of the kitchen, carrying a tray with four steaming lattes. She set the tray on the counter, and two *tiny* lines formed between her eyes when she nearly frowned.

"You lost a client, Daphne? How? What happened? Does it have to do with the fact that you keep getting involved in murders and locked in freezers?"

Actually, I'd only been locked in one appliance, and it had been a refrigerator.

"The loss of this client—while admittedly related to the homicides—is actually a good thing," I told Mom. "Bernie—aka Bubba—has found a forever home with Max Pottinger, who doesn't need a pet sitter, since he hardly ever leaves the forest."

Piper shot me a confused look. "I thought you said Max didn't want the dog."

"Yes," I confirmed, taking a sip of my latte, which was a perfect balance of bitter espresso and sweet milk and sugar. I tried not to think about all that the coffee maker had probably endured at my mother's hands, just so I could have a treat. Swallowing, I added, "But Jonathan texted me this morning to say that he'd convinced Mr. Pottinger that the dog wasn't a bad omen. Which probably wasn't very hard to do. Mr. Pottinger is lonely, and he loves Bernie."

"I suppose that is nice," Mom agreed, looking around Flour Power. "And you do have two sources of income now. . . ." Then something caught her eye, and she frowned again, ever so faintly. "What in the world is *that*?"

I followed where she was looking, and Moxie must've done the same.

"You mean that?" my best friend chirped proudly, pointing to a golden trophy that she'd prominently displayed on a shelf that also held canisters full of small treats. "That's the Overall Best Entry award that Daphne, Artie, Sebastian, Bernie, and I won at the Cardboard Iditarod."

"I can't believe Elyse didn't win," Piper observed, leaning against the counter and crossing her arms. "Her Cinderella carriage was unbelievable!"

"The judges thought so, too," Moxie said. "They didn't believe she'd really made it. And it wasn't even cardboard. It was Styrofoam."

I actually believed that Elyse had crafted her own entry. But I could understand why she'd been disqualified. It *was* a *Cardboard* Iditarod.

"I thought it was really nice of Elyse to stop by today," I noted. "She bought a lot of treats for Paris and Milan."

Elyse had also thanked me for helping to solve Lauren's murder. Apparently, Detective Doebler had been homing in on her as a suspect, based upon the discovery of the bottle at Big Cats of the World.

Joy had thanked me, too, when she'd shown up at Flour Power to film that morning. The experience had been surprisingly painless. She'd kindly, but firmly, ordered Kevin to stay out of the way as much as possible, and he'd complied. I had a feeling she was going to be okay as a producer.

"I hope Elyse didn't feel badly when she saw the trophy," Moxie said. "I didn't mean to rub her nose in our win by displaying it."

Socrates snuffled, like the comment amused him. He obviously agreed with me that Elyse no doubt had plenty of awards of her own, most of which were probably a lot nicer than the ugly plastic trophy that Moxie had foisted on me.

"Are you sure you don't want to display it at Spa and Paw?" I asked her. "I didn't do anything to earn it."

"Sure you did," Moxie disagreed. "You dressed Sebastian!"

At the sound of his name, the rat poked his head out of one of Moxie's apron pockets.

"What the . . . ?" My mother reared back, resting one hand on her chest, which was smothered under a chunky necklace. Her eyes were wide and blinking rapidly. "What is that thing?"

"That's a very sweet rodent," I said, holding out my hands. Smiling, Moxie lifted Sebastian out of the pocket and handed him to me. His little nose twitched and I could feel his heartbeat when I cradled him close to me. "You just have to get used to him."

Piper rolled her eyes, then tapped Mom's arm. "Come on. I think this is our cue to return to our own businesses." My sister lowered her chin and looked at me over the wire frames of her eyeglasses. "I believe Daphne has plans this evening, too. Right?"

I shrugged and handed Sebastian back to Moxie, who tucked the rat into her pocket again. Then I absently adjusted the vase of cut flowers that Gabriel had sent to wish me luck. "I'm not sure what I'm doing."

Gabriel had also stopped by Flour Power to interview me for what I hoped would be a favorable article in the *Gazette*. I'd made sure he only took pictures of the store, not me. And I hadn't given him an answer when he'd asked me to join him for dinner that night.

I knew that Gabriel really hadn't been involved in Lauren's murder. And I also knew, from Piper's past experience, what it was like to be a suspect in the death of a significant other. Some people might always look at Piper with suspicion, after she'd been implicated in the murder of her ex-boyfriend. That wasn't fair, and I didn't want to discriminate against Gabriel, whose name had also been cleared.

And yet, I'd told him—honestly—that I was busy with customers and would answer later.

"Sebastian and I have to run, too," Moxie said. "He's overdue for a cheese break, and I have a late client coming in."

"Well, thank you all for supporting and helping me," I said, following them to the door, with Socrates at my heels. He'd been reluctant to leave my side since helping to save me. I spun the lock so they could all exit. "You all helped to make this day a success," I added. "I'm even grateful to you, Piper, for forcing me to dive right in."

My sister wasn't one for displays of emotion, but she gave me a quick hug. "I knew you could do it."

Moxie, who loved bonding moments, embraced me, too.

Under pressure, Mom air-kissed both of my cheeks.

Then they all walked out into the snowy, dark evening.

"Thank you, too, Socrates," I said, as I closed the door and spun the lock again. "Without you, I'd probably be . . ."

I was about to say "dead in a fridge" when something caught my eye. A plant, which someone had left on the windowsill. I hadn't noticed it before and had no idea how long it had been there.

"That's weird," I muttered, reaching down to pick up the pretty, Asian-inspired clay pot, which held twisting stalks of bright green bamboo. There was a card tucked in the foliage. I carried the plant over to the counter and set it next to the flowers Gabriel had sent. "Who do you think it's from?" I asked Socrates as I opened the envelope. "I'm guessing Max Pottinger, because he loves plants and—being a hermit—would slip quietly into the store and leave."

Socrates shook his head briskly, like he thought I was way off base. His long ears swung.

"Well, I guess we'll see," I said. Then I opened the card and read aloud. *"I'm sure that you have some 'long story' about traveling in Asia and already know that bamboo is considered lucky in many Asian cultures. Not that you will need luck, Daphne. I'm sure your venture will be a success."* I hesitated before reading the signature, which would prove that I'd been wrong. Then I told Socrates, "Jonathan. It's from Jonathan Black."

Socrates gave a restrained wag of approval. Clearly, Jonathan had won him over by listening to his canine direction and saving me.

Then I looked at the card again, because Jonathan had added a postscript, which I didn't read aloud.

"You ARE lucky to be alive, Daphne. Stay out of refrigerators—and away from homicides!"

Smiling, I tucked the card back into the envelope. Then I took a deep breath and spun on my heel, surveying my new enterprise—and catching a glimpse of my old VW, which was parked outside.

"I think we're doing okay, huh, Socrates?" I asked, smiling more broadly.

He obviously agreed. For only the second time I could recall, my favorite baleful basset hound flashed a happy, doggy grin.

Recipes

I have been having a great time tracking down and dreaming up new recipes to stock the shelves at Flour Power, where business is booming. And Socrates and Tinkleston have been enjoying their new roles as official taste testers. In fact, Socrates has been taking an extra walk every day to burn off the additional calories, and I've even been trying to get a harness onto Tinks, so he can get some outdoor exercise, too. As you can imagine, that hasn't gone too well. But we'll get there. In the meantime, I hope your furry friends enjoy some of the recipes that have been hits at my new bakery!

Cinnamon Roll-Overs

I promise you, most dogs will roll over for one of these treats! Not Socrates. But most dogs.

   2 cups whole wheat flour
   1 tsp. baking powder
   ¼ tsp. salt
   ½ cup milk (or water if your pup is lactose intolerant)
   1 large egg
   ¼ cup canola oil

2 tbsp. honey
1 tsp. cinnamon
½ cup finely chopped walnuts or pecans

Preheat your oven to 350 degrees. Line a cookie sheet with parchment paper.

In a large bowl, combine the flour, baking powder, and salt.

Get a small bowl and stir together the milk (or water), egg, and oil. Add this to the dry ingredients and mix gently, just until it forms a soft dough.

On a lightly floured surface, pat the dough into a rectangle measuring about 9 by 12 inches.

Drizzle the dough with honey and sprinkle on the cinnamon and nuts, then roll up the dough, starting at the long edge, and pinch the edge to seal it.

Using a sharp knife, cut the log into half-inch-thick slices and place them, cut side down, on the cookie sheet. If the knife gets sticky, dip it in water.

Bake the Roll-Overs for fifteen minutes. (I check at twelve to make sure they're not burning.)

Note: You can make an easy cream cheese "frosting" for these by mixing about four ounces of cream cheese and milk or water. Add just enough liquid to thin out the cheese. You can also make a bunch of these at one time and freeze them. Socrates thinks they taste just as good thawed!

Mutt Loaf

There's something comforting about an old-fashioned meatloaf on a cold winter day. I even make a vegetarian version for myself. But Socrates insists upon the real thing. This is his favorite comfort food recipe.

  1 large egg
  ¼ cup milk or water
  1 pound lean ground beef
  ¾ cup finely grated carrot
  ½ cup breadcrumbs

Preheat your oven to 375 degrees.

Find a big bowl, and first add the egg and milk or water. Whisk these together. Add the ground beef, carrot, and breadcrumbs. Get in there with your hands and combine. (I'm not a fan of that part, but it's the best way to combine things well.)

Form into mini footballs. (You pick the size, based upon your dog. Bernie could probably do with just . . . one.) Arrange in rows in a baking dish.

Bake for about a half hour, until nice and brown.

Make sure to let them cool before serving!

Reel-y Good Tuna Tidbits

I'm not sure why cats love fish so much. I don't think I've ever seen a cat sitting next to a stream, waiting to catch a trout or salmon. But if you open a can of tuna, they will always come running. This treat can even tame a temperamental Tinks—for a few minutes. And your feline friend will love the secret ingredient: catnip!

> 1 (5 oz.) can of tuna in oil, drained of *most* of the oil
> 1 cup whole wheat flour
> 1 large egg
> 1 tbsp. catnip

Preheat your oven to 325 degrees. (These cook quickly even at a low temperature!) Line a cookie sheet with parchment paper.

Mix all the ingredients together in a food processor until well combined.

Using a ¼ tsp. measuring spoon, scoop up the mixture and form it into small balls.

Place the balls on the cookie sheet and flatten them, slightly, with your fingertip. You should end up with about three dozen treats.

Bake for about 12 minutes, watching them closely.
When they're lightly browned, they're ready.

Cool thoroughly and serve. Extra treats can be stored
in the refrigerator.

Woofles

Nothing is cuter than the sight of Artie eating a Woofle while wearing one of his adorable sweaters. He always gets the yogurt "whipped cream" on his nose. Jonathan and Socrates would disagree about the sweater being cute.

 2 cups whole wheat flour
 ¼ cup brewer's yeast
 ½ tsp. baking powder
 1 large egg
 ⅔ cup beef broth
 ½ cup peanut butter
 1 (6 oz.) container plain yogurt
 1 tbsp. honey

Get your waffle iron ready, if you have one. If not, preheat your oven to 350 degrees and line a cookie sheet with parchment paper.

In a large bowl, whisk together the flour, brewer's yeast, and baking powder. Add the egg and beef broth, and stir to combine thoroughly, making a batter.

Scoop out about 1 tablespoon's worth of batter per waffle and cook for about 12 minutes in either your waffle iron or the oven. (The oven won't leave cute marks, but they will still taste good.) The Woofles should be dense and fairly dry when they're done.

While still warm, spread a small amount of peanut butter on each Woofle. Allow treats to cool.

Mix together yogurt and honey and place a dollop of "whipped cream" on the Woofles, too.

Hint: You can find brewer's yeast wherever protein powders are sold.

Praise for Bethany Blake's
Death By Chocolate Lab:

"When murder is unleashed in the idyllic town of Sylvan Creek, it's up to spunky pet sitter Daphne and her darling duo of misfit mutts to catch the killer. A doggone charming read from start to finish!"
—Cleo Coyle, *New York Times* bestselling author

"I had such a delightful and fun time reading this book! . . . The characters are hilarious and quirky and I just fell in love with them and the small town of Sylvan Creek. The mystery was unpredictable, suspenseful and brilliantly plotted. I can't wait for the next installment! Bethany Blake, the author, has a fan for life!"
—*Night Owl Suspense*

"This is already marked to be on my Best Books of 2017 list."
—*Kings River Life Magazine*

"*Death by Chocolate Lab*, is the best first in a new series of 2017. I am calling it now. . . . Even though I can only give five stars, this book is easily eight paws and two hands up!"
—*Bibliophile Reviews*

"I loved this book. . . . The book is engaging from the very beginning and kept me entertained throughout. . . . I can't wait for book 2."
—*Sleuth Café*

"Bethany Blake gets a blue ribbon for her 'paw'sitively charming dog cozy, *Death by Chocolate Lab*. From the get-go, the pets steal the show. . . . Adorable dogs, a good murder mystery and a dash of romance make *Death By Chocolate Lab* a delicious concoction that mystery and dog lovers alike will adore."
—*Mutt Cafe*

Books by Bethany Blake

Death by Chocolate Lab

Dial Meow for Murder

Pawprints & Predicaments

ST. MARTIN'S

MINOTAUR
MYSTERIES

GET A CLUE!

Be the first to hear the latest mystery book news...

With the St. Martin's Minotaur monthly newsletter, you'll learn about the hottest new Minotaur books, receive advance excerpts from newly published works, read exclusive original material from featured mystery writers, and be able to enter to win free books!

Sign up on the Minotaur Web site at:
www.minotaurbooks.com

PRAISE FOR LINDSEY DAVIS AND
THE MARCUS DIDIUS FALCO SERIES

"Marvelous . . . If Sam Spade traveled back in time to A.D. 76, he'd be Marcus Didius Falco."
— *Booklist*

"Every book in this series is a delight, the characters so finely drawn that they have become good friends and the plots so unusual and frothy with humor that it comes as a surprise when the climax is so shocking and original."
— *Library Journal* (starred review)

"A delight, combining suspense with a fascinating look at ancient Rome's manners and morals."
— *San Diego Union-Tribune*

"Wickedly convoluted . . . Falco's facetious tongue and domestic complications are the real fun."
— *Time*

"Roman history and culture are nice accessories for the more durable tool that Davis employs—hilariously good writing."
— *Washington Post Book World*

"It has everything—mystery, pace, wit, fascinating scholarship, and, above all else, two protagonists for whom . . . I feel genuine affection."
— Ellis Peters, author of the Brother Cadfael novels

"Davis is both a deft storyteller and a scholar . . . A top-drawer series."
— *Newsday*

"The Rome of Davis' imagination is licentious and entertaining."
— *San Jose Mercury News*

"Excellent . . . a cross between *I, Claudius* and *Mystery*."
— *Rocky Mountain News*

"A pure delight . . . brilliantly [immerses] us in the marvels of ancient Roman life."
— *Good Book Guide*

"An irresistible package of history, mystery, and fast-moving action, all punctuated by a sense of humor that few writers can match."
— *Cleveland Plain Dealer*

"Davis brings life to Rome better than anyone else ever has."
— *Detroit Free Press*

"Falco remains as delightfully irreverent and insightful as ever; and Davis, as usual, brings the time to life while handling the eternal—worry, danger, love, and in-laws—just as deftly."
— *Publishers Weekly*